Dr. OB

THE DOCTOR IS IN
BOOK ONE

max
monroe

New York Times & USA Today Bestselling Author

Dr. OB

The Doctor Is In, Standalone Novel #1

Published by Max Monroe LLC © 2017, Max Monroe

Editing by Silently Correcting Your Grammar

Formatting by Champagne Book Design

Cover Design by Peter Alderweireld

dedication

To Michael Scott, the best regional manager in the greater Scranton area. Without your guidance, we'd be supremely lacking in our ability to turn anything anyone says—ever— into a "that's what she said" joke.

Also, to Shonda Rhimes, for killing so many characters in your drama, *Grey's Anatomy*, we had no choice but to do the exact opposite.

And to the combination of the two for inspiring this twisted docuseries.

CHAPTER*one*

Nostalgia overwhelmed me as I pulled into the quiet driveway of my parents' suburban New Jersey home. It had only been a few weeks since my last visit, but it felt like longer—and there was always a welcome sense of familiarity.

Several memories played back like trailers for a movie as I took in the two dormers that popped out of the roof—one of which led directly into my childhood room—and guided my car to a stop behind my sister and brother-in-law's SUV.

My little sister, Georgia, a toddler at the time, hightailing it across the front lawn—naked—while I'd chased after her, and my oversexualized parents made out on a lounge chair folded out in front of the garage.

My dad standing in the door and laughing as I'd walked my first date to the car, opened the door, and tried to sit her down directly on a box of condoms he'd placed there.

George coming home from masturbation camp—yeah, that's a long story—and crying to me about murdering our mother as I'd sat next to her hip on my bed.

In the end, she hadn't gone through with the murder, and I hadn't been able to do anything to stop the tears, but we'd bonded that day. Somehow, the awkward, well-meaning doings of our parents quieted the normal sibling antagonism that lived between us and turned it into something more mature. Something that still teased and poked, but by and large, focused on understanding and love.

Lost in my thoughts, I startled when the storm door slammed open and a naked toddler came shooting out of it and onto the front lawn. I jumped into action, swinging out of my car door and leaving it open just as my frazzled brother-in-law Kline leapt from the front porch onto the grass and dropped to a squat, ready to corral her. I took the other side, and together, we herded my niece Julia like she was a lost calf and we were the cowboys.

As sweat broke out down the line of my back, I realized something: toddlers are basically just smaller versions of drunk adults, but cuter. But I wondered when the transition happened, when cute wasn't quite so cute anymore. *At what age do we expect them to dry out, go to rehab, that kind of thing?*

I'm kidding, obviously.

But there's no denying the similarities between a toddler and drunk twenty-one-year-old guy at a frat party are uncanny.

When Kline had her safely squirming in his arms, my mind drifted straight back to my trip down memory lane.

"Like mother, like daughter," I remarked at the *same time* Kline said the *exact same* thing.

Both of us froze.

"What are you talking about?" we asked *in unison again.*

His face took on a carnal quality, and I recoiled.

Oh, gross. And awkward.

"Never mind," I mumbled, blinking my eyes rapidly to try to scrub the mental image.

My sister and brother-in-law were one of those perfect pairs that made each other better. He was a brilliant businessman, loaded with more money than I could even fathom, and one of the humblest guys I'd ever met. She was just as brilliant, successful in her own right as a marketing director with the New York Mavericks, and the happiest part of his day.

That said, she was also a nutcase, and he was far too good at being her enabler.

"Where's Gigi?" I asked, and his whole face lit up.

"Inside with her feet up."

My eyebrows squished together. "Is she feeling okay?" She was pregnant with their second child, and as far as I knew, the fatigue hadn't been hitting her too hard.

"Oh, yeah," Kline remarked lasciviously, and once again, I was sorry I went there.

"Oh, gross. I was asking about morning sickness, not orgasms, for fuck's sake. My mom is rubbing off on you."

My mom, Dr. Savannah Cummings, was a sex therapist, and the scars of having a parent like her ran deep. I found my moments to enjoy the gifts her occupation had bestowed on me as a brother looking for ammunition against his sister and the like, but Kline, as an outsider, didn't have the same personal traumas to slow down his enjoyment. Most people run *from* their crazy in-laws; he ran *with* them.

"Oh, come on. If I were really trying to torture you, I wouldn't have protected you from the fact that Savannah has been in there trying to convince Georgie that, and I quote, *'It'd be the most natural thing in the world* for you to be her obstetrician.'"

Internally, I cringed. Externally, I cringed. In fact, it felt like Kline had just jabbed me in the back of the throat with his finger, and my gag reflex was doing nothing more than reacting accordingly—hacking cough, choking sensation, slight nausea.

I loved my career as a physician in obstetrics, but I'd sign up to flip burgers at the nearest fast-food joint if it meant avoiding doing vaginal exams on my sister. The mere thought was worse than that disgusting horror flick called *The Human Centipede.*

Seriously, if you've never seen that movie, don't fucking see that movie.

That flick is more traumatic than the blue waffle and that "Two Girls One Cup" site combined.

Jesus. Don't Google those either.

I immediately wanted to scrub my brain with acid bleach and found myself cringing again.

Kline grinned triumphantly. "Exactly."

Honest to God, a vagina, in a professional setting, didn't have much effect on me anymore. In a personal setting, say, three beers deep on a Saturday night in Manhattan, I was all about the effect it had on me— but that was another subject entirely. However, as well adjusted to the overwhelmingly intimate aspects of my job as I was, I still couldn't get on board with being George's regular OB. An emergency? I'd be el-bow-deep in a heartbeat. Otherwise, my sister and I were just about close enough, thank you very much.

Done talking about my sister's reproductive pleasure, capability, and organs, I stretched out my arms and wiggled my hands. Kline handed over my squirming niece immediately.

"Come on," Kline called as he headed for the door, looking over his shoulder as I blew raspberries on my niece's tiny stomach. "We better get inside so we don't miss your big television debut."

Butterflies danced in my stomach at the state of my life. Several months ago, a TV production company had approached me and two other doc-tors at the head of their departments at St. Luke's Hospital and done their best to convince us to sign on to be a part of what would be a do-cuseries with several episodes about each of us. They'd decided to call it *The Doctor Is In.* I honestly thought they could have taken more cre-ative liberties with the title, but I guessed keeping it professional and to the point wasn't a bad approach either.

To me, it had sounded like a blast from the beginning. A way to spice up work, a little extra initiative, and maybe something I could show my kids someday—and use as an opening with women in the meantime.

Dr. Scott Shepard, head of the Emergency Department, had the same positive take on the opportunity, but Nick Raines, the newest addition of all of us to St. Luke's and the head of Neurology, wasn't so sure. Apparently, he had some ground to make up with his daughter, whom he'd been estranged from for most of her life, but with some pressure from us and the board of directors at the hospital, he'd caved. It'd be good publicity for the hospital as a whole.

If I was being honest, I was more excited about the publicity it'd give me…*personally.*

Grey's Anatomy had taught me that the "hot doctor" was a thing.

Telling people you watch Grey's Anatomy *probably isn't a hot doctor thing,* my mind advised.

Julia started to thrash as soon as we stepped inside the door of my childhood home—after a quick detour to shut the door to my car—so I set her down without protest. Sometimes toddlers needed to be free to roam, and, for lack of better words, go apeshit.

"Willy!" my father yelled in greeting, charging toward me and the door and completely boxing Kline out of the way. He grabbed my face between his hands and pretended to kiss the air beside my head. This was new behavior, but it wasn't entirely unexpected. My mom was always reading some article on love, affection, and the effect of said expressions on your kids. This was probably something she'd told him was good for the health of my sex life.

"I'm right here, Dad," I muttered back, a smile on my face. "You don't have to yell."

He ignored me and kept right on booming. "You're looking long today, son."

Oh, good. Another odd behavior, but this one wasn't at all new. The day I saw my dad and he didn't have a penis joke waiting for me, I'd also be attending his funeral. Dick had purposely named me William so that we'd be forever bonded as father and son with Johnson-themed nicknames.

What? Isn't that how your parents named you?

Still. Preparedness never softened my reaction. You can't ever be ready for your parent to open the conversation with the state of your genitals. "Oh Jesus."

Georgia buried her face in Kline's chest behind Dick's back to swallow her amusement. That wasn't new either. If anyone knew what I was going through, it was her.

As soon as she composed herself and turned around, I gave her *the eye.* The one that said *hey, these are your parents, too.* She gave me a look back, but hers conveyed how happy she was to be sharing some of the humiliation.

She'd borne the brunt of it for most of our recent past. First, while I was in medical school and doing my residency, both endeavors that consumed nearly every hour of my days, and then when she got married to a man my parents adored, settled thirty minutes from their house, and then went and had a child.

She can only blame herself, if you ask me. Everyone knows grandchildren are a surefire way to ensure your parents have an all-access pass.

But she'd received more than one shipment of sex toys—*even while on her honeymoon*—from our mother in her tenure as humiliation buffer, so I guessed it was my turn.

"Come on, come on," my mom said, shuffling us into the living room. "Your show is about to start, but I have snacks inside!"

"Snacks?" I asked hopefully. I hadn't had anything to eat since this morning before work, and I was starving. Unfortunately, Kline's laughter and a few slaps to my shoulder dampened my hope rather quickly.

"What? No snacks?" I asked.

"Oh, there are snacks," Kline corrected. "Just you wait."

"Get in here, you three!" Savannah yelled. My sister's eyes gleamed with the knowledge of things to come.

I glanced at the door, vivid dreams of escape temporarily taking over my vision, but Georgia's slap to the top of my arm snapped me out of it.

"Come on. Your television debut awaits."

How weird. Me on television. Talk about a turn of life I didn't really expect, seeing as I was a doctor.

Officially lured in, I followed my sister and brother-in-law down the hall. Julia shot out of a doorway and tripped me, but I managed both to catch myself before hitting the ground and avoid stepping on her.

"Whoa, JuJu. You almost took your Uncle Will out," Kline teased with a smile as he scooped her up and into his arms.

"Boom boom, dah-dee," she answered, and even I laughed.

Boom boom, indeed.

My mom and dad were waiting in the living room when we arrived, but that didn't last long.

"Shoot, Dick. Come help me. I forgot the champagne out in the garage."

"Champagne?" I protested. "It's just a show, Mom."

She ignored me, and so did my dad. He didn't hesitate to jump up and follow her down the hall.

Georgia covered Julia's ears, the constantly moving little girl now on her lap, and said the words we all knew to be true but didn't want to say. "They're definitely going to have s-e-x."

I shrugged in affirmation. I couldn't think of a time when Dick and Savannah weren't sneaking off to have sex. And good for them, I guess. I just wished I knew a little less about it.

The smell of food caught my attention, and it didn't take me long to zero in on its origin—the coffee table.

Ah Jesus.

"Are those vagina-shaped crescent rolls?" I asked, but I knew the answer. *Goddammit, my parents are weird.*

Kline nodded enthusiastically. "I helped shape them."

"And those? What are those?"

"Deviled eggs with the tops on and a pickle speared garnish," Georgia said, her eyes wide and innocent.

"And?"

She huffed and giggled a little. "A fertilized egg, obviously."

"The Twizzlers?"

"Fallopian tubes."

"See?" Kline said with a laugh. "I told you there were snacks."

"Christ."

Still…I was really hungry. *And I do like eating pussy,* I reasoned. Grabbing three bread vaginas, I popped the first into my mouth and searched the table for penis-shaped hot dogs. I really needed some protein, even if it was of questionable origin and phallic in shape.

"Ooh, it's starting! Look, look!" George squealed excitedly. "Turn it up, Kline."

He jumped to do as she bid, and I took a seat on the couch beside her and Julia as he did.

The music started, a fast tempo with a ton of B-roll footage of the hospital, its halls, and the busy streets of Manhattan. The intensity was exciting, so much so it made my heart beat a little faster. It flashed to the front entrance of St. Luke's Hospital off of 59th Street, and then zoomed in the front doors and through the halls, stairwell, and around the corner to the front entrance of St. Luke's Obstetrics and Gynecology at superspeed, almost as if they'd strapped the camera to a rocket.

But when the doors of my office opened, the actual camera shot faded and the graphic for the show formed, the last words to fade in: Dr. OB, and a picture of me.

Gigi squealed and squeezed my knee, and Kline gave me an encouraging smile from the chair beside us.

The camera shot picked up again as the cameraman walked down the hall lined with our exam rooms to my office at the end. As soon as my face filled the frame, a knot formed in my stomach. I wasn't sure why; up until this point, I hadn't felt anything but excitement. But in that moment, there was a strange sense of foreboding. I didn't know if it was the expression on my face or just the uncertainty of it all.

But, it wouldn't be long before I knew why.

I introduced myself and the practice and explained that I couldn't wait to invite viewers into my world. It was all very innocuous. But then the image of me froze, a flirtatious smile on my face, and rapid-fire, so fast you could barely make out the words as they flashed, a list of everything in my world—or the one they intended to paint—scrolled across the screen.

The one I expected—medicine. One I encouraged—innovation.

And then, a whole litany of adjectives that were sure to haunt me for the rest of my life.

Sex.

Scandal.

Intrigue.

Secrets.

Lies.

I sat immobile.

The graphic for the show filled the screen again, and the indication of my segment, Dr. OB appeared at the bottom. Only this time, a ghost of the letters "s-c-e-n-e" filled the space right after.

Dr. OBscene. *Dr. Obscene.*

Me. They're talking about me.

Several minutes of footage following me around the hospital ensued, but I was numb to it all. The only thing that penetrated was Kline jumping from his seat and Georgia leaving the room with my niece. Dick and Savannah came back at some point, and they could have yelled for all I knew. But to me, everything was silent.

My whole life was flashing before my eyes.

The camera shot followed me into the locker room of the hospital, something I'd had no clue they even had permission to do—*an ignorance I had a feeling they intended if the shaky recording and barely cracked door were anything to go by*—and continued filming as I pulled my shirt up and over my head and started to pull off my scrub pants. There was nearly a full ass cheek exposed by the time the shot panned away.

A *Grey's Anatomy*-like scenario where they actually filmed you taking your clothes off and having sex in the on-call room wasn't nearly as appealing in real life. I'd thought they'd follow me around, present me with opportunities to show off my expertise and show the difference I wanted to make in my patients' lives—not belittle my intent with creative editing and show me getting naked instead of the emergency C-section I'd performed not even an hour earlier. There was a difference between looking hot and capable and looking inappropriate—and this crock of shit was definitely painting me as the latter.

Christ, my *career* was on the line here.

Before I even realized what I was doing, I had my phone out and in my hand, searching for the number of someone who would have some answers, and I really only had one question. What in the *fuck* was going on?

Settling on Tammy Schuler, a member of the board for St. Luke's and one of the biggest advocates for all of the *positives* the show would bring to our lives, I hit Call and pressed the phone to my red-hot ear.

She answered on the second ring, and her voice was cautiously chastising. "Will, calm down."

I hadn't even said anything, but I guess that was the power of my fury as it radiated through the phone.

"Calm down?" I asked, deathly quiet. "You want me to calm down?"

"Listen—"

"They've got me on camera undressing, Tammy!" I exploded. "How the hell were they allowed to film in the locker room anyway? Where was Legal on this one?"

"They didn't exactly detail in their contract that they'd be filming you undressing, Will."

"Then let's go after them! This is an invasion of all professional privacy and a complete misrepresentation."

"Will…" She paused. "God, Will."

"What?"

"They didn't outline that they planned to do it on their side, but we didn't outline that they couldn't on ours. I'm sorry."

"So…what? I'm just supposed to sit here and let this happen for the next *twelve weeks*? I thought this was a goddamn docuseries, not one ass cheek away from the start of a porno!"

"*Our* hands are tied for the next thirty-six, Will. We've checked with the lawyers, I assure you, but we have no legal recourse. Every single planned episode—yours, Scott's, and Nick's—*will* air."

"Fucking shit."

"Will."

"Yeah, yeah, I know. That's not exactly professional language."

She actually laughed a little, and I considered what kind of technology it would require to have my hand reach through the phone and strangle her. *Have they invented it yet? Can my brother-in-law afford it? He's fucking loaded, so I'm sure he can.*

"No, it's not, but it's fine. I was just going to tell you the positive news."

"I'm not really seeing how you can spin this one in a good direction, Tammy."

"How about five hundred thousand hits in an hour?"

"What?"

"That's how many people have visited the hospital website in the last hour."

I rolled my eyes. "And? I've always thought of hospitals as one of those things that sell themselves. People get injured, they come. It's not like they're choosing a spa."

"You'd think that, but you're wrong. People do choose hospitals, Will, and as much as you don't like this personally, people are choosing our hospital because of this show."

"And they're all checking in to the psych ward?"

Deep down, I knew she was right. People really did choose hospitals. I'd seen it enough in my time as a physician, but still…this was about me and I was pissed. Emotion sometimes skews rational thought.

"Will."

I sighed. *Goddammit.* "Fine. I guess it is what it is."

"It is."

"Then you better keep me on salary until I'm dead, close, or convicted of an actual crime."

It was her turn to sigh. "The hospital cannot actually promise to keep a job for you, but I can guarantee the circumstances have been noted."

"My *sacrifice* has been noted."

"Now you're just being dramatic."

Maybe she was right. Maybe I was being dramatic. Or maybe this really was the end of my life as I knew it. Either way, I said my goodbyes, hung up the call, and forced myself to go back into the living room to watch the rest of the show.

The truth was, as angry as I was with Tammy and the board, and as livid as I felt with the production company, neither of those had anything on the loathing I felt for myself. I'd been excited. Naïvely thinking the show would improve my social life, for fuck's sake. *Oh, you're so impressive, Will*, I'd thought women would say.

But the show had taken a direction completely different from what they'd pitched—a harrowing account from St. Luke's most elite doctors—and turned it into a lighthearted romp on everything ethical and professional.

Unfortunately, with my guard down and my head up my ass, I'd given them the material. I'd been the man on camera, and there wasn't anyone but myself to blame for that.

Goddammit.

On the edge of my seat, I watched with disgust as the man on the screen— me, apparently—said something bordering on offensive and winked… while doing a dilation check on a harmlessly pregnant woman…just before the show faded into the final commercial.

Good. God.

I didn't even remember doing it, winking for the camera like that, and I certainly didn't remember doing it with my hand inside of a woman.

The camera had been right behind her head, and a gown was covering all the skin of her legs, but, for shit's sake, it was never appropriate to wink at a woman while giving her such an intimate exam. I wonder if she'd felt uncomfortable? If she'd thought I was winking *at* her?

Even though I knew I'd never act that way without some kind of pseudo-reasonable explanation, panic and hysteria swirled inside me until the disbelief wore off and let them explode.

"I look like a predator!"

No woman was ever going to come near me again. Not for medicine and certainly not for sex. I was going to have to move. To somewhere remote. Without television. And live in a hut or something. Oh my God. *No one is ever going to blow me again.* I was going to be the male version of a spinster, but instead of cats, I'd just have a collection of pocket pussies.

Sweet Jesus, I am going to throw up.

"Don't worry, Willy. If anything, this will probably up the ante on your female attention and dating life. Women are notorious for seeking out things that are bad for them," my dad remarked.

Kline gave a low whistle, and Georgia stood up from her seat in affront. "Um, *excuse* me?"

"Dick," my mom said. But being *my mother*, she said it through a goddamn chortle.

Being the center of such discord, I figured it was my familial duty to wade in. Plus, if I didn't say what I was thinking soon, I feared I'd burst into something from *Men in Black*. "No, Dad. Crazy women seek out things that are bad for them. The smart ones run in the other direction." My voice dropped to a dejected mutter. "Which is exactly what they're going to be doing with me now. Jesus."

"I bet no one is even watching," Georgia chirped hopefully, trying to make me feel better through a backhanded insult. I'd spent all day hoping the opposite, but at this point, I wanted nothing more than for my sister to be right.

My phone, the opportunist, chimed tauntingly in my pocket. I half considered not reading the text message that beckoned, but in the long run, I wasn't sure ignoring this little problem would actually make it go away. Instead, it might just make me a bigger fool.

My family continued to debate my now questionable eligible bachelor status in the background as I pulled my phone from my pocket and swiped to read the message without pausing to see who it was.

In hindsight, I probably should have taken the moment.

Thatch: Hot damn, son. You've been pretty good at hiding your freak-a-leek all these years. Cassie already has her legs in the air around the clock, trying to get pregnant again, but if that doesn't work out, you're officially our new doctor. Hell, even if it does. Her pussy makes all the others you see on a regular basis look like amateurs.

There it was. An endorsement from Thatcher Kelly, my brother-in-law's best friend and one of the most ridiculous human beings ever born. He was an adolescent in a giant's body, and he didn't like things that didn't have a big, obvious pair of tits prepared, just waiting to be suckled. He was the worst judge of normalcy and the exact opposite of my target demographic—and he *liked* the show.

I was fucked. Really and truly fucked.

My head fell back in frustration as my inner voice mocked me with the real truth. *You aren't fucked, Will Cummings. You're never to be fucked again.*

CHAPTER *two*

THERE WAS ONE CERTAINTY IN THIS MOMENT, SCOTT EASTWOOD LOOKED PERFECT naked.

And he looked even better naked in my bed.

"Good morning, Melody," he said with that signature grin of his and pulled me on top of his ridiculously beautiful body—toned, firm, and sculpted, it was the kind of physique that Greek gods aspired to have.

"Morning, Scott Eastwood," I said, and his smile grew wider.

"I think you can drop the formalities," he teased, and I blushed. "We're married now, honey. It's about time you started getting used to just calling me Scott."

Even though this is most likely a dream, Mel, we'll never stop calling him Scott Eastwood...

Shit...am I dreaming?

I stared into Scott Eastwood's heavenly blue eyes as he looked at me like the sun rose and set inside of me.

"You're so beautiful in the morning, Melody," he complimented and brushed a lock of hair out of my eyes.

Hmmm... Yeah... This seems a little too good to be true...

"I could spend the rest of my life just staring into your eyes," he whispered and pressed a soft kiss—that included a little tongue—onto my just-woken-up mouth.

"You taste so perfect," he told me.

I took pride in good dental hygiene, but even the cleanest mouths couldn't escape the morning breath culprit.

Goddammit. I'm probably dreaming.

"We're married, Scott Eastwood?" I asked.

"Yes, Mrs. Eastwood," he responded through a soft chuckle, pressing his lips to mine once more. "We're married."

"Did I sign a prenup?"

He shook his head. "I'd never make the love of my life, *my soul mate,* sign a prenup."

Fucking hell. Definitely a dream.

Shades of pink and yellow started to filter over Scott Eastwood's face, and I knew it was only a matter of time. "Kiss me again," I demanded and he listened.

A man who listens instead of arguing? Most assuredly a motherfucking dream.

"Fuck me, Scott Eastwood," I insisted, but it was too late. My dream husband's face and our luxurious white bed started to vanish into thin air as the morning sun finally worked its way beneath my lids.

I opened my eyes and immediately groaned at the sight—pink walls, cardboard boxes, and work-out equipment. In a matter of thirty seconds, I'd gone from floating dreamily on cloud nine with Scott Eastwood's naked body pressed against mine to one of the seven circles of hell that was actually my reality.

My parents' two-bedroom nightmare in Hell's Kitchen. Bill and Janet thought it was a dream, though. One provided by the grace of two little words: rent control.

But I didn't really see it that way. Not right now. My life had been reduced to six cardboard boxes stuffed inside my old bedroom, and every effort I'd put into being my own woman for the last six-plus years was gone. I was back home. With my parents. In the place I grew up.

Although, it no longer looked like my teenage youth. The beige walls used to be littered with posters of eighties' New Wave bands like Modern Talking and Rick Springfield.

Hey, don't judge my teenage music preferences.

I might've been an outcast in the early 2000s because I refused to jump on the boy band and mainstream pop wagon, but no one could resist songs like Modern Talking's "Brother Louie," and let's be real, even to this day, everyone wants to be "Jessie's Girl."

But now, the room had turned into something out of a bubblegum pink jazzercise nightmare—aka my mother's "fitness" room. Apparently, pink was one of those colors that motivated people to strive for buns of steel.

To make a long story short, my life outlook was grim—twenty-nine years old, and I had officially moved back home into *my parents' apartment.* I was newly single, had no job, and would be spending my nights sleeping between a treadmill and a thigh master.

Ugh. *Come back to me, Scott Eastwood!*

Shit had just gotten real. Well, real sad. And depressing. And fucking pink.

"Rise and shine, Melody!" My mother announced her entrance with two soft taps to the already half-opened door. The hinges squeaked, and before I knew it, Janet Marco's smiling face was in full view from my perch on top of my new bed—*a mother-flipping air mattress from 1982.* It was old enough to be vintage—and not in the fun way—and you couldn't even use an air pump to inflate it. This baby required the kind of lung capacity that usually resulted in passing out.

Jesus. What in the hell time is it? It felt too early for Workout Barbie to be in here working up a sweat. I snatched my phone off the cardboard box—otherwise known as my nightstand—beside the air mattress. I tapped it to life, and the bright screen all but blinded my tired eyes. I ignored the bullshit *How's the weather by you?* text from Eli—*my newly appointed ex-boyfriend*—and focused on the time. The numbers 9:30 a.m. glared back at me, and I mentally gave my bubbly mother the middle finger.

"How's my favorite girl?" Janet singsonged as she walked her spandex-covered ass into the room. She left no time for a response before hopping onto her treadmill and jogging at a leisurely pace.

"It's too early," I answered, and she immediately cupped her ear in my direction, giving the universal signal for *I didn't hear you.*

"What was that, sweetheart?"

"I said, it's too early," I repeated, and she offered no response, seemingly still unable to hear what I was saying. I was no rocket scientist, but I'd say the recurrent pounding of her feet against the treadmill track wasn't helping our conversation.

"Speak a little louder, Mel," she instructed and tapped her finger against the controls to increase her speed.

Fantastic idea, Mom. Because increasing your speed will definitely help us converse like normal human beings.

A little-known fact about Janet: she was a little hard of hearing. She blamed it on aging and genetics, but considering she'd always had issues, I had a feeling it had something to do with all of the rock concerts she and my father used to go to when they were young and wild. Back in the day, Bill and Janet were hard-core Black Sabbath fans and attended no less than twenty concerts in a span of five years. Not to mention, they moonlighted as KISS groupies on the side.

I was no expert, but it seemed logical that years of Ozzy Osbourne and Gene Simmons shouting into her eardrums didn't increase my mother's hearing capabilities.

"I said, *I'm fine*," I tried again, and she glanced down at her watch.

"It's just a little after nine, sweetheart, but you still didn't answer my question," she said with a smile. "How are you doing this morning?"

Someone help me. I generally had more patience with my mom, but considering the time of morning and the fact that I'd yet to have a drop of coffee, I pretty much just gave up on having a successful conversation with her and focused on entertaining myself. "I'm a mime," I said, and she nodded but stared at me skeptically for a few moments.

"Are you sure you're fine?" she eventually asked. "You've had a rough few weeks."

Interesting, I noted in my case study. *Saying something ridiculous to her is actually more successful than honest discussion.* Maybe I had just uncovered the secret to productive conversation with Janet Marco. "Yep. I'm a mime."

"Okay, Mel." She nodded and offered an apologetic smile. "I guess it's a little too early for me to start meddling, huh?"

I held up my forefinger and thumb and gestured *just a little bit* in her direction.

Her smile grew wider, and she nodded again.

Hmm…maybe the whole mime bit isn't a stretch after all…

"Okay…just one more question, and then I'll leave you alone—"

"*Mom*," I groaned.

She held up one determined hand. "Look, I'm your mother, Mel. It's my job to worry about you," she said through panting breaths. "You basically just uprooted your life in a matter of weeks. I mean, a little over a month ago, you were living in Portland with the man I thought you were going to end up marrying, and now, you're back home and single. You've ended a relationship, quit your travel nursing job, and left the city you had been living in for the past five years. It's just very abrupt is all," she added and glanced in my direction. "I just want to make sure you're doing okay."

The air mattress squeaked and creaked as I tossed the comforter off my body and got to my feet. I rubbed the sleep out of my eyes and walked the four steps to stand directly in front of my mother, who was still running like a lunatic on the treadmill.

"I'm okay, Mom," I reassured her with exaggerated pronunciation.

She quirked a questioning brow, and I nodded.

"Seriously. I'm okay," I said, and it wasn't a lie. Although my life had changed dramatically over the past few weeks, it had all occurred by my choice.

I wanted to move back home.

I wanted to leave my relationship with Eli.

I wanted a new start.

And yeah, I'd much rather not be sleeping on an air mattress in my parents' place, but I couldn't deny that I felt overwhelming relief by my initial steps toward change. My relationship with Eli was all about give-and-take; I gave and he took.

I had stayed in Portland because of Eli. I had stayed at a hospital nursing job I wasn't all that fond of because of Eli. I had done a lot of things because of that relationship, and it was time I found my own way and lived the life I wanted to live. I loved Eli, but I didn't love him enough to lose myself to a relationship I wasn't even certain he was fully committed to.

"Will you do me a favor, Mel?"

I tilted my head to the side skeptically. "What kind of favor?"

"Do you remember Savannah Cummings?"

"Your weirdo sex therapist friend?"

She nodded. "Yep. Her."

My eyes bugged out of my head. *"You want me to go to sex therapy?"*

"Don't be ridiculous." My mother laughed and shook her head. "Her son Will is an OB/GYN, and his practice is currently interviewing for an office nurse. His office is only about ten blocks from here, and since you've been doing labor and delivery for the past five years, I think you'd be a perfect match for the job."

"I don't know, Mom," I sighed. "I mean, working in an office setting? I think I'd rather just apply for an actual labor and delivery position at one of the hospitals here."

"You'll also get to assist Will in deliveries at St. Luke's. You'll get the best of both worlds with this position."

"You seem to know a lot about this job…"

She shrugged it off. "I had lunch with Savannah last Thursday, and she happened to mention it."

I scrutinized her facial expression and found a couple of cracks—mostly in the skin between her eyebrows, a Janet Marco tell. "What aren't you telling me right now?"

"Nothing."

"Mom."

"Fine," she muttered. "I told Savannah to have Will's office manager schedule you for an interview on Monday."

"Monday?" I questioned in annoyance. "As in this Monday? Like, to-morrow, Monday?"

"I had to, Mel," she defended. "I was afraid the position would be gone if you waited any longer."

"What if I didn't want that job? Did you ever think of that?"

"But you love nursing, Mel."

I fought the urge to roll my eyes. "What time is the interview tomorrow?"

"Eight thirty."

"In the fucking morning?"

"Language, Melody."

I refused to feel bad for dropping an f-bomb over this news. I mean, my mother had just gotten me an interview for a job I wasn't even sure I wanted. Not to mention, she'd scheduled it for eight thirty in the goddamn morning. I'd been working night shift for the past five years—I was the furthest thing from a morning person. My internal clock was accustomed to sleeping at eight in the morning, not waking up to be interview-ready and fight the morning NYC rush.

Hello, God. It's me, Mel. Can I go back to my dream life with Scott Eastwood? He'd definitely be on board with staying in bed all day.

"8:30 was the only available time they had left for an interview," she explained. "I didn't want you to miss this opportunity."

Fucking hell. I considered miming a very distinct gesture, but only briefly. No amount of bird-flipping was going to get me out of this one.

Click. Clack. Click. Clack. The rapid sounds of my heels tapping against the sidewalk berated my tardy ass as I rounded the corner of 10th Avenue. My Monday morning had started out like only a true Monday morning could. First, I'd slept through my alarm and woken up to my mother's shrill voice shouting that I was going to be late for my interview before she hopped on her treadmill and started jogging while the Bee Gees serenaded her with "Stayin' Alive."

Of course, then, since I'd only had fifteen minutes to get ready, I'd found myself fixing my hair and makeup on the subway. It was pretty much an exercise in futility, applying mascara on a metal contraption speeding across tracks with enough bumps and grinds to make R. Kelly proud, but I'd done it anyway. And then there'd been the old man sitting behind me who'd appeared absolutely fascinated with making creepy eye contact with me in my compact mirror.

Did I mention Mondays are my favorite?

And even more than that, the best kind of Monday is one where you have to wake up at the ass-crack of dawn to attend an interview your mother scheduled for you.

An interview you don't even really want.

An interview that would keep you in a career you aren't even sure you like.

Happy motherfucking Monday.

As my lungs struggled for oxygen and my feet screamed inside of my heels for a reprieve, I realized I'd forgotten what three New York city blocks actually equated to in terms of distance. Sure, walking three blocks at a leisurely pace with a pair of comfy Converse on was no big deal, but practically sprinting that distance in a pair of heels was the equivalent of *Mean Girls'* queen bee Regina George—a real fucking bitch.

As I headed for the finish line—Dr. Cummings's office—I tried to pick up the pace. I was already fifteen minutes late, and I had a feeling most medical practices preferred applicants who could get to work on time.

Interviewing 101: Be on time to the fucking interview, Melody.

There was a good chance I'd already screwed this opportunity before I had the chance to hand them my resume. I was a fighter, though, so I kept onward.

I did my best impression of *The Matrix* as I maneuvered through the workweek foot traffic cluttering the sidewalks. But it was of no use. My elbow still managed to bump into a man in a power suit holding a cup of coffee. The liquid splattered out of his cup and onto his dress slacks.

"Hey, watch where you're going!" he shouted toward me.

"Shit. I'm so sorry," I muttered, but my legs kept moving toward Dr. Cummings's office. I knew not stopping made me seem like an inconsiderate asshole, but for one, I was already running late, and, well, that guy appeared to already have a job. And thirdly, the damage was already done. What was I going to do? Stop in the middle of the sidewalk and lick the coffee off of his crotch?

A girl could only handle so much bullshit on a Monday morning.

The words *St. Luke's Hospital* shone like a beacon as I stopped in front of the entrance closest to Dr. Cummings's practice, and quickly headed through the front doors, down the hall, up the stairs, and through the doors of the office. Apparently, Janet had been so excited about this opportunity that she'd invested in the research, drawing me a schematic of the hospital's layout and the fastest route to the office last night after dinner.

The instant my heels hit the hardwood floors of the waiting room, everyone, including the receptionist, glanced up in my direction. I had a feeling my entrance was less than graceful. It could've been the whole out of breath with my hands on my knees performance I was displaying or the windblown hair and wrinkled dress shirt that I hadn't worn since high school.

Whichever it was, both things pointed to me being a bit of a mess.

"Can I help you?" the young female receptionist asked around a mouthful of gum.

"Uh, yes," I muttered and walked over toward the desk. "I'm here for an interview. My name is Melody Marco."

She stared at me for a good thirty seconds while she made popping sounds with her gum. Eventually, she sighed, blew a giant pink bubble from her lips and sucked it back into her mouth, and then moved her fingers to the computer and tapped her long, acrylic nails against the keys.

"Your interview was at 8:30," she announced.

"I know. I was a running a little late," I excused. "I just moved back to the city from Portland, and I guess I forgot how busy New York is on a Monday morning."

"It's 8:50."

"I'm really sorry."

"You were supposed to be here twenty minutes ago."

Good Lord, this receptionist was sassy. And repetitive.

"I know. And like I said, I'm really sorry."

Melissa, as her name tag indicated, sighed and picked up the phone. "Melody Marco is here for her interview. She's twenty minutes late."

Wow. Thanks, Melissa.

"Okay. I'll send her back," she responded into the receiver before hanging up the phone. She tapped the button for the doors that headed toward the offices, and they swung open on command. "Even though you're late, Betty will still see you. You can go on back."

"Uh, thanks," I said and glanced toward the doors. "Which office is hers?"

"You'll find it."

"Gotcha." Perfect. I'll just stroll through the hallway and, hopefully, find Betty's office. No worries about me accidentally stumbling into one of the exam rooms while a woman is getting a pap smear or something.

Luckily, Betty's office actually said *Betty*—well, it said her full name, *Betty Matthews*, with the title *Office Manager* below it. And it was easily spotted a few doors down from the reception desk.

The door was shut, so I rapped my knuckles against it three times.

"Come in," she responded. I opened the door, walking in and shutting it softly behind me.

Betty sat behind her desk, tapping her fingers across the keys of her laptop at a rapid-fire pace. *What is that? A hundred and twenty words per minute?* She didn't even bother to look up at my entrance, her eyes staying completely fixed on the computer screen.

"Uh, hi, I'm Melody Marco," I announced. "I'm here to interview for a nursing job."

"You're late," she stated, but she did at least look up in my direction.

"I'm so sorry. I just moved back to the city from Portland, and I guess I misjudged how busy New York is on a Monday morning," I repeated my earlier excuse in hopes it would help for something and ran two sweaty palms down the wrinkles of my skirt. This whole interview thing was off to a phenomenal start. Everyone I'd met in the office appeared to completely despise me. I wasn't a psychic, but I felt like a prediction of me not getting this job wasn't too far off base.

"Please, take a seat," Betty said as she finally looked up from her laptop and gestured toward the leather chair in front of her desk.

I handed her my resume and sat down.

"Is tardiness an issue for you…" she started and glanced down at my resume, "Melody?"

"No," I answered confidently. "I've never had any issues with tardiness or absences with any of my past jobs."

"You did travel nursing for a few years, I see," she stated and continued to browse through my credentials. "And it looks like for the past few years your sole focus has been labor and delivery."

"Yes. I have over five years of experience as a labor and postpartum nurse."

"And what made you move back to the city?"

Because I broke up with my asshole boyfriend, and now I'm stuck sleeping on an air mattress beside a treadmill at my parents' home. "My family is here. I just felt like it was time to move back home."

"And what made you apply for this job?"

Because my mother loves to meddle in my life and actually scheduled this interview for me without my knowledge. I don't even think I want this fucking job. "I have a passion for obstetrics and loved the idea of having a more set schedule. My last job in Portland, I was working twelve-hour night shifts," I informed her. "Working night shifts occasionally isn't bad, but after a few years of doing them full time, it really starts to wear on you."

"All right, Melody," Betty said. "I'm the type of woman who likes to cut through all of the crap, and seeing as I've already interviewed over fifty women for this position in the past week, my patience is starting to wane, and I'd rather just get down to the important shit."

"Uh…okay."

"Have you seen the show?"

"What show?"

"The show."

I looked back and forth, half expecting to see a camera hiding behind her potted plant, and then back to Betty. What in the hell was she talking about? "I honestly have no idea what you're talking about."

"The documentary that Dr. Cummings is on."

"He's on a documentary?" Now? Cripes. I didn't want to be on camera.

She tilted her head to the side and scrutinized my expression. "You honestly haven't seen it?"

"No. I've honestly never seen it." I could feel my eyebrows drawing together to form my *what the fuck* face, so I tried to fight it. I'd been told it made me look really bitchy.

"Okay. Well, I have a few more interviews scheduled this week, and then we'll give you a call sometime next week to let you know either way."

"Oh. Okay. That sounds good to me."

"Would you like me to give you Dr. Cummings's phone number in case you have any specific questions about the job?"

"Um…" What? "I'm not sure that would be appropriate… Couldn't I just contact you?"

Betty smiled and clapped her hands together in excitement. "Oh, thank God!" she exclaimed and hopped up from her chair. She walked toward the front of her desk and pulled me—*literally pulled me*—out of my chair and into a tight hug.

"Uh?" I mumbled, but she completely ignored my confusion.

Once she was finished embracing me, she let go and held out her hand in my direction.

"Melody, I would like to offer you the job."

"You're offering me the job?"

"Yes," she said with an enthusiastic nod.

"But I was like twenty minutes late for the interview," I blurted out.

"Yeah, but you have the right experience, and you're not here to seduce Dr. Cummings."

My eyes went wide in confusion. *Seduce Dr. Cummings? What in the ever-loving fuck?*

"So, Melody Marco, is that a yes? Would you like to accept the position?"

Did I really want the position? Probably not.

But did I need money? A thousand times yes. I could only handle having Janet and Bill as roomies for so long.

Was I a little creeped out with how this whole interview process had just gone? Definitely.

But money, Mel. You need money…

I nodded and smiled. "Yes. I would like to accept the position."

"Fantastic," she said and shook my hand. "Paul from Human Resources will contact you to discuss benefits and pay and start date," she informed me and handed me a folder filled to the brim with new-hire information. "He sounds a lot tougher than he actually is, so whatever he offers as your base pay, I'd counter with something at least ten percent higher," she whispered and winked.

"Uh…okay, thanks." Was the office manager really giving me tips on how to get more money from the hospital? *What in the hell is this place?* I thought to myself as I glanced around her office again to make sure there weren't hidden cameras for some kind of prank show.

But they weren't there.

And Betty just kept smiling like she'd won the lottery.

"And don't hesitate to call or email me with any questions that you might have." Her fingers tapped the folder. "All of my contact information is in that folder."

As I walked out of Betty's office, a bit dazed and a lot confused, I couldn't deny that I'd just experienced the weirdest interview I'd ever attended. I felt like one of the main reasons I'd gotten the job offer was because I hadn't seen the documentary with Dr. Cummings, and if not having seen the documentary was *that* important, I only had one question.

What in the *hell* kind of documentary was it?

CHAPTER *three*

Will

ANXIETY GRATED ON MY NERVES LIKE A FRESHLY SHARPENED KNIFE AS I PUSHED OPEN the door to St. Luke's Obstetrics and Gynecology that morning. I'd taken over the practice just two short years ago, but I'd seen so many patients, delivered so many babies, it felt like I'd been doing it forever. Coming into the office wasn't something that normally spiked my blood pressure, however.

But on regular, *before the goddamn show* mornings, I usually didn't feel like a social pariah, the death of my sex life with sane women fresh in my mind, and I didn't *know* that all of my employees had information lying in wait to use against me.

I knew they did now. Good God, the first episode of the show had been a disaster—like a nightmare I had absolutely no chance of waking up from. So much so, I'd begged off of work for a full week to cry into my ice cream and mourn the death of both my career and all of my favorite places to put my dick.

It hadn't really helped much. With social media as my constant roommate and a virtual footprint I couldn't escape, being away from work seemed just as bad as being at it. According to Twitter, women were still interested, but it was the kind of interest that made me feel icky inside. Doctor, patient innuendo. Offers to bang me once, just to say they'd done it. One woman had even offered me a kinky prostate exam.

Though, I doubted the office would actually be a reprieve. It was more like six of one, half dozen of another. Especially since I'd been a moron and waited long enough for the second episode to air as well.

I'll give you one guess as to how it was, but if your answer isn't "god-fucking-awful" or "way-way-worse," you lose.

"Good morning, Dr. Cummings," Marlene, one of the most seasoned nurses on my staff, a "leftover" from the old practice, sang as soon as the door cleared my face enough to confirm my identity. "Nice of you to join us."

She was the one I'd been most worried about, a smartass old bag of insults through and through. She'd done it all, seen it all, and if she hadn't, you'd better pretend she had for fear of her wrath.

"Morning, Marlene," I called back as casually as I could manage.

She licked her lips, the evil in her eyes lighting in a way I'd only seen once before—in my brother-in-law's cat. And believe me, Walter was the kind of cat you didn't want to know, didn't want to meet, hell, you didn't even want to think his name.

Shit.

I guess the shit wasn't going to wait to hit the fan until after I'd had my coffee. And I probably wouldn't get to have it afterward either. I wasn't sure I'd even feel like drinking it while covered in feces.

Shit-stained and caffeine deprived. That'd probably make for an interesting day of seeing patients.

But she didn't say anything about the show as I made my way to the desk and nodded my hellos at the receptionist, Melissa, and Beth, one of the medical assistants who helped with the filing and check-in and check-out of patients when things got really busy.

Instead, in a shocking twist, Marlene seemed interested in if I'd done anything fun during my time off and asked to see a picture of Julia. They hadn't helped in the delivery of my sister's baby any more than I had, but they had a skewed sense of extended family all the same. Any babies were their babies, no matter whose babies they actually were.

"Here," I said, putting my briefcase up on the counter to dig around in it. "This is a picture from Saturday."

"Oh! How cute!" Marlene mooned. "I used to play naked in the sprinkler all the time when I was little too."

I tried not to picture it—failed. Except, I wasn't picturing Marlene as a toddler at all. *Oh God.*

I forced my thoughts back to my niece. "Yeah. Truth is, you'll be hard pressed to get a picture of Julie where she isn't naked. Kline and Gigi haven't been able to keep clothes on her for anything. Apparently, she even takes her diapers off during her naps."

Melissa and Beth were quieter than normal. In fact, I could usually barely get a word in edgewise for all their chatting, but they still smiled and peeked at the picture of Julia as if interested, so I let any wondering about why fall away.

As soon as they handed the picture back, I made my way down the hall toward my office.

Okay. That hadn't gone so badly.

My step got a little lighter, and for the first time in days, the pressure behind my eyes started to ease.

Maybe work wouldn't be so awful. The show was terrible, but maybe people really weren't watching, or it didn't look as bad to those who weren't seeing themselves look like an idiot. I wasn't completely sure, but I wasn't going to do something stupid like look a gift horse in the mouth either.

I didn't want to hate my job. If you'd asked me what my specialty would be back at the beginning of medical school, I don't know what I would have told you, but I do know it wouldn't have had anything to do with vaginas that wasn't recreational.

Still, I felt like it fit, like I had something to contribute—like life wasn't the kind of thing you could live on a plan for a reason.

I felt like I had a way of understanding women, and, as much as I grumbled about her, I probably had my mother to thank for that. She was always open and honest about menstruation and sexuality in a way that made me comfortable enough to see the people behind the reproductive system.

I cared about these women—my patients.

And I didn't want some trumped-up version of a documentary about me and everything I tried to achieve to ruin what I was actually trying to do—to negate the difference I was trying to make.

"Shit," I muttered to myself. I'd forgotten my mug up in the break room, which was just behind the front desk. I'd been so focused on escaping the impending shitstorm and predicting the consequences, I hadn't thought to grab it on my way. And I *needed* coffee.

Dropping my briefcase and the picture on top of my desk, I headed straight back down the hall toward the front.

Melissa's and Beth's once-again exuberant voices caught my attention just as I moved to step through the door to the break room.

"I know!" Beth agreed to something enthusiastically.

For some insane reason, one I immediately wished I'd ignored, I stopped to listen to their conversation.

"With how good of a flirt he is, I'm just glad he's never tried it on me. I'd have my panties down and my legs open so fast—"

Involuntarily, my body moved, back out the door and around the corner to the space just behind their chairs. I moved almost silently, and truthfully, I didn't even really feel like I was in control of my own body. It was as if my gut instinct engaged at the barest hint that they were talking about me.

"Oh my God. Speaking of opening your legs… Did you hear what he said about the vagina being a beacon of—"

I cleared my throat in shock and recognition—now *knowing* they were talking about me—and Beth almost fell out of her chair trying to get Melissa's attention and make her stop talking. "Shh!"

Melissa's face flushed and dropped to ease her focus on the carpet as she addressed me. "Oh. Hey, Dr. Cummings."

Fucking great. I guess the office wasn't going to be a safe place after all.

"Hi again, ladies. Just forgot my coffee cup. I hope you're having a lovely day." My teeth were gritted, but fuck me, it sure as hell wouldn't help to curse them out. Mentally, sure, but not professionally. I had to work with these people day in and day out. As much as I'd have liked to be, I wasn't made of money.

They tittered a little, surprised not only by my presence but also the casual and kind way I addressed them, and the teasing, knowing smiles slipped from their faces and melted into embarrassment.

"Um, you too, Dr. Cummings," Melissa muttered. Beth, on the other hand, had once again gone mute.

"I'll be ready for the first patient in about ten minutes or so."

Melissa nodded.

"Marlene," I called, and she jumped from her spot in the corner. She hadn't been avidly participating, at least not at that particular moment, but she'd been listening intently. She just hadn't thought I'd be including her in this awkward little tête-à-tête.

"Get the room ready, please."

"Of course, Dr. Cummings."

I nodded with a smile and turned to leave. Then, and only then, did I turn back, my voice soft and smooth like butter. "For the record…" They all jumped at the sound of my voice again. "I didn't say the vagina was a beacon of anything. That was a forty-minute speech on fertility that they spliced together for a fifteen-second clip of nonsense. So let's get back to work, okay?"

Aggravated that I had to explain myself to people who'd been working with me for years, I stormed back to my office—stopping briefly to get my goddamn mug—slammed the switch for the coffeepot on and listened raptly as it started to brew. I needed to take my ten minutes, have my coffee, and get my shit together before I went out there and started seeing patients.

The last thing they needed was a doctor whose head wasn't in the game. My priority was their health. Period.

I tucked the picture of Julia back into my briefcase and checked my phone one last time before setting it to silent and shutting it inside of my drawer.

There was only one message, from Thatch no less, so I figured now wasn't the time to read it. Not when I was trying to calm myself down.

Thatcher Kelly was a goddamn incendiary device.

I pulled off my suit coat and hung it on the hook in the corner, and then I pulled out my chair to sit down and look through patient files. I liked to get a jump on the day by reminding myself of their history before they even darkened our door. Once the day was rolling, I'd barely have any time at all, and patient care was at least fifty percent knowledge.

Each person needed and expected different things, and I tried my best to give it to them.

It didn't take me long to let go of my personal troubles and take on the burdens of my patients. Whether it was fertility issues, a cancer scare, or endometriosis, each of them had something they needed my help with. Something they came to me to make better, bearable, or even just offer some support.

A knock on the doorframe of my office pulled my attention from the file I was studying and up to Marlene.

I lifted my eyebrows in question.

"Just brought your first patient back, Dr. Cummings."

"Okay. Thanks."

She jerked her chin and turned to leave, but I called her back. "Oh, and Marlene?"

She stepped back into the door and listened. "I'm going to be expecting more from you going forward. You've been here long enough, and you're experienced enough, to know that someone needs to hold down the fort, keep the rumor mill under control, and make sure that patients are the first priority. That someone should be you. It should be all of you, but you should know better than anyone."

She ground her jaw, but she didn't talk back. Perhaps a first for Marlene. "Is that all?"

I smiled, an attempt to smooth the water under our bridge, but when she turned without waiting for me to answer, I knew I'd probably be paying for that little speech for quite a while. I was technically the boss, but according to the *Life and Times of Marlene Donahue*, no one was her boss but herself.

I sure hoped someone packed my life jacket.

Three raps on the door to exam room one later, my first patient called out for me to come in.

I stepped through the door and moved to the counter, where Marlene had already run a urinalysis that indicated, as designated by the birth control note on her file, the patient lying on my exam table with nothing more than a paper gown on was maintaining her preferred status of *not pregnant*.

"Hello, Alyssa," I greeted, opening her chart on the counter and scrolling through some of the particulars one last time before turning to face her.

"Hi, Dr. Cummings."

"How are you today?"

"Good, thanks."

"Any problems we need to talk about, or is everything pretty much business as usual?"

"No problems."

It wasn't surprising that her answers were curt and simplistic. I found that was how it usually was while they were undressed and vulnerable. Once the clothes went back on, most patients were much better at chatting.

"Okay, good. We'll just do your breast exam really quick, and then we'll get the rest of it over with, okay?" I asked as I moved toward her.

"Yep."

Pulling back her paper gown one side at a time, I applied gentle pressure, checking in a circle around the circumference of her areola and radiating out. No hard tissue or suspicious textures jumped out at me, so I closed that side of her gown and moved on to the other. All well there too, I pulled it closed and reassured her.

"Everything seems good, Alyssa. Just make sure you keep doing monthly exams yourself, okay?"

She nodded.

"You're young and healthy, but it is literally never too early to be proactive."

She smiled a little.

"Okay. Let's go ahead and do the pelvic exam then, and you can get back to regularly scheduled programming."

Her eyes widened a little, and then seemed to harden with determination. I tried not to recoil in fear.

"Speaking of programming, I saw your show last night, Dr. Cummings."

Has anyone not seen this fucking show?

I worked hard to smile, give a little nod of thanks, and keep my eyes from closing in despair. But inside, my humiliation was hot and gooey like melted chocolate.

"Oh, yeah?" I asked casually, pulling a pair of gloves from the box and taking a seat on the stool before wheeling closer. She nodded, her eyes lighting up with something I didn't like but couldn't exactly decipher. Was it mocking? Distaste? Judgment?

"Yeah. You were…"

Oh Jesus, here it comes.

"Different than I expected," she finished. Her voice rasped with something I recognized distinctly, but couldn't fucking believe without seeing it with my own eyes.

I shifted to look her in the eye, around her gown-covered legs, and almost recoiled at what I saw.

Lust, raw and uninvited, shone from every facet of her being.

Well, fuck. From terse to flirtatious in the span of a moment. At least I'd known how to handle the first.

"Oh, well, editing and TV and smoke and mirrors and all that," I mumbled clumsily.

She bit her lip and smiled, her head dipping closer to her shoulder.

"Okay, so, yeah, let's get the exam going, shall we?" I said, stumbling to move away from any remote possibility that the woman currently waiting to have her reproductive system examined by me was considering asking me to do something way too unsanitary for a medical facility.

"Lie back, scoot all the way down, and put your feet in the stirrups, and we'll get started."

She did as I instructed, opening her legs and pulling the blanket up to expose herself as she did.

"Are you sexually active?"

"Occasionally," she said, sitting up to meet my eyes over the blanket and giving me a wink.

I cleared my throat violently. That goddamn wink for the camera on the show. I knew it'd been a colossally bad idea. But I'd been over and over it in my head since then, and two nights ago, I'd finally remembered. The cameraman had asked me a question. Something completely unrelated to the exam, and what I assumed was an off-the-record type of moment. Obviously, I'd gotten the ass end of assuming.

"Okay, then. Any pain or discomfort during?"

"No. Not the bad kind anyway. I don't mind a little bite—"

Oh sweet Jesus.

"Right, right." I tried to force a laugh.

Next question. *Where do I go from here?* Oh! Periods. Something considerably less sexy. Fantastic!

"How about your menstrual cycle? Any concerns there?"

I inserted the speculum carefully and swabbed the cervix quickly.

"No, ah—" She winced at the invasion.

"Sorry about that," I consoled. No matter how awkward the appointment was for me thanks to her flirting, I had no doubts this part was more awkward for her. And it was my job to make it all right.

"There. Done," I said as I removed the speculum. "I'm just going to feel a little, make sure everything feels like it should—"

"Knock, knock. Dr. Cummings?" I heard a female call from the other side of the door. "Marlene instructed me to go into this exam room," she added, and I was so caught up in escaping the uncomfortable cloud filling the room, I didn't think about how much calling out for her entry so enthusiastically might add to the discomfort.

"Yes, God, please come in."

Awkward was nothing more than a memory when her body cleared the door and her enticingly hazel eyes met mine.

A rubber band of intensity stretched between us as I took the soft tendril of uncontainable hair that draped over her forehead and down her cheek. I struggled to keep my eyes from exploring anything below the neck.

She was new, I knew that much, and she gave the best physical first impression, to which I'd ever been fortunate enough to bear witness. But her eyes weren't smiling in a way that said she was currently falling in love with me in this one perfect moment, and they didn't say she thought I was making a good first impression.

I finally—painfully—understood why when the vagina currently wrapped around my fingers—not hers, as a reminder—contracted noticeably.

Ah Jesus.

I couldn't claim to know everything about the female psyche, but I was absolutely certain halfway through a pelvic exam of a *different* woman wasn't the most opportune time to win one over with small talk and half-assed compliments.

Find out why she's here, my mind instructed.

"Can I help you?" I asked, doing my best to comply with the limited tools presented by my scattered thoughts.

She looked to the patient, then my hand—still inside a different woman, by the way—and back to my face. "I'm, um, the new nurse." She shook her head slightly before correcting, "*Your* new nurse."

Excited about the news that this wouldn't just be a chance encounter, that I'd have the opportunity to actually get to know this woman, my actions once again outraced thinking it through.

"Oh, wow," I chirped—yes, fucking *chirped*. "It's so nice to meet you."

And then.

Oh God. And then…I pulled my hand from its place—*inside of another woman's body*—and held it out for her to shake.

She was horrified.

Both shes were, actually.

"Um, hello?" the now agitated patient called from the table. I wasn't sure if she was more upset that I was doing something abhorrently disgusting or that my attention was no longer focused on her, but either way, I couldn't say I blamed her.

My new nurse made big eyes before trying to play it off with a pat on my shoulder. Three pats, in fact, each more awkward than the previous. What she didn't do, however, was shake my contaminated hand.

For fuck's sake, Will. Pull it together.

Grabbing the glove at the collar, I ripped it off my hand so that it flipped inside out, and I tossed it in the garbage quickly. Moving to the sink and turning on the tap to wash my hands, I spoke rapidly, taking advantage of the fact that I didn't have to look either one of them in the eye.

"So everything seems good, Alyssa. It'll take a couple of days to get the results back on the pap smear, but we'll get in touch with you if anything comes back abnormal."

"Nurse, uh…?"

"Melody," she answered for me.

"Melody, yes." Fucking hell. "Let's step outside."

Please, please, get me out of this room.

CHAPTER *four*

I WAS STARTING TO GET CONCERNED THAT MY NEW JOB WAS ACTUALLY THE TWILIGHT Zone of weird, absurd, and comedically awkward.

I'd been hired on the spot after arriving late to the interview for some insane reason. A reason that appeared to revolve around the fact that I wasn't applying for the position to get inside of Dr. Cummings's pants. Then, on my first official day on the job, instead of getting a normal, new-hire orientation of the inner workings of the office, I was told by an old nurse named Marlene—*who bore an uncanny resemblance to Grandma Moses and literally gave zero fucks*—to go into exam room one.

It'd gone something like this:

"Are you Melody?" she spat out with an irritated sigh.

"Yes," I responded with a smile. "Hi. It's very nice to meet you."

Marlene ignored my proffered hand and grabbed a file from the desk. "Well, what are you waiting for?" she questioned with a raise of her brow. "You're Dr. Cummings's new nurse, and he's already in exam room one."

She'd given me no time for questions. No welcome to the office basket or encouraging smile. No tour of the break room or where to find the supplies—or even helpful pointers about the best places to hide and cry.

Just her, cantankerously telling me to *get the fuck in there*, basically. That was that. My official orientation.

Unfortunately, Marlene's list of undiscussed topics didn't end there. No, she'd also failed to mention that inside exam room one wasn't just Dr. Cummings. It was actually Dr. Cummings in the middle of a pap smear.

Now, I'd had no issue with the pap smear itself, just the fact that my official introduction to my new boss had occurred while he was wrist-deep inside of a vagina.

And funnily enough, that hadn't been the worst part of the situation.

No. The awkwardness had reached its climax when Dr. Cummings had pulled his hand out of a vagina and then promptly held that gloved, vaginal-fluid-covered hand out toward mine *to shake.*

Uh… thanks, but no thanks, Doc. I'd never been the type of girl to shy away from bodily fluids, but I'd also never been the type to embrace bodily fluids without the proper protective equipment.

As I followed Dr. Cummings out of the exam room, I honestly wasn't sure where else this could go. And if I was being frank, I kind of wanted to strangle my mother for thrusting me into the insanity that was my current place of employment. *Who are these people?*

"Let's head into my office for a minute," he said, glancing over his shoulder and gesturing toward the end of the hall.

"Sounds good," I lied. Because yeah, it was a lie. Absolutely nothing sounded good at this stage in the game, especially not several more minutes of awkward as fuck interaction between me and anyone in this office. I'd have much rather been relegated to dealing with only the patients, as I still held out hope for their normalcy, via access to the outside world.

As I glanced up at the ceiling, I wondered if maintenance needed to come check for poor air quality or carbon monoxide contamination. Anything to explain the oddities of the people inside this office.

At least it's getting close to lunch time, I thought to myself and glanced down at my watch for confirmation. When the numbers 9:01 a.m. glared back at me, I groaned internally. It was a bad, bad sign when you felt like you'd worked for five hours, and nary an hour had passed. Not only was

I in the Twilight Zone, but it was an alternate dimension of the Twilight Zone where time stood still.

Holy screaming goats. This day is never going to end. I will literally die in this place.

Dr. Cummings opened the door to his office and gestured me inside. "Please, take a seat," he instructed and I complied. I didn't have much choice in the matter, but as I sank into one of his old leather chairs, I thanked circumstance that if I was going to be consigned to hell, at least the seating was comfortable.

Good design work, Satan.

"Good God, that was awkward," he said and moved around his desk. My eyebrows lifted in a statement of *yeah, fucking obviously* while his back was turned, but as he shrugged out of his white exam coat, my brain made a U-turn from its route to a well-deserved mocking and straight back toward arousal.

His muscles flexed and moved beneath his well-fitted dress shirt, and his waist was lean without seeming skinny. With the way his muscles stood out in stark relief—through the freaking fabric for kittens' sake— he didn't need any more bulk. Dr. Cummings was a man who made the statement *less is more* ring true.

Believe me, it was more. Oh boy, was it more.

My traitorous gaze moved down his shoulders to his back and landed on his perfectly firm ass.

Sweet baby pigeons in a kayak, my new boss was an Adonis.

I wonder what he looks like naked. That perfect ass...those wide shoulders...his trim hips that no doubt hold that sexy as hell V...

Holy hell. Was I just fantasizing about my boss? The very boss who'd no less than five minutes ago attempted to shake my hand with a glove covered in more than just latex?

God, what was it with this place? It was like I'd stepped onto the set of the medical version of *The Office*. The only difference was that this boat of crazy wasn't commanded by Captain Michael Scott. It was Dr. Awkward Adonis.

I cleared my throat nervously and watched as Dr. Cummings threw his exam coat haphazardly across the back of his chair and sat down. He rested his elbows on the mahogany wood of his desk and ran a frustrated hand ran through his golden-brown locks. I fought my brain's urge to daydream about running my own hand through those sexy tresses and gave my best attempt at professionalism, crossing my legs and sitting up straighter in my seat.

Eventually, his gaze met mine, and he offered an apologetic smile, blue eyes crystal clear with unpretentious sentiment. "Can we have a do-over?"

"A do-over?" I asked, taken aback by his question.

"Yes." He nodded. "I'd prefer our first introduction didn't occur while I was in the middle of a pap smear," he explained earnestly. "I'd also prefer that you'd wash that embarrassing and, honestly, really unsanitary, attempt at a handshake from your memory."

"Oh, so you don't always try to shake new hire's hands right after performing a vaginal exam?" I teased.

"Definitely not." He smirked and shook his head. "That was the first time I've ever tried that intimate of a welcome to the office."

"Wow," I responded with a smirk. "I'm not sure if I should feel special or concerned."

I felt the rough vibration of his soft chuckle in my chest—and squeezed my legs together to stop the feeling from spreading to other places. "I guess it's safe to say you're never going to forget that, are you?"

"Probably not." I shrugged. Truthfully, the comedic value was too good. I'd likely be jazzing up this story to tell to my grandkids one day about how tough it was to be me. My version of walking both directions uphill in the snow, to school, barefoot. "But, in the name of getting into my new boss's good graces, I'm willing to allow a do-over," I added with a smile and held out my hand toward him. "Hi, Dr. Cummings, I'm Melody Marco. Your new nurse."

He took my hand in his and grinned. "It's nice to meet you, Melody. And please, just call me Will."

"It's nice to meet you too, Will," I said and instantly loved the feel of his first name sliding off of my tongue.

His grin grew wider and finally gave way to one of the best smiles I'd ever seen in my life. A smile was one of those things that was so universal even an infant knew it by heart. A smile could tell you a lot about someone. And with the way Will's smile encompassed his lips and his cheeks and his ocean-blue eyes, my gut instinct told me he was a down-to-earth guy at heart. Maybe a little awkward at times. Definitely sexy as hell underneath that white exam coat. But I had a feeling he was one of the good ones. The kind of guy every woman searches for and only a few have the luck to find.

I wanted to know him. Like really, really know him.

And see him naked. Don't forget you want to know him naked.

Jesus. I blushed at my mind's brief detour into the gutter. It was one thing to be intrigued by someone, but it was a whole other ball game when you were fighting your brain's desire to picture that person sans clothes.

"Thank you for obliging me with a do-over, even if it was under the pretense of extortion. I feel a lot better about our introduction now," he said with a little wink. "Now, seeing as it's your first day on the job, I want to make sure you feel at home here. Do you have any questions for me? Is there anything I can show you?"

Your penis.

Oh. My. God. Even though the words never crossed my lips, the shock of them flooding my head made my eyes go wide and my lungs forget how to maintain the normal flow of oxygen in and out. Saliva clogged my throat, and I couldn't stop the fit of choking coughs that followed.

Had I really just thought the words *your penis*?

As in *yes, please, Will, show me your penis*?

Holy hell, I was a pervert. A total fucking pervert.

"Are you okay?" he asked in concern when the coughs continued for an uncomfortably long time. "Do you need some water?"

I need more than just water, I thought to myself. *A lobotomy. A new job— preferably one where my boss doesn't make my brain think about his penis.*

I nodded in response because it was literally the only thing I could do. For one, speech wasn't really feasible between the coughs, and two, I feared if speech were an option, I'd blurt out something ridiculous about his balls. I mean, if Penis was stop one, my train was two short chugs away from pulling into Testicle Station.

He pulled a fresh bottle of water from his drawer and slid it across his desk.

I took it willingly, and thankfully, the slightly cool liquid managed to clear my throat and calm my lungs.

"Better?" he asked, and I nodded again.

"Thank you," I said when I felt confident enough to use words and set the bottle onto his desk. "I swear, I normally have the whole breathing and talking thing down without dying."

He chuckled at that. "Kind of like how I don't normally try to shake hands right after performing a pap smear?"

Hmm. I guess he makes a point. I smiled. "Yeah. Kind of like that."

"Did Betty show you around this morning?"

"No." Will's brow furrowed in confusion, so I explained further. "Actually, she had Marlene show me around."

He sighed and shook his head. "Yeah. That's not going to work. I'll make sure Betty takes the time to show you around and then has another nurse give you an actual orientation."

Obviously, Marlene's give-no-fucks attitude wasn't something new.

The overhead vents inside his office creaked and groaned, and suddenly, the room started to fill with hot air. And it wasn't the good kind of hot air. It was like ten times hotter than a sauna kind of hot air. It didn't take long for my pores to respond to the desert-like warm temperature.

"Christ," Will cursed under his breath. "Can you give me a minute?"

I nodded.

Picking up the phone on his desk, he tapped one of the speed dial buttons. "Harry," he greeted. "How's it going?"

I tried to ignore the heat while he continued with this phone call, but eventually, I couldn't take it anymore. I needed to de-layer or else I'd find myself in another awkward situation of fainting in his office.

Be proactive—that was my goal.

"That's great, man. I'm glad to hear it," he responded into the receiver. "Listen, I'm still having issues with the temperature in my office. The vents are blowing more heat than the sun. I can actually feel my skin shriveling."

He was right. Not even lizards could live like this. *Good God, it's hot.* I moved into survival mode, removing my button-up scrub jacket and sliding up the sleeves of my long-sleeve white shirt. Even though the room was still insanely hot, I sighed in relief from the slight decrease in temperature less clothing had allowed. Anything was something when the vents in Will's office were on a mission to kill us both via heatstroke.

"Okay, perfect," he said and looked toward me for a brief moment. His eyes went wide, and he blinked several times before hurriedly moving his gaze in the complete opposite direction of the room. "Yes… No… Shit… I'm sorry, what did you just say, Harry?" he stuttered into the phone.

What the hell?

Will's eyes moved toward me again, and his reaction only got more absurd when he nearly dropped the receiver in his hand.

Okay…seriously…what was happening? Did I have something on my face? Did I have pit stains from sitting inside the office that could now be used as an actual steam room?

Surreptitiously, I glanced down at my shirt. I wished the reason for his hysteria had been less obvious, but it wasn't. Not even a little. There for all to see were my braless boobs—*underneath a white shirt no less*. I didn't know if I should sprint from his office like my ass was on fire or crawl under the desk and curl up in the fetal position.

How in the hell had I forgotten to put on a bra this morning?

I wasn't the kind of girl who just free-boobed without a care in the world. Hell, I only ever free-boobed in the privacy of my own home.

Could this day get any worse?

A part of me wanted to say that there was no way anything could top this, but then again, I'd naïvely thought the whole vaginal-fluid-hand-shake thing was the climax of awkward. It wasn't. Not even close. The true peak of embarrassment had just officially occurred—with my nipples on display like donuts beneath a clear-glass cabinet in a bakery shop.

Quickly, I tossed my scrub top back on and stood up from my chair once navy blue was securely over areolas and white. Will watched as though my breasts were a car wreck before jerking roughly away and staying gone.

"Uh…" I fumbled for something feasible to say that would allow me to exit Will's office. "I'm going to go see if…Betty can give me a walking tour… Yeah…I'm going to go see Betty…" I stammered. Will nodded with the phone still firmly pressed to his ear, but his eyes never met mine or *me*.

I couldn't blame him.

My first day on the job and I'd inadvertently given my boss a peep show.

Happy motherfucking first day of work, Mel.

CHAPTER *five*

Will

FOR THE PAST WEEK AND A HALF, I'D BEEN DOING MY BEST TO AVOID THE ONE woman I thought I wouldn't be trying to avoid at all.

After the Vagina-gate and Nipple-ghazi scandals of Melody's first day, neither one of us had been able to do more than mutter a few words to one another while studiously avoiding looking into each other's eyes. In fact, direct eye contact felt like a solar eclipse—stare too intently and one of our special parts would pop out and blind the other before they had the chance to look away.

But, as one might imagine, avoiding someone you work with wasn't without failings.

"Dr. Cummings?"

I lifted my head from the prescription on my desk and looked straight into the hazel-green eyes of the woman herself.

See? Hard to avoid.

Looking away quickly and back to my desk, I scribbled my signature and concentrated on simultaneously seeing what she wanted as best I could. "Yes?"

"Your next patient is in exam room two, and your two thirty is early. Do you want me to go ahead and bring her back or wait?"

"You can bring her back." Without meaning to, I looked up, and everything about her sharp gaze hit me right in the gut. Soft auburn-brown hair back in a respectable ponytail and creamy peach skin peeking out from the professional V-neck of her scrub top were the perfect complements to the enthralling green-gold color of her eyes.

God, she's pretty.

Shit. I was staring. I nearly knocked over the cup of pens on the corner of my desk in my haste to look away. Thankfully, she ignored the ensuing scramble to catch them.

Eyes back to my desk in protection, I spoke again. "It always seems like people are happier to wait in the actual room than out in the waiting room."

A brief pause settled between us, but I fought against its urging to look up at her again. Was she staring at me now? What was she thinking?

"You got it."

I lifted my gaze as soon as she turned and watched her take a few steps down the hall before forcing myself to look away again.

I didn't want her to feel unwelcome, but I didn't want to make it harder on her either.

Fuck, being awkward sucked. I didn't know how my sister Georgia had done it her whole life.

Ripping the prescription from my pad, I held it up to give it a once-over before taking it to the front desk for the patient checking out.

And thank fuck I did.

Because there, scrawled in my handwriting for all to see, were the words: **God, Melody Marco is pretty as fuck.**

Good going, Will. There's something that'll help your reputation.

⌇∞⌇

Melody met me outside the door to my next patient's room and handed me her file. I opened it quickly to double-check the name. *Linwood, Colleen.*

"Knock, knock," I called as I rapped my knuckles against the door.

"Come in," Mrs. Linwood invited, and I turned the handle to oblige.

She was just about my mother's age, but she still hadn't hit menopause. Unfortunately, her periods were needlessly heavy and a huge burden we'd been fighting for the past couple of years. Cryoablation hadn't helped adequately, so today we'd be seriously discussing the merits of doing a hysterectomy.

"Hi, Mrs. Linwood," I greeted.

I smiled my normal smile, but I could tell as soon as she didn't return it that this wasn't going to be as pleasant as our previous appointments had been. I mean, the subject matter and her suffering were never exactly a good time, but she was always sweet to me and pleasant to chat with.

She'd lived a pretty interesting life and never balked at sharing stories as I did my exam.

"Dr. Cummings."

I tried not to sigh heavily as Melody followed me into the room and made a bid to Mrs. Linwood. "I'm just going to sit in if you don't mind, Mrs. Linwood. Help the doc out."

"Well, that'd be fine," Colleen acquiesced, obviously a bigger fan of sweet little Melody than she was of me right now.

Though, on that account, I really couldn't blame her. I was a much bigger fan of Melody than myself these days too.

"You need a chaperone anyway," Colleen scolded me.

I bit my lip to stop myself from laughing and answered as calmly and neutrally as possible. "And why do you say that, Mrs. Linwood?"

"I saw you on the TV. I saw you bat your eyelashes at those women and take off your clothes while all of America watched. I'm not going to let you do anything inappropriate with me, sir."

Melody sucked her lips into her mouth to stop from laughing, but I just shook my head. I couldn't believe this shit.

"You've been coming to me for years, Colleen. You know me. Have I ever tried anything inappropriate with you?"

"Of course not. But I know how you young people get when you get on TV. Get a big head, think you can touch anyone's anything anytime you want."

Melody made big mocking eyes from behind Colleen's head.

"Well, I assure you," I comforted, "I have no interest in doing anything but making you relaxed and healthy."

"I know you'll behave yourself. We've got a chaperone. And by the way you're looking at her, it's *her* you've got the hots for."

I choked on saliva and had to clear my throat violently. Melody looked away, clearly uncomfortable with the insinuation.

"Mmm-hmm," Mrs. Linwood hummed.

Shit.

"Mrs. Linwood," I implored. "There is nothing unprofessional going on in this room. I promise."

Though, I couldn't say the same for the things I'd *imagined* doing to Melody in this room. And out of it—in my apartment, on the street, anywhere, really.

"All right."

"Can we talk about you now?" I asked. "Aren't you tired of talking about me?"

"I believe I am."

"Okay, good." I agreed. "Me too."

I grabbed the stool and took a seat, wheeling over so I could look her in the eye. "How are you? Any changes?"

"If by changes, you mean have I gone through them?"

I shrugged and nodded.

"No."

I smiled in sympathy.

"Am I still bleeding all over everyone and everything like a stuck pig?" she went on. "Yes."

I couldn't help it. Her colorful description made me smile even bigger.

Unfortunately, thanks to my good nature, the smack to the back of my head took me by surprise.

Apparently, she no longer found me funny.

"Oh my God!" Melody squeaked, clearly as surprised to be witnessing my assault as I was.

She stepped forward clumsily, unsure how to intervene or if she should, but I waved her off.

"It's okay. It's fine."

I stood up and moved away from Mrs. Linwood as calmly as I could, but really, frustration ran rampant within me. *Jesus.* I just wanted to do my job without walking around on eggshells all the time. I was a good guy with good intentions, and I didn't want this to be my purgatory for the rest of my goddamn life.

"I think it's best if we transfer your care over to Dr. Elders, Mrs. Linwood."

I didn't even wait for her to answer before scooting toward the door and asking, "Take care of that, please, Melody?"

"You bet," she agreed easily.

The door slammed behind me. I headed for my office, but after two minutes inside, everything that was going wrong with my life started to overwhelm me, and there were too many eyes watching through my open door to have my reaction here. Even if I shut it, they'd just move closer to listen. An unexpected location was the secret to a good breakdown.

Out the door and around the corner, I stomped to our supply room and stepped inside, closing and locking the door, and turned immediately to rest my forehead against the cool wood.

"What *is* it with my life these days?" I shouted to no one as soon as I'd taken a breath. Maybe God. I wasn't sure who I was yelling at or if it would do me any good, but ever since the stupid show had aired that first night, every woman I encountered either hit me or hit on me and nothing in between.

It was getting old. I bruised easily, for Christ's sake.

Unfortunately, it wasn't until the sound of Melody clearing her throat stirred the otherwise stagnant air that I realized I was not, as I had thought, alone in the room.

Good one, God. I get it. My stupid behavior is in no way your fault.

"So you're in here," I stated without turning around.

I could hear a smile in her voice as she replied. "Uh-huh."

"I'm not alone."

"Nope."

"Great," I muttered as I turned around.

Her soft eyes and sweet smile made it worth the initial embarrassment.

"Don't worry," she teased. "I have no bricks. No pitchforks. No weapons at all." She held up her hand full of new gowns to show me. "Though, maybe I should. You know, just to protect myself."

"So you heard about the show, huh?"

A soft smile curved the corner of her mouth before she dipped her head and stole away her eyes to look at the ground. She was laughing at me, I could tell, but she was nice enough to try to hide the fact that she was doing it. That made her just about the only one in the office or in my family. Basically, no one but Melody was nice enough to cushion the blows even a little bit. "Uh, yes. It seems to be a favorite topic around here."

I groaned without meaning to and sank my head into my hands.

"Great. Just great."

"Hey, obviously, it's a hit. You should be happy."

"Are you kidding me?" I asked with a laugh. "Have you actually watched the show?"

She nodded sheepishly. "After listening to Marlene talk about it yesterday, I had to watch last night."

"Well, then you know I look like a seriously creepy dude. Inappropriate and all kinds of shit I wish I could erase from the memories of everyone around me."

"It's not that bad."

I leveled her with a look, and she caved quickly, bursting into a smile that made the ridicule a little more worth it. *She's got a great smile.* "Okay, so you look pretty bad. A little creepy, *really* flirtatious, but more than that, in my opinion, cavalier. Like everything is kind of a joke."

I winced and leaned into the door in defeat. "Christ, that's even worse."

"But I've been here for almost two weeks now, and I've never seen you act like that. I don't really get it."

"Me either," I admitted. "Some of it is creative editing, that much I know. But some of it, I think, was me just trying to be impressive on camera." I shrugged. "Unfortunately, it comes off more…"

"Jackass."

"That's the word." I snapped my fingers in self-deprecation. "Way more jackass than inspiring."

"Look, Will, I'm far from perfect. I was late to the interview and my first day, and I showed you my nipples within fifteen minutes of meeting you. I'm not exactly a judge and jury here."

"Wow. Late to the interview *and* your first day? Why is it we hired you?"

She smiled again, and every ugly thing boiling inside of my chest cooled. "Beats me."

I shook my head. "Not me. I think I get it just fine."

She blushed, and I took that as my cue to make my exit. "Thanks, Melody. I needed this."

"This? What this?"

I shook my head, turned the knob on the door, but admitted the truth quietly. "You. I needed you."

The door shut behind me soundlessly. Having left so fast after uttering the words, I didn't even really remember stepping through the door.

But it was true. I'd needed her. She was professional and courteous and didn't look at me like I was the guy on the show. And most of all, she'd comforted something inside of me, settled the churn of my stomach and calmed the chaos in my mind.

Maybe God wasn't such a smartass after all.

CHAPTER *six*

———————— ∽∾ ————————

"**H**OW FAR APART ARE YOUR CONTRACTIONS?" MARLENE HUFFED OUT INTO THE phone beside me. I rolled my eyes.

We were holed up in the nursing office, returning a few triage phone calls that had come through while we were busy with office patients, and I couldn't deny that I had a love-hate relationship with my fellow nurse.

Her sarcastic remarks while talking to patients were useful for my personal enjoyment—as well as for implementation as a device of a distraction from a sexy as hell doctor who liked to say things like *he needed me*—but I also kind of hated listening to it at the same time. Christ on a crutch, I'd spent way more hours than I'd like to admit wondering what he'd meant by those words and if I wanted them to mean anything at all. Did he like me? Was he just happy to have a nurse other than Marlene? Was my vagina a beacon of his desire? I didn't know.

In a way, I had to be thankful for Marlene's theatrics for finally smothering all of my overanalyzing.

But there were only so many times you could overhear your fellow nurse telling patients that her hemorrhoids were more painful than Braxton Hicks contractions and that said patient just needed to "Netflix and chill."

I honestly didn't even think Marlene knew what Netflix and chill really meant.

And I sure as hell didn't want to know about her goddamn hemorrhoids.

She was a brilliant nurse. She knew her shit when it came to Obstetrics and Gynecology, and she'd seen and experienced more than anyone around her—even Will. But that brilliance was overshadowed far too often by her lack of compassion and patience. After working the same job for far too many years, she'd become jaded and, most likely, bored.

Plus, she was, like, seventy years old. By the end of one eight-hour shift, I knew more about her spider veins and bunions and back problems than any human would ever want to hear.

But sometimes, when she wasn't insulting people callously or giving me the stink eye just because I was in her vicinity, overhearing Marlene's phone triage conversations with labor patients was one of the highlights of my day. She had no filter. Like, *no filter.* She said all of those things normal human beings think but don't voice out loud. And it certainly didn't make me feel pure inside, but some of the shit she said was just too funny to ignore. I'd even started to catch Will milling around from time to time trying to listen.

"No," she sighed into the receiver. "One contraction in two hours doesn't equal labor. You probably have gas and need to fart," she paused and then shook her head in annoyance. "Honey, if you're in labor and deliver at home, then you're a medical marvel. Fertility statues should be made in your honor."

She rolled her eyes in response to whatever the patient was saying and brushed a crumb from her coffee cake off her pants. "I'm the head nurse. I'm giving you the best medical advice anyone can give you in this office. Stay home. Rest. Drink some water. Try to fart or take a crap. And call the office back if you reach the point where you've had five contractions an hour for two hours straight."

Try to fart or take a crap. Beautiful and professional medical advice from Nurse Marlene Donahue.

Once the call ended, she hung up the phone, and at a snaillike pace, she pulled the patient's medical chart up on the computer. I watched out of the corner of my eye as she started to type her version of the phone conversation into the patient's chart.

9:55 a.m.: Patient called office to update that she has had one contraction in two hours. Contraction only focused on lower abdomen and does not spread around abdomen to her lower back. Patient rates the contraction pain a 2 on a scale of 0-10. She denies vaginal bleeding or leaking fluid. Nurse advised that patient drink water, rest, and attempt to fart or take a crap. Nurse instructed patient to call office back if contractions increase to five contractions an hour for two hours straight.

I had to give it to the woman, she didn't hesitate to put her exact words into the patient chart.

As I finished up the notes on my earlier triage call, Melissa peeked her head into the room. "Load-y, Dr. Cummings's ten o'clock is here."

I glanced up from my computer with a furrowed brow. "Load-y?"

What the fuck is a Load-y?

Marlene slammed her fingers on the keyboard and cursed about technology under her breath, making me jump. I wondered how many weeks of working here it would take to get me used to her lack of finesse.

"Yeah," Melissa said and popped the pink gum inside of her mouth. "That's your new office nickname. Isn't it great?"

Load-y? My nickname? Like someone just shot their freaking load on my face? Was she shitting me?

"Uh…not really," I responded. "How about I just go by Mel?"

"Because I'm the Mel in this office."

Of course.

"But everyone calls you Melissa."

"Yeah, but sometimes I go by Mel."

Sometimes? More like *never*. Two weeks into the job and I'd yet to hear anyone call her Mel.

"Okay… Then, I'll just go by Melody," I decreed and hopped up from my seat before she had a chance to argue. "And we can put the new patient in exam room six."

"Whatever." She rolled her eyes and handed me the patient's chart before sashaying on her heels into the hallway. I followed her lead and noted that Melissa was walking straight toward an unsuspecting Will. He sat at a desk in one of the small alcoves in the main hallway and appeared busy reading through a patient's medical file.

Instead of watching what would most likely be an entertaining exchange, I shuffled into exam room six to get the room set up. Melissa had turned into Nancy Drew, sleuthing on a daily basis in an effort to figure out which staff members Will had possibly slept with.

Not her, I'd deduced. Not her.

Which, I had to admit, made Will all the more impressive. She made it pretty obvious he'd had opportunity.

Not that I didn't understand her a little. I wanted to be near Will too—but I'd also been fighting that feeling. The last thing I needed was another guy who wasn't looking for something serious.

I didn't know much about him. Maybe he wasn't a player. But I knew all too well that women from all over Manhattan were willing to help him give it his best go.

"Dr. Cummings, your ten o'clock is here," Melissa's far too loud voice echoed down the hall and into my ears while I busied myself with pulling fresh white paper onto the exam table.

"Okay," he said at what I guessed was a normal volume.

"Load-y should be bringing her back to exam room six now."

Jesus Christ. *This bitch.*

"Load-y?" he asked, confused. Justifiably motherfucking confused. No one on the planet should have a nickname based on a come shot.

Melissa sighed. "The nurse."

Silence descended between them until she elaborated. "*Your* new nurse."

"Are you talking about Melody?"

"Yeah. Load-y. That's what she likes to go by."

"She likes to go by *Load-y?*" I could literally hear the disbelief combined with amusement coloring his voice. If his tone had an actual color, I'd say it was aubergine—*because what the fuck kind of color is that anyway?*

"Yep. She loves it."

Yeah, it was safe to say that Melissa was probably going to be my least favorite coworker in the office. She spent most of her time browsing BuzzFeed and watching YouTube makeup tutorials behind the reception desk. That, on its own, I could support. I was just as down to see what my McDonald's order said about my sex life as anyone else.

But she also had a penchant for attitude, laziness, and obviously, horrible nicknames. *Load-y.* Holy water in a wineglass, that was by far the worst name anyone had ever come up with. It made me sound like a washed-up old porn star who had taken one too many money shots, and I had a feeling that was her exact intent.

With both Marlene and Melissa at the helm, I was honestly starting to wonder how this office ran smoothly on a daily basis without any major issues or lawsuits. Quite frankly, it was a modern fucking miracle. I mean, *try to fart and take a crap* wasn't the world's best nursing advice.

As I set out the instruments for a pap smear, Will peeked his head in. "Are we all set, Load-y?" His grin was all I needed to see to know he was fucking with me.

I rolled my eyes and smirked. "Yeah. All set."

"Interesting choice in nickname…"

"Oh, yeah. I love it. And it has absolutely nothing to do with Melissa trying to deliver a virtual tit punch," I explained in sarcasm. "What can I say? I just love going by *Load-y*. It has a certain sophistication to it, don't you think?"

He chuckled softly. Unlike listening to Marlene, I didn't have any doubts that seeing Will's smiling face and hearing his laughter were one of my favorite parts of my day.

The man had a great smile—knock you to your knees type of stuff.

And a sexy laugh. And a sexy body. And a—

Good Lord, my brain needed a filter.

"Oh, yeah. It's amazing it's still available for use. I heard the Queen was looking to trademark it," he teased.

My cheeks pulled up as I smiled.

"I'm going to make a quick call in my office, and I'll be ready in about five minutes."

I nodded. "Sounds good."

It had taken a good two weeks for us to get past the ridiculousness that was my first day on the job, and a good week and a half of that was achieved through semisuccessful avoidance.

But it finally felt like enough time had passed to let go of the embarrassment of his unsanitary offer of a gloved greeting and my unexpected peep show. Even the encounter in the supply closet had felt relatively normal in comparison. And we'd fallen into a good working relationship, with the added bonus of actually being able to make eye contact ever since.

And now that I was paying attention, I'd learned a few things that had me wanting to do the opposite of avoiding him.

Will was fucking awesome to work with. He was never a dick to staff and always treated his patients as individuals, and he was never in a bad mood—at least not with me. He made jokes and lightened my day instead of stressing me out.

In the world of medicine, those kinds of physicians were hard to come by. Especially when you took in the fact that Will Cummings wasn't your average physician. He was the lead physician in his practice and the Chief of Obstetrics at St. Luke's. The man had achieved some serious professional milestones in his young career, and with it came a ton of pressure.

Not to mention that he was gaining quite the popularity with his show.

The Doctor Is In.

I'd been hearing about Will's show through office gossip and chatter since my first day. Well, if you considered the odd interview I had with Betty, I guess I'd actually been hearing about it since the moment I stepped through the practice doors.

The staff in this office had a lot of opinions about Dr. Obscene—some good, some bad, and some so inappropriate that I had to walk away rather than listen.

Marlene, though, appeared to be enjoying the hell out of it every episode that aired—probably even recording them for future viewing pleasure.

For an old lady who'd been living in the medical world for nearly forty years and honestly never seemed too concerned with doing the actual work that was needed to keep the office running on a daily basis, she was more than concerned with Will's episodes of the series.

It had only taken me a week to realize that each episode aired on Tuesday evening.

How did I know this?

Because Marlene was her happiest on Tuesday afternoons. Once the clock neared four, the woman had a pep in her step and actually took the time to greet patients, leading them into the exam rooms with a gallant wave, versus herding them in like cattle and offering nothing more than a frustrated sigh and annoyed eyes.

And it had everything to do with *The Doctor Is In*.

The show portrayed him as Dr. Obscene, but I didn't get it. From my perspective, the title didn't match the man.

I'd inadvertently shown him my boobs, for Pete's sake, and he'd done everything humanly possible *not* to look. Based on that awkward as hell situation, if anyone was obscene out of the two of us, I'd say it was me.

After overhearing whispered conversation after conversation about *The Doctor Is In* star, my curiosity had reached an all-time peak. The episodes may have been weekly, but the office chatter was endless. I couldn't stop myself from tuning in and finding out what all the fuss was about with my own eyes.

The first episode had felt weird. The Will I knew and the Will that was schmoozing and charming his way across my TV were two different men. On camera, he was a force to be reckoned with—flashing flirty winks at nurses, chatting to patients with a sexy smirk permanently across his full lips.

Off camera, he was professional and had a fantastic bedside manner. He was equal parts caring and concerned, while managing to get straight to the important tasks at hand. Sure, he had tried to shake my hand after pulling his own hand out of a vagina, and he did have a flirtier smile than some, but who was I to judge? Six hours into my first day, I'd re-enacted *Girls Gone Wild*.

I'd only known Will for a short period of time, but my impression of him didn't at all match the man nicknamed Dr. OB*scene*.

But even I couldn't deny I was a bit addicted to the show. Sure, I was nowhere near Marlene's level of excitement, but I definitely had the sucker set to DVR every Tuesday night. Which was interesting in itself. I'd really never been one to watch TV, especially reality shows. I'd much rather spend my time browsing eBay for weird, abstract art or curling up behind a good book. Television had never really done it for me.

Until now.

Until Will.

I wasn't sure if it was because I enjoyed the show itself or if I just enjoyed the man on the show—or at least, my version of him—an enigma of sexy and brilliant and adorably awkward.

My version?

Well, shit.

Two weeks in, and I'd already done something enormously stupid.

Why the hell do I have to like the guy?

CHAPTER *seven*

M Y CELL PHONE RANG IN THE POCKET OF MY COAT AS I HEADED FOR THE cafeteria in the hospital. I was inducing two women today and rounding on the bedrest of a third. I'd expected to go into the office for appointments first thing this morning, have my coffee, and get things moving before I headed over here, but one of the babies didn't like my plan.

Sarah Jeffries was in active labor; she'd come in about three hours ago, and I'd just gone in and broken her water to try to keep her dilation progressing. She'd stalled out around five centimeters, and even though she'd had an epidural, she still wasn't exactly thrilled with the idea of being in labor for all of eternity.

I checked the screen quickly and saw that it was the number of the office.

"Hello?"

"Hey, Dr. Cummings. Load-y just called in to say she's running five minutes late. Something about the subway and a banana. I don't know. She never makes much sense to me."

I shook my head at Melissa's theatrics. "Fine. Just send her over to the hospital when she gets in. We've got one in active labor and another induction in two hours."

"Okay. Will do."

"Great. Thanks."

This would be Melody's first day at the hospital with me, but I'd done some searching—cough, research—once I'd met her, about her past experience.

That's not creepy, right?

I guess it wouldn't have been if I hadn't done it for more personal reasons than professional. I couldn't help it, though. I couldn't get the picture of her out of my head. But at least half the time, she was clothed. That's something, right?

Anyway, she'd been working as a night shift labor and delivery nurse for the last five years, so I had no doubts she could handle being thrown right into the hospital fire.

Hell, she was probably dying for a little excitement after being confined to the office with Melissa and Marlene for three weeks.

The cafeteria was already bustling with the breakfast crowd when I stepped inside, but I had only one thing in sight. Coffee shone like a beacon on the far wall, radiating its energizing brilliance as though a Columbian with a donkey stood beside it, so I kept my head down and avoided eye contact to ease my passage.

The last thing I needed was to have some kind of interaction or discussion about me or the show or any-fucking-thing before I guzzled about a gallon.

Victory sounded inside my head as I made it there without incident and yanked a cup from the stack. Glorious heat spread through my palm as my cup filled with the hot liquid, and the smell of full brain function and better decisions made me smile.

I was just reaching for the jug of milk when I made the mistake of looking up and across the room.

Damn. Spotted.

Scott Shepard beamed at the sight of me, and then he wasted no time following it with his distinctive, playful boom. "Will Cummings!"

I smiled in spite of myself. Scott's brand of fun was contagious. He flirted with life—and everything female within it—with a fervor I could only dream of. If I was a player in the game, he was the whole damn team.

I didn't yell back, though. I waited for him to make his way across the room and get within a respectable distance before opening my own mouth.

See? Notwithstanding all of the evidence to the contrary, I'm a respectable human being.

"Scott," I greeted with a handshake.

His mocking smile made me want to punch him in the fucking stomach. "Stop looking at me like that."

"Touchy, touchy. Someone's in a bad mood."

"Just you wait," I grumbled, using a little red straw to stir the milk in my coffee. "You will be too."

He laughed. *Naïve prick.* "You're assuming everyone is as good at looking like an asshole as you are." He reached out and jostled me by the shoulder patronizingly. "You really are the best."

"Oh, no, Scott," I disagreed magnanimously, a hand to my chest. "I assure you, as much as the rest of us try, we'll never top you in the asshole department. Just ask Mandy. And Sarah. And Monica."

For the first time during our encounter, he started to look a little less than sure of himself. The smug smile still held, but his level of confidence wavered. I could see it in his eyes. He didn't like hurting women, even if he'd done it so much he could make a living out of it.

"I guess you really are in a bad mood."

Fuck. Now I feel bad.

"Sorry, Scott. Just…with the show and everything…and I haven't had my coffee." I held up my full cup as evidence. "I guess you're right. I am the biggest asshole."

His signature smirk came back with a vengeance. "Well, at least you recognize it now." He patted me on the back and made his exit before I could say anything else.

Fucker. Always tricking me into apologizing when he was the real schmuck.

I swallowed a mouthful of hot coffee as I watched him go, but it didn't come without consequences.

"Oh, fuck!" I whisper-yelled, grabbing my throat as that shit burned me all the way from the tip of my tongue to my stomach.

Obviously, it was one of those days.

Just as I pushed my way out the door of the cafeteria, a familiar back turned the corner up the hall, and for once, he didn't look like he was rushing from one surgery to the next.

"Nick," I called to get his attention. He turned around at the sound of my voice, but he didn't stop walking. Still, I didn't need him to be fully immobile to catch the look on his face.

Oh, shit. He did *not* look happy to see me.

I liked Nick. He was a good guy, if a little serious, and deviously brilliant when it came to neurosurgery. I didn't want to be on his shit list.

I broke into a jog to catch up to him.

"Nick, hold up."

"No, Will. I don't feel like talking. I don't feel like commiserating over your fallen reputation, and I don't feel like forgiving you for talking me into this mess." He shook his head, the ends of his mouth turned down, all while I jogged along next to him. He was still walking.

Jesus. How long are his legs?

He finally turned and came to a stop to look me in the eye after another fifty feet of jogging on my part, and he did it with a heavy sigh. "Winnie already called. She's worried about my episodes and what they'll mean for Lexi. She already has enough trouble fitting in as it is."

Winnie was a badass doctor and a woman I'd worked under for most of my residency. But now she was the team physician for the professional football team, the New York Mavericks, and married to Wes Lancaster, one of my brother-in-law's best friends. But she was also Nick's ex from way back and the mother of his daughter, Lexi.

I wouldn't want her to have my balls in a vise either. Especially not when seeing my kid was the item at stake.

"I didn't know… I had *no idea* it would be like this, man. I'm sorry."

He took a deep breath and ran a frustrated hand through his hair. "Me too. I know this isn't your fault, Will. I just…"

Have a remarkable kid that I've spent years trying to turn my life around for, I silently thought the words for him.

"I get it. Seriously. Don't worry about me, dude."

He very nearly broke into a smile. "Wow. Close call," I teased. "You're almost smiling."

That tipped the scales, and the corners of his mouth actually turned up. "Wouldn't want that, would we?"

"I gotta run grab some shit and then get back up to four. Catch up later?"

"Sure, man." He held out his hand, and I shook it. Something was still plaguing him. I could see it in the fatigue around his eyes, but I wasn't about to delve into it.

I currently had my own problems.

Not knowing when Melody would make it there, I pushed through the door to the stairwell and drank my coffee as I climbed to the fourth floor, also known as the maternity wing.

The last drops left the cup and hit my tongue as I moved through the door and onto the floor. I ducked inside a room and threw away the empty cup in the trash inside the door and then continued down the hall to the supply closet.

I needed a suture kit in case my patient tore during delivery and to find something to give her as a push gift—society's modern-day reward for having endured the trials of labor. It wasn't exactly a hospital-approved use of supplies, but I agreed with this new era—these women deserved a little something extra for their trouble—and paying for each gift on my own would make me broke in no time.

The door to the supply closet creaked as I pushed it open, and as if provoked, other sounds exploded around me: several supplies hitting the floor in violent succession, an amusingly creative expletive involving the words "pickax" and "cockpecker," and finally, the heavy breathing of someone trying their best to go unnoticed and failing spectacularly.

My initial plan was to give them what they wanted, get in and get out with the stuff I needed and do my best to ignore whatever couple I'd found in a starkly nude, professionally compromising position. I'd been in this situation myself a time or two, and like any good boy, I was trying really hard to live by that *treat others how you want to be treated* credo. Plus, just because my sex life was officially ruined by the show from hell didn't mean everyone else's was.

And I would have followed the plan, I really would have, if it hadn't been Melody I found and she hadn't been wearing way more clothes than I was expecting. Though, if I was honest, Melody in fewer clothes probably would have decreased the probability of me leaving without incident even further.

"Mel?" I asked, my mouth curving up into a smile as her body jerked unnaturally and rotated woodenly to face me. She seemed disappointed that her back's powers of invisibility had worn off but not all that surprised.

"Oh, hey, Dr. Cummings," she tried to remark casually, brushing some loose hair off of her face with one hand and keeping the other behind her body. "What brings you here?"

My smile deepened. "Supplies. And you?"

"Oh, you know. The same."

I wanted to let her off the hook because she was so fucking cute, but the little tiny voice in the back of my head that actually helped me pass my boards spoke up like an annoying parakeet. *Squawk, what if she's stealing drugs, squawk.*

"Oh, okay," I said with a nod. Her face eased and she moved to go past me, but I stopped her with a gentle hand at her elbow and dropped my voice to a playful whisper. "What, oh what are you hiding, Melody?"

Her shoulders sagged as her eyes rose slowly from the ground to meet mine. She looked embarrassed but resigned, so I steeled myself for whatever horrible deed I was about to uncover and the horrendous circumstances of dealing with it.

"Tongue depressors," she replied in a rush, the gust of her expelled breath hitting me right along with my surprise—and the box, which she shoved hard—in my chest.

"Tongue depressors?" I asked, but my shock did nothing to slow her painfully embarrassed, highly comical confession. I looked down, and— *hot damn, look at that*—tongue depressors.

"I know. Stealing them from the hospital is wrong and unethical and completely unacceptable. I'm always telling myself, *Mel, why don't you just order them online or, for fuck's sake, steal something more interesting if you're going to put it all on the line,* but they're just so useful."

"Useful," I muttered, dumbfounded, and she nodded.

"I make a jar of the week's tasks and pull one out to keep myself on my toes and prevent my already pathetic life from seeming mundane, and I use them to wax my legs with those at-home kits because the ones they include are so flimsy, and sometimes I use them to write personal affirmations—"

"Tongue depressors?" I asked again, cutting her off with a smile.

"Yeah."

I cleared my throat and stepped even closer into her space, pulling the box from her hand—we'd both been maintaining our hold on it—as she backed nervously into the shelf behind her and made it rock. "And why is it again that you don't just order them online?"

She shrugged helplessly. "Easy access?"

Immediately, unbidden and uninvited, my motherfucker of a male mind flashed to an image of sweet Melody, *my nurse*, bent over in this very supply closet, hands on the shelf and her ass out and inviting, a skirt pulled up around her perfect round hips. *Easy access.*

Danger, Will Cummings. Motherfucking danger. I'd managed a spotless record of not fucking my actual employees since getting the practice up and running, but that record currently felt like I might run it off of a cliff into a catastrophic explosion scenario. *Back away slowly.*

"Ha…ha." I forced a laugh. *Jesus, I sound crazy.* Wrinkles formed at the corners of Melody's hazel green eyes and sucked my focus in like little tributary rivers.

What am I supposed to be doing again?

"Will," she called, her lips so close I could practically taste them. Okay, a good foot away, but still, they were good lips.

"Yeah?" I asked softly, mesmerized completely.

"Are you…um…"

"Yeah?" Two more seconds like this and we were going to kiss.

"Are you gonna—"

"Yeah."

Are we going to kiss?

"Oh, yeah."

"You're going to rat me out?" she peeped, her voice rising a full octave in despair.

Wait…rat her out? What?

"Wait. No. Rat you out?" My mind struggled to pull the blood back from my dick quickly enough to catch up. Not kissing. *She's not thinking about kissing at all, you fucking schmuck.* "For the tongue depressors?" I managed around the knot of would-have-been embarrassment clogging my throat.

"Well, yeah."

Despite the disappointment of circumstances being considerably different than I'd been imagining for the last two minutes, I smiled.

"No, *Load-y*. I'm not going to rat you out for stealing the tongue depressors."

She smiled and exhaled a breath of relief.

"Rat you out? No. Tease you mercilessly until the end of time about it? Yes."

"*You* tease *me*? That's rich."

I crossed my arms over my chest and settled into a grin. For the first time ever with Mel, I thought I might actually manage something other than acting like a bumbling idiot.

"Right? Seems like it might be refreshing, though. You know, spreading some of the office ridicule around."

"Uh…Load-y? I think Melissa's got that covered."

"She's just jealous because she's the lesser Mel."

Her breath caught a little, and I knew I had to get out of there. If I didn't, I'd end up doing something I'd regret. Or she would. Because, yeah, I probably wouldn't regret it.

I forced myself to move away and over to the door. The cardboard in my hand flexed under the overall pressure running through my body and reminded me to turn around.

"Hey," I called. "Think fast."

I tossed the box of tongue depressors, and she caught it adeptly.

"Come on," I told her when she didn't move. "Haven't you heard? We've got a lady doing her best to become a lady with a baby."

CHAPTER *eight*

"**F**EEL LIKE TAKING A WALK, LOAD-Y?" WILL ASKED WITH AN AMUSED SMIRK.

I glanced up from my comfortable perch in the break room where I was currently browsing through the pictures of the newest issue of *Vogue*. "Not if you keep calling me that."

"But I thought you loved that nickname?" He feigned confusion, and I scratched the side of my face with my middle finger. He moved closer to my chair and peeked over my shoulder. "Oh. Wow. You're probably too busy, huh?"

I smiled and dramatically turned the page of the magazine, demurring, "I'm so busy right now doing my best impression of Melissa." But my heart didn't protest, not even in jest. It jumped in my chest.

A few days ago, Will had asked me to come over to the hospital for the first time. Of course, it wasn't like he'd asked me on a date or anything. Just the hospital…for work.

And I'd been running late anyway, so really, Melissa had sniped the direction toward me as soon as I'd walked in the door.

But I wasn't surprised half of my brain was trying to twist it into something it wasn't. See, labor and delivery was a hella messy job. Sure, we suit up with protective gear, so to speak, but by the time one of our patients had gotten to the hospital that afternoon, she'd been crowning. Will had done nothing more than don a pair of gloves and get right in there.

A twisted part of me wondered if she was one of the ones Marlene had threatened with death if she came to the hospital before she was actually in active labor.

Still, all of the fluids had done a number on his shirt, and I'd walked in on him changing. He was surprised to see me—to be fair, I *had* walked into the men's locker room by mistake—but I wasn't surprised at what I saw. No, I'd been fantasizing about it for an embarrassing number of days now. Sleek, toned muscle, tan, smooth skin, and some of the best obliques I'd ever laid eyes on were just the beginning.

It made me wonder about the things I couldn't see. Mainly, his penis.

He grinned. "Hey, she's a good kid. Maybe a little lazy at times, but she works hard."

I raised a pointed brow. "Define hard, please," I joked, but honestly, the joke was on me. My brain went straight to the dirty.

Will…*hard*.

Holy hell. My penchant for thinking about Will's penis was starting to get a little creepy. It wasn't normal to think about one penis this often. Especially when the owner of said penis was my boss. For some reason, his penis had become some kind of phallus-shaped mythical character in my brain. I had to find a way to stop it.

Find a way to see it. If you see it, then you'll know.

Yeah. I'd have to keep brainstorming…

Will's grin grew wider, and my cheeks flushed pink. I'd veered way too far off the path of what was considered normal. It was one thing to understand the sexual innuendo with the word hard, but it was another to bypass hard and speed toward imagining Will's penis naked and hard.

I needed help. A shrink. Brain surgery. *Something.*

His grin was so perfect, it looked like an artist had etched it directly on his face. I sighed.

"Oh my God. I didn't mean that kind of hard." If he only knew.

He waggled his brows. "You said it, not me."

"The expression on your face said everything I needed to know."

Will winked, and I immediately wondered, was Will flirting with me?

Yes, please. Flirt me so hard, Will.

Whoa. *Pump the brakes.* There was no way he was really flirting.

Ugh. Sometimes, I really hated my brain. It was like it had gone all haywire since I'd broken up with Eli. Maybe I was too sex-deprived? I mean, the last time I'd actually had sex was starting to get further and further away, and a girl only had so much time to masturbate when her bed was located in the same room in which her mother loved to do jazzercise at all hours of the day.

Yeah. I probably just needed sex.

Sex with Will's penis.

Oh, for fuck's sake. I had to steer this conversation somewhere else. Medical questions. Patient updates. China. Sweater knitting. *Anywhere else.*

Listen, I swear my brain isn't generally a kaleidoscope of dicks and cocks.

Seriously. It isn't.

"Where are you taking a walk to?" I asked in hopes that it would help me not feel like such a pervert.

"Since Dr. Meadows is slammed with inpatient deliveries, I offered to head over to the hospital for an hour or two and handle some of the triage patients while she finished the deliveries."

My brow pinched in confusion. "So, you just want me to walk over to the hospital with you?"

"Well, I'd actually like you to see the patients with me," he explained with a grin.

"Oh boy, I've got you spoiled, huh?" I teased. "I'm such an awesome nurse, you don't even want to go over to the hospital without me. What do you do now when it's your turn to be on call for twenty-four hours?"

"I generally just cry," he jested. "Hell, sometimes I even cry during the deliveries."

I giggled. "You're going to start losing patients that way."

"See? Now you have to come. My career is on the line here."

"Ugh," I groaned. "You're not going to leave me alone until I say yes, huh?"

He shrugged. "Probably not."

"And who's going to see your patients? You still have four more appointments before the day is through."

"Surprisingly enough, Dr. Elders agreed to man up and do some extra work."

I grinned. "Color me shocked." What Will's disposition had in spades, Dr. Elders's lacked completely. It was amazing how different two doctors in the same practice could be in virtually every way. I also doubted Dr. Elders's penis was anywhere near as nice as Will's.

Dammit!

Will winked. "I know, right?"

"I think there's more to it than you just asking and him agreeing. I bet you had to bribe him with something…"

He didn't even deny it—just shrugged shamelessly. "Mavericks tickets."

"I knew it!" I pointed at him with my index finger. "How good are the seats?"

"Well, it's when they play New England, and they're box seats."

I let out a low whistle. "Sheesh…must be nice to just have tickets like that lying around."

"It probably helps that my brother-in-law is best friends with the owner, and my sister runs their marketing department, *and* I didn't have to pay for them."

"Friends in high places kind of thing?"

"Something like that," he said. "But I think it's more like 'friends with equally low morals in high places.'"

I shook my head. So his friends were obviously good people.

"So, is that a yes?"

"Is what a yes?"

"Are you going to come with me?"

"Come with you?"

Come with Will? Yes. Yes. I'd love to come with Will, preferably with his penis inside of me.

"To the hospital," he explained.

Holy hell. I *really* need help. Maybe I could look up a number for a hotline at the hospital…

"Oh! Oh, right," I stuttered. "Yeah…sure… I mean, you didn't really give me any other option since I'd have to deal with Dr. Elders for the rest of the day."

"You don't like Dr. Elders?"

I glared at him. "He's old. He's mean. And he pretty much hates everyone."

"He's basically the male version of Marlene," he whispered conspiratorially, and I laughed.

"Okay, Dr. Cummings." I hopped out of my chair. "I'm at your service. Since you can't live without me and all."

He grinned and gestured toward the hallway. "After you, Nurse Load-y."

I flipped him the bird over my shoulder, and his soft chuckles followed me all the way through the office and out the entrance doors.

I'd never had more fun at work, and I wasn't really even sure I liked my job.

God, you're in trouble.

After a quick tour of all the things I hadn't explored the other day, especially the triage area, Will and I settled in, seeing patients in a smooth and orderly fashion. We'd been handling triage for about two hours and had managed to lower the number of patients waiting to be seen from fifteen to two.

Generally, when it came to labor triage patients, they were at the hospital to see if they were *in* labor. Once we assessed that, they got passed on to the doctor on call. Lucky for Dr. Meadows—who was currently elbow-deep in several deliveries happening one right after the other— only one of the patients we'd seen got admitted to the hospital.

Between playful banter and patient care, Will and I had managed to send the rest home with instructions on when to call the office or come back into the hospital.

While Will finished up charting, I started to review the next patient's medical file.

Carmen Dominguez. Age 25.

Reason to be seen: Abdominal pain.

Gestation: Not confirmed. Patient believes she is 8-9 months pregnant.

Last prenatal visit: No prenatal care.

Last period: Patient is unsure.

Past obstetric history: One prior pregnancy at age 18 that resulted in a miscarriage at 3 months, and a D&C was performed in Venezuela.

Past surgical history: Appendectomy at the age of 12 in Venezuela.

Past medical history: Unknown.

Relevant social history: Patient recently immigrated to the USA one year ago.

Throughout my nursing career, I'd always made a point of doing my research on the patient before entering the exam room. Personally, I'd never much enjoyed sitting on the exam table while a medical professional scrolled wordlessly through my chart in front of me. Those types of interactions made me feel more like an item on a checklist instead of an actual living, breathing human with medical questions or concerns.

And today, for these people, it was no different. They wanted someone who read for content, not an asshole who skimmed.

I browsed through the rest of Carmen's medical chart outside of her exam room, and her lack of medical records and prenatal care put me on high alert.

Sadly, these types of situations occurred more than most people would think. Oftentimes, it had to do with socioeconomic status, poor education, language barriers, financial burdens, and a lack of insurance. But no matter the reason, with obstetrics, it meant possible adverse effects for two patients instead of one.

I stepped into triage room four and found Carmen sitting on the exam table, leaning to the side with a wince on her face.

"Hi, Carmen," I greeted and clicked the door shut. "I'm Melody, Dr. Cummings's nurse."

"Hello," she responded in a thick Spanish accent. Her eyes watched me hesitantly as both hands rested protectively around her pregnant belly.

"What brings you in today?"

"My stomach has been hurting," she admitted, caressing it from top to bottom slowly.

"How long has it been hurting?" I asked as I slid on a pair of gloves. Some pain could be natural, as even Braxton Hicks contractions presented mild pain.

"For a few hours," she responded, and her face started to strain with discomfort.

Oh, man. This might be more than Braxton Hicks.

"Okay, well, if you don't mind lying back on the table, I'm just going to check your belly."

She followed my instructions, but I couldn't miss the way her brow furrowed and her mouth pinched into a firm line.

"Is this the pain that made you come in?" I asked and gently placed my hands on her abdomen.

"*Sí*…Uh…Yes," she whispered, near agony toning her voice.

Her stomach was tight and firm like a drum. *Contractions.*

If she was as far into this show as I suspected, Carmen was one tough cookie.

"And you said you've been feeling like this for a few hours?" I asked as I glanced at my watch and noted the length. *Thirty-five seconds.* "Do you remember about what time it started?"

"Uh…before breakfast," she responded as she worked to catch her breath.

Before I could continue my exam, another contraction started to work its way across her abdomen. Carmen gripped her belly in discomfort, and I gently encouraged her to breathe through it. "Big, deep breaths, Carmen. In through your nose and out through your mouth," I said and grabbed the fetal monitor and ultrasound gel to place on her belly.

I moved the monitor across her rounded abdomen in search of the baby's heart tones.

Nothing.

"Is everything okay?" she asked with gritted teeth, and I offered a reassuring smile.

"I promise I'm going to take very good care of you and your baby, Carmen," I said calmly. "Now, I just want you to turn on your left side and focus on making sure you're giving your baby lots and lots of good oxygen, okay?"

"Okay," she said, fear working its way into the creases at the corners of her eyes.

As I continued to search for heart tones and came up empty, I reached toward the wall and clicked the button that let the staff know I needed immediate assistance.

Bum-Bum. The first sounds of the baby's heart rhythm finally reached my ears, but it wasn't the normal, gallop-like noises that reassured. It was slow, much, much slower than it should be.

I gently pressed my fingers to Carmen's wrist to make sure I wasn't detecting her heartbeat on the monitor and immediately came to the ominous realization that I did, in fact, have baby's heart rate.

"Carmen, have you been having any pressure in your vaginal area? Do you feel the urge to push?"

She nodded frantically. "I feel like I need to go to the bathroom right now," she moaned, and then her eyes went wide. "Oh, no. I feel like I'm peeing."

"It's okay," I said soothingly. "I think your water just broke." I switched out my gloves—removing the blue ones for a pair of sterile ones off the exam table. I moved toward the middle of the bed and sat on the edge. "Carmen, I need you to relax your legs a bit. I'm going to check to see how far dilated you are, okay?"

"Okay," she whispered.

"You're going to feel some pressure," I instructed. "I just need you to stay as relaxed as possible and breathe through it, okay?"

"Okay."

The instant my fingers reached her cervix, I knew what the issue was. Not only was Carmen six centimeters dilated with ruptured membranes, but she also had a prolapsed cord. Which was the exact opposite of a good situation. A very, very bad situation, actually. Prolapsed cords were fairly rare, but when they occurred, delivery had to be straight-away. And in Carmen's case, since she wasn't fully dilated, it most likely meant an emergency C-section.

It was at that moment that Dr. Cummings stepped inside the room. "Everything okay?"

"She's six centimeters. Gestation is unknown, but patient believes she's around eight months. Her water broke about forty-five seconds ago. And now, we have a prolapsed cord. I'm holding the baby's head above it. Fetal heart tones were fifty but have stabilized a little at 110 with the baby's head off the cord."

Will immediately peeked his head back out of the room and instructed the triage receptionist to notify the OR and neonatal team. "You know it's for sure the baby's head and not breech?" he asked and immediately shrugged out of his white exam coat and started donning OR gear.

"Yeah, I can feel fontanels."

"Is everything okay? Is my baby okay?" Carmen asked, her accent thicker with distress, and my eyes glanced toward the continuous fetal heart monitor noting that even with baby's head off the cord, the heart rate was continuing to dip below one hundred at times.

"Carmen, I'm Dr. Cummings," he introduced. "We have a bit of an emergency right now. The baby's head is on the umbilical cord, and we need to get the baby out as soon as possible. We're going to take you back to do an emergency C-section."

Her eyes went wide. "*Pero*…Right now?"

"Yes," he responded. "But I promise you I'm going to take very good care of your baby." His eyes met mine, and he nodded for me to get comfortable on the bed. "Ready to ride, Mel?"

"Let's do it," I said and pulled my legs onto the bed—with my hand still securely keeping Carmen's baby's head off its umbilical card—as Will pushed us out.

"Think your hand can hold up until we're scrubbed in and I can get the baby out?" he questioned as he pushed the bed down the hall and toward the obstetric ORs.

"Yep. I'll be fine." Luckily, it wasn't my first prolapsed cord experience.

Carmen's eyes met mine, and I could see the sheer terror of being a powerless mother in her gaze.

"Carmen, you're in good hands, okay? All you need to do is stay calm and keep taking those deep breaths like you have been. You're doing great."

"Okay," she whispered, and one lone tear started to drip from the corner of her eye.

"Did you come to the hospital by yourself?" I asked as the bed made its way to the OR doors and OR staff members started to help us suit up before heading in. A mask was placed across my face and a scrub cap over my hair.

She nodded as an OR nurse placed a surgical cap over her hair.

"Is there anyone we can call to come to the hospital?"

She shook her head, and a few more tears dripped down her cheeks. "My husband is at work and doesn't have a cell phone."

"It's okay, Carmen," I reassured again as OR staff helped moved both Carmen and me onto the sterile and draped surgical table. "What's your husband's name?"

"Miguel."

"And where does he work?"

"A *construcción* company."

"Do you know which one?"

"Phillips and Neiman."

I glanced over my shoulder and met the gaze of who I thought was the circulating nurse. "Can you do me a favor and call out to triage? Ask them to find the number to Phillips and Neiman construction company and see if they can get in touch with her husband."

"Sure thing," she responded. "What's her husband's name?"

"Miguel Dominguez."

"Did we get fetal heart tones?" Will asked as he moved toward the OR table.

"Yes," one nurse responded. "Tones were one hundred."

"Let's get moving, then," he announced and stood beside the patient. "Okay, Carmen," Will said behind his surgical mask as he gripped her hand tightly. "We're going to have you breathe in some medicine that will put you to sleep so we can perform the surgery quickly," he instructed while the anesthesiologist placed the mask over her face. "Just take deep breaths. I promise everything is going to be okay."

As Carmen started to fade to sleep, Will prepared for surgery. His eyes met mine, and he nodded toward my hand that was still striving to keep the baby's head off of the umbilical cord. "Can you hang in there for about thirty more seconds?"

"Yep." Honestly, looking into his confident, *proud* eyes, I felt like I could do anything.

Once the patient was under anesthesia, Dr. Cummings got to work. He didn't waste any time, making a clean cut and working at a quick yet smooth pace. I'd seen a lot of physicians perform C-sections, and I'd seen a lot of physicians perform C-sections under stressful situations, and it was apparent that Will was the Chief of Obstetrics for a reason.

When it came to emergent situations, he stayed cool, calm, and collected. He never raised his voice at the staff, and that alone made a world of difference, keeping everyone else relaxed and focused as well.

It took a lot to impress me when it came to the medical field, especially obstetrics.

And I couldn't deny that Will had impressed me.

Moments later, healthy cries filled the room as Will held up a pint-sized baby girl. The waiting neonatal nurse took the baby from his hands, and I think everyone in the room breathed a sigh of relief when the first minute Apgar was announced as nine.

"You saved her life, you know," Will said, and his eyes met mine. "You saved that little girl's life."

I stared back at him.

"You did good, Mel," he added as he continued to finish the surgery. "You did really good."

There was a part of me that was happy, excited, and grateful that I was able to act quickly and do what needed to be done. And I definitely felt warm about Will's recognition and trust in my ability.

But there was another part of me that felt sad.

Sad that Carmen had slipped through the cracks. Sad that she had gone nearly her entire pregnancy without any prenatal care. Sad that if she hadn't come to the hospital when she did, she could have lost her baby.

There was a big issue with the way the health care system worked.

There shouldn't be any woman out there, no matter her ethnicity or socioeconomic status, who didn't have access to the health care she needed.

Maybe if there had been a women's free clinic within St. Luke's, Carmen would have gotten the prenatal care she needed.

It was something to think about.

And it was definitely something a lot of women in the city would benefit from.

And what better place than St. Luke's?

After all, it'd sure been doing a good job of giving me what I needed.

CHAPTER*nine*

Will

TRIED NOT TO READ THE SPARKLING CRYSTALS AS THEY WINKED UP AT ME UNDER THE fluorescent lights. I mean, I was a goddamn professional. But professionalism only went so far.

Especially when each crystal, placed precisely and with intent, played a part in spelling out the words "Date me, Dr. Obscene."

Dr. Obscene? Fucking seriously?

"It's what they call you," the exposed woman offered without prompting. Obviously, my face wasn't completely with the professional program.

Shit. Maybe this is why I always lose at Thatch's poker nights.

I glanced up to Melody, hoping she'd save me, but she just shook her head. She had no idea what the fuck was going on either.

At least I'm not alone.

Wait… My eyes narrowed as Melody looked to the ground and smiled.

Fuck. Maybe she did know what the hell was going on. She was just good at pretending like she didn't. The more I scrutinized her expression, the more certain I was that she, unlike me, wasn't surprised by the words adorning our current patient's vagina.

I tried to get her attention, but it didn't work. She was a like a Jedi at avoidance, and I only had myself to blame—I'd given her all that practice right off the bat. She knew my weaknesses.

She is your weakness, my mind whispered. *Shut up*, I told it.

Not that it would have mattered if she'd looked up. What was I going to do? Mouth *what the fuck is going on?*

No. As much merit as the idea held in theory, I didn't think feigning invisibility—or at the very least, discretion—would work in practice. Mel had the right idea by ignoring everything.

I tried my best to follow her lead.

Grabbing Jamie Abrams's chart from the counter, I pulled it in front of me and focused on the words as hard as I could. "So it says there that you came in today for a suspected urinary tract infection?"

"Oh," she mumbled. "I thought maybe I did, but all of the symptoms seem to have cleared up."

I looked over my shoulder at her urine sample on the counter and studied the test strip on top of the cup. All clear.

"Well, you didn't test like you have one either, so I think we can rule that out. But let's talk about those symptoms a little more. Get to the bottom of what's going on."

She was young, twenty-one according to her chart, and unverified symptoms of a urinary tract infection without an actual cause were concerning. So I wasn't about to write this off as nothing, even though something smelled like fish.

And no, it wasn't bacterial vaginosis. She was just as fresh and clear as the crystals glued to her.

"They really weren't that bad."

I looked back down at her folder.

"Your chart says it was urgent."

Her cheeks flushed bright red, but I had to hand it to her, she looked me directly in the eye and swallowed any and all shame. I didn't think I would have had the balls at her age. And maybe, therein that very anatomy, lay the problem.

"Okay, so I lied. I'm sorry, Dr. Cummings. I just wanted to meet you. I've been watching the show—"

She must have noticed the corners of my mouth turn down because she switched tactics pretty quickly.

"And I've heard you are an incredible doctor, but your waiting list for new patients goes out a while."

One of the crystals caught the light and subsequently my eye. Shit. Reaching forward, I pulled the paper blanket back down to cover all of her skin completely, being careful not to touch her or even come close in the process.

"All right, Jamie. I appreciate your honesty here, so here's how we'll handle it. When you leave, go ahead and schedule your annual appointment for next year. I see that you've just had this year's in your records."

She nodded sheepishly.

"But I appreciate your enthusiasm about our practice."

I smiled and moved toward the door and a rather wide-eyed-with-amusement Melody when Jamie called me back.

"Dr. Cummings?"

"Yes?"

"What about the date?"

So close.

I didn't really understand why the guy on my show—unfortunately, me—was so appealing, but I was conscious enough to be sensitive to her feelings. I dropped my voice, trying to soften the rejection around the edges.

"Sorry, Jamie. I have a strict rule against dating patients, and it seems you just signed on for the long run, right?"

Her mouth opened and closed, gulping air like a fish out of water for a few seconds before a hint of a grin pulled her lips closed.

The expert player has been played.

She nodded. "See you in a year, Dr. Cummings."

"Looking forward to it, Jamie."

"Take your time getting dressed," Melody told her as I headed for the door. "I'll meet you at the front desk with your paperwork so you can schedule your appointment for next year."

Several minutes later, Melody found me studying the next patient's chart in my office and called my attention with a soft knock.

"Can I come in?"

"Sure," I offered, curling my fingers toward my body.

She stepped inside and shut the door, locked the knob and took a seat in the chair in front of my desk. My eyebrows pulled together in confusion.

"What's up?"

She tapped her ear like it was a secret code and pointed everywhere around herself in a circle.

Ah. Prying ears everywhere.

Hope mushroomed in my stomach as I conjured up all of the reasons she could want to keep this conversation private.

Maybe she felt it too? Whatever this thing between us was.

"So…"

"Yeah?"

"Looks like you're a pretty hot commodity."

I shook my head and rolled my eyes.

"You're great, so I get it."

She thinks you're great. Ask her out. Just do it.

I opened my mouth, but no words formed before she filled the space with some of her own.

"Her vagina actually sparkled."

Oh. So we're going to talk about the patient.

"I honestly didn't think you could make the female anatomy that attractive."

"Hey, the female anatomy doesn't need that much help to be beautiful. Kind of like makeup. Less is sometimes more."

She laughed, carefree and easy, and I immediately craved more of it. Had to have it. Wondered how many organs I'd have to sell on the black market to get enough money to pay someone to break in to her apartment and make a video of her doing it on a loop.

Okay, that's creepy. Where the hell did that come from?

"We men like to feel powerful and caveman-like. It might not be right, but the power feeds us. That kind of instruction, insinuation, really, that I should become more acquainted with her takes away all the power."

She rolled her eyes, but she was still smiling. "Is this like asking for directions? Her vajazzle is like a map, and as a man, you're just not down with that?"

"Yes," I laughed. "It's exactly like that. Tremendous analogy."

"Shut up."

I winked, stupidly, and caught off guard, she turned her gaze away in a hurry. She gathered herself quickly and spoke again, though. "You're going to have to work hard to salvage your reputation after this. Every day I'm here, your problems from the show seem to be a little more substantial. I don't think I'd ever go to the trouble of faking a UTI to meet a man."

A big metaphorical arrow started flashing above her head with the words *this is your opening* written in neon above it. I couldn't put my finger on the particulars of my attraction, what it was that seemed to draw me to her so strongly, but understanding or not, it was there all the same—in a way that I knew wouldn't dissipate without any evidence to support the reasons it should. *She fucking works for you, and things could get hella awkward* apparently wasn't good enough.

"The problems are real, but maybe salvaging my reputation won't be so bad."

She laughed mockingly. "Yeah, you're right. It'll probably be a piece of cake."

High on her renewed laughter, I went for it. "Maybe dating you would do the trick."

All sounds of laughter cut off as though I'd physically choked her. I might have even heard a set of imaginary tires squeal as they forced themselves to a stop on the pavement. "What?"

Still, it wouldn't do me all that much good to back out now, so I per-severed. "Dating you. Maybe that would solve some of my problems. You're well-liked. I'd be off the market for all of the crazy women. And I won't even ask you to make an appointment or vajazzle yourself."

Her face settled into a mixture of pity and understanding. Her big eyes turned down at the corners, and half a dimple formed a hollow in her cheek. There was a smile there, but it was veiled in the sadness of a frown. The expression wasn't my favorite, but she still looked beautiful.

"This is a bad idea, Will. You can't date me to rebuild your image."

I could give two flying fucks about my image. Just say yes.

"Can I date you because I want to?"

"Will."

"Come on," I pleaded. "One date. What's that going to hurt? Seriously, I can be really endearing. I know I haven't done such a great job of show-ing that to you, but I swear I can."

And now you're begging. Oh, Will, how far you've fallen.

All traces of happiness fled her face, leaving only the pity to comfort the coming blow. "I'm sorry. It's not just you. It's me too. There's so much un-settled. So much I don't know about what I want and who I am. I just…"

I shrugged. Disappointment took the form of a full-body throb, but I ignored it. She was obviously right. It wasn't a good idea at all. I'd have to get out tonight. Find someone to fuck, balance out the obviously fucked-up hormones inside me, and move on.

"You're probably right. It might salvage my reputation, but think of the horrible things it'd do to yours." A ghost of a grin lifted the corners of her lips. "Saaaave yourseeelf," I cried, and her smile deepened just enough to be real.

Silence stretched between us for what felt like years but was likely no more than a few seconds before she stood up.

Hooking a thumb over her shoulder, she pointed to the exit. "Well, I should probably…"

"Right. Yeah, okay. Next patient. I'll see you out there."

"Okay," she agreed before stepping through the door and shutting it gently behind her.

Which was probably good. I needed a minute to get over myself and get back to business.

I stood up and pulled my coat back on when an old tongue depressor caught my eye on top of my filing cabinet.

I wasn't sure if the talk about not knowing things about herself was just talk, a way to take some of the focus off of me and soften the blow, or if she really felt that way, but our conversation in the supply closet of the hospital blared throughout my mind in response.

Tongue depressor affirmations.

I grabbed a Sharpie from my drawer, and without even thinking, the words flowed out of me and onto the thin piece of wood.

Open wide! Everything you're looking for is inside yourself.

I startled when she knocked on the door, and I slammed a hand down on top of it to cover it.

"Yeah?"

It sounded like there was a frog in my throat. Her eyebrows pinched together, but she didn't say anything. She probably just thought I was having a mental breakdown.

"Your next patient is in exam room eight."

"Okay, thanks. I'll be right there."

She studied me briefly before nodding and making a retreat down the hall.

I watched her go until I was sure the coast was clear and then lifted my hand. The ink had bled a little into the wood, but all in all, the affirmation was still legible. I read it a couple of times.

God, that's corny.

Opening the middle drawer of my desk, I picked up the tongue depressor and tossed it in.

Maybe I'd give it to her someday, but I'd already put myself out there enough for one day. Humiliation really is the sort of thing to which you have to acclimate—one painful encounter at a time.

CHAPTER *ten*

F**RIDAY WAS MY SECOND FAVORITE** F **WORD.** A**ND SINCE MY OTHER FAVORITE** F **WORD** wasn't appropriate to use in a work environment, I settled for repeating the one word that I could. Both of them brought me joy.

"Friday. Friday," I singsonged as I finished cleaning up exam room five. "Thank God it's Friday." I continued the tune as I skipped toward the nursing office to make sure there weren't any outstanding voice mails from patients waiting to be called.

"If you say Friday one more time, I will strangle you with this blood pressure cuff," Marlene huffed in her designated chair in front of her designated computer. I scrunched my face behind her back.

No, we didn't all have our own chairs and desks and computers—just Marlene. She'd claimed hers, thirty-five years ago, according to her, and it was a certainty that unless you wanted to see the giant white light guiding you toward the pearly gates, you stayed the fuck away. The torn-up piece of masking tape haphazardly placed across each item even said that in black Sharpie. *This is Marlene's. Stay the fuck away.*

"Oh, c'mon, Mar," I said with a grin. "Everyone loves Fridays. It's like a universal religion. It melts people from all over the world into one big pot."

Though, the truth of it was, I'd had a fucking knot in my stomach ever since I'd turned Will down, and some of my weekend cheer was probably a means to cope. But she hadn't turned down one of the nicest guys she'd ever met for the date she'd been fantasizing about ever since she'd met him.

Had she?

"Not me," she muttered. "Especially when it's my weekend to be on call."

See what I meant earlier? Tuesdays were Marlene's favorite day of the week.

I honestly didn't know what she did on her days off. I'd often try to imagine it, but I usually ended up picturing her yelling at a young grocery store cashier about the rising prices of pork loin.

"You shouldn't have too many calls, though," I reassured, even though I knew it was useless. "There's only a handful of patients that could deliver this weekend, and most of them are on their second and third pregnancy. It's old hat for them."

"Yeah, right," she huffed her disagreement. "I'm sure one of the thirty-weekers will gorge themselves on chili dogs and then call in a panic because they're confusing gas pain with contractions."

"Always the optimist," I teased with a laugh.

"Keep laughing. But I know you'll be just like me one day," she stated with a pointed brow in my direction.

"What's that supposed to mean?"

"Remember this conversation after you've been doing this job for another twenty years, and then you'll understand."

Doing this job for another twenty years?

Jesus Christ, I hoped not.

I mean, I didn't mind this nursing job. I often found myself enjoying the patient interactions, and since Will had recently added hospital deliveries to my list of job responsibilities, I hadn't found myself getting bored.

But deep down, I knew this wasn't my final career stop. Eventually, I wanted to do something else, something more. I wanted to feel like I had a true purpose.

Running a women's clinic for the underserved population.

It had been on my mind since Carmen's prolapsed cord delivery. I couldn't shake the nagging thought that her situation could have ended terribly. Sure, no medical professional can predict emergent situations like a prolapsed cord, but in her case, she could have been more educated. She could have actually received prenatal care throughout her entire pregnancy. Her baby's fate wouldn't have had to rest on a stroke of luck.

Because Carmen and her little girl were lucky.

If she hadn't been at the hospital the exact moment her water broke, the baby wouldn't have made it. If something had been wrong with Carmen's baby, it would not have been detected until delivery, and then, it might have been too late. So many factors, and thank God, fate was in Carmen's favor that day.

I also hoped I wasn't a lonely bat with poor dental hygiene at her age. I wanted a husband, not seventeen cats.

"Tell me, what has you so happy about the weekend?" Marlene asked and waggled her brows. "Hot sex?"

A shocked laugh escaped my lungs. "Uh…no."

"Hot date that could possibly lead to hot sex, then?"

"No, you horny woman," I said on another laugh, and Marlene grinned wide and unashamed. "No hot date. No hot sex."

But you could have a hot date…

And hot sex. Hot, hot, hot *sex with Will and his penis.*

I could've gone on the date with Will. I *wanted* to. He'd asked me, and at first, I'd felt my stomach climb up and into my throat, but the bottom had dropped out just as quickly. It all seemed like it was in jest. Like he would've been dating me just to help his reputation.

Can I date you because I want to?

His words repeated inside my brain.

Did he want to date me?

I didn't know. He seemed earnest in those words, but his earlier words… *Dating you. Maybe that would solve some of my problems?*

Yeah, not so much.

But you really like him.

I did. I really liked Will in all of his handsome, brilliant, funny, and sometimes hilariously awkward glory. He made me laugh. God, he made me laugh. And smile. My days had become better just because he was in them.

"All set, ladies?" Will poked his head into the nursing office with his briefcase in his hand and his suit jacket slung over his arm.

"Quitting time?" Marlene asked, and Will nodded with a smile.

Marlene didn't waste another moment. She was logged out of her computer and grabbing her purse before anyone could say otherwise. For a woman who didn't like Fridays, she sure looked happy to be strolling out of the office.

"Have a good weekend, Mel," Will said with a smile. "See you Monday?"

My chest panged at the idea of having a whole weekend without his stupid smile and any hope of having it just for myself being missing when I did see it again. "See you Monday," I said, but the words felt all wrong. And the situation felt all wrong as I watched him turn out of the doorway and head down the hall.

My body jumped into action before I could process what I was doing.

My legs moved at a rapid pace down the hall. "Will!" I called toward his back. "Wait a minute."

He stopped in his tracks and turned toward me. His head tilted to the side in question. "Everything okay?"

"Yeah." I nodded and took a deep inhale to catch my breath. "Yeah, everything's great."

"Okay," he responded with a confused smile.

I stared into his deep blue eyes as I tried to find the right words, but I didn't know what to say. I figured shouting the words *Date me!* would be a little weird. But it was those two words that just kept sitting behind my tongue, ready to shoot out of my mouth like a rocket.

"Is there anything else or…?" he asked when the silence had reached an awkward amount of time.

Now or never, Mel. Just say it. Say. It.

"Date me!" The words burst past my lips before I could stop them. *Oh. Jesus.* My eyes went wide in embarrassment. "I mean," I started and nervously cleared my throat. "Is the offer still on the table?"

Will's eyes creased at the corners once his smile consumed his face. "The dating offer?"

I nodded.

"When it comes to you, I'm not sure that offer would ever be off the table, Mel," he said, and the tone of his words matched the earnest expression on his face.

Good God, that was one of the sweetest things anyone had ever said to me.

"How about tonight?"

Will smiled. "Tonight is… Shit. Tonight is bad."

My smile fell. He reached out and grabbed my hand, a tingle shooting up my arm at first contact.

"No. I mean, I really wish I could. But I promised my sister I'd babysit my niece tonight through Sunday morning. She's pregnant with their second and wants to take a little couple's trip before the new baby comes."

My smile came back at the thought of him and his niece.

Jesus. Why don't you just swaddle my heart, God?

"Monday?" he offered, and I winced. I'd promised Janet I'd go shopping in New Jersey for a new set of weights on Monday night. She'd understand, but something inside me was too nervous to deal with switching plans with my mother.

"I can't."

"Tuesday," we both said at the same time.

But it was his next words that would stay in my head for a good long while. "Tuesday is perfect."

Tuesday is perfect, he'd said. And in that moment, I'd thought, *Yeah, Tuesday* is *perfect.* But as I stood in the guest bathroom applying a fresh coat of lipstick, a flock of nervous butterflies took up residence in my stomach. Tuesday may have been perfect in the sense that it was our first free day, but it was completely fucked in the sense that I'd had *three and a half days* to run every stupid dimension of this scenario through my mind.

Was this really a good idea? Dating Will?

It hadn't been that long ago that I was living in Portland and in a long-term relationship with Eli. And Will wasn't some random guy I'd met on a night out. He wasn't just some random guy at all. He was my *boss.* Yesterday and today at work had given me plenty of goddamn time to reinforce that one. Sure, he was carefree and respectful and totally trusting of my skill and capability, but he was still the guy in charge of my checks.

Does that make me a hooker?

"What time is he picking you up, honey?" my mother shouted from the hallway. "Do you think he'll want something to drink? Oh! Maybe I should make a quick batch of muffins!"

I sighed. "Will doesn't want muffins, Mom." Muffins. *Fucking* muffins. Will was a thirty-four-year-old man. Not a fifteen-year-old boy in the middle of a growth spurt.

"I'd love some muffins, Jan!" my father called out.

A part of me wondered if my biggest issue with going on a date with Will right now was that he'd have to pick me up at my parents' house. Maybe that was really why I'd turned him down in the first place.

I wasn't a fan of introducing potential lovers to Bill and Janet before I'd had the chance to actually go on a date with them…*or see them naked.* Meeting the parents was something reserved for date five, not before date one even got started.

The intercom buzzed, and my mother's giddy voice filled my ears. "Oh! I think he's here, Mel!" I could practically hear her skipping toward the front door from the bathroom. "Sit up, Bill, and look presentable."

My father groaned. "Christ, Jan, he's not the king of England."

"Come on up!" my mother singsonged into the intercom, and then moments later, chastised my dad. "Stop being so cross, Bill." Her voice went from angelic to possessed in an instant. "It's like you've completely forgotten that he's Dick and Savannah's son. *Sheesh.*"

"Forgetting and caring are two different things," my father muttered to himself.

"What was that, Bill?"

"I said, *I can't wait to meet Dick's son.*"

Oh boy, this was going to be interesting.

Instead of moping, I put on my big girl panties and finished applying an extra coat of mascara before grabbing my purse off the bathroom sink. I took one last look at my appearance in the mirror, taking in my long, wavy locks resting on my shoulders and my soft but classic makeup.

I'd be lying if I said I hadn't put a lot of effort into my appearance. Hell, it'd taken me a good thirty minutes to decide on my outfit—black thigh-high boots, black skirt, and a fitted, rose gold blouse. I'd put far too much thought into what was the perfect yet appropriate amount of cleavage. Going by the finished product, apparently, there was nothing wrong with a healthy amount of boob.

It's not like he hasn't seen them before.

"Ready or not, Mel, there's no going back now," I whispered to my reflection and took a deep breath before walking out into the hallway and toward the living room.

Will stood in the doorway, smiling down at my mother as she prattled on about something that was the opposite of important. The instant my heels hit the hardwood floor of the entry, his eyes met mine and a soft, handsome, erotic smile crested his lips. Good God, just his face held the power to make your panties disappear. *Maybe he is Dr. Obscene.*

"You look beautiful, Melody."

So do you, I thought, my nipples perking up noticeably.

He did. Will Cummings cleaned up nicely outside of the office. Like, *real* nice. Put him in a dish, and I'd eat him with a spoon kind of nice. Between his gorgeous blue eyes, his sexy hair, and the button-up lilac shirt that fit in all the right places, I didn't know which I liked best.

"You're not looking too bad, either," I teased with a wink, and Will grinned. "I see you've already met my wonderful mother, Janet."

"I did." His grin grew wider. "For a second there, I thought she was your sister."

"Oh, Will!" Janet giggled and gently tapped his shoulder. "I don't like fishing. Thank you so much for inviting me. Maybe we can do something else."

Fishing? He asked my mother to go fishing? Confused, I looked at Will and noted the puzzled expression on his face. Yeah, he didn't ask her to go fishing. It was just Janet's hearing issues acting up again.

Will's eyes shot to me in question, and I tapped my ear as discreetly as possible. The last thing I needed was my mom catching me in the act.

Two minutes into their meet-and-greet and she was already in love. If I didn't move quickly, she might try to go on the date without me. "All right, let's get a move on it," I insisted, raising my voice to avoid further confusion, and moved toward Will's side. I half hoped we'd be able to slide out the front door without my father leaving his perch on the couch.

"But wait," my mother urged and glanced back toward the living room. "Bill!" she whisper-yelled through gritted teeth. "Get off the couch and meet Melody's date."

My father groaned and moaned and finally gave in to her demands, getting up off the couch and shuffling toward the three of us.

"Dad," I started before my mother could take the reins on introductions. "This is Will Cummings. Will, this is my dad, Bill."

"It's a pleasure, Mr. Marco," Will greeted and shook my dad's hand.

"You like KISS?"

Will's brows scrunched together. "Kiss?"

"The band?"

"Oh!" he responded in relief. "Yeah, I like KISS. No one can pull off stage makeup and spitting fire while simultaneously belting out some of the best lyrics in rock history like Gene Simmons."

The hint of a smile crested my dad's lips. "What about Black Sabbath?"

"Ozzy Osbourne. Enough said," Will responded. "There's never been anyone like him."

"Never will be either."

"Probably not. He's rock royalty. One of a kind."

"Oh, yeah," I chimed in. "One of a kind for sure. Pretty sure there's never been another human being that could consume as many drugs as Ozzy did and still live to talk about it."

Bill flashed an annoyed look in my direction, but he quickly returned his focus to Will. He slapped him on the back and grinned proudly. "I like this one, Mel. I think you should keep him around."

Will winked at me, and I wanted to roll my eyes. If I weren't careful, Will would end up spending more time with my parents than me. Fishing dates with Janet and concert tours with my dad. Yippee.

"All right," I said and wrapped my hand around Will's arm. "Consider the rock history lesson done for the evening. We're going to head out before we miss our reservation."

Will glanced down at me in confusion, and I whispered, "Just go with it."

There was no reservation—at least, I didn't think. But I sure as fuck didn't want to stand around chatting about drug-addicted heavy metal bands with my father. Someone had to put the brakes on it before he got out the vinyl records and started playing air guitar in his underwear.

"Take good care of my Melly," my father said as he opened the door for us.

Will smiled and nodded. "Don't worry, I will."

"Have a nice evening, you two," my mother added with a smile as she wrapped her arms around my dad's waist.

Go. Go. Go! My brain shouted. *Go before someone says something inappropriate.*

My parents were notorious for saying the most off-the-wall shit. Honestly, I think they were avid acid users back in the day. I mean, how else could anyone stand listening to Black Sabbath in concert that many times?

"It was really nice meeting both of you," Will said, and I was half tempted to strangle him. He needed to move his ass and not leave any more time for my parents to show their true, weirdo colors.

"Melody, please send me a text message if you decide to stay at Will's tonight," my mother said and then lowered her voice, "you know, *for the sex.*"

There it was. And here I'd naïvely thought we had a chance to get out unscathed.

"Wow," I muttered. "Yeah. We're leaving now."

"If you two end up doing the sex, be safe," my father added, and I wanted to melt into the hardwood floor. "Do you have condoms, Will?"

Scratch that, I wanted to teleport my body to somewhere else. Hell, I wanted to time travel to a different time period and switch families entirely.

Will, though, looked like this might be the best time he'd ever had in his life. "I strive hard to make sure all of my patients are well-educated on safe sex, Mr. Marco. It is priority one for me."

My dad stood proud and tall like a peacock at his response. "Good man," he stated with a grin.

"Bye!" I all but shouted as I shuffled Will out of the door before my parents could add anything else to the conversation.

The instant the elevator doors closed in front of us, I sagged against the wall. "I'm so sorry about that," I apologized. "My parents are kind of weird. Some days I think they're still on an acid trip from the seventies."

"Believe me, you have nothing to apologize for. Just wait until you meet my mom and dad. Dick and Savannah take the cake on crazy," he said. "I must say, it's way more fun from the outside."

Just wait until you meet my mom and dad.

Oh boy. Was Will really picturing me meeting his parents some day?

Maybe this date really wasn't about fixing his reputation.

CHAPTER*eleven*

Will

"**C**OME ON!" I YELLED, PULLING HER TO A RUN AS THE DOUBLE-DECKER BUS slowed to a stop up ahead. "We're going to miss it!"

The city was in full motion, the energy of Tuesday night in Manhattan alive and well, and I'd already bumped into approximately one million people loitering in my way since leaving Melody's parents' apartment. Tuesday wasn't a typical party night, but some kind of sugar rush had obviously descended on the city this week.

On active nights like this, there was really no other choice than to use your body as a human battering ram if you wanted to make it anywhere in a timely fashion.

Melody hadn't told me she lived with her parents, and the surprise of her mother answering the door honestly threw me for a loop. The weird part was that the more it played out, the more uncomfortable she seemed about the whole thing, the more it started to feel like a good loop—like one on an extreme roller coaster I'd been waiting in line for thirty-four years to ride.

"Miss what? Why are we running?" she yelled as she tried to keep up from behind. "I have to warn you that on a sliding scale of enjoyment from one to ten, the fact that you've already got me engaged in exercise has this date starting at a negative two." I smiled as I slowed my steps and swung her up and into my arms to carry her.

"Ahh," she shrieked. The people around us jumped out of the way to avoid her flailing feet while she scrambled to make sure all of her parts were covered. I very nearly made a joke about it being nothing I hadn't seen before, but I realized how terrible of an idea that was before it ever even got off the ground, thank God.

"What the hell are you doing, Will?" Melody questioned with a slap to my chest.

I crossed the street, avoiding cabs and cars as I did instead of answering, and I didn't put her on her feet until we made it to the bus. Only then did I set her down to pull out our tickets and hand them to the driver as I ushered her on board.

"What the hell? What are we doing?" she repeated, tired of no answers. But this wasn't really the kind of thing you could explain without visual aids. If I popped my cork too early, it'd be disappointing for both of us.

The cork.

The.

Not my.

Though, really, popping *my* cork early would be pretty fucking disappointing too.

Again, I ignored her line of questioning—after briefly considering teasing her if she lost ninety-nine percent of her vocabulary when she stepped outside of the office—and motioned for her to precede me. "Let's go upstairs. Much better view."

She dug her heels in, holding me at a stop behind her. "Why are we on a bus full of tourists?" Hell of a pair of heels they were, by the way. Stiletto, thigh-high boots that just skimmed the bottom of her, short— *God, painfully, beautifully, short*—black skirt.

I snapped my fingers in excitement. "Ah, thanks for reminding me." I reached into my back pocket to hand her a disposable camera. "So you don't miss anything."

She almost tripped as I pushed her up the stairs, and when her angry eyes met mine over her shoulder, I worried for the first time that maybe this hadn't been such a great first-date idea after all. But under all of that anger lived passion—a side of Mel I'd been dying to see since I'd laid eyes on her in that awkward exam room the first day—and curiosity over intelligence won out. *I blame my Y chromosome.*

"Will—" she started again when we reached the top of the stairs to an almost packed bus.

Turning her body to mine with a hand at her hip, I slid the other hand up and into the loose curls of her crimson hair. "Have I told you how happy I am that you changed your mind? How happy I am that some small part of you found me irresistible?"

"Will," she said again, but this time it was a whisper.

The emotion of her word yanked the cord attached to my chest and sucked me in, luring me as if the call were designed specifically for me. In that moment, I was nothing but her prey.

Desperate for gratification, for some physical reassurance that I wasn't fourteen steps into the twelve it would take me to lose my mind, I touched my lips to the skin of hers. Heat, raw and exotic spread from my mouth to my chest at first contact, but when she pushed up onto her toes and touched *her* lips to *mine*, once, twice, the blaze spread all the way to the end of every limb.

When the bus started to move, rocking us so hard that I had to catch her with an arm around her back and the other hand to the railing, I forced my lips to back away.

She smiled, and I realized at once that sometimes moving away has its perks.

Directing her to a seat, I let her scoot in first and settled beside her before wrapping an arm around her shoulders and leaning in to whisper in her ear. "Is this a bad idea? Do you hate it?"

I moved closer as I scented the intoxicating fruity allure of her skin. She shivered and leaned in to whisper in my ear. "Not anymore."

"Good. I didn't want this first date to be like any other first date you'd ever been on. I know you know the city, but this way, from now on, I'll have memories of this everywhere I go."

And, hopefully, so will she.

Truthfully, I was also hoping posing as tourists would aid in anonymity. I didn't exactly get recognized everywhere I went, but it happened a whole lot more than you'd want it to on a first date.

She laughed. "Well, you're definitely succeeding there."

"I promise dinner at the end of the bus tour, though."

"Well, well, look whose grade just shifted up the scale to a four point five."

"Four point five?"

She winked. "What fun would it be if there weren't any room to improve? I know how you doctor types are. It's the challenge that drives you."

I shook my head with a chuckle. "I don't know, Mel. In this case, victory sounds pretty good to me."

"Excuse me?" I heard as a soft tap rapped on my shoulder.

Mel's face scrunched, especially at the corners of her eyes. I knew from watching her with Marlene that this was her face when annoyed. Ironically, the sight of it kept me from being the same.

I turned to the moment-interrupter with a smile. "Yes?"

"Would you mind taking a picture of us? Times Square is coming up, and we really want to get one of us with all the lights!"

"Sure," I agreed, watching as Melody's crabby wrinkles deepened. Absently, my hand lifted to the side of her head so I could smooth a finger over them. They cleared immediately.

"Oh, thank you so much!" the stranger gushed from behind us. "Did you want us to take one for you too?"

"Got your camera?" I asked Melody.

She shook her head, but the seed of a smile I'd planted on her face with my touch started to grow.

"We'd love a picture," I told the woman behind us as I noted our location—54th and Broadway. "You better get your phone out. We're close."

"Oh! Thank you! You've been to New York before?"

Mel made big eyes, but I ignored her. "A couple of times. First time was our honeymoon."

As Melody's mouth widened in shock, I waggled my eyebrows.

"Oh, how romantic!"

"It is, isn't it?" I asked. Melody pinched the inside of my thigh so hard I jumped.

I winked. "Don't worry, baby. There'll be plenty of time for that later."

Rose stained her cheeks, spreading out rapidly like food coloring in water.

The bus slowed to a crawl as we made it to the iconic Midtown location, the flashing lights of each sign swirling and mixing across the red of Melody's blush and coloring it every other hue.

I grabbed the tourist's camera and counted down. "Three, two, one.… smile!"

The normally blinding flash of the photo blended in with the show of lights for us, but by the way they blinked, I guessed it didn't feel quite the same on the other side.

"Sorry," I apologized. "Night pictures are tough."

"Oh, that's okay!" the woman said, waving her temporary blindness away. She apparently did most of the talking for the two of them, and quite frankly, her fellow looked glad of it.

"Here," she went on, holding out her hand. "Let me get your picture before it's too late."

"Oh, that's—" Mel protested.

But I cut her off with a yank of my arm, pulling her into my side and shoving my face into her neck as I handed off the disposable camera. "Memories, Mel."

The light of the flash going off made me smile deeper before looking up for one posed picture of the two of us smiling.

As soon as it was done, I reached out for the camera with my left hand and held out my right to shake.

"I'm Will, and this is Mel," I introduced.

"I'm Susie, and this is Frank." Frank gave a halfhearted wave.

"Where are you folks from?" Susie asked, carrying the conversation once again.

"California," I said before Mel could ruin the fun unknowingly.

"Oh, wow!" the woman exclaimed excitedly. "California! We're from Kansas. Always wanted to see the big city! But, oh my gosh, the West Coast sounds so exciting too! What's it like?"

I turned to Melody and invited her to speak with an encouraging grin. It wasn't the most orthodox way to hear about her life on the West Coast, and California wasn't where she'd actually lived, but it helped me get to know her all the same. And being in on the little fib together gave us something to share right off the bat.

"Well, it's actually really peaceful. We're from northern California, not Hollywood like you see on TV. We love to make day-trips up north to the real Pacific Northwest. Seattle and Portland are some of the coolest towns we've ever been to. If you want to go to the West Coast, that'd be our suggestion. There's a real family feel in the air even though they aren't small towns."

Funny thing was, as she spoke to Susie, Melody's eyes never once left mine.

Slow motion.

The bounce and swirl of her curled auburn hair, the swing of her hips— even the time it took for the long lashes of her eyes to meet and move away again.

All of it seemed to take forever, and yet, the night had gone scream- ing by like a high-speed train. Two hours of laughing at each other and breathing in the energy of the New York air on the double-decker bus, an hour and a half of pizza and beers at a pub down the street, and the last hour here at this bar, watching and feeling Melody lower her walls and dance with me, over in an instant. But I remembered each moment in vivid, terrifying detail.

The feel of her fingers clenching my thigh as she settled into our tourist ruse, the speck of tomato sauce she licked from the corner of her lips with just the tip of her magenta tongue, and the bounce of her breasts as she jumped in excitement at the beginning of each new song all vied for my attention, only to be pushed out of the way by each and every single new thing she did.

This was the best date I'd ever been on, and by some stroke of luck, I'd managed to keep us in dark enough corners that outsiders were equally in the dark on my identity. It was also the longest, and somehow, I still feared its premature end.

I pulled her closer, inhaling the hints of soft vanilla seeping from her skin, and continued leading our bodies to the rhythm of the music playing inside the bar while silently hoping that I could find a way to stretch this night out longer.

CHAPTER *twelve*

Melody

GOD, THIS WAS THE BEST DATE.

Will was the best date.

The night had been a blur of laughter and Will's smiles and Will's beautiful blue eyes and Will's teasing commentary and… *Will. Will. Will.*

I wasn't sure if it was the alcohol flowing through my veins or the fact that he was unlike anyone I'd ever met. But five hours into a night alone with him and I never wanted to leave his side. He was sweet and kind, and yet, innately charming in a way that made me want to permanently fuse myself to his lap so I'd always be there to hear all of the things he had to say.

With Will's hands on my waist and his warm breath on my neck, every single part of me felt good except for the nagging clench in my stomach reminding me our time was nearly up. I wanted to bottle up this intimate moment of dancing with him and keep it forever.

But we'd been dancing for what felt like hours at Chez Noir and, unfortunately for me, my feet were starting to announce their disdain for being in heels.

I needed a break, unless I wanted to end up breaking something.

As the ending beats of Rhianna's "Love on the Brain" left the speakers hovering over the dance floor and the song ended, I fell forward into his arms.

"Will!" I said with a giggle and leaned in, pressing my lips to his ear to be heard over the music. The close proximity and warmth of his skin against mine sent a shock straight up my spine.

God, he smells good. I bet he tastes even better.

He grinned down at me, curiosity mingling with interest and want in the most intoxicating way.

"My feet hurt," I complained on a whine, and he laughed softly.

"Should we call it a night?" he asked neutrally, but his expression didn't match the tone of his voice. He looked disappointed at the thought.

Ditto, Doc.

"Maybe we should close out our tab and grab one last drink?" I suggested, and his face brightened at my words. If he kept looking that happy to be around me, I couldn't be held accountable for the things I would do.

"Grab a table, and I'll get the drinks."

I nodded and he grinned before leaning forward and pressing a soft kiss to my cheek.

Moments later, we were sitting cozily at a table in the corner of the bar, located conveniently away from the bustling night crowd. He'd gotten the drinks in record time, seemingly as eager to get back to me as I was for him to return.

"Tomorrow night at eight?" he asked into the skin of my neck, an arm draped warmly around my shoulders. I smiled at first—obviously enthralled with even the most basic of things he had to say—but quickly realized I had no idea what he was talking about.

I tilted my head in confusion and asked, "What's tomorrow night?"

"Our second date," he declared with a smirk, and I giggled.

I blamed it on the alcohol. One glass of wine and I tended to giggle like a loon. I might have been self-conscious about what I sounded like if Will didn't look like he liked it so much. I'd never been on a date with a guy so open with his emotions. He wasn't trying to play some sort of game. Or if he was, it was my new favorite.

"Already looking for a second date?" I teased. "I'm pretty sure I'm still a little busy with the first one."

"And how is the first one going?"

"Horribly," I lied with a sly grin. "Probably the worst date I've ever been on."

"I know, right?" He played along. "Between the laughter, the nonstop conversation, and your insanely pretty…everything, I've never been more bored in my life." He paused, running a soft hand up the zipper of my boot and stopping just at the top, the tip of one deliciously long finger tracing the line of skin there. "And don't even get me started on your legs. Jesus, those things go on for miles. It's like they never end. Definitely a turn-off."

God, just that touch made my pussy ache. "I should've gone with the sweat pants," I said shakily, unable to fight the growing arousal with a squeeze of my legs, thanks to his hand now calmly resting on my thigh. If I pulled my legs together now, his hand would get trapped in between.

Maybe that's not such a bad idea.

"They might've made it a little easier for you tolerate me."

"Oh, yeah, because you're completely intolerable," he said on a laugh, his fingertips flexing into the flesh of my thigh and nearly making me moan. But his expression morphed into something much more serious as he used his other hand to slide a lock of my hair behind my ear. "You're amazing, Melody," he whispered. "I feel like a real lucky bastard that you found me so irresistible you changed your mind."

I smiled and bit my lip, completely enthralled by his ability to tease and compliment in one sentence.

He looked down for a moment, and my eyes enjoyed the show, watching him intently and taking in every minute detail that equaled Will. I had never been the type of woman to think a man's face was beautiful. Masculine? Sure. Handsome? Of course. But *beautiful*? No way.

At least, not until now.

Well-defined, with a sharp jaw and angular cheekbones and a genuine warmth you couldn't cook up in a genetics lab, Will had a *beautiful* face. But it wasn't the kind of beauty you'd see on the cover of a magazine; it was different. Captivating yet subtle. Soft yet firm. And when the slight olive complexion of his skin mixed with the ocean blue of his eyes, it made it nearly impossible to look away.

While he brought his beer to his full lips, I sat mesmerized. It was as if the alcohol that slid down into his throat had a direct link to my body, bolstering the warm sensation already living deep inside my belly.

When his chin came back down after his drink, he joined me in my perusal and didn't once question the silence. The jovial sounds of bar patrons and the serenading voice of Beyoncé filled the background, but that's all it was in that moment—just background noise. With Will's avid attention fixed on me, everything else felt nonexistent. Hell, Beyoncé could've been standing in the middle of the dance floor singing "Single Ladies," and I wouldn't have noticed. I felt drunk off of him. Well, I was probably already a little drunk, but the buzz from the alcohol paled in comparison to the vibrating, heady energy that flowed between us.

His hand flexed on my thigh again, and my walls based on traditional first-date boundaries all but crumbled.

I wanted him. More than just dinner, more than just dating, I *wanted* him. Naked. Hard. Clawing at my skin. Kissing my neck. Sliding inside of me.

The room darkened as the lights inside the bar flashed with the techno beat of the next song, and I savored the feel of being cloaked in privacy. Will and I, sitting at a small high-top table toward the corner of the room, had now become unrecognizable to the other patrons. And before I could stop myself, I turned on my barstool, my back to the crowd, and faced Will directly. He watched me intently, his eyes fixed on mine, until I slowly parted my legs.

Without inhibitions and fueled by desire, I took his hand from my thigh and into mine and ran his index finger higher, under the material of my skirt and along my hot skin. His gaze locked on the apex between my thighs where only a hint of my panties was visible beneath the material of my skirt.

Touch me, I silently begged, and he didn't disappoint.

I stopped helping him, but he kept going, his fingers leaving an electric trail until they reached the tiny sliver of silky material covering the place where I ached and throbbed for him.

I thought maybe he'd shy away from the public setting, but he took what I was thinking and did me one better.

With his gaze back to mine, he moved my panties to the side and ran his index finger through my arousal—*once, twice, three times*—and my hips jolted forward in response. His touch was calculated yet gentle as his thumb found my clit, pressing firm enough to spur a shot of pleasure up my spine.

"Does that feel good?" he asked, leaning forward enough that his lips skimmed the skin of my neck, and I nodded.

At least, I thought I'd nodded. For all I knew, my head had escaped my body—the only two places I knew with certainty were there were the ones Will was touching.

His thumb set up a rhythm of smooth, mind-blowing circles on my clit, and I swallowed my moan.

Good Lord, I wanted more. *Needed* more.

"Come home with me tonight," he said into my ear. He lifted my chin with the tip of his finger, locking our gazes once more. "Let me spend the night with you."

"Yes," I whispered. I'd had the answer prepared before he even asked me the question. Whatever he wanted, I wanted.

Fingers still toying with me, he moved his lips from my ear to my mouth, and I gasped in surprise. But as soon as the tip of his tongue touched mine, I immediately responded with fervor, pulling his bottom lip into my mouth, sucking on his tongue, until both of our mouths and lips and tongues were dancing the same rhythm together.

"Let's go," he moaned against my lips. I didn't want to stop, not at all. Not to move from this spot or to come up for air or anything. I just wanted him to keep touching me forever.

My disappointment was audible when he pulled his fingers from my pussy and put my panties back in place, but it didn't last long.

In perhaps the most erotic move I'd ever paid witness to, he lifted his fingers to his mouth, right in front of my face—close enough that I could smell myself there—and sucked them inside.

"Yes," I said finally, in answer to leaving—in answer to everything—and he didn't waste any time, all but dragging both of our bodies toward the exit.

Time had turned into a blur of hurried kisses and brushing touches and stealing, desirous glances. Somehow, we'd left the bar and hopped into a cab. Somehow, we'd gotten to Will's apartment. And *somehow*, we'd found ourselves standing face-to-face, still fully clothed, in the middle of Will's bedroom with the foot of his bed beside our hips.

The night had morphed from the speed of light into slow motion.

We just stood there, looking at one another, the intensity so high it felt like I might come out of my skin. Still, there was something about this moment, this intimate encounter, that had forced both of us to take our time and savor every look, every touch, every tiny little second of time that equaled us, Will and me, together.

Without words and with his heated gaze locked with mine, his fingers slid up my wrist, to my elbow, until they stopped at my shoulder blade. They rested there for a breath and then slowly, oh so slowly, moved my shirt to the side. His fingers danced, skirting between not moving at all and just barely whispering against my skin.

I wasn't sure why, but that one innocent touch, *his* touch, felt more erotic than the act of sex itself. Maybe I was horny. Maybe I'd reached my threshold of sexless days. Or maybe, just maybe, what had started to occur between Will and me was something words couldn't explain.

The electricity of the moment slid up my spine as he started to undress me, first with his eyes, and then with his hands, removing every item of clothing—my bra, my panties, even kneeling in front of me to take off my shoes, with slow, calculated, and unhurried movements.

Bare and naked and vulnerable for his gaze, I felt him take me in. He didn't touch me. Kiss me. Say anything. But make no mistake, Will *savored* me. His blue eyes caressed and whispered against every single inch of my skin so vividly it felt like a real touch.

I followed his lead, looking into his eyes, and without haste, I removed his shirt, his pants, his socks and shoes, and I didn't stop until his boxers were on the floor and his tan and toned and muscular form was gloriously naked.

Will naked.

Oh boy.

I had fantasized about this.

Hell, I'd probably spent far too much time daydreaming about this very moment. But by the looks of things, I hadn't been doing a good enough job.

Without shame, I let my eyes move across his skin, starting with his face and taking my time, moving down, down, down until I reached his hard and straining cock. My breath caught in my throat at the sight of him. He was beautiful. And *big*. And he was just as turned on as I was.

Holy moly, his penis is far, far better in real life.

"Fuck, Mel. You are unreal," he whispered into the barely lit room, and I moved my gaze back to his. "You are," he repeated, and I could've gone for a swim in the blue depths of his eyes. The waters were that warm and inviting.

Without touching any other part of my body, his fingers found my hair and gently slid a loose lock behind my ear.

I moaned at the feel.

I had never experienced this kind of intimate intensity with someone. Our attraction was almost *visible*. It could be seen and felt and tasted all around us. I was just tipsy enough to admit this sexual tension had been building from day one, from the first awkward moment Will's eyes had met mine, and tonight, all of that want had transformed into *need*.

My breaths escaped in short, whimpering pants. My nipples grew tight and my breasts were heavy, and I throbbed and ached between my legs. When my hands started to run down my thighs, I wasn't sure how much longer I could last. The urge to touch him, kiss him, feel him inside of me was unbearable.

"Spread your legs," he ordered, sensing I needed something and needed it now, and I obeyed.

Riveted, I watched as he knelt in front of me, and his new position put him in the perfect place to turn his power of seduction to my pussy. Honestly, I'd never felt more turned on, and fully confident in my body, in my life.

"Look at you. Just fucking look at you." From under his lashes, his gaze met mine again, his index finger softly grazing my aching skin. "This is the prettiest cunt I've ever seen," he said. He'd seen a lot of them, that I knew, but the funny thing in that moment was that there wasn't even a tiny fraying part of me that didn't believe him. My hips jolted forward of their own accord, begging for him, desperate for more than teasing.

Grabbing my hips so hard I gasped, he yanked me toward his face and licked through my arousal, taking the taste of me inside and leaving a moan behind.

It was rough and needy, and the vibration of it felt even better than my very favorite toy.

"God, Mel, you must mainline sugar, you taste so fucking sweet," he teased and licked once more, before flicking the tip of his tongue against my clit. I smiled at both the feel and his words, and then he flicked my clit again.

Oh, fuck.

"God, you taste so fucking good," he growled against my skin. "I could eat you forever."

Seconds later, he moved to his feet, standing before me again. I laughed my annoyance, a scene from *Titanic* popping unbidden into my head

"You're just as bad as Rose," I accused. "Promising Jack she'd never let go just before she fucking did it."

He smiled and grabbed both sides of my face to bring me close enough that our lips almost touched. "I need to feel you," he explained. "Us. You and me."

"Yes," I whispered.

"Now," he demanded through gritted teeth. "I need to feel your perfect cunt wrapped around my cock, Mel."

God, yes.

"Get on your knees," he instructed with one hand gently wrapped around my neck. "Let me see that glorious ass in the air."

He didn't have to ask twice. My knees hit the bed seconds later, and he helped me tip my ass farther into the air.

"Fuck," he gritted out, connecting us in one swift thrust.

A guttural moan escaped my lungs, and sparks danced behind my eyes. God, he felt so good.

"Never stop doing this," I whimpered as he picked up the pace, sliding his cock in and out with deep and heavy strokes. "Never ever stop doing this."

"Never," he groaned in agreement.

Honestly, it was the best thing I'd ever felt. I'd be willing to sign on to live like that movie *Groundhog Day* as long as today was the one on repeat.

The tip of his cock rubbed just the right spot, like his length was made to pleasure me, and by the way he was grunting behind me, I could tell he felt the same. Incomprehensible moans spilled from my lungs while Will pushed his cock deep and pulled it back again, speeding up until I developed a keening cry. "Fuck, fuck, fuck," I chanted.

"Let go, Mel."

I shook my head against the blinding pleasure, completely against the prospect of letting this blissful heaven end, but the perfect biology of our two bodies together worked against me. I cried out as everything good and right hit me so hard I thought I might black out, and Will, pressed to the hilt, climaxed inside of me simultaneously.

Time. Space. *Safe sex.* None of it existed in that moment. Still connected, all we felt was our perfect, intimate joining and the mind-blowing orgasms that had washed over both us until we were lying breathless and panting on Will's bed.

But slowly, as he pulled his cock free from me, everything came filtering back.

Time. Space. *Safe sex.*

Holy hell. What in the fucking fuck?

I'd never slept with someone unprotected in my life. Even in my five-year stint with Eli, I'd been mindful enough to at least discuss birth control.

With his back on the bed and his chest moving up and down with deep breaths, Will turned his head to meet my eyes. "What was that?"

"I have no idea," I answered honestly, a little scared by the prospect of how powerful it all was—how fully I'd let myself go.

"That was…" he started, only to run out of words immediately. I didn't blame him. I couldn't find any words to describe it either.

"I know."

"I think my orgasm made me lose brain cells."

A soft giggle fell from my lips at the starkly honest truth. "Ditto."

"Question," he said, his gaze turning serious as it searched mine. "This is painfully late…but are you on birth control?"

I nodded, relieved I at least wasn't *that* big of an idiot. "Now, sir, I see your bet and raise you one…"

He grinned. "Shoot."

"Have you been tested?" I asked, melting into his happiness like a loon. *God, he's distracting.* I shook my head to clear it of his voodoo and re-member the responsible things. Adult things. Things I should know bet-ter than to wait to ask until *after* fucking my boss. "No STDs or weird fungal infections I should know about?"

"Clean as a whistle."

"That's good to hear."

He shook his head, closing his eyes—apparently just as embarrassed as I was. "It's real fucking sad that an obstetrician and a labor and deliv-ery nurse didn't have the safe-sex talk before the sex actually occurred."

"Yeah," I agreed. "That's not something I...uh...do often...or ever, actually."

He grinned. "The last time I did anything without a condom, I was a fifteen-year-old virgin and played just the tip with my teenage girlfriend. It had lasted all of thirty seconds before her minister father came strolling in the front door."

I laughed at that.

"Yeah," he added. "This isn't how I usually do things."

"Me either."

"I just wanted you so bad," he whispered. "Honestly, Mel, I'm not sure I was even conscious."

"Me too," I agreed. Me fucking too. And as insane as it made me feel, I couldn't think of anywhere I'd rather be.

"Wanna go again?"

He didn't even blink. "I can't think of anything I'd rather repeat."

Sold!

Melody's heart, for the price of one comment.

CHAPTER *thirteen*

T HIS MORNING, FOR THE FIRST TIME IN MY NEW YORK TENURE, I RODE THE SUBWAY without watching the people around me.

Normally, even when I was reading or pretending to sleep, I had one eye strategically sweeping the area around me. Call it paranoia. Or maybe it was the amount of time I'd spent during my residency suturing some kind of injury from a mugging on the platform or a crazy guy with a knife on one of the cars.

I mean, overall, riding the subway was just as safe as walking in Manhattan. Though, as a side note, I'd sewn up a pretty healthy number of wounds from mugging while walking as well.

But really, New York is lovely. You should visit.

Not to mention, since the first episode of the show had aired, I'd had to make a concerted effort to hide my face from gawking strangers as they snapped pictures with their iPhones.

But last night, with Melody, had been so much more than I'd expected. The conversation, the vibe, the overall easy flow of every single moment—all of it had been incredible. The best date of my life.

Also—side note again here—the sex.

To say I was off my game and just about tapped out for concern about keeping a semblance of personal privacy was an understatement. Luckily, the cloud of all of those things combined, and their power against my command of observation hadn't resulted in a trip to the hospital in something other than a professional capacity. Though, it probably would mean a few more pictures of me floating around in the cybersphere.

I pushed through the door to St. Luke's Obstetrics and Gynecology without hesitation for the first time in weeks, excited for the day, and immediately started scanning the space for her.

It was stupid, really. Mel was always fucking late. But rationality wasn't an emotion, and frankly, it was no match for one either.

"Interesting night, huh, Dr. Cummings?" Marlene asked as I passed her.

Melody's knees high and spread, her hands clenching my throat as I rode her hard and fast the second time. Her eyes blazing up at me like I might just be the best thing she'd ever felt. God, yes. Last night had been more than interesting. It'd been everything.

Smiling, I nodded my affirmation and continued down the hall, only turning back to look when I realized Marlene didn't know anything about me and Melody, but she was already gone.

I wonder what she's talking about.

Whatever it was, I didn't feel like dealing with it right then.

I went straight to my office to drop off my briefcase, but I checked the inside of every exam room as I passed about as discreetly as I could, just in case Melody had chosen the night after we'd slept together to be prompt for the first time in her life.

She hadn't, by the way.

God, I'm going crazy.

Things had ended well, far too late into the night to help Melody get up this morning, but there'd been kissing and general contentment on both sides.

But it'd been six hours since she'd climbed into the cab I'd called for her—after she refused to stay over and deal with explaining to Janet—and five since I'd felt any real sort of certainty about where we stood.

We'd slept together on the first date, and while I wasn't even remotely complaining, I also couldn't shake one nagging question. *Does first-date fornication ever lead to a real relationship?*

It sure as hell never had for me. Not with Lana or Megan or Seela… *yeah, the number isn't important here…* It was the principle. Could sex—and significant but fairly superficial interest—ever be a good foundation for more?

I wasn't convinced it could.

Though, to be fair, I'd never lasted more than four months in a relationship anyway. Georgia always told me it was because I chose the wrong women, but I don't think that was it. I was pretty sure it had more to do with the fact that being with the same woman for the rest of my life sounded like just about the worst thing I'd ever heard…until recently.

And no, it wasn't the moment I laid eyes on Melody.

It was just around the time I slid inside of her.

Kidding.

Sort of. It was *really* good.

Glancing up to look out in the hallway for her, I noticed the time on the clock above my door. 9:05 a.m.

Shit. I had better get busy seeing patients even if my nurse wasn't here to help me. She was lucky last night had gone the way it had.

Ugh, Will. No. Thinking those kinds of things is the reason dating your subordinate isn't a good idea.

In reality, part of me was just nervous she wouldn't show up at all. Like somehow, I'd conjured the whole thing—even imagined her—in my mind. I smiled at quite possibly the most insecure conversation I'd ever had with myself and grabbed my coat to scoot up to the front and bring my own patient back. It'd be better if I at least multitasked—worked and talked myself off of the emotional ledge simultaneously.

"Did you see *Dr. Obscene* last night?" I heard Melissa say as I made it to the front.

Goddammit. Would there ever be a time I traveled to the front of my office and didn't hear someone talking about me anymore?

Also, I'd completely forgotten that episode had even aired last night. I'd been busy.

"Oh, for fuck's sake. Don't call him that. I can't work with a man named Dr. Obscene," Marlene retorted.

"It's not like it's his *actual* name. Relax. It's just fitting after he…well…he…"

"God, you're blushing," Beth commented on a whisper.

"Of course, I'm blushing! It looked like he was whacking his mole!"

"Oh my God!" Beth's whisper was now more like a shriek. I couldn't say I blamed her. I felt a little like screaming myself.

"Beating his meat. Slapping his stick. Stroking his ore."

"We get it!" Marlene snapped, and for once, I agreed with her. My brain felt like it was on overload. Good God, did she mean what I thought she meant?

Fuck, I might come out of my skin.

"There's no way he was doing that."

"It *really* looked like he was."

"I don't know. They probably edited him. You remember the last time he caught us talking? Besides, have you ever seen him act like that around here?" Beth defended me. It wasn't like she was a saint, but fuck, I guessed I couldn't be choosy about my allies anymore.

"No. I can honestly say I've never seen him *jerk off* around here."

"Melissa!"

"Well, that's what it was. And I'd know if I'd seen it here. Trust me."

"But I talked to him. Hinted about what an *interesting* night last night was. He didn't object," Marlene interjected again.

"Like he was gonna *actually* address it? He doesn't like office gossip."

Okay. Bad news… I apparently looked like I was fucking *jerking off* on the show last night? Jesus Christ!

My brain felt like it was bleeding, but I fought desperately against going full aneurysm.

Silver lining…think of the silver lining. Well, I guessed they didn't know Mel and I had slept together last night.

Is that even really a positive? my brain questioned doubtfully. I didn't know.

I did know, however, that I didn't want the women I worked with on a daily basis thinking they'd seen me engaged in a little self-love and fucking blabbing about it!

Stepping forward and around the corner, I did my best not to speak with any of the actual rage I now felt. "He sure doesn't."

Especially not with a waiting room full of patients. *Or ever.*

"Crap," Marlene huffed.

"You three," I addressed them. "My office."

They looked down at the carpet but pushed out of their chairs, and Marlene pushed away from her spot against the wall, to follow me, but none of us made it more than a foot before the door opened and Melody walked in.

She got one look at our faces, and her eyebrows pulled together.

And then, unfortunately, accusing eyes shot to me. *Does she actually think I told them about us?*

"Melody," I snapped, far harsher than intended. She jumped at the sound of my voice, and she wasn't the only one. I cleared my throat and worked to smooth out the line between my eyebrows. "Sorry," I apologized. "Just…sorry. But as soon as you're settled, bring back the first patient."

"Sure, Dr. Cummings," she said softly. She sounded fucking hurt, and I felt nearly helpless with the direction this day had taken. *And I was in such a good mood when it started.*

I looked back to Marlene, Beth, and Melissa, but all I could say was, "Later." Even I couldn't tell if it was a promise or a threat.

But just as before, none of us made it even a foot before the main office door opened again, and something we'd never seen before walked in.

A man.

Okay. Obviously excluding myself, the other male physicians in the practice, and the occasional husband. Otherwise, no men whatsoever.

Shut up. Obviously, lots of men walk through these doors,

but that's not the point, okay?

This one, I didn't recognize.

Unfortunately, someone else knew him…and by the looks of it, she knew him well.

CHAPTER *fourteen*

"**E**LI?"

I stared in shock—and maybe a little bit of horror, too—first at his face, then down at the bouquet of flowers held out in his hand, and then back into the chocolate hues of his eyes.

"Hi, Melly," he said, standing tall and proud in a sleek black suit with a white button-up shirt. He looked handsome, albeit a tad overdressed for the reception area of a medical office, but just as attractive as ever.

Of course, his looks had never been the problem.

"W-what are you doing here?" I stuttered. My voice wasn't strong, but inside, I was yelling. What the hell was he doing here? In New York? At my *place of employment*?

"I wanted to surprise you." He smiled.

Why in vaginas was he smiling?

This wasn't exactly a picture-worthy moment—me in my scrubs, Eli dressed like he was about to go to the goddamn Oscars, and an entire waiting room full of pregnant women who were seconds away from grabbing some popcorn and settling in for a show. Not to mention the fact that we'd *broken up* months ago.

"I'm definitely surprised," I muttered, and his smile grew wider.

Jesus Christ. This was just like him, being too absorbed in his plan to read me. I wasn't thrilled with his arrival, and I *knew* it was written all over my face.

I had never been the type of girl who could school her facial expressions into neutrality if the urge to freak the fuck out was overwhelming. No. I was the girl who freaked the fuck out. Today's emotional meltdown just happened to be in the form of a little wooden Melody, slack-jawed, eyes wide, and spine as stiff as a board.

"I miss you," he said, urging me to take the outrageous bouquet of flowers—*that I was most likely allergic to*—from his hand.

The monstrosity would've made a fantastic prop for *Saturday Night Live*, and with my excessive allergy to most bulbs, pollen, and buds, a slapstick skit wouldn't be too far behind.

Despite all this, as a means to avoid a goddamn scene, I did the polite thing and took them from his hands. Pastel petals of tulips and daisies and roses dancing before my eyes, I couldn't see anymore.

I attempted to look above them, then to the left of them, and then to the right, but it was useless, and once my nose started to itch and my face began to tingle, I wasn't sure if Eli was trying to profess his love or kill me.

If the plan was murder by anaphylaxis, surely, I had to give him props for creativity.

"You came all the way to New York because you missed me?" I asked and set the flowers on the reception desk in an effort to get them away from me. Melissa gave me a catty smile, apparently gearing up for her next move.

One sneeze. Two sneezes. Three more sneezes and I'd say it was official, the death petals had permeated my nose. *Fantastic.*

"Uh…" Melissa sighed in annoyance from her perch behind the desk. "Those are blocking my view of the waiting room, Load-y."

And there it is.

I understood her frustration because, yeah, Eli had officially bought the world's largest bouquet, but I also didn't really care. It was fucking Melissa. She only spent five percent of her workday looking out on the patients anyway. She could handle one minute of flowers blocking her view of reception.

Plus, I was still a little fucking busy.

"Are you okay? Are you sick?" Eli touched my shoulder, and his eyes assessed me with concern.

"No," I said with a shake of my head and a most likely disgusting sniffle of my nose. "I'm not sick. I'm just allergic."

"Allergic?"

"To the flowers."

"You're allergic to flowers? When did that happen?"

"Uh…it happened about twenty-nine or so years ago." He still looked confused. *Goddamn*, why had I liked him again? "Around my time of birth."

"Seriously?"

I nodded, but he still looked confused.

"But I used to buy you flowers all of the time."

"No," I refuted. "You actually bought me flowers once, and you stopped once you realized flowers weren't the way to my heart unless you wanted to kill me."

"Shit," he muttered and watched me apologetically blow my nose into a tissue I'd snagged from the reception desk. "This isn't going the way I wanted it to."

"I was hoping this would be romantic," one woman whispered behind me.

"I know," another one added. "I don't think it's going as planned."

"He's going to need to change up the game plan if there's any hope," a third woman chimed in.

"Does her face look a little swollen to you?"

"Yeah. I think it's from the flowers. She said she's allergic."

I'd never wanted to burrow into the floor more than I did right now.

Once I'd stopped sneezing and snorting and itching my face, I focused on getting to the point of this ridiculous charade. "Seriously," I started. "What are you doing here? In New York?"

"For you," Eli started but paused briefly. "Well, I was kind of in the neighborhood."

"In the neighborhood?"

"Investors' meeting," he explained. "The firm gained a huge potential client, and I came out here to close the deal."

Of course he'd come to New York with the priority of a business trip. I was just an added convenience.

Let me tell you...that was the story of my life when it came to Eli.

This trip had nothing to do with me. He didn't want an actual, committed relationship with me. He might have missed me to some degree, but I knew he didn't miss me enough to fly across the country just for me.

That was the difference between Eli and me.

Five years ago, I *did* fly across the country for him. And I'd stayed there, for him.

I moved away from my home, my family, and friends—for him.

Sure, I still cared about him. I still wanted good things for him. But I didn't want to be with him. I wasn't in love with him.

You're in love with Will.

Holy hell that had come out of left field. There was no way I was in love with Will…right? The idea seemed ridiculous. We had only known each other for a short time.

Like Will? Of course.

Love Will? That sounded crazy.

"Isn't that so sweet?" another bystander from the waiting room whispered behind me, and like a runaway dog on a retractable leash, those little words yanked me right back to the present.

I felt like shouting, *Listen, lady. This isn't sweet. This man is probably one of the most self-absorbed human beings you will ever meet, and he had five years to make an effort. Now is not the fucking time. And I'd really love an antihistamine and a nap.* You know, as long as I was ranting.

But luckily, I kept my cool and forced my face into something less confrontational.

"I'm really glad to hear things are going well with the firm," I said, and honestly, I meant it. Just because I didn't want to be with him didn't mean I didn't want him to be happy. "But—" I started to explain my true feelings but got interrupted before I even got started.

"Everything okay, Mel?" Will asked from somewhere close. So close, the hairs on my arms stood on end.

I turned to find him standing behind me, eyes questioning, brow furrowed.

Jesus, this was getting worse by the minute. The ex-boyfriend and the guy I'd fucked five times last night.

"Y-yeah," I stuttered while I struggled to find an escape from this hellish situation.

"Who's this?" Eli asked.

"Uh…this is Will…er…Dr. Cummings." *My lover,* I thought. But instead, I said, "My boss."

"Hi," Eli greeted and shook Will's hand. "I'm Eli, Mel's boyfriend."

Oh, for fuck's sake. I closed my eyes and cringed, but I realized pretty quickly I'd better open them if I was going to be able to prevent anything worse from happening.

Will looked at Eli and Eli looked at Will, and my lungs burned so much they felt like they were being sucked into a vortex. But before I could do anything to soothe the chaos—not that I had any clue what the fuck I was going to do—Melissa called Will's attention. "Dr. Cummings, Marlene is asking for you to head into exam room six immediately."

Will turned at the beckon, and panicked, I reached my hand out and gripped his bicep. "Will...wait..."

But he just shook his head and strode through the reception doors and down the hall toward, I presumed, exam room six.

Shit. Shit. Shit.

"Why did you say that?" I asked Eli through gritted teeth. "You're not my boyfriend. You're my *ex*-boyfriend."

"I know," he said, but it didn't really feel like he knew it. It felt like he was just doing what he always did—capitalizing on situations when it was optimal for him. "But I don't want to be your boyfriend or your ex-boyfriend. I want to be more than that, Mel. I want to spend my life with you."

My jaw dropped. Literally. Dropped to the floor. "Excuse me?"

"Oh my God," a woman whispered behind me. "Do you think he's going to ask her to marry him?"

I fucking hope not.

Are you there, God? It's me, Melody. And this better be a freaking joke.

"Don't you think we should have this conversation somewhere else?" he asked and glanced around the room to several sets of riveted eyes. They practically glowed like a herd of deer in the dark forest.

We had officially become the live soap opera in the waiting room.

And, yeah, we probably should've had this conversation somewhere else. The whole situation felt like one giant clusterfuck of disasters. But this shit was Eli's fault, and I'd be damned if I was going to give him anything he wanted, even if it was the thing I most wanted myself.

"Listen," I said with determination in my voice. "I'm not sure what your motives are—"

"Motives?" He cut me off with a shake of his head. "There are no motives, Melly. I love you. I miss you. That's why I'm here."

I sighed. "You're here because you had an investors' meeting, and it was convenient."

"Oh, come on, Mel," he tried to argue. "Do you really think that little of me?"

Let the record show Exhibit A of Eli's notorious ways: turning the blame on me. Eli had a talent for finding a way to use guilt against me. And a year ago, I would've crumpled like a piece of a paper.

But not today. Not now. I'd just started to find myself again. I'd just started to repair what I'd lost in that relationship. I'd just started to feel like me. *I'd just found Will...*

I met his gaze and didn't back down. "It's been over four months since I left Portland," I argued. "Over four months and this is the first time I'm hearing from you in any form other than a generic text message. If you've been missing me so badly, why have you waited until now to tell me? Why did you wait until you were conveniently in New York for a work thing to reach out?"

"It's not like that."

"Then what is it like?" I questioned. "Tell me, Eli. What is it like?"

"I want to marry you," he said as if it was the most normal thing in the world.

He wanted to marry me.

I called bullshit.

"No, you don't."

"How can you say that?" he exclaimed with a frustrated wave of his hand. "How can you just discount what I'm feeling like that?"

"I'm not discounting anything," I explained. "Your actions speak louder than your words ever have. And your actions, Eli? Well, they show a man who doesn't know what the fuck he wants."

"I want you."

"You want me? You want to marry me?"

He nodded, resolute. "Yes."

"Okay, Eli. Then tell me why."

His head moved back and forth in little tiny shakes.

"Tell me *why*. What is it about me you can't live without? What is it about me that makes your heart beat faster? What is it *about me* that makes you feel like you can't hold back until you have me, can't go on unless you keep me?"

"Come on, Melly. You know why."

I shook my head. "You want the idea of me. You want the Melody who was willing to give-give-give while you took-took-took. You want things to go back to the way they were. And guess what? They will never go back to the way they were. I don't want to go back. I want to stay right where I am." The second the words left my lips, relief overwhelmed me.

Maybe I didn't know everything that I wanted, but I knew I liked where I was heading. And even though I was working a job that I didn't necessarily feel was my purpose and I was currently waking up every morning to my father blaring Black Sabbath, I knew I'd made the right decision.

"So, that's it?" he asked, and I immediately nodded.

"That's it."

"You'll regret this, you know," he said, and the fact that it didn't bother me one bit said more than words.

I kissed his cheek and whispered what I figured were the last words I'd ever say to him.

"Goodbye, Eli." Closure. That's what that goodbye meant to me. I'd finally closed the door on that relationship for good.

And as I turned away from my ex and headed through the reception door, I had only one person on my mind. *Will.*

CHAPTER *fifteen*

Will

BACK IN MY OFFICE, I TRIED TO CALM MYSELF DOWN. Being summoned to exam room six had been the reason for my escape, and at first, I'd headed there.

But my brain was like an unsolved crossword puzzle at the moment, and I didn't think making up words based on the number of spaces in the answer was a solid strategy for practicing medicine.

Obviously, I couldn't fucking go see a patient like this, so I hoped like Christ Marlene dug deep and found some people skills while she was waiting.

I wasn't prone to emotional outbursts of any kind, and I couldn't remember the last time I'd been this close to hysteria. Normally, I was level-headed and rational, and I didn't do Wild West showdown type scenes in the middle of my goddamn workday.

But last night with Melody had been more than a date. It'd been more than a couple of hours of monotonous conversation and flirty looks, and the sex had been more than two bodies rubbing against each other until somebody came.

It had been, quite literally, the best date of my life and then some, and the fact that some fucking *guy* was here, today of all days, acting like Melody was *his* made me want to tear this fucking place apart.

Smash things, slam priceless medical equipment into the wall, grind every last splinter of my mahogany desk to dust.

But Georgia had had Julia make me artwork for my desk, and fuck if I was willing to risk destroying it. So instead, I channeled my anger at the one thing I didn't mind beating up a little—myself.

Grabbing the stupid fucking project I'd worked on instead of getting any real sleep last night, I slammed it into the garbage in the corner so violently it made a resounding clang as wood met metal.

It felt good to get out some of the surface rage, so I walked over to the wastebasket, pulled out the bouquet, and slammed it down again.

The reverberations of the second clang hadn't even quieted when Melody opened my door, stepped through without asking, and closed and locked it behind her.

"Will," she whispered softly, cutting through my anger and using a torch of memories to melt it all into hurt.

When she didn't say anything else, and the back of my throat started to tingle with unshed tears, all I could do was raise my eyebrows. *What the hell did she want from me?* I wasn't the one with the information.

God, my brain breathed in panic. *Maybe there is no explanation.* Last night, the weeks leading up to it, maybe all of it was a made-up fantasy. She *hadn't* wanted to stay over. Maybe Melody was just like all the other crazy women out there—out for a night of scandalous fun with *Dr. Obscene. Jesus, that's a depressing thought.*

"I'm so sorry for the scene out there," she finally apologized. "I can't believe he came here and did that in front of all of those people…"

My insides froze, waiting for the rest, unsure whether to prepare for elation or heartbreak.

"And?" I found my voice.

"And…I know it's unprofessional."

"Unprofessional?" My head started to pound in time with my heart, and neither of the two took it at an easy pace. The vacuum was strong, sucking me toward despair at a rapid speed and threatening to keep me there.

"Yes. I wouldn't want you to see me that way."

"That's it?" I questioned disbelievingly.

"I…" She chewed her lip nervously and wrung her hands together. "Yeah, that's it."

Every single part of me revolted. My skin tried to shred, my bones turned to dust, and my heart raced to a strain before exploding.

The memory of the sensation of her so fresh in my mind I could feel it physically, I locked it down and poured virtual salt into my wounds.

The woman you're mourning doesn't exist.

"Wow." I shook my head, my voice so thick with disgust it tasted like molasses. "Don't worry, Mel. The way I'm viewing you now is *nothing* but professional."

Crowding her, I moved to the door and grabbed the handle, hoping she'd get the hint and move out of the way. When she didn't, I vocalized the implication. "Marlene needs me in exam room six."

She didn't move, so I forced it.

"Will, wait," she cried as I pulled the door open a sliver, slamming it closed with her weight and her back.

"Mel—"

"No, Will. Wait. Please?"

I took a deep breath and backed up a step to look her in the eye. If everything I'd felt for her was really going to die, I was going to have to let her hold the hammer for the final nails.

"I'm not handling this well, I know. But I wasn't expecting this." She paused and sighed. "And I wasn't expecting last night either."

A spike of anxiety mingled with hope made a sharp pain contract in my chest. *The shock of the defibrillator on my heart.*

"And, what? You just thought you'd have one night with me and then go back to your boyfriend?"

Her eyes widened in horror. "No! God, no. He's my *ex*-boyfriend." Her voice dropped to a mutter as she spoke to herself. "Christ, Mel. Way to bury the *very fucking important* lead."

Ex-boyfriend. Christ. Well, that was at least a little better. Still, I needed more of an explanation so I pushed on. "You thought last night was what, exactly? Help me get on the same page here, Mel."

"I don't know!" she huffed, frustrated. "At first I thought it was about your reputation, and then when the sex happened, I thought it was more about having fun."

"Having fun?"

"Well, yeah."

Is it really possible she didn't feel what I did? Am I losing my mind here?

Christ. Maybe I was. I'd only known her for a month.

Forcing myself to remember what I was like, what I'd been looking for from a woman until Melody had walked into my life about two point five figurative seconds earlier, I took a deep breath.

I was a player. I slept around, I did it with people I worked with and didn't, and I did it often. I met women in bars, took them home, slept with them, and never spoke to them again. I wasn't exactly a pillar of society.

That, combined with the way I was being portrayed on TV and the fact that Melody didn't actually know me that well at all suggested it wasn't only fair of her to think this way, it was pretty much expected. If she were any other woman, I'd be worried if she *wasn't* thinking this.

She couldn't presume the way she made me feel, just like I couldn't presume she felt the same. Only time could prove that.

In the meantime, I would just have to make sure she knew the difference between her and everyone else, that she felt the difference I so clearly did, and it wasn't going to happen in a conversation. At least, not entirely.

There was no way I'd say the right thing.

No, actions were going to have to be my words, and I was going to have to be really fucking eloquent.

Too bad I'd been nothing but a big bag of awkward since I'd first laid eyes on her.

Fuck. *Make the best of this, Will.*

"You're right. It was fun." It was safe to say I paraphrased my inner monologue a bit. "And I want to keep having more of it. But I was kind of thinking our fun would be a two-person, no exceptions kind of activity. Aka, not having guys like *Eli*—"

His name reeked of disdain as it rolled off of my tongue.

"—show up with flowers for you. If you get flowers, they're from me, and they're made of fucking tongue depressors, goddammit."

Okay. Maybe I should have taken another breath in the middle of that little speech. Seems the good attitude wore off by the end.

"What?"

I thought she was confused, naturally, but if I'd been paying attention to her more than my own mental breakdown, I would have noticed she wasn't confused at all before she moved.

She pushed me aside, her hand reaching for the garbage behind me, and as I turned to look, I spotted what I already knew was there—the bouquet of tongue depressors I'd made this morning lying almost pristinely on top. Did I mention the five hours of uncertainty I'd had after she left? Well, turns out, I also had an old box of tongue depressors in my home office.

Goddammit. I would have thought I'd destroyed those things a little more.

Plucking one from the bundle, she held it up for closer inspection and read aloud the ridiculous words I'd written.

"There's nothing depressing about your tongue."

I looked away. Christ, that was a bad one.

"The back of your throat has never looked prettier."

Okay, that one was worse.

"Will? What are these?"

I shook my head, but the intensity of her stare forced the motion to a stop. "Will."

"They're tongue-depressor-themed affirmations. You said you like to use them—"

"I know what I said," she interrupted, her voice dropping to a whisper and her eyes dropping to the sticks in her hands. "I just can't believe you did."

I shrugged and told the truth. "I like you, Mel. It's not that hard to remember when you say things. It's not that hard at all."

CHAPTER*sixteen*

"**H**i," I STARTED TO GREET, BUT I HAD TO GLANCE DOWN AT THE CHART IN MY hand in search of the patient's name. "Elise," I finished and gestured her into the exam room. "I'm Melody, Dr. Cummings's nurse. I'll be assisting him with your checkup today."

"Oh, I don't think an assistant is necessary for my appointment," she said and sashayed into the exam room on her black stilettos. "It's just a yearly pap smear. I've done them, like, a thousand times."

I internally called bullshit. This woman didn't look a day over thirty. One thousand pap smears was either a gross exaggeration, or her prior OB/GYN was giving out pap smears like condoms at the free clinic.

"It's actually our new policy," I corrected and moved toward the cabinet and started to set out the needed sterile supplies on the counter. "Moving forward, all of our physicians have a nurse with them during exams to ensure patients are comfortable and the physicians have all of the assistance they might need."

Also, now that I was officially dating Will, having a chaperone in the room with this woman was *my* policy. She looked like she was ripe for more than a pelvic exam.

We hadn't told our coworkers about our current dating status yet, and considering who they were, I honestly didn't know if I'd ever want to, but things had finally settled.

Two weeks after the *Eli Incident,* as we were now calling it, and things between Will and me had maintained a steady pace of getting to know each other in all the ways that included the ah-mazing, toe-curling sex that occurred when we were together.

Ironically enough, my ex-boyfriend randomly showing up at my place of employment had actually done us a little favor. If I hadn't been forced to confront Will directly, if I hadn't seen the look on his face as I blew off our night together as if it was no big deal, I don't think I ever would have gotten around to facing my feelings.

I wasn't making wedding plans or anything, but I didn't have any doubts Will liked me. In fact, he told me he did.

I guess you could say he was my boyfriend. Which shouldn't come as a surprise, I mean, he'd made me a tongue-depressor bouquet and told me it wasn't hard to remember when I said something, for shit's sake. I wasn't one hundred percent emotionally available, but I wasn't an idiot either. When the object of most women's fantasies spends his time making you a bouquet of affirmations, you fucking date him. Period. Consequences pending until later.

"We can just ignore the policy. I won't mind," Elise added suggestively. I rolled my eyes before turning back toward the exam table to get her vitals.

Much to my dismay, Elise had already made herself comfortable—actually, a little too comfortable. Without removing her clothes or putting on a patient gown, she'd hopped up onto the table and placed her feet—still clad in stilettos—into the stirrups. Her panty-less crotch was on display for anyone and everyone to see. If I weren't certain I was at my job, in a physician's medical office, I would've thought someone had teleported me on to the set of *Cocktor Pound,* a B-rated porno. Any second the male lead, John E. Deep's boner would have been popping in for its onscreen debut.

Holy moly, what is going on here?

"Knock, knock," Will said as he opened the door. "All se—" he started to say, but once his eyes made contact with Elise's crotch, he quickly averted his eyes. "Uh…I'll give you another minute or two," he muttered and glanced at me with wide eyes. "Melody, I'll be in my office. Just come get me once the patient's ready."

"Oh, but I am ready, Dr. Cummings," Elise purred, but Will continued his path, straight toward the hallway with the door firmly shut behind him.

The patient sighed in frustration, but I found myself smirking. It wasn't every day you got enjoyment out of watching your boyfriend get flashed with a crotch shot from another woman. But with the way he'd reacted, I couldn't help but smile.

Luckily, Elise seemed to get the picture too—if only temporarily—and took her heels out of the stirrups and sat up straight on the table, legs crossed and hiding what I'd decided to nickname *The Beave.*

"I'm just going to check your vitals and ask you a few questions, and then we'll be ready for your exam."

"Whatever," she muttered, put out with me. *She* was put out with *me.*

Wow. You're kind of a bitch, I thought to myself, but somehow, I managed to school my face into a neutral expression and move along with the appointment. The sooner I got her assessed and examined, the sooner her stiletto and miniskirt wearing ass would be out the door.

But seriously, who dressed like that for a doctor's appointment?

Especially one where you were going to get a pap smear.

The last time I'd had a pap, I'd worn yoga pants, a sweat shirt, and Converse. The idea of a physician sticking his hand and a speculum up my hoo-hah had never been a situation that made me feel like getting dressed up like a hooker on a Friday night.

Either pap smears made Elise horny, or Dr. Will Cummings—*my Will*—made her horny.

I had a feeling it was the latter, but self-preservation and jealousy I didn't expect made me cut that thought off at the knees.

"When was your last period?" I asked and pulled up her medical file on the computer in the room.

"Two fucking weeks ago," she responded in a frustrated tone.

Yeah, I take that back. You're actually a total bitch. Not just a little bit, but full-on *bitch.*

"And how long did it last?" I questioned in my sweetest voice.

"I dunno," she said with a sigh. "Like…five days or something."

"Do your periods generally come every twenty-eight to thirty days?"

Do you know that you're a total bitch?

"Yes."

"Are you sexually active?"

Are you pretty much the worst person ever?

"Obviously," she answered with another eye roll. *HA! Walked right into that one, didn't you?*

"When was your last pap smear?"

When was the last time your brain had an intelligent thought?

"Like, a year ago, I think."

I continued the assessment, asking questions and getting bitchy—but quite humorously perfect to my own imaginary line of questioning— responses, and checked her vitals before grabbing the chart and moving toward the door. "Are there any medical conditions Dr. Cummings should be aware of before the exam begins?"

"I have a very, very tight pussy," she replied as if it was the most normal thing in the world.

It'd been a while since I'd been in nursing school, but I didn't recall "a very, very tight pussy" being a diagnosis question on the NCLEX.

"All righty, then," I responded, just stopping myself from losing my mind, and opened the door. "Go ahead and remove your clothes from the waist down and put on the paper gown. Once you're comfortable and appropriately covered on the exam table, Dr. Cummings will be in to do your exam."

"About fucking time," she muttered and hopped off the table.

I shut the door behind me, and before I moved down the currently empty hall to get Will, I turned back toward the closed exam room and gave Elise the middle finger. I knew it wasn't the most professional thing I'd ever done, but holy hell, that chick was a piece of work, and it wasn't the good kind. If she were a painting in a museum, she definitely wouldn't be a Monet. No. She'd be that weird piece of art like pictures of toenail clippings or a mummified dog sculpture made out of papier-mâché and cow manure that no one could ever wrap their brain around its actual meaning.

"She's that fantastic, huh?" Will said quietly into my ear, and I jumped.

"Jesus," I muttered with a hand to my chest. "You scared the hell out of me."

He just smirked in response and rested his elbow against the doorway.

"How long have you been standing here?" I whispered, and his smirk grew wider.

"Long enough to see you flip off the door for a good ten seconds."

"The hallway was empty ten seconds ago," I said in annoyance and moved toward the small alcove beside the exam room to finish putting Elise's assessment into her medical chart. "It's like you appeared out of thin air."

"It wasn't empty," he corrected and followed me, making himself comfortable in the chair beside mine. "You were just too intent on giving that patient the bird."

"Yeah, well, she deserved it," I added and typed her vitals into the computer.

"Excuse me," Elise called out from behind the closed door. "Nurse Lyric? I'm ready for Dr. Cummings now."

Nurse Lyric? Really?

At least it sounds better than Load-y...

Will groaned, and I grinned at his anguish. Somehow watching him suffer so adorably made me feel better.

"She seems *real* excited to see you."

"Jesus," he muttered.

"And she would also like you to know about her medical condition."

"Medical condition?"

"Yeah," I answered, swallowing my urge to smile. "When I asked her if she had any current medical conditions that you needed to be aware of, she said, and I'm repeating this word for word...*I have a very, very tight pussy.*"

His jaw dropped, and his eyes narrowed. "Are you fucking with me right now?"

"Nope," I said with a little to pop to the p.

"And she's a huge fan of your show," I added. "She wanted you to know that as well."

"Oh, for fuck's sake."

I smiled and hopped out of my seat with Elise's chart in hand. "C'mon, *Dr. Obscene.* We've got a patient waiting on you."

"For the love of God, never call me that again."

I just giggled in response and knocked on the exam room door. "All set?"

"Yes."

I opened the door and found that Elise had managed to put on the paper gown but appeared intent on airing out her vagina while her feet were perched in the stirrups.

"Oh God," Will muttered to himself as we both entered the room.

"Hi, Dr. Cummings," Elise purred with a provocative smile. "I'm Elise," she greeted with her hand held out in his direction. "Elise Allen."

Will shook her hand while simultaneously avoiding the giant beaver in the room. "It's, uh…it's nice to meet you."

"Oh, believe me," the patient continued, "the pleasure is all mine."

Boy, this chick was laying it on thick.

"Melody, could you place another gown over Mrs. Allen's legs?" Will asked, and I nodded. *You bet I can.*

"Oh, I don't mind," Elise started to chime in, but I ignored her, haphazardly tossing another paper gown over her legs. She flashed a glare in my direction, but I chose to ignore that, too.

"Dr. Cummings?" Elise questioned as Will sat down on his rolling stool and started to put on a pair of sterile gloves.

"Yes?"

"It's *Ms.* Allen," she corrected with a wink. "I'm newly divorced."

Will just nodded in response and set his focus on setting up his sterile instruments. "So, we're just here for your yearly pap smear, is that correct, Ms. Allen?"

"Please, call me Elise, and yes, just a yearly pap smear."

"You're just going to feel a little pressure as I insert the speculum," he instructed and started the exam. "Now, I'm going to swab your cer—" He paused midsentence with a perplexing look etched on his face. Two seconds later, after grabbing for an instrument that looked a hell of a lot like oversized tweezers, Will pulled a small piece of laminated paper out of the patient's vagina. He set it down on the metal table and just stared at it, his face equal parts shocked and horrified. He looked so cute, a little wrinkle between his eyes, but I'd never seen him make that face before.

Morbid curiosity got the best of me, and I moved toward his side to read the wording written across the laminated paper.

212-555-1111

<3 Elise Allen <3

A gasp left my lips before I could stop it, and Will looked in my direction.

Not only had the patient dressed up like a hooker and not worn underwear to her appointment, even flashed *The Beave* to him before the appointment had gotten started, she'd also come to the fucking appointment with her phone number inside of her vagina.

Inside of her vagina, people.

What in the ever-loving *fuck* was this?

And quite frankly, wouldn't a piece of laminated paper inside your hoo-hah hurt?

Elise sat up on her elbows and smiled down at Will. "I'm a huge fan of your show, Dr. Cummings," she purred, and I had the irrational urge to vomit. "I'd love for you to call me sometime."

On top of the irrational urge to vomit, I felt like sprinting out of the exam room. I didn't want to be anywhere near Elise, or Will for that matter, as jealously turned to alarm.

Was this the kind of shit I would be dealing with all the time?

I wasn't sure if I could handle a relationship like this. Women weren't just visibly flirting with him during appointments, now they were using their actual vaginas as wingmen to hand out their phone numbers.

What else was next?

Holy hell, I didn't even want to think about that. Women were crafty. And horny women were crafty *and* determined. I wasn't sure I could handle all of this. Will wasn't exactly a normal guy anymore after the show. He wasn't just a successful physician. He was more than that now. Women all over the country, hell, probably even the world, knew him.

And they knew him as *Dr. Obscene.*

That nickname didn't exactly discourage vaginas stuffed with phone numbers.

I couldn't stop myself from wondering, *Is it really a good idea for me to be involved with Will?*

CHAPTER *seventeen*

"WILL, WE NEED TO—"

Looking both ways for witnesses, I pushed her toward the door to the empty patient room and opened it, ushering her through before she could finish her sentence. She went easily enough, too busy trying to figure out what I was doing or how to say what she wanted to say to fight me. It didn't really matter to me which it was, as long as she was distracted enough to let me get started.

From the moment of the inappropriate treasure discovery, it'd felt like the rest of the exam of *Ms.* Elise Allen had taken forever. Lust rushed over me so powerfully it was blinding, and it had nothing to do with a woman desperate enough to put her number in her vagina.

Instead, it was the other woman in the room, the one who'd looked on as Elise flirted, drumming up enough self-control not to say anything in response when I wouldn't have blamed her at all if she had.

I pushed Melody toward the table with a firm hand to her stomach and laughed internally as her bouncing eyes tried to make sense of it all.

My lips went to her ear to speak before she could, and when I did, it came out in a raspy whisper. "That little gasp," I explained, a weakness I couldn't avoid acting on. "When you figured out what it was, I heard you gasp."

All that self-control ruined by one sharp inhale.

"Will," she breathed back shakily.

"I lost my mind when I heard you gasp, and I haven't been able to think about anything else but making you do it again."

"Will," she murmured again, her heart racing so hard I could feel the vibrations of her chest against mine.

"I have to be inside of you, Melody."

Somehow, I'd managed to put the right words together to explain my teenage-like hormonal response to a simple reactionary noise eloquently enough that she understood—and not only that, but wanted me too.

"Jump up," I told her but put my hands to her hips so she didn't have to do the work all on her own. The paper crinkled beneath her ass as it landed, and for the first time ever, the sound of it fired something erotic inside me.

Grabbing the fabric at the top of her scrub pants, I bunched it in my hands and yanked it down as she lifted her hips to ease my way. They caught on her shoes, so I took everything off at once and spread her at the knees.

With practiced efficiency, I pulled the stirrups up and locked them into position. I couldn't have missed the widening of her eyes.

"You've got to be kidding me."

I didn't reply verbally, not at first, instead lifting her feet and placing them pointedly in each position. She eyed me carefully, clenching her knees tightly together in denial.

But I didn't even have to think about how to bring her around to my way of thinking. Her skin was soft and alluring and invited me further into her space with every inch my hands skimmed. As I moved up the line of her calves and around to the inside, her knees parted at my push, and her hips jumped at the approach of my touch.

"I'm serious. About this and you and the fact that you'll be in a whole lot of trouble if you move your knees even…one…inch…closer together."

Her throat bobbed as she swallowed, and I leaned forward to touch my lips to the apex of her thighs as if called.

"Just relax, Mel," I whispered there, right against her warm, humming skin.

Pulling away slowly—and quite painfully—I backed out of the space between her legs and rounded the table to the cabinet. I opened the one with samples and scanned the contents until I found what I was looking for.

Grabbing one from the box, I shut the door and moved back to Melody, unbuckling my belt and undoing the button of my pants as I did. The color of her face ripened as she realized where I'd gone.

"Oh my God."

I laughed a little and leaned toward her with the condom between my pointer and middle fingers. "What? There are perks to doing this here."

Her eyebrows pulled together, and I knew the question without her even having to ask it.

God, I'm an idiot. I was joking, and she was thinking, *Have you ever done this here before?*

"Never," I answered, even though the question had never been spoken.

And I hadn't. Not in my office and not with one of my office staff. The younger version of me didn't think about things the way I did now, so I couldn't say hospital hookups hadn't happened in the past, but Mel was the exception to the rule, not the rule itself. Always. I wanted her to know that, but I didn't want to spend any more time than necessary talking about it. We'd only have so long before people noticed us missing individually, and then eventually, noticed we were missing as a pair. And that would have a hell of a lot bigger impact on us than any transgressions from my past would.

"I promise."

She nodded, not in agreement but belief. If I said I hadn't done it, she trusted that. I didn't think I'd ever had a woman other than my sister have that much faith in me before.

"Now," I whispered. "Spread those legs wide, baby, and keep them there." I flicked the condom up onto her chest and leaned in closer as she watched it land. "And hold on to that for me. I'm going to need it soon but not until I have a little something to eat."

She shivered before my tongue even touched her. As it turns out, words *can* be foreplay when you're short on time.

"Mmm," I moaned as my lips closed over her pussy and sucked on the already waiting arousal. Her legs started to shake with the effort to keep them open, and I couldn't pass up the opportunity to tease her. "Bet you're glad for those stirrups now, huh?"

She smacked my head with a scowl, but when the violence was over, her hand didn't bounce off of my head and away. Instead, her fingers laced through my hair. She yanked it back, pushing my mouth to her pussy and smiling. "We don't have a lot of time here, *Dr. Cummings.*"

I think my name was meant to knock some sense into me, but all it did was turn me on. "Keep talking like that, and all you're going to get is my cock, Mel. A meal isn't meant to be rushed. It's meant to be enjoyed."

"Yeah, well, unless you want the whole office to see you shoot your load in good ole *Load-y*, you better get your shit together."

I laughed, moving up her body to touch my lips to hers and softening my voice to a cajole. "Relax, Mel."

She pursed her lips.

"I locked the door."

Her green-gold eyes narrowed, and I fell a little deeper. Into her, into the moment, on my way into in love. "Okay," I agreed. "I'll hurry."

She smiled then, triumphant.

"But only until we get to the good parts," I amended.

Slowly, she moved her lips over mine, one side to the other and open until I let her tongue inside. Only then did she whisper her approval. "Deal."

"Go ahead. Lie back, and we'll start the exam."

"What, are we playing doctor and patient now?"

"Why not?" I asked with a laugh.

"Because it's creepy."

I winked. "Good. I'd much rather play doctor and nurse."

She smiled and shook her head. "Then get in there, Doctor. They need you."

I just bet they did.

Bending low, I lifted her thighs with a jerk so that her ass left the table, and I settled my hands there. With one long lick, I pulled her taste back into my mouth and savored it. She wasn't like anyone I'd had before, sweeter in all the ways that counted. And the taste of her pussy was sure as hell one of them.

She gasped, the same sound she'd made in the other exam room, and my dick pulsed in my pants.

"Again," I rasped against her, and her hips jerked. With a quick stroke, I punched my tongue inside her, and only then did she gasp again.

"Again, Mel," I ordered. She didn't listen, not that I expected her to, the difficulty of a genuine gasp on command above even my pay grade. But it was part of the fun, telling her to, and then finding a way to make her.

Fingers to her ass, I pulled her closer to my face and swirled her clit until she gasped at the final flick.

She writhed now, close to climax, and I wanted nothing more than to taste it as she flooded my mouth. Up and down, her hips punched the air and guided my face as I ate. "That's it, Mel," I encouraged. "Chase it. Make me give it to you."

"Will," she called, closer to a yell than either of us expected.

"Quick, baby," I told her. "Before someone finds us."

Her eyes widened and then closed in ecstasy, the threat of discovery and the swirl of my tongue combined with three quick pumps of my finger finally enough to push her over the edge.

She sat up violently at the unexpected knock on the door.

"Hello?" Marlene called from the other side.

I smiled at Melody's sheer panic and scooped up the condom from the center of her chest before leaving a kiss behind in its place.

"Guess we're going to have to save this for another time."

She shoved my shoulder and mouthed, "Marlene!" angrily.

I winked. Cleared my throat. And then raised my voice to a yell. "Be out in a sec, Mar. Just needed a minute to collect myself."

Melody's eyes shot to my very hard dick as Marlene grumbled an unsatisfied *okay* back.

I laughed softly. "I wish you had time to help me collect myself too."

Another slap to my chest.

"Go!" she mouthed. "She's outside that door waiting for you."

I looked down. "Do I look like I can go now?"

"Well…think gross thoughts, then. Quickly."

"Gross thoughts?"

She scowled. "To make him go back to normal."

"Oh, please," I said with a chuckle. "Please give me examples."

"Susie sucking Frank's dick."

Oh God. The NYC bus tourists. I cringed.

"Exactly!" she cheered nearly silently, offering another suggestion immediately. "Your mom."

"Ew. That's more twisted than I'd like, thanks."

"Hairy knuckles. Bowel obstruction. Applesauce on a mustard sandwich."

I pouted as the blood filtered its way back into my head, but she leaned forward and touched her lips to mine to make it better, promising, "Later."

God, yes. Later.

"Now, I'm hard again." I teased, rubbing my thumb over her perfect, plump bottom lip. "You ruined all of your hard work."

"Just go!" she said with a shove.

I straightened myself, grabbed my coat from the stool, and threw it on before walking to the door and looking back at her.

"See you soon, Melody Marco."

All of her features gave up only a hint of their sternness, but it was enough. "See you soon, Dr. Cummings."

CHAPTER *eighteen*

Melody

ANOTHER DAY, ANOTHER DOLLAR, AND ANOTHER GLORIOUS OPPORTUNITY TO WATCH Will's firm ass strut around the break room as he doctored up his coffee—*with what I presumed was someone else's creamer*—from the employee fridge, while I stood with a hip to the counter.

That man, *my* man, had a fantastic ass. And yeah, maybe he wasn't exactly strutting, but I had a vivid imagination and could easily insert memories of him where *actual* strutting had occurred. Particularly the ones where a naked Will had strutted toward me with a magnificently hard cock.

He'd been doing a lot of naked reassurance in the last few days since Elise Allen had used her genitals as a delivery service. First, here in the office, and several times on a variety of masculine furniture in his apartment. I wasn't at all opposed.

Yes. Yes. Those are good memories.

After he'd poured a healthy amount of creamer into his mug, I caught sight of a familiar name with a familiar masking-tape label.

Marlene's Creamer. Drink it and you die.

Death threats via dairy. That was a new one and only proved that Marlene had no scruples when it came to what was considered within the normal boundaries of appropriate workplace behavior. Lawsuits for harassment be damned, the woman meant business when it came to what she thought was rightfully hers.

"Looks like someone is in the mood to live dangerously today," I whispered, and he glanced over his shoulder as he shut the fridge door.

"You didn't see anything."

"Hmmm…" I squinted my eyes and crinkled my lips at the corners. "I'm not so sure about that…"

Will stood beside me and rested his back against the counter. "I was never here," he whispered conspiratorially.

"I'm pretty sure Mar—" I started to say, but he covered my lips with his hand.

"I. Was. Never. Here," he said with serious eyes, and my mouth crested into a grin against his palm. "This isn't funny." He affected concern. "This is life or death here."

I didn't take the bait, though. Instead, I just licked his hand like a puppy until he pulled it away, chuckling.

"How long have you been living on the wild side and stealing her creamer?"

He smirked. "I have no idea what you're talking about."

"If she ever finds out, your ass is grass."

Will just laughed in response and took a sip from his coffee. After he'd successfully caffeinated up for the last half of the day, he looked at me with a mischievous grin.

"Feel like playing a little hooky from work?"

"Always. This place blows," I teased, and he feigned annoyance. I played it off like it was no big deal, but the thought of heading out on some kind of adventure with Will made my heart jump in my chest. We'd been out on our first date obviously, but since then, if we were together outside of the office, it was probably at his apartment. Sure, we spent a lot of our time naked in a place with a convenient bed, but a little part of me nagged that it wasn't natural.

"This place doesn't blow."

"It's probably the worst job I've ever had," I added, and he reached his hand around my back and pinched my ass. I couldn't help but squeal out my surprise.

"Quiet down," he said and shushed me. "Don't draw any attention to us or else my plan isn't going to work."

"Don't pinch my ass, then," I whispered back. He just chuckled softly.

"Anyway, how are you going to manage sneaking out before noon? You have five more appointments before the day is through."

"Mark has a resident working with him today."

"So?" I questioned with a skeptical brow. "Dr. Stewart isn't exactly known for going the extra mile and taking additional appointments. That man is out the door at five p.m. on the dot."

He flashed a wink in my direction. "I might've also given him my Mavericks tickets for their game against Pittsburgh."

"Ah." I nodded in realization. "Now, I'm understanding. Low morality bribing at play again. At this rate, you won't have any tickets left for yourself this season."

"Don't worry, if you're interested in going one day, I'm sure I'll be able to scrounge some up. Plus, I think you need the rest of the day off."

"Oh, really?"

Will nodded with concerned eyes. "I think it's important that nurse Load-y gets a personal day every once in a while."

"Can you never use that nickname again?"

He shrugged. "That depends."

I raised an eyebrow as I waited for his demands.

"If you ditch work with me for the day, then yeah, I'll never use it again."

"Am I hearing you right?" I asked with a smirk. "My boss is asking me to leave work early, even though he knows my paycheck will pay me for a *full* day's work."

No hooky for this chick without pay. *Come on, Mel*, I chastised. *You're turning yourself into a prostitute.* Still…a day off was a day off.

"Yep."

"Count me in," I agreed and then added, "But I get to choose what we do." If I was in control, there was a guarantee we were going out to enjoy the sun and the city. I didn't know if his choice would be the same.

But he calmed my irrational fears without much effort at all when he agreed instantly. "Deal."

I guess dating the boss wasn't such a bad thing after all…

"Okay…what's the plan?" I asked on a whisper. "The old bait and switch? Shell game? A good old flimflam?"

"You have no idea what any of those really mean do you?"

"No, but I know it sounded good."

He grinned in amusement. "Oh, yeah, it sounded like skipping out of work is old hat. Like you've done it a million times. Maybe I should be concerned?" he asked in pretend shock. "Have you done this before? Jesus!" he exclaimed. "Have you done this while working here?"

"Shut up." I slapped his shoulder playfully. "Get to the point, Dr. Cummings. How are we going to blow this popsicle stand?"

"Okay," he said and moved in closer. "We're going to get our shit, and then…we're going to walk straight out the front door."

I leaned back and looked at him with a furrowed brow. "That sounds like a shitty fucking plan. Everyone will see us."

"Indeed. *But* you're lucky enough to be with a forward thinker. Some might call me brilliant, even."

I scoffed, but he just smiled.

"Everyone thinks we're leaving for an important meeting with a pharmaceutical rep."

I laughed. "You're such a tease."

"You have no idea, Ms. Marco." He waggled his brows. "Wanna meet me in exam room six to find out how much of a tease I can be?"

I shook my head on a laugh.

"Another time?"

"Maybe if you're a very, very good boy and follow all of my rules today…"

"Are you playing coy with me?"

"Maybe." I shrugged and fluttered my eyelashes dramatically. "Is it working?"

A sexy smile consumed his mouth. "Maybe. Will you keep doing it?"

"Only if we actually leave work for the day instead of just talking about leaving work for the day."

"Let's hit it," he said and moved toward the doorway. "Meet me at reception in five."

I grinned. "You got it, Doc."

Two hours later and Will and I had managed to eat two hot dogs, a slice of pizza, a cupcake from a mom-and-pop bakery, and walked about a million blocks toward the East Village.

Instead of hearing Marlene grumble about her bunions, I got to breathe in the warm, fresh air of a New York spring day. Blue skies and the rays of the sun peeking out between the buildings had replaced hearing Melissa pop her gum one thousand times while filing her nails behind the reception desk.

And instead of watching patients trying to give my boyfriend their numbers via vag-mail, I was strolling hand in hand *with* him, people watching and chatting about the most random but hilarious things.

Granted, he was my boyfriend in disguise—a baseball hat pulled low and sunglasses covering the perfect blue of his eyes, but he was my Will all the same when it came to personality. He'd also changed out of his professional garb and into a pair of dark jeans and a plain white T-shirt, but when I'd teased him about all of it, he'd had a succinctly genuine explanation. Apparently, wildly popular attention from the show had spread beyond the office and had been following him around in the form of paparazzi as well.

I shouldn't have been surprised, but I was. I never traveled to or from work with him, even though I spent most nights at his apartment, so I hadn't seen it. I was always running twenty minutes behind his schedule. Well, everyone's schedule, actually.

As sorry for him as I felt, it did make me feel a little better about the fact that we weren't taking daily strolls through Central Park.

But as Will leaned forward and touched his lips to the line of my jaw, a chuckle still clinging to his tongue, one thing was clear. Playing hooky from work was everything it was hyped up to be.

Will's phone chimed inside of his pocket, and he pulled it out to read a text message. "Hold on," he said, and our leisurely walk through the city came to a halt. "It's my sister."

We sat down on a bench beside an old, Victorian-style church, and Will held his phone in his lap while he typed a quick response. No less than a minute later, his phone chimed again.

"Jesus," he muttered and moved the phone so that I could read the messages.

Georgia: William. I need your help. Is it normal to have contractions at 6 months pregnant?

Will: Is everything okay? Seriously, Gigi, if you're having contractions, you need to call your OB now.

Georgia: I'm not. But I knew that would get you to respond.

"My sister is a huge pain in my ass sometimes," he said and typed out a response.

Will: Wow. That's low. Even for you.

But Georgia didn't waste any time, firing back within seconds.

Georgia: Like you should talk. When we were kids, you told everyone at school Mom sent me to Masturbation Camp for the summer.

My eyebrows pulled together in curiosity. "Masturbation Camp?"

He grinned and nodded. "My mother, the sex therapist, was all about setting a foundation of healthy sexual habits and open minds when we were kids."

"Wow." I couldn't hold back my urge to laugh.

"Yeah," he agreed on a soft chuckle as he typed out a response on his phone. "I'm pretty sure my sister is still dealing with PTSD from those summer camp memories."

Will: That was like a million years ago. And Mom DID send you to Masturbation Camp. I was merely telling the truth.

Georgia: It wasn't Masturbation Camp!

Will: It was called Camp Love Yourself, Gigi. I can connect the dots.

Camp Love Yourself? Holy Moses in Crocs. And here I thought Jazzercise Janet took the cake on crazy mothers. No wonder our moms were friends. They went together like two nuts in a shell.

His phone chimed again, but he still never hesitated to move it away from my view, seemingly relaxed and content with letting me read the conversation between him and sister.

Georgia: Ugh. You're annoying.

Will: I love you too, sis. Mind telling Kline I'm in for Poker Night next week? You're the best. Bye.

Georgia: DON'T IGNORE ME, WILLIAM.

Will: What do you need, Gigi?

Georgia: Have lunch with me and Julia? She misses her uncle.

"Goddammit, she knows my weaknesses," he muttered and tapped out an answer.

I couldn't blame him. I'd seen pictures of Will's niece on his desk, and I was certain no one on the planet could resist her dimples or pretty blue eyes. That little lady was bound to break some hearts when she grew up.

Will: Tell Julia I'll be there. Name the time and place.

Georgia: Noon at that Italian restaurant on Broadway.

Will: Okay. See ya then.

Georgia: Oh man. Julia just told me she's busy Monday. She won't be able to make it.

Will: Julia is two, Gigi.

Georgia: Shoot… And here I already made the reservation. Looks like you're locked in or else we'll lose the table. That restaurant is notorious for not letting you order until the entire party is there.

"I should've known," he said on a sigh. "In person, my sister is the world's worst liar, but through text messages, she could mastermind a plot to take over the universe."

Will: Entire party? How many fucking people are going?

Georgia: Just me, Cassie, Winnie, and now, you. A reunion of sorts. I'm so glad it worked out! See you tomorrow at noon!

Will: You're evil.

Georgia: :) Love you. Bye!

"I love my sister dearly, but sometimes she meddles worse than our mother." Will shook his head as he slid his phone back into his pocket. "Do you think it's too late to hire a decoy to go for me?"

"A Dr. Obscene look-alike?" I teased and he groaned.

"Jesus, I hope that doesn't exist." His eyes met mine, and a pleading expression covered his face.

"No," I protested before he even said the words. "I'm not going to lunch with your sister for you."

"Not for me," he corrected. "With me." His expression morphed into something that resembled a word that was more than like, and it nearly melted me into a puddle of swoon on the pavement. "I want you to know all of the important people in my life, and more than that, I want them to know you, too. Just think about it, okay?"

Considering Will had to meet my crazy parents before our first date even got started, it made sense for me to go to lunch with his sister.

And more than that, I did want to meet her. I wanted to know the people in his life.

I wanted to be a constant in his life and him in mine.

Sure, I didn't know where we were headed exactly, and I was still finding my own way after a long relationship, but when I looked toward my future, I found myself picturing Will there, *with* me.

"Okay," I agreed on a whisper, and he leaned forward to press a gentle kiss to my lips before sitting back on the bench with his arm around my shoulder.

"Now, what shall we do for the rest of the day, Load-y?"

I smacked him hard on the shoulder and he winced, but that discomfort only stayed put for a blink of an eye before it was replaced by pure amusement.

"You promised that nickname would be banished from your vocabulary."

He shrugged. "Minor amnesia from Mrs. Linwood."

"Amnesia moment, my ass. She hit you weeks ago," I muttered and he laughed.

"Banished nicknames aside…what's our next stop, Mel?"

"Umm…" I looked around the little neighborhood that made up the East Village and knew instantly once my eyes locked on a place that always brought back some of my fondest memories.

It was an area of the city I didn't get to explore often, but it had one of my favorite little antique shops nestled inside of its neighborhood. Obscura Antiques and Oddities, a store full of vintage items that were about as far out as my parents. You could literally shop there every weekend for a year and not leave without finding something seriously strange and intriguing.

"Follow me!" I exclaimed and hopped off the bench to my feet.

"Where are we going?" Will asked as I locked my hand around his wrist and tugged him off the bench and toward the crosswalk that led to eclectic heaven.

"It's a surprise." I grinned and glanced over my shoulder as I navigated us across the street and down the sidewalk until we were standing in front of the shop. Its sign hung like a beacon of allure on the space that was once used as a funeral home.

"Obscura Antiques and Oddities?" Will read with a question in a voice.

"Have you ever been here?"

He shook his head with a soft smirk. "I can honestly say that I haven't."

"Get ready to be amazed," I said, shoving him inside playfully. The bell rung proudly as the door swung open with a creak.

I glanced around the store with a nostalgic smile etched across my lips. God, it looked exactly like it had fifteen years ago. Not a single thing had changed. It was as if it was my very own time capsule of good memories that had stayed preserved just for me.

Will put his hands to his hips and quietly scanned the shop, his eyes roaming across each nook and cranny. "An antique shop?"

"The *best* antique shop," I corrected. "My grandmother used to bring me here every Sunday when I was a kid. And she always had one rule. We couldn't leave without bringing one thing home."

God, just the smell of the store—dust mixed with wood mixed with that universal scent of old books—brought back good memories. Some of the best memories I still had of my grandma.

"I like that rule," Will said and pressed a soft kiss to my lips. "I think we should keep it."

I grinned against his mouth. "I think we should, too."

He leaned back and stared into my eyes with a challenging smirk lighting up his face. "But let's up the ante on it."

I quirked a brow. "How exactly are we going to do that?"

"Whoever gets the best find gets to choose where and what we eat for dinner tonight."

Considering dinner with Will always ended in sexy times with Will, it was a no-brainer. *Count me motherfucking in.*

"I've never been one to back away from a challenge," I said with a determined hand to my hip.

"Me either." Will leaned in close, his lips just brushing mine.

Without hesitation, I left him standing near the entrance and moved toward the back of the store, where I knew the weirdest items were located. I was a woman on a mission, and I didn't let his occasional comments of "Oh! I think this is it!" or "Man, I've got so many good things, I don't even know how to choose!" deter me.

His mind games wouldn't work on me.

And if I was being honest, I really fucking wanted Chinese tonight. Ever since I had to watch Marlene stuff her face full of Chicken Lo Mein last week, I'd been craving egg rolls like a son of a bitch.

"How's it going, Mel?" Will called from the front of the shop.

"Just fine," I replied and grinned to myself as I rummaged through a stack of obscure medical magazines from the fifties. These weren't it, but I was getting close. I could feel it.

"Don't be too sad when you lose," he added, and I could literally hear the smile in his voice.

"Uh-huh. Whatever you say, Will."

The man didn't know what was coming. My childhood years scouring antique shops with my grandmother had gotten me ready for this moment. And dammit, I would be victorious…with a mouthful of egg rolls.

And then, like God himself had opened the gates of champion's heaven, I spotted my winning item inside of a wooden box lying on the floor near the stairs that led up to the shop's storage space.

There they sat, like the golden ticket for Chinese takeout, *Russian flight goggles.*

Let the winning commence!

"Get ready to feel like a loser!" I shouted victoriously and looked toward the front of the shop, but Will was nowhere to be found.

Where in the hell did he go?

Not even a minute later, my phone chirped inside my pocket with a text message, and I immediately pulled it out to read.

Will: Meet me outside. But I should warn you, prepare yourself for defeat.

Me: Did you already pay for it?

Will: No. I stole it.

He didn't give me any time to respond before firing off another text.

Will: Kidding. Of course, I fucking paid for it. Lol. Get your item and bring that cute little ass outside. I'm ready to taste victory.

Me: You're minutes away from having to eat those words.

It was on like Donkey Kong, and I was at the register and checking out in two minutes flat.

"Do you want a bag?" the clerk asked me, and I shook my head.

"No thanks," I said, and without any explanation, I took the Russian flight goggles from his hands and slid them securely over my eyes.

"Groovy," he said with a smirk.

"Definitely groovy," I agreed and strolled out of the shop entrance with a confident pep in my step.

But the instant my goggle-covered eyes met Will, standing proudly on the sidewalk without a care in the world, I stopped in my tracks.

You've got to be fucking kidding me.

He stood like a caped Adonis in the middle of the pavement. No, seriously, he had a cape. A goddamn black, floor-length cape adorned with skulls and crossbones and an inverted white stitch on the seams.

"Nice goggles," he said with a proud smile.

Jesus with a juice box, it was the coolest fucking cape I'd ever seen in my life, and I didn't know how I'd missed that trophy of vintage inside the shop.

"Cool cape," I muttered petulantly as I walked toward him, my stupid Russian flight goggles starting to feel like a cheap pair of sunglasses.

Seriously? How did I miss that cape?

The instant my body was within reaching distance of his arms, he pulled me toward him and cocooned me beneath the cape and against his chest. "It's okay, Mel," he whispered into my ear. "You don't even have to say that I'm the winner."

"Shut up."

"But," he continued on a whisper. "Since I'm a stickler for rules, you need to know that I'll be eating your little cunt for dinner."

I pressed my face into his chest and grinned.

Yeah, fuck that cape. I'd take Will's face between my legs.

He might've snagged the coolest cape in the history of capes, but I was definitely the winner of the day.

Who needed egg rolls?

CHAPTER*nineteen*

Will

I SPOTTED THE TRIO OF TROUBLE THE MOMENT WE STEPPED INSIDE THE RESTAURANT. THEY were loud and disruptive, and they looked like they were having so much fun that none of the patrons around them even looked annoyed.

"I can't believe you talked me into meeting your sister," Melody griped, swiping at her hair in an effort to look *presentable*. Truth was, she looked flawless.

"Why? Are you actually worried she isn't going to like you? Have you met you?"

"Yes!" she whisper-yelled. "I have. And quite frankly, I'm a little bit of a bitch."

Laughter, uproarious and unchecked, burst from my chest at the lie.

Three sets of interested eyes—those of Georgia, Cassie, and Winnie—locked on to us immediately. "Whoops," I whispered, pushing Melody slightly in front of me with a hand at her back. "Looks like we're busted."

She moved the first few steps like her feet were encased in cement, so I used my hand and pressure to suggest she move a little faster.

"It'll be fine," I whispered right before we got to the table. "They're going to love you."

Melody's eyes bounced over her shoulder, and I knew it had to be the tone of my voice. It said the words I didn't: they're going to love you. *I know because I do.*

I surprised even myself when I didn't panic. I wasn't completely sure if I was actually in love with her, but I knew what I felt was a little more than affectionate. I also knew we'd been together barely any time at all, but we spent literally every day together. Working, talking, laughing— all of it made me that much *fonder* of her.

"Hey, brother!" Georgia greeted, jumping up from her seat to give me a kiss on the cheek. "I didn't know you were bringing a friend."

"Yeah." I looked to Melody and back to the group of women. "I hope that's okay."

Georgia waved my comment away. "It's fine! The more, the merrier."

"Great. But actually, Melody is—"

"We get it, Will," Georgia cut me off, waving her napkin back and forth before putting it back in her lap. "You're not dating. Winnie taught us the important lesson of what a woman 'too smart to date Will Cummings' looks like."

"Yeah," Cassie remarked with a laugh. "Hot. Stacked. Fire in her eyes. She's definitely too smart for you."

A tiny little river of hurt carved its way through my chest, the doubt it left in its wake making me wonder if they were on to something. Melody was good. She was positivity and a real conduit for change. And she was the most beautiful woman I'd ever laid eyes on. The sum of all those things easily outnumbered the total of what I deserved.

"Actually," Melody cut in, her hand snaking out and linking itself with mine, "I'm not too smart."

Fuck me. Doubt effectively dried up, I felt a little like puffing out my chest.

Winnie's eyes were the first to light up. "Yessss." She banged a hand so hard on the table it made everyone else jump. "I'm finally here for the fun stuff."

Melody's expression turned uncertain, so I leaped to explain with a pointed glare in Winnie's direction. "She's got a brilliant mind, but Winnie is just as deranged as my sister and Cassie. Ignore her words until they actually make sense."

Cassie took no offense. "Don't mind us. We just love to watch the drama."

"You love drama?" Melody asked, slightly horrified at the prospect of what I'd gotten her into.

Cassie was once again unfazed. "Go through it, no. Watch it, yes."

"There's no drama," I interceded. Fucking hell, this lunch was going to be long.

"Of course there's no drama…" Cassie muttered. "Yet."

"No. No drama. Ever."

"Pshh!" She laughed. "Okay, William. Good one."

"Cassie!" Georgia scolded. "Back off. You're scaring Melody." My eyes narrowed. I appreciated the backup, but normally Cassie and my sister played on the same damn team. I didn't trust this new development.

"I'm okay," Melody offered. "Really. A day in our office is a little bit like an episode of *Dallas*."

"You work together?" Winnie asked excitedly, and Melody's eyes jumped to mine.

No. I hadn't shared that little detail.

"Yes," I confirmed. "Melody is my nurse."

"Ohh," Cassie breathed, grabbing Melody by both hands and yanking her toward herself. "Are you his naughty nurse? Thatcher and I could really use some ideas for that role-play."

"Gross," Georgia muttered, grabbing her tea to take a sip.

Carefully, I reached down and untangled Cassie's hands from Melody, asking, "Can we sit down now, please? We're hungry and on a schedule. It took a little effort to sneak both of us out two times in less than a week."

I looked at Georgia pointedly. She'd all but insisted that we come to lunch today.

"Fine, fine," Cassie acquiesced. "Sit down. Eat pussy. Doesn't bother me."

"Oh, Cass, geez," I snapped, noticing Melody's eyes were now the size of saucers.

Georgia had employed her own tactic, covering her ears and chanting, "La La La, that's my brother, La La La!"

"Sorry, Melody," Winnie apologized. "Cassie has zero filter."

Melody's cheeks were pink, but all in all, she recovered nicely. "Oh, that's okay. I'd be in trouble if I were bashful with this guy around. The other day he had a woman come in for an exam with a laminated phone number in her vagina."

I sank my head into my hands. "Oh, here we go!"

"*What?*" Georgia yelled. "That is incredible! You have to tell us everything!"

"Dish, diva!" Cassie commanded.

And she did. For the next twenty-five minutes, I watched, enthralled, as Melody inserted herself into their little circle seamlessly. I didn't even really mind that ninety percent of her material came from embarrassing stories about me. I'd sacrifice myself as long as she felt comfortable.

"You should hear the way she—" I said, hoping to actually add something to the conversation.

"You know what I just realized," Cassie interrupted now that someone with a penis was trying to talk. "There's a chance we could have a little birthday baby!"

"What?" I asked. "Whose birthday is in late July?"

She rolled her eyes. "No one's. But Big Dick's is at the end of June."

"But then she'd be having the baby a month early," Winnie pointed out, and I nodded.

"And?" she said, waving her off with a swat.

Winnie looked to me and bugged out her eyes, prompting, "Will?"

Cassie's hard stare turned to me swiftly. Her look was nearly as sharp as I knew her tongue could be, so I dropped my sandwich onto my plate and cleared my throat as a means to gather my courage. "As a medical professional, I'd have to advise against it if at all possible."

"Ugh," she huffed. "What do you know!"

Melody's eyes came to me, and let me tell you, they were wide. "Um, you're only the head of obstetrics at St. Luke's Hospital," she leaned close and whispered.

I smiled, turning to kiss her on the cheek before whispering back into her ear, "Trust me, that doesn't matter at all."

"Anyway, how great would it be to have Big Dick Junior share a birthday with his dad?" Cassie went on.

"Would you stop?" Georgia shouted. "My baby is a girl! She doesn't have a dick, big or small, for shit's sake."

"Meh." Cassie shrugged. "I'm not convinced."

"It's a girl!"

"I'll wait until Big Dick's birthday to find out."

"My baby isn't coming that early!" Georgia continued to shout.

"Relax, George," I advised. "Calm is better for the baby."

She took a deep breath, smoothing the air down with her hands like it would actually help her calm herself.

And then a gleam entered her eye.

"Oh my God, I know!" Gigi squeaked excitedly, bouncing up and down like a teenager. My eyes shot to her stomach. *Okay, a pregnant teenager.* "You guys should come over to my house tomorrow to watch the new episode of *Dr. Obscene.*"

That little fucking schemer. I bet that's why she'd wanted me to come to lunch in the first place—so she could force me into another horrific family gathering for one of my episodes. She knew seeing her all pitiful and pregnant made it harder to say no.

"Ugh," I groaned. "Don't call it that."

"Why, William?" Cassie cooed seductively. "You can't fool us."

Melody's eyes shot back and forth between Cassie and me in question, and I shook my head no. *No.* Sure, I'd joked about a fictitious affair between her and me in the past as a means to get under Georgia's skin, but there was a little too much crazy in her recipe for me. Too much spice and I broke out in a sweat.

"But seriously," George implored, grabbing on to Melody's hand and squeezing. "You guys *have* to come! Please, please, please! You can't say no to a pregnant woman."

"You really can't," Winnie advised with a shake of her head. "I tried, like, three times when she invited me to this lunch. And yet, here I sit. Eating."

I groaned. "Mel?"

She shook her head, but what I took away overall was her smile. "I guess we'll see you guys tomorrow."

CHAPTER *twenty*

Melody

AFTER A TWENTY-MINUTE DRIVE THROUGH SOME SERIOUSLY RICH PEOPLE SUBURBIA, Will pulled the car up in front of his sister's New Jersey home. As soon as the engine's growl quieted to the tick of a hot car cooling, I unbuckled my seat belt and started to open the door, but I didn't get far before Will reacted.

"Wait," he urged and wrapped his fingers around my elbow. "Are you sure you're ready for this?"

I dropped my hand away from the door handle and looked at him inquisitively. "Ready for what, exactly?" I asked, curious as to what he could think I wasn't prepared for at this point. The vagina-shake, the nipple display, Marlene, Melissa, the vajazzling, Cassie at lunch yesterday… I wasn't sure how much worse it could get.

He sighed the beleaguered sigh of someone who knew better than I did that there was always something worse around the corner.

"My parents are going to be here tonight."

I knew that. Georgia had called him earlier to let him know. In his words, *another layer to her fucking onion of a scheme.*

"Yeah…I'm meeting your parents tonight…" I paused for a moment and searched his eyes for an explanation. "It all sounds pretty straightforward to me."

He shook his head slightly. "Nothing is straightforward with Dick and Savannah."

The stressed-out expression on his face pushed a slight giggle from my lips.

"Don't laugh," he said, but the faint smirk on his lips betrayed his words.

"I'm not laughing."

"You are *so* laughing."

"Okay, fine," I admitted. "I'm laughing a little, but the look on your face wasn't helping anything."

"What look?"

"This look," I answered and mimicked the anxious creases of his eyes and firm set of his lips. "Like, you're either constipated or two seconds away from putting the car in Drive and slamming on the gas."

His face eased into amusement, and a small chuckle left his lips. "It's the latter."

"I'm just meeting your parents, Will. How bad can it be?"

"Bad? More like dangerous."

A surprised laugh escaped my lungs. "They're not serial killers."

"No, but what they don't hit in death count, they make up for in meddling about my sex life and inappropriate comments about *their* sex life."

"Your mom's a sex therapist. I won't be shocked by her being a little more open-minded than most."

"I wish it were just open-minded," he muttered.

"C'mon, William," I encouraged and opened my door. "Let's go meet your parents. Lord knows, it can't be worse than meeting mine. I mean, my dad asked you if you had condoms, and that was right before our first date."

He just smirked in response, and I didn't give him any more time to dally in the car. I hopped out of the passenger side and grabbed my purse off the floor. Will followed my lead, getting out of the driver's seat and rounding the car to meet me.

With his hand placed to the small of my back, we walked toward the front door of his sister's home. "Remember," he started once we reached the porch. "I warned you."

"Oh, shut up," I teased and grinned up at him. "Everything will be just fine."

He rang the doorbell, and within seconds, the door swung open and a giant of a man appeared with a toddler on his hip. "William!" he greeted. "It's so nice of you to stop by."

"You realize this isn't your house, right?"

"Yeah, well, Savannah put me in charge of greeting guests. She said I've got the sexiest smile she's ever seen," the giant responded with a smirk and wink. "And who might this be?" he asked and held out his non-toddler corralling hand toward me.

"Thatch, this is Melody," Will introduced us. "Melody, this is Thatch, my brother-in-law's best friend. And the little guy in his arms is his son, Ace."

"It's nice to meet you." I shook Thatch's hand. "And it's really nice to meet you, you little cutie," I said to Ace and tickled his belly.

He giggled in response and then held both of his tiny hands out in my direction. "Hole me, pease."

Both Will and Thatch chuckled.

"You come on too strong, little man," Thatch whispered to Ace. "You have to ease into it with the ladies. Dinner first before cuddling."

"Un-ca Will!" a tiny voice exclaimed as she ran toward us. Her pigtails bounced in the air as she made a beeline straight into Will's arms.

"How's my favorite girl?" Will asked and settled the little girl—who I knew from pictures was his niece, Julia—onto his hip.

She kissed his cheek, and Will grinned.

"Who dis?" she asked once her eyes met mine.

"Julia, this is my girlfriend, Melody," he answered and smiled in my direction. "Melody, this is my niece, Julia."

"Hi, Julia," I greeted and gently tugged on the silk material of her pale pink dress. "Your dress is so pretty."

"Tanks," she said with a grin and then looked toward Ace, who was still in Thatch's arms. "Ace-eee!" she exclaimed and squirmed out of Will's arms. He set her to her feet, and Thatch followed suit, setting Ace onto his tiny Nike's.

Ace smiled at Julia, and she smiled back at him. They exchanged a little toddler babble of their own before giggling like hyenas and running down the hallway together.

"I get you, Lia!" Ace shouted toward her, and Julia continued running, giggling the entire way.

"Look but don't touch, son," Thatcher advised, and I couldn't stop a shocked laugh from leaving my lips.

"You'll get used to that," Will whispered into my ear. "Thatch is the opposite of conventional in every facet of his life."

"His wife is Cassie, right?" I asked quietly, and Will nodded.

"Now it's all making sense." Because it was. Cassie wasn't your average woman. She was outspoken and confident, and it only took a few seconds upon meeting her to deduce that she was a bit wild. Maybe a little crazy, too.

Plus, I was ninety-nine percent sure she hadn't been wearing a bra. Only a certain kind of woman has the confidence to free-boob on purpose.

Thatch turned back toward us with his large arms crossed over his chest.

But he didn't say anything, merely just stood there, grinning down at us without a care in the world, and things started to get awkward.

"Do you mind if we come in?" Will asked with a sarcastic smirk. "You know, inside the house, my sister's house?"

Eventually, Thatch gestured us in the door while bellowing, "Dick! Savannah! Georgia! Will's here!"

The second we stepped through the door, I spotted a horse of a dog snoozing on a dog bed with a fat, fluffy cat curled up to his side. Honestly, it was one of the cutest fucking things I'd ever seen.

"I'm guessing they're best friends?" I asked Will with a nod toward the dog bed.

He snorted in laughter. "Uh…a little more than that."

"Stan and Walter are lovers, actually," Thatch informed me. "Oh, and watch out for Walter. He's an asshole."

"Walter is the dog, I'm guessing?"

"Nope. He's that evil fucking demon cat. If I were you, I'd just avoid eye contact, and stay away from his boyfriend, Stan."

I looked at Will in confusion, and he smiled.

"Trust me, it's a long story."

"Pretty sure I need to hear that story." Because I did. I mean, a Great Dane and demon cat that were in love? Where was a television show producer when you needed one? That was reality TV gold.

"Later," Will whispered and guided me down the hall with a hand pressed to the small of my back. Before we reached the spacious living room, a jolly specimen of a man rounded the corner with a petite and gorgeous woman pressed to his side. Both were smiling widely, and by looks alone, I knew instantly they were Will's parents.

"Willy, my boy! Have you grown?"

My eyebrows pulled together as Will's cheeks tinged with pink. I didn't think I'd ever seen him blush before. *What's got him embarrassed?*

"Hey, Dad," Will greeted, but under his breath, he muttered, "Lord help me."

"Oh, William, you look so handsome this evening." His mother kissed him on both cheeks. "And I'm assuming this is Melody?"

"You assume correctly," he said and wrapped his arm tightly around my shoulder. "Melody, these are my parents, Dick and Savannah Cummings."

"She's stunning, William," his mother complimented. "Long legs, fantastic rack, and a gorgeous face. Isn't she gorgeous, Dick?"

"So pretty that I'm wondering why she's dating our son."

I fought the urge to giggle and looked up at Will. He appeared slightly exasperated, but mostly, just smiled down at me proudly.

"Well, come in, come in." Savannah gestured us toward the living room where everyone—including Georgia and Cassie—seemed to be sitting cozily in front of the big-screen television.

"Georgie," Dick chimed in, "Get off your lazy pregnant ass and greet your brother's girlfriend."

Georgia flipped him the bird, and Cassie laughed. "Damn, Wheorgie's in a mood tonight."

"Dick," Savannah chastised. "You know she's probably tired from all of the pregnancy sex that she and Kline have been having. Her sexual aura is practically encompassing us all." She looked around at all of the characters who'd assembled there and smirked. "It's making us all horny."

"Jesus, Mom," Will breathed out on a sigh.

"Oh, don't be such a prude, William. You know I taught you better than that."

A ridiculously handsome guy hopped out of his seat and held out his hand toward me. "I'm Kline, Georgia's husband, and Will's brother-in-law."

"Hi, I'm Melody."

"Oh, believe me," Kline said with amusement. "I'm more than aware of who you are after your lunch date with Will and the gossip queens."

"I take offense to that!" Georgia exclaimed, but Kline just grinned in response.

"We're not gossip queens," she added and looked toward Cassie. "Back me up, Casshead."

Cassie smirked and shook her head. "We're totally gossip queens. And you're the worst of the bunch."

"I am not!"

"You definitely are," Thatch added as he sat down beside his wife and wrapped his arm around her shoulder, pulling her close to his side. "And the fact that you can't lie or keep a secret if your life depended on it makes it even worse."

"I can lie," Georgia refuted and looked around the room, but when no one spoke up in agreement, she looked toward her mom. "Mom?"

"Sorry, honey, but you're the world's worst liar," Savannah disagreed, and Dick chuckled.

"Yeah, Georgie," he chimed in. "You were even a shit liar when you were a kid."

"I was not!" she argued. "I hid loads of things from you guys."

"Honey, we knew about your hump pillow about a week after you started masturbating."

"Mom!" Georgia's cheeks flushed pink.

Dick appeared more than amused. "It's true, Georgie," he continued the conversation. "Your mother had to sneak into your room every month just to make sure that thing got washed."

Will laughed at his sister's embarrassment, and she flipped him off. "Shut up, Will. Everyone in the house knew those hour-long showers weren't for hygiene purposes."

"Wow. Thanks, Gigi."

She flashed a curt smile in his direction. "You're welcome."

"Wait a minute…" Cassie said and looked at Thatch. "Did I just hear that my little Wheorgie had a sex pillow?"

Thatch grinned. "I know, right? Tonight is fantastic."

"Everyone shut up about the pillow!"

"We still have it in the attic at home if anyone wants to see it," Savannah added kindly, and Georgia sighed in frustration.

"Oh. My. God."

Kline grinned and wrapped a comforting arm around his wife's shoulder. As he pulled her close to his side and let her hide her face against his chest, he mouthed toward Savannah, "I want that pillow."

Savannah winked and mouthed back, "Stop by tomorrow."

"Oh!" Cassie exclaimed and turned up the volume on the television. "It's about to start."

Will sighed and muttered, "Yay" in the most unenthusiastic voice possible.

As the opening credits for *The Doctor Is In* started to appear on the screen, I dragged Will toward an empty love seat and forced him to sit on the couch beside me.

"I think we should go," he whispered in my ear moments later. "Yeah…I think we should leave and spend hours upon hours naked in my bed."

I grinned and shook my head. "You're not getting out of this by trying to ply me with sex."

"God, I love this fucking show," Thatch said with a giant smile stretched across his lips.

"I wonder if Dr. Obscene is going to get naked again in this episode?" Cassie questioned as she popped a few pieces of popcorn in her mouth.

"I'm right here," Will said, but she ignored him.

"Or maybe they'll get another shot of him where he looks like he's jerking it?"

"One can only hope," Thatch responded around a mouthful of pretzels. "One can only fucking hope that Dr. Obscene will get wild and nasty tonight."

"You know, I'm still right here, guys."

"Yep," Thatch and Cassie responded in unison.

The show started with a shot of Will walking down the hospital hallway toward the nurses' station and a blond nurse—wearing a pair of scrubs so tight that she must have glued them onto her body—stopped him before he could reach his destination.

"Dr. Cummings?" she asked with a flutter of her lashes and a seductive grin. "Do you have a minute?"

"For you, Mandy," he said with a flirtatious smile, "I always have a minute."

"Ohhhhhhh! Dr. Obscene is going to bone Mandy!" Dick called out, and I immediately felt like puking. It wasn't even just a little bit of nausea. No. I literally felt like hurling all over Kline and Georgia's living room.

"Aww...you're so sweet, Dr. Cummings," Mandy said with a playful tap to Will's bicep. "Oh my, have you been working out?"

"She loves Dr. Obscene's guns!" Thatch cheered toward the TV.

Jesus Christ. Was this about to turn into a goddamn porno?

I had never felt more uncomfortable than I did in that moment, sitting with Will's family, watching him flirt on screen with a slutty nurse named Mandy.

Which was dumb…right? It was just a stupid reality show that was filmed months ago. I mean, I hadn't met Will until after the first episode had aired. I had no claim to him when this was filmed. He was just a single guy at the time…

But God, it hurt like a motherfucker to watch it.

What in the hell was happening to me?

You're jealous.

Was I jealous? Okay… Yeah… I was woman enough to admit that I was. I was fucking jealous. *Will is mine.* He wasn't a piece of meat for slores like Mandy to sink their slorry claws into.

Will is mine? Holy hell, had I really just thought that? Like some territorial chick who was about to piss a circle around her boyfriend?

I'd never been the jealous type in the past. Hell, I wasn't sure I'd ever felt this kind of jealousy before, not even with Eli. But holy mother of macaroons, had the green-eyed goddess made herself known.

I searched and searched the recesses of my mind for the answer to one question—why in the hell was I so jealous?

But I was completely caught off guard by how easily I figured out the answer.

Because you love him.

CHAPTER *twenty-one*

MEL STOOD IN THE CORNER, MAKING NOTES ON THE CHART, AND I HAD TO TEAR my eyes away from her to focus on my job. She was always distracting, her creamy skin and bold features enough to pull me in on any given day, but today was something else.

I couldn't put my finger on it.

Last night at my sister's house had gone surprisingly well under the circumstances—those circumstances being Thatch, Cassie, and my parents all in one room.

But on the drive home, Melody had been pensive—never something you want your new girlfriend to be without you. She'd actually wanted to go back to Bill and Janet's to sleep on her air mattress instead of sleeping at my place.

Red flag.

Sure, she didn't sleep over every night, but usually, when I put on a pretense of begging, she pretended to be put out and then accepted. Not last night.

Last night had been, *"I think I'll just go home. I'm tired, I need clothes, and I'd like to actually be on time for once."*

I'd argued that I could guarantee her timely arrival if she stayed with me, but she declined.

She hated that air mattress and her mom's version of *Workout Barbie*, as she put it, yet her excuses seemed potentially valid.

Thanks to the insecurity monster, I'd also asked her if everything was okay so many times I was bordering on doctoring her, and every single time, she'd smiled her smile and promised she was just tired.

I was running out of ideas to get her to be honest with me. I didn't have the practical relationship hours to know what I was doing—all I knew was that the relationship plane had controls I didn't know how to use without flight school.

I'd finally settled on the possibility that what she said was actually what she felt. It wasn't what we're trained to believe about women in Man School, but it was also the only theory I had left to come up with.

Yeah, there's no Man School per se, but when you grew up with a father like Dick Cummings, your adolescent youth included long talks about what makes women happy.

Ironically, it's only now that I'm wishing those discussions would have hit more topics than just "how to find the G-spot."

Unfortunately for me, Melody still seemed off today, and I had to let it go. My patients needed concentration.

"We'll start with the breast exam, so just lie back and relax for me," I told our current patient with a genuine smile.

She complied immediately, pulling the top of her gown off completely and massaging her own breasts jovially. Out of the corner of my eye, I noticed Melody's eyes widen.

"I haven't felt anything, but there's just so much tissue," Samantha Wilson teased. "You're better at covering all of it."

I smiled and shook my head at her seemingly forward advances. But it wasn't like that—not really anyway.

Samantha wasn't a new patient, as the majority had been lately, and I knew her and her case on a deeper level. She'd already been through the wringer, breast cancer at the age of thirty-six four years ago, and she'd followed that up by having reconstructive surgery to, in her words, *get the boobs she'd always wanted anyway.*

We joked regularly after she'd taken the lead that first appointment, opening up about how alive it made her to freely engage in humor and harmless flirting whether it was entirely appropriate or not. She'd never made any actual advances, and I'd never stepped out of line. Hell, I even knew her husband Justin pretty well. We saw each other on the golf course a few times a year.

But the most important part about our patient-doctor interactions was that we both left each appointment feeling good. And that's all I wanted out of my job.

"Well, I *am* the doctor."

She laughed.

"Let me see how you're doing."

She moved her hands from her breasts, sliding them under gracefully like one of the models on *The Price is Right.* "Have at it, Doc."

I smiled at her as I started the exam, but the nature of my touch wasn't playful. It wasn't the same as when I used breasts for pleasure, and it wasn't hot in any way. It was the same old exam I'd done thousands upon thousands of times.

Concentrating on searching all of the tissue, conscious of a relapse in a case like Samantha's, I glanced up to find Melody's pinched, almost pained face watching my hands intently.

I stopped automatically, calling Samantha's attention. "Everything okay?" she asked, anxious.

My face, I knew without seeing it, was one of genuine concern, but it wasn't because of the patient. It was because of my girlfriend. Still, I forced my concentration back to the patient where it was supposed to be.

"Yes," I comforted. "I'm sorry, Samantha. Everything feels great. Absolutely nothing to be worried about, okay?"

Her relief was pungent.

I worked not to look at Melody for the rest of the exam and made my best effort to be courteous but professional with Samantha. She didn't seem to mind at all, and it was actually nice to get through an entire appointment with a patient without feeling like a huge fuck-up.

"I'm going to write out a script for your ultrasound and mammogram, and I know I don't have to tell you how important it is that you go to your appointment. You're free, you're beautiful, and you're a survivor. Let's keep it that way, okay?"

She bobbed her head in affirmation and pulled me into a hug. "I know. Thank you for always caring so much, Dr. Cummings."

After a quick squeeze, I let her go. "Of course. See you next time, Sammy. And tell Justin to give me a call if he wants to play again in the St. Luke's Charity Golf Tournament next spring."

"I'm sure he'll be game for that," she said with a smile.

Finally done with my medical responsibilities, I headed for the door and let myself look at Melody directly. The crease between her eyebrows had eased, but she still wasn't looking at me directly.

"Mel?" I called, and her head came up unnaturally fast.

"Yes?"

"Meet me in my office when you're done, okay?"

She nodded and moved over to Samantha to complete her exit responsibilities. "Take your time getting dressed and then just come out and meet me in the hall. I'll have your paperwork and walk you up to the front to make your next appointment."

I stepped through the door as Samantha offered her thanks, and I headed straight for my office.

Grabbing the necessary papers, I quickly wrote up all of Samantha's procedure orders and waited for Melody to come for them. I had something else I wanted to do, but I also didn't want to get caught in the act.

A short minute later, Melody stepped just inside of my door and asked succinctly, "Paperwork?"

Normally a gentleman, I would have gotten up to hand it to her, but today, I kept my ass planted in the chair and held it out—to force her into my office.

She stepped forward and grabbed the papers, but I didn't let go when she pulled them.

Her face took on an immediate air of annoyance, but she smoothed the rough edges of her irritation when I smirked.

"Come back after you take this up to her, okay?"

She gave a jerky nod, and I finally let go.

As soon as she cleared the door, I pulled out a tongue depressor and got to work.

Is that your uvula, or are you just happy to see me?

I know. These are so bad. But they usually make her smile.

Standing up, I waved it around to help the ink dry and then tucked it into my pocket. After two minutes, I started to get antsy, so I walked around the big desk and settled my ass into the front.

When another two minutes passed, I pushed up to standing straight again.

When the final two minutes passed—and still no sign of Melody—I walked right out of my door and up the hall toward the front, checking every open exam room as I went, but all of them were empty.

A commotion at the front was apparent the closer I got, so I hurried my pace a little.

"What's going on?" I asked when I got to reception to find Marlene and Melody in the middle of a showdown.

"It was Marlene's day to get lunch," Betty explained with a shake of her head.

I glanced over my shoulder to find a waiting room full of patients staring at my staff like they were an actual reality show playing out for their viewing entertainment.

Shit. I stepped forward to intervene.

"Ladies." Two angry faces turned toward me with a near growl.

I recoiled slightly but recovered enough to hold my ground.

"What's going on?" Both of them started to speak at once. I rolled my eyes, speaking over them, "Melody first."

"I ordered an Italian sub and a Coke from Marlene, and she screwed it up."

"I didn't screw it up!" Marlene objected loudly.

"She totally screwed up Load-y's order," Melissa happily chirped from behind the reception desk, and I shot a pointed look in her direction.

"Melo…Mar… *Melissa*, this is none of your concern."

Good Lord, did every woman in my office's name start with an M?

Just get to the crux of the matter, Will, before patients start to get out their phones and posting videos on YouTube. The No Cell Phones *sign is only going to hold up for so long.*

"Everyone just relax for a minute," I said on a sigh and looked at my beautiful and very frustrated girlfriend. "Okay… What exactly happened?"

She sighed but jumped into her story quickly. "Marlene was taking lunch orders. I ordered an Italian sub and a Coke and gave her ten bucks. And when she got back, I went to collect my order. Our interaction went something like: *'Hey, Marlene. Is this a good time to get my lunch?'*

Yada yada… she grumbled and said, 'What'd you order?'

'An Italian sub and a Coke.'

She rifled through her bag again and came up empty. 'I don't have that.'''

"I didn't have that!" Marlene exclaimed in the middle of the story, but Melody just shot her a glare and continued on.

"And then I responded, '*Um, but...I ordered it.*'

She looked through the bag again and offered, 'I've got a piece of toast and a pickle. You want it?'

'*A piece of toast and a pickle? I gave you ten dollars for a sub and a Coke.*'

She shrugged and just shoved the pickle and toast into my hands. 'Here.'

'*But I gave you ten dollars.*'

'*Yeah, well, them's the breaks.*'

And scene."

Melody's breathing was heavy as I looked down into her hands. *Toast and a pickle.*

Good Christ, Will. Do not laugh. Do. Not. Laugh.

"Are you gonna let me speak?" Marlene snapped. I just pinched my lips together and shook my head...taking a deep breath to gather myself.

Finally, when I had control over the urge to explode into laughter, I spoke. "No, I'm not," I told Marlene.

Reaching forward and easing the now smashed piece of toast and dripping pickle from Melody's hands, I deposited them in the trash can and waited for her eyes to meet mine.

"Come on. I'll take you to get a new lunch. On me."

Quite frankly, this situation played right into my hands. I'd taken other staff to get lunch before after Marlene fucked it up, so the whole thing would seem rather innocuous. But it would also give me the opportunity to clear the air with my girlfriend once and for all.

"Get your stuff," I instructed gently as everyone looked on. Marlene cursed under her breath, and I shot a warning glare in her direction. "Everyone else get back to work, or take your lunch to the break room."

Melody complied, walking woodenly down the hall and coming back with her purse tucked over her shoulder.

Luckily, I already had my wallet in my pocket, so we moved right for the door.

Silence descended as we walked to the corner deli and ordered her another Italian sub and a second one for me and sat down at a table in the back—practically in the kitchen, actually. This was the absolute last time I needed prying eyes following my conversation and recording it to post on Instagram. Luckily, the owners knew me well, and as a favor, had started to keep this table empty for me, just in case.

"So…" I ventured, when she started to eat in silence.

Her eyes met mine over the bulk of her sandwich.

"What's going on?" I asked.

She chewed quickly and set her sandwich down. "You saw what Marlene did! God, that woman is infuriating sometimes."

"I did. But I'm asking what's going on with you and me. You're acting weird, Mel. Did I do something?" I asked earnestly. Because I honestly had no fucking clue.

She sighed once and then again before opening up to me. "No. I guess sort of, but not really. You're just you."

"Well, that narrows it down," I teased, and for the first time today, she gave me a half smile.

"The show last night. You were so flirty. Flirtier than normal. And with a nurse." She shrugged. "I guess I'm feeling a little jealous."

I laughed and she scowled.

"I'm sorry," I apologized. "It's just…you have nothing to worry about. You're the only woman I'm interested in. I swear."

She nodded, but she still didn't look sure.

God, I hated that uncertainty in her eyes. I didn't want anyone else but Mel. She'd burrowed herself under my skin so deeply that I literally didn't see anyone but *her*.

"Mel," I started, just about ready to tell her *I love you* when she interrupted.

"I know. Really, it's fine. It's just been an off couple of days, you know. All the patients flirting with you all the time, watching you on the show. It just seems like someone turned a dial on these fucking women ever since you jerked off on camera. I'm fine, really."

"I didn't jerk off on camera, and you know it!" I defended on a near shout. I'd been loosening the laces on my sneaker, for fuck's sake. But it was amazing what a camera angle could do.

She pursed her lips.

Noting that the moment felt a little too sour for first-time declarations, I reached into my pocket and slid the only other thing I had to offer over the table with a sigh.

"Another tongue depressor?" she asked, a small smile curling one corner of her mouth.

"Obviously," I teased in my best Valley girl voice.

"Where do you keep them? Like, honestly, this is starting to get creepy."

"Just read it," I advised.

I watched as she looked down and studied my scrawl for far longer than it took to read that many words, but when her gaze finally met mine again, I had my Mel back.

"I'm pretty sure I'm always happy to see you."

That makes two of us.

CHAPTER *twenty-two*

Melody

"**G**OOD EVENING," WILL GREETED ME AT THE DOOR OF HIS APARTMENT AFTER three short knocks.

The expediency with which he answered made it seem a little like he'd been waiting just on the other side.

Butterflies took off in my stomach at the thought of him being that anxious to see me.

Of course, he looked as handsome as ever, dressed in black slacks and a pale blue button-down, collared shirt that made his eyes appear even bluer. And Lord almighty, it looked good on him—snug in all the right places with both sleeves rolled up and showcasing his strong forearms.

"Uh…" I paused and glanced down at my slightly casual black summer dress that I'd paired with open-toe wedges. "I think I'm a little underdressed…"

He shook his head, his eyes lighting with a gleam to reinforce his words. "You're perfect."

Will leaned in to press a soft kiss to my cheek and then led me through the door and into the loft-style apartment that was starting to feel like a second home.

It really was a spectacular place—floor-to-ceiling windows highlighting the open and airy space, paired with just the right amount of sleek yet comfortable furniture and décor to make it feel cozy.

I loved his apartment, and it definitely fit him like a glove. And if I was being honest, it made me a little jealous on those now rare occasions when I wasn't at his place that I was still living inside Bill and Janet's humble abode. With my mother's meddling and insane work-out routine and my father's obnoxious music habits, their apartment was starting to feel smaller than a sardine tin—in reality, in New York, it was palatial.

"Let me be the first to welcome you to our first official date," he said with a gallant sweep of his arm and a smirk once we'd entered the living room.

"This isn't our first date," I disagreed with a quirk of my brow. Ever since I'd admitted how jealous I was, Will had become persistent with this whole first official date thing.

Considering we'd been nearly attached at the hip since the night of our *real* first date, it was a bit insane. I mean, it was an infrequent occurrence when I *didn't* stay the night at his place. Hell, I'd even started keeping extra clothes and underwear in his closet.

But he'd been preparing for this night since Wednesday, after Marlene had tried to convince me toast and a pickle was an actual lunch option. And since Will wasn't on call this weekend, once the work clock struck five p.m., he instructed me to head to my parents' apartment, get ready, and be at his apartment at seven on the dot.

"Okay… It's our first official date *as a couple.*"

I wasn't sure that was true either. But our real first date had been wildly above the national average, so if he wanted to use that as his basis for all future encounters, I wasn't going to complain.

"Whatever you say, Doc." I shrugged, and Will smirked his satisfaction.

I followed his lead into the kitchen and set my purse down on the counter while he busied himself at the stove. "So, what's on the agenda for tonight?"

Will glanced over his shoulder while he stirred a white cream sauce inside a pot on the burner. "I'm wining and dining my favorite lady."

I silently hoped said wining and dining included foreplay and Will's penis.

His eyes searched mine studiously, and when all of my cues finally clicked together into a complete puzzle, a sexy smile eased its way across his full lips. "Oh, don't worry, there'll be time for that, too."

Good lord, he was getting good at reading me.

"Lots and lots of time," he added, and I felt my cheeks heat up from the intensity of his gaze.

"Stop looking at me like that. You're making me blush," I said and put my hands to my face to hide my pink cheeks.

"Eh," he muttered. "Not likely. I love your blush. It doesn't happen often anymore, but when it does, it drives me fucking crazy. If just this look does it for you, you can expect me to be giving it to you for the next one hundred years," he said with a soft smile before turning his focus back toward the stove.

And while he stood there with his back to me, relaxed and calm and finishing up dinner, I froze in my tracks. His words might as well have been jumper cables, sparking a fast and steady pounding inside of my chest. *The next one hundred years?*

Whoa.

Whoa.

Whoa.

That was the first time Will had ever referred to us in a future tense like that, and I wasn't sure which was more potent—the way those words made me feel or how badly I wanted them to be true.

Jesus Christ, what was happening to me? We hadn't even exchanged I love yous, and my heart seemed intent on keeping Will for the long haul. *Not just the long haul. You want to keep him forever...*

"I hope you're in the mood for Italian." The crisp cadence of his voice snapped me out of my shocked trance, and while he moved toward the sink to drain pasta from the big pot in his hands, I ran two, now sweaty, palms down my dress in an attempt to pull my shit together.

I know, I know. Sweaty palms. Supergross, right?

I can't help it, though. I always get sweaty when I'm stressed or anxious or like right now, internally freaking the fuck out.

Holy mahogany-bound books and cigars, I needed to take a deep breath and try not to ruin the night by acting like a weirdo. I was afraid I'd do something extreme like sprint out of his apartment or get on my knees and propose marriage.

Yeah, don't *do that. Calm down. Act natural. Say something normal. Anything normal…*

"Uh… Is that garlic bread I smell?" I asked, and Will winked in my direction as he moved back toward the stove.

"Uh-huh."

Yeah. That's good. Talk about the food. You love food.

"And Alfredo sauce and uh…cheese?"

"Yep."

I moved closer to the stove and peered over his shoulder as he finished up heating the sauce. "Either you're trying to kill me with carbs or win my heart."

Too late for that. He's already won your heart.

Internally, I sighed and wished my brain would just shut up for two fucking minutes.

Will turned around and pulled me into his arms. "It's the latter," he said and pressed a smacking kiss to my lips. "Which is why I also picked up a cherry cheesecake from that bakery by the office you love so much."

"I don't love it *that* much…"

I totally did. It was a sweet-treat lover's heaven, and I'd contemplated putting my application in to work part time just so I could spend a few hours a week smelling and staring at the pastries.

He grinned and lifted me onto the counter near the stove. He fit his large frame between my spread legs before I had a chance to protest. I watched as he slid two long fingers up my thighs and rested his hands at the hem of my dress.

"You're a little liar," he whispered into my ear. "I've watched you bring in donuts and cookies and cupcakes from that little bakery no less than three times a week."

"I do that because I'm being nice…for the staff…" I lied and he laughed softly.

"Uh-huh," he said with his lips pressed against my neck. "I guess that explains why you always take your favorites out before you share with anyone else."

"Jesus, you're nosy," I muttered. "Who are you? The pastry police?"

"I also know that you've been sneaking patient numbers into your phone so that you can call them outside of office hours."

My face fell in panic. How did he know that?

"How…I didn't…" I stuttered as I tried to figure out what to say.

"Relax," he soothed, pulling back to look me in the eye, tucking a loose piece of hair behind my ear, and smoothing the deepening wrinkle between my eyes with a gentle swipe of his thumb. "Syreeta Johnson. Bethany Hyland. Rolanda Diaz. I know what you're doing for all of them," he whispered. My eyes moistened, and my nose stung as his features softened to near reverent.

"How do you know this?" I whispered back, rolling my lips in on themselves at the end. After Carmen, any time I ran into a new patient in dire need of support, I gave them my cell number—just in case they needed someone. But even that didn't feel like enough. I'd become so troubled by the numerous women, even under our care, who didn't have family or anyone to lean on, I'd taken to stealing their numbers out of their charts and calling them occasionally, just to check in. I'd been doing it for weeks now.

But I didn't think anyone else knew.

When he touched his lips to my cheek, I felt his smile against my skin. "I'm merely an expert in all things Melody Marco."

My heart pounding so fast I didn't know what to do, I did my best to calm it down with a little levity.

"If I didn't like you so much, I'd probably think that line was a little creepy."

Will chuckled and moved back to the stove, letting the moment pass exactly like I needed him too. It was starting to scare me how well he knew me.

"How much do you like me exactly?" he asked with a waggle of his brow.

More like love...

Ugh. Not that train of thought again...

I wasn't sure which freaked me out the most: that I was already thinking that four-letter word and the idea of settling down when it came to Will, or how perfect those things really felt.

Will and I hadn't been dating for that long, and I'd just gotten out of a very long relationship. The mere idea of being in love with Will was a bit too sudden...*right?*

"*The heart wants what the heart wants, Mel.*" My mother's words of advice rang loud and clear in my head. She'd told me those words time and again—when I waffled about moving across the country to follow Eli...when I decided to come back across to get away. And I agreed with her on the basic sentiment. I was just having a hard time wrapping my mind around the fact that my heart was so damn willing to fall in love again so quickly.

"Are you okay?" Will asked and tilted his head to the side as he scrutinized my facial expression.

I could only assume said facial expression had changed from relaxed and smiling to deer in highlights. *Jesus. Get it together, Mel…*

"Of course I'm okay." I schooled my face into a neutral expression and nodded. "Now…if I do recall, you were asking me how far my like for you goes, *aka, you're fishing for compliments…*"

Will grinned. "Too scared to answer the question, Mel? I understand. I'd be overwhelmed by me too."

"No," I retorted, rolling my eyes. "I think you should answer the question first."

"How much do I like myself?" he asked and winked in my direction. "Well…I consider myself a nice guy. I'm pretty good at my job. Insanely hilarious and charming. I don't think I'm too bad to look at. I don't have a small dick… So, yeah, I'd say I really like myself."

I giggled. "*I don't have a small dick?*" I repeated his words, and he nodded.

"Well, I don't," he answered. "I'm about average."

Average? Pfffffft. It wasn't average. Honestly, it was *above* average. Will's penis was a one of a kind. Smooth, thick, *long,* and curved in all of the right places. He had a good penis. A great one. *The best one.* Michelangelo's David wished he had Will's penis.

I snorted in laughter. "You're so full of it."

"What did I say that was so wrong?"

"Your penis isn't average. It's more than average, Will."

"Uh…yeah, it is," he retorted. "It's a nice, average penis. I think it gets the job done."

"It definitely more than gets the job done," I agreed with a waggle of my brows. "But it's not just *average*. How many inches, William?"

"How the fuck would I know?"

"Haven't you measured it before?"

"Um…no. I don't spend my free time sitting in my living room holding a measuring tape up to my cock."

"The average penis size is like five to six inches," I stated and glanced down at the crotch of his pants. "You're *way* bigger than five to six."

He shrugged. "Okay…I'm slightly above average."

I hopped off the counter and started rummaging through his drawers.

"What are you doing?"

"Looking for a ruler."

I only managed to get through one of his junk drawers before Will wrapped his arms around me tightly and pulled me away from the counter. "You're not measuring my cock, Mel."

"Yes. I. Am."

"No, baby," he said with a chuckle. "You're not."

"Aren't you a little curious?" I asked and turned into his arms. "Like, just a *little* bit curious? Seven or eight *inches* of curious?" I pushed.

He shook his head and kissed the tip of my nose. "I give zero fucks."

"Ugh."

Will just laughed and pinched my ass. "Guess what?"

"You're going to let me measure your penis?" I asked hopefully.

He shook his head. "Dinner's ready."

"Ugh."

He pressed his lips to my ear. "Maybe…just maybe…after dinner…I'll let your *tight little cunt* measure my dick."

"Ugh…Fine," I said on a sigh, but on the inside, I shivered. *Man, he gives good dirty talk.* He chuckled.

"Now that's the spirit!" A sharp spank to my ass punctuated his excitement.

I probably would've forced the issue more had it not been for the garlic bread…and the fettuccini alfredo…and the cheesecake…and *the sex…*

A girl could only hold out for so long when carbs and sugar and hot sex were involved.

And her heart can't hold out at all when Will Cummings is involved.

CHAPTER *twenty-three*

GOD, SHE'S STUNNING.

I pulled her lips to mine and ran across the seam of them with my tongue. She moaned, a hot puff of air moving from her mouth to mine as she did, and immediately, my dick jumped at the thought of that kind of warmth around it.

Apparently, we were on the same page, pure joy breaking out like a fucking virus inside my chest and spreading until it filled all of the cavities as she sank to her knees and nipped at the rough fabric of my jeans covering my pulsing dick. She was in some mood.

Mental note: Make pasta alfredo and garlic bread for Melody at least once a week.

I wasn't sure if that really had anything to do with how feisty she was at the moment, or if it had more to do with the three glasses of wine she'd consumed with it. But *good God almighty*, I thought as she looked up at me from under her lashes, the ends of her lips curling up with mischief. I was more than willing to repeat everything about today ritualistically, just in case.

"God, Mel," I whispered and she giggled. Just the soft rasp of internal laughter, but I felt it all the way inside my bones. Her eyes danced in the low light of my living room lamp, and her mouth already looked tortured from the moments we'd spent making out as we sat cuddled on the couch in a post-meal-consumption haze.

It wasn't hard to imagine all of that hair and the hum of her laughter wrapped around my cock as she looked up at me with those big, innocent eyes.

Shit. I wasn't even sure I'd survive it.

Still, it was more than worth the risk.

I reached down to unbutton my jeans, but she shoved my hands away, looked up sexily, bit her lip, and shook her head playfully. "Uh-uh. That's my job."

Christ. My dick throbbed at the authority in her voice. I wouldn't exactly call myself a beta personality—in fact, not at all—but fuck me sideways, the pure carnality and confidence of her tone put me on the path to climax.

Undoing the button and pulling my zipper down with a rasp, she licked her lips, reached straight into my boxers, and grabbed on to my dick with a nice, firm squeeze.

My eyes nearly rolled back in my head.

Skin to skin, she started to stroke slowly, squeezing harder and giving two soft pumps at the bottom every third pass. My hips rocked in tune with her, striving to get deeper, closer…wetter.

"Fuck, Mel," I groaned. "Suck it. Put it in that fucking sweet mouth of yours and swallow it deep."

She didn't hesitate to do as she was told, opening her mouth wide, rounding her lips, and sucking until her chin brushed my balls.

Instantly, and without warning, a tingle shot up my spine, and I had to close my eyes to stave off a premature climax. I wanted to savor this—savor her. Watch her eat me alive like I was her last and favorite meal.

"You like my dick, baby?" I asked, smoothing a hand into her loose hair and tangling it with the strands.

"Mmm," she moaned, wet and wild as she moved up and down my shaft.

Her eyes wide and aroused, almost as though she was enjoying sucking me just as much as I was enjoying watching her do it, I forced my focus to lowering the tenor of my voice until it was just rough around the edges.

"What about your pussy? What does it think of my cock?"

"Mmm," she moaned again, and unsatisfied, I yanked her mouth off of my dick with a pull of her hair. She gasped.

"What was that?"

"My pussy loves your cock," she clarified immediately, shifting jerkily on her knees.

"Does it ache now, baby?" I asked, bringing her mouth back to me where she began to suck on my balls.

"Goddamn," I groaned as she took one fully inside. "Keep that up, and I'm gonna fuck you so hard you ache."

Releasing me with a wet pop, she spoke in nothing more than a rasp. "Yes, please."

"Is that what you want, Mel? You want me to be rough?"

She licked her lips and slid her hand down, lifted up her dress, and started to touch herself. "God, yes."

I couldn't wait another minute. Reaching down and sliding my arms under her armpits, I lifted her and twisted at the same time before giving her a little toss. She landed on the couch, knees to the seat and elbows resting on the back edge.

"Spread your legs and lean forward as far as you can," I commanded. She was all too happy to comply.

I lifted her dress up over her hips and shimmied her panties down until they were stretched tight enough that they bit into her thighs. "Don't move."

I slid a hand over her perfect ass and hissed as I took the first step away to go get a condom. Sensing my movement, she turned to look over her shoulder in a near panic.

"Where the hell are you going?"

"To get a condom."

She shook her head rapidly. "No. I *need* you."

"Mel—"

"I'm on birth control, Will. Fuck me right now. I want your come all over me."

Sweet Jesus. Definitely making pasta alfredo at least once a week.

Unable to turn down an offer like that, I moved back to the couch, grabbed on to her hips hard enough to make a mark, and surged inside.

A guttural moan left her sweet lips, and I had to bite my lip so hard I tasted blood to stop myself from coming right then.

Her breasts were perky and full, and I took one in each hand and pinched the nipples as I began a smooth rhythm. She gasped at the end of each stroke, shoving her hips back to meet mine violently each time.

"Faster," she ordered.

I pumped two strokes for my every previous one and leaned forward to touch my tongue to the skin of her back. She tasted like berries and sugar and *Melody*, my new favorite summertime snack.

Skimming her skin with my fingertips, I moved from her breasts to her hips and leaned back to get a perfect view of her ass. The new position put me at the perfect angle. I could tell by the way her breathing came in short, keening pants.

"Oh, oh, uh, uh, ahh," she moaned.

"That's it, Mel. Come. Get so wet and tight that your perfect pussy sucks me in and doesn't let go."

Her world shattered immediately at my words, locking my dick in a vise so tight I had no choice but to come right along with her.

I leaned forward so that my chest met her back and smoothed her hair up off the skin of her neck so I could whisper there, "Feel good, baby?"

"So good."

Pulling my cock out slowly, I watched as my come leaked out to coat the trail I left behind. Mesmerized, I reached forward and swiped my fingers through it, spreading it all over every part of her pussy, up over her asshole, and onto one perfect cheek. The feel of it on her skin pulled me in, and Melody kneeled completely still, watching me over her shoulder.

Both of us moaned when I brought my hand down on her decorated ass with a sharp slap.

I nodded. "Yep. I'm thinking we're going to have to do this again in the future."

She laughed; I turned serious, my eyes locked on this insanely beautiful woman still perched on her knees with her body bared and vulnerable for my eyes.

"God, Mel, you're fucking perfect."

I love you.

I caught the faint pink tint of her cheeks, and I smiled. Yeah, she was perfect. *For me.*

After a few kisses to her lips, I moved to the bathroom and got a wet washcloth to clean her up while she waited there in the same vulnerable position. She watched as I wiped myself from her skin with gentle care.

"You okay?" I asked, and once again, she nodded.

"Time for bed?" I questioned further, and her face melted into a smile.

"What time do you want your cab in the morning? You want to be late like usual or strive for on time?" I teased. She still wouldn't let us go to work together or leave at the same time, but tonight, in this perfect moment, I had absolutely no desire to dwell on what that could mean.

She laughed and leaned in to touch her mouth to mine one more time, and that kiss turned into two. By the time we got to five, I knew she wasn't going to answer my question.

But Mel was in my arms, happy, and on her way to at least one more orgasm for the night, and I couldn't think of a reason to dwell if I tried.

CHAPTER *twenty-four*

"H ERE," MARLENE GRUMBLED AND TOSSED DOWN A SMALL WHITE BOX ONTO MY keyboard—while I was still physically typing on it, mind you.

But considering it wasn't a Tuesday or a lunch she wasn't responsible for providing, it wasn't like she was acting abnormally.

I glanced down at the box and read the words, *"Goddess Cup"* aloud.

It was a menstrual cup that had recently been released to the market, and I only knew that because of my job. I hadn't ever been a menstrual cup user or advocate—which made me wonder what kind of horrible reason prompted her to give it to me in the first place. "Why are you giving me this?"

"You need to test it," she said but didn't offer any other explanation.

God. I just *knew* the reason for her unplanned air delivery wasn't going to be a good one.

"Test it?"

She nodded and plopped her ass down into her designated chair. "Yeah. Test. It."

What in the fuck is happening?

"This is a menstrual cup, Mar. Why would I have to test it?"

Three huffs of irritation left her lips one right after the other. Apparently, *she* was the one put out here. "Because I don't have a uterus, and you do. Plus, you're on your period this week," she explained as if *that* would aid in clearing up my confusion.

Why in the hell does she know I'm on my period? Am I dreaming right now?

I closed my eyes tightly for a good ten seconds to scroll through all of the reasons that even justifiable homicide would land me in prison, and then, when I finally had myself talked out of the cardinal sin, I opened them again.

One thing at a time.

"Okay… First of all, how do you know I'm on my period?"

"Because you're moody, and you're eating M&Ms like candy."

"M&Ms *are* candy," I retorted, and she sighed in annoyance.

And I wasn't eating *that* many M&Ms. Like a bag a day. A small bag. Well, not a supersmall bag, but like a medium-sized bag. Okay, fine. I was eating a lot of M&Ms, but Jesus Christ, I was on my period, and I had to work with Marlene and Melissa on a daily basis. If anything, they should've been thanking me. The M&Ms were probably the real reason I hadn't strangled one of them to death. Fuck ten-second pep talks about being someone's bitch in prison—candy was the game changer.

"You know what I mean," she added with a roll of her eyes. "Plus, I saw you put your giant box of tampons in the bathroom."

Holy hell. Was this old broad spying on me in the bathroom? Panicked, I looked around like I'd find cameras at reception, too.

"That's creepy, Mar."

She stared back at me unfazed. "The fact that you'd need that many tampons for one cycle is creepy."

"I buy in bulk," I explained for some unknown reason. "Doesn't mean I use all of them in a month's time."

"Anyway…" She completely ignored me. "We promised the manufacturer that some of our staff would try their new Goddess Cup and give feedback."

"Thanks, but I don't want to use a fucking menstrual cup." I refused, what I thought under the circumstances was politely, and slid the box back in her direction. "I'll stick with my giant box of tampons, thank you very much. And for the love of God, stop spying on me in the bathroom."

"Whatever you say," she muttered. "I mean…you'd get an extra five hundred bucks in your paycheck for it, but I'll let Betty know you're a no-go."

Wait… What? Five hundred bucks?

I slid the box back toward myself. "And how many days do I have to test it?"

Sure, menstrual cups made me want to gag, but five hundred dollars seemed like a nice addition to my *get the heck out of my parents' apartment* fund. I'd been saving like a penny pincher, and I was getting pretty damn close to reaching the little nest egg of savings that would get me out of Jazzercise purgatory.

"The contract with the manufacturer states you have to test it for at least twenty-four hours."

I looked down at the box and back up at Mar. The idea of testing the Goddess Cup wasn't exactly number one on my bucket list—*more like my fuck-it list*—but it was just for one day… *How bad could it be?*

"If I still had a uterus, you can bet your bony ass I'd be shoving those menstrual cups up my cooter for five hundred bucks without a second thought," she stated without an ounce of shame. "Hell, if they paid per cup, I'd stick more than one of those suckers in."

I fought the urge to projectile vomit across the nursing office. I, personally, didn't want to think of any situation where Marlene's *cooter* was involved. The fact that she called it a cooter was bad enough.

"Okay, I'll do it," I agreed. "Is there anything I need to do before I try one? Some kind of disclaimer to read? A contract to sign?"

"Just shoot Betty an email that you're going to do it, and then she'll have you fill out a questionnaire once you've completed the test trial."

"Okay." I shrugged and stood up from my chair with the box in my hand. "Sounds easy enough."

I glanced at my watch and noted the time as I headed for the employee bathroom. It was half past ten, which meant I only needed to get through the rest of the day and part of the morning tomorrow to be done with the official Goddess Cup test.

That didn't sound too difficult. Hell, I'd be free of it before lunch tomorrow.

Thankfully, the employee bathroom was a private one-stall kind of deal, so I locked the door, got myself ready for the menstrual cup insert, and opened the box without feeling like anyone in the office was lurking around.

The instructions showed numerous pictures of the drawn female figure standing up with her legs spread as wide as they could go. I cringed.

"Good Christ in a ballet," I muttered, wishing for perhaps the first time in my life I had the flexibility of Misty Copeland. Maybe an Olympic gymnast…someone other than me.

I had a feeling this wasn't going to be as easy as the standard seated-on-toilet application of a tampon, so I made myself *really* comfortable by removing my shoes, scrub pants, and underwear and turning myself into a human frog.

Okay, I can do this.

The first attempt, well, it didn't go so well. The damn thing flipped out of my hands before I could even insert it and bounced on the floor. Eyes wide, I took it to the sink and scrubbed it down and got set to try again. The second attempt was just a repeat of the first.

Jesus Christ, this thing was more complicated than a NASA spaceship manual.

How in the hell do women get this thing inside?

After three more attempts with all of the same results, I resorted to pulling my phone out of my scrub pants and tapping on the YouTube app. Yeah, I, Melody Marco, nurse of obstetrics and gynecology, was YouTubing "how to insert a menstrual cup." I was a disgrace to my profession. But my hands were getting dry from washing the goddamn thing so many times, and eventually, they were going to start to miss me out there doing my *actual* job.

Five minutes' worth of a tutorial later, I thought I was ready. Videos always make understanding things easier. It also helped with my mental readiness that Renee, the chick on the video, appeared quite fucking peppy and enthusiastic about her menstrual cup. If Renee loved her feminine oil filter so much, maybe I would too.

So, using Renee's endorsement of *"Everyone needs to switch to these! They make life so much easier!"* for motivation, I grabbed the Goddess Cup and spread my legs like I was riding a horse.

You better not be fucking with me about this, Renee. More importantly, Marlene better not be fucking with me about the five hundred dollars. Christ, why hadn't I considered that until now?

I made a quick mental note to call Betty when I wasn't practically spread-eagled and shoving a menstrual cup up my vagina.

Luckily, things were going smoothly. Slowly, but surely, I had the Goddess Cup inside, and my fingers were easing it into the "settled" position.

Unfortunately, like a flip of a switch, things got real fucking ugly.

The cup slipped from my fingers a little and *bam!*

It popped open.

I mean, it *popped the fuck open*, before I'd gotten it settled.

Stars literally danced behind my eyes. Those little bastards were hand in hand doing the fucking mamba while an endless stream of curse words flew out of my mouth.

"Motherfuckinggoddammithelpme!"

Pain. Red-hot pain inside of my body. I feared I'd just killed my vagina for a measly five hundred bucks and I was never going to be able to have sex again.

What in the hell were they thinking when they made this?

I was half convinced the manufacturer was trying to kill women. Obviously, they weren't, but holy cannoli, it was bad.

Seriously, if you think childbirth is painful, trying having a menstrual cup pop open inside of you before you get it settled.

Actually, don't try it.

Just. Don't.

Fucking Renee and her peppy attitude about her menstrual cup. Renee was a goddamn liar!

God, I had to find a way either to get this thing out or to get it to fucking settle. Whatever the hell that meant.

I stared down at my vagina with concern. "I'm so sorry I did that to you."

She didn't respond—after all, she was a few gasping breaths away from death—and I knew I had to woman up and get us out of this situation fast.

With my eyes closed shut, I reached my fingers back inside and nudged on the cup a little. Thank God, it moved with ease, and eventually, it found its way to the settled position.

How did I know it was in the right position?

Well, I no longer felt like a tiny elf had crawled inside of my vagina and was trying to physically remove it from my body.

Note to self: Never agree to test anything. Not even if they are offering you a million dollars. Don't do it.

Once I got my clothes back on and washed my hands, I glanced down at the time on my phone and saw that it was now half past 11.

One hour.

A motherfucking hour?

Dear God. It had taken me *a whole hour* to put that goddamn menstrual cup in. How did women do it on a daily basis?

I had a hard enough time with tardiness at work as it was. If I used this stupid cup all the time, I'd probably have to just call off for an entire week. *"Oh, hey, Will, it's me. I won't be in to work today. Well, actually, all week. I'll be too busy inserting my menstrual cup."*

As I walked—well, hobbled—out of the bathroom, I set my focus on patient care. Lord knew, I didn't even want to think about the fact that I was going to have to *remove* the menstrual cup at some point in the day.

Help. Me.

Luckily, after my hour-long bathroom break, the day had run smoothly. My vagina stopped hurting. Patients were on time. Will was in a good mood. Marlene wasn't grumbling too much. And Melissa managed to do more than five minutes' worth of work at reception.

This office of medical misfits was running like a well-oiled machine.

I peeked into Will's office and found him with the phone pressed to his ear. "Your two o'clock is here," I mouthed.

He covered the receiver with his hand. "I'm almost finished with this call."

"I'll bring the patient back, then, and get her ready. We'll be in room eight."

Will nodded, and I headed toward reception with the patient's chart in my hand.

"Mable?" I asked toward the waiting room, and a petite, white-haired lady stood from her seat.

"That's me."

I smiled and helped her through the door and into the exam room.

"How are you feeling today, Mable?" I asked as I took her blood pressure.

"I can't complain," she said with a cute little grin.

"I'm glad to hear that. Is there anything important you would like to discuss with Dr. Cummings today?"

"No." She shook her head. "Just here for my yearly exam."

"Okay," I responded as I finished up her assessment. "Everything looks and sounds good. Go ahead and get undressed and put on the paper gown. Dr. Cummings will be in in just a few minutes."

I left Mable to change in privacy and walked toward one of the computer alcoves to chart her assessment, but when I tried to fire up the screen by clicking the mouse, nothing happened. Impatient, I tapped on a few keys. Still, nothing.

It was moments like this when you realized technology could be a real pain in the ass.

Knowing that the computer was most likely turned off or unplugged, I squatted toward the floor and started scanning the wires and monitor for an answer. The instant my fingers touched the top of the monitor, dust bunnies scattered through the air

Housekeeping had obviously missed a few corners.

I waved the dust out of the air and tried to set my focus on getting the computer to work, but the dust had officially reached my nose. It tingled and itched until, spontaneously, a sneeze left my nose before I could find a way to stop it.

And then, like a goddamn fountain, a rush of warmth slid down my legs.

Oh, God…

I glanced down at my pants, and my jaw dropped in utter mortification when all I could see was red. Dark, red stains covered my crotch, my thighs, and God only knew what else. At some point during the sneeze, the Goddess Cup had left the building, and as a result, the Red Sea had officially fucking parted.

Oh, fucking shit monkeys.

My eyes darted back and forth around the hallway for witnesses. When I noted that no one was near, I hopped out of my squatting position and sprinted toward the employee bathroom. Once the door was locked, I took a deep, controlled breath and stood in front of the mirror, staring at my reflection.

Jesus Christ on a baseball team, I looked like I'd been shot. My scrub pants were covered in period blood to the point of no return. Stain pens would weep at the sight of me. A gentle hand-wash of the affected area would mean taking the entirety of my pants and dunking them in a bucket of water.

There was no fixing this situation without a shower and new clothes.

Panicked, I pulled my phone out of my pocket and texted the first person that came to mind.

Me: *There's been a murder. Help me. I need help.*

Not even thirty seconds later, my phone chirped with a response.

Will: *WHAT? WHERE ARE YOU?*

I immediately realized my mistake.

Me: Calm down. Not a real murder. But I do need help. I'm in the bathroom.

Will: Are you sick?

Me: No… I'm…well…I just need help in the form of new clothes.

Ah, shit. I had forgotten all about little Mable sitting in the exam room.

Me: And you should probably have another nurse go in and check on Mable in room eight.

Will: Okay. I'll be right there.

It only took fifteen rounds of pacing the bathroom before three soft knocks rapped against the door. "Mel, it's me," Will whispered.

I pressed my ear to the door. "Is anyone close by?"

"Nope."

"Are you sure?"

He sighed. "I'm sure. Just open the door, baby."

I pulled open the door enough to meet his eyes, and he searched my face with concern.

"Are you okay?"

"Yeah. I just need those clothes," I added and nodded toward the scrubs in his hands.

He didn't hand them over, though. "Mel, you're scaring me a little. Can I come in and make sure you're all right?"

"I don't think you want to do that."

His expression turned serious. "Trust me. I do."

Christ. *Am I okay with him seeing me like this?* I did another short circuit of his concerned blue eyes and realized that I was. Or, rather, I *didn't mind* if he saw me like this. There was a really fucking short list of people whom I trusted this much, and he was the only name on it.

Still… "Remember that I warned you."

"Just let me in."

"Fine," I huffed and slid the door open enough for him to sneak inside.

The second we were securely locked in the bathroom, he scanned the room with anxiety in his eyes until he spotted my pants. And instantly, the anxiety fled and surprise took its place, widening his eyes.

"Oh."

"Yeah, *oh*," I muttered. "Marlene convinced me to test the Goddess Cup today, and well, let's just say, things didn't go so well."

His lips crested into a smile, and I pointed an accusing finger in his direction.

"Do not laugh."

Will raised both hands in the air. "I swear. I'm not laughing."

"Ugh," I groaned in frustration. "I'm not even sure how the fuck to get out of these scrubs without it looking like someone was murdered in here."

A soft chuckle escaped his lips, and I couldn't stop myself from smiling.

"Stop it," I said through a few quiet giggles, and he grinned wide.

"Can I help you?" he asked with sincerity in his eyes.

"Uh…you want to help me take off my menstrual-blood-soaked pants and see the crime scene left behind?"

"No," he corrected. "I want to *help my girlfriend* who seems like she's having a *rough fucking day*."

"You're not grossed out by this?"

"Seriously, Mel?" He flashed a pointed look. "This isn't the first time I've seen a bleeding vagina."

I guessed he had a point. Will's job basically revolved around bleeding vaginas.

"Uh…okay…yeah…" I found myself agreeing, and he didn't give me any time to change my mind.

Will moved toward me, squatted to his knees, and started untying the strings of my scrub pants. "I'm sorry you've had a shit day," he said and looked up at me from beneath his long, dark lashes.

Man, he's handsome.

"Me too," I muttered, running a hand through his perfect hair. As I watched him gently remove my stained clothes, I started to think this day wasn't so bad after all.

I've got one of the good ones.

"Mind if I help make it better tonight?"

I quirked a curious brow. "What'd you have in mind?"

"Stay at my place tonight, and you'll find out," he said with a soft smile. "But I promise, it will most likely revolve around pizza, ice cream, and a movie of your choice."

I smiled and nodded, teasing, "Aw, that sounds amazing." I shook my head dramatically. "And to think, all I got you was a bloody pair of scrubs."

Will flashed that perfect smile of his in my direction, and within the blink of an eye, the day wasn't seeming so bad after all.

CHAPTER *twenty-five*

Me: Where are you? Are you in hiding?

I'd left Melody fully dressed and ready, her purse on her shoulder, keys in hand, and prepared to leave the apartment directly behind me. I couldn't understand how she still wasn't here, seeing as I'd arrived fifteen minutes ago.

Melody: I'm running late.

How was that even possible? I shook my head to myself, thinking, *Starbucks*. She'd probably stopped at Starbucks.

Me: How do you still have your job?

Melody: I'm fucking my boss.

Me: HAHA! That probably isn't how we should lead into telling the rest of the staff about our relationship today.

Melody: Maybe we shouldn't.

Me: WHAT? This was your idea, I'll remind you. After two showings of I Am Britney Jean, you went on and on about how thoroughly misunderstood Britney Spears has always been and declared that she was my soul sister.

Melody: I was drunk. I'd had a seriously bad day.

Me: I think not. You didn't break out the hard liquor until after the discussion about coming out in the office as a stand for my truth. I Am William Morris, I think you called it. They need to know the real you, you said.

Melody: I was just excited about learning your middle name.

Me: Sorry, Charlie, but this was your idea. Though, I'm completely behind it, baby. Love you.

Oh, fuck…

You haven't said that before, Will, my brain taunted. For weeks, I'd been trying to figure out the time to say it for the first time, and *this* was how I did it? Time sped up and slowed down and turned motherfucking backward as I desperately searched the hollow recesses of my mind for something to say that would fix this. Or erase it. Fucking something.

A full two minutes passed, and I still had nothing.

Melody: Well, this is awkward.

Me: Well. I guess it is. Maybe we'll deal with it later? Also, it's not as awkward as you showing me your nipples on the first day. I'll take a repeat of that when you finally get here, by the way.

Melody: No more hanging out with Thatch for you.

Complete avoidance. I guess that meant she was on board with dealing with it later. A tiny cloud of disappointment mushroomed in my chest. I used my memories of last night together to smother it.

Me: Why?

Melody: Because I've noticed a substantial increase in the amount you talk about my nipples since we hung out with them the other night. Like, substantial. Marked. Like, you've mentioned them forty times.

Me: Forty? Pshhh. No way. Maybe two dozen. At a push. But they are nice nipples. Can you really blame me here?

Melody: Don't you have patients to see?

Me: Not until my nurse gets here and tells everyone she's my girlfriend.

Melody: You expect **me** *to tell everyone?*

Me: I suppose I could serenade you with a song...An Ode to Melody's Nipples.

Melody: I'll tell everyone.

Me: See you soon.

Me: Oh, by the way...get me a blueberry muffin at Starbucks, would you?

Melody: Uh-oh... Busted.

I chuckled to myself as I set my phone to silent and dropped it onto the top of my desk. Truth was, I had to get busy. I did have patients to see whether Melody was here or not.

Grabbing my coat from the hook as I stood up, I swirled it up and around my shoulders, put my arms through, and pulled the ends of my dress shirt sleeves out at the bottom to make it comfortable.

Unfortunately, Melody's tardiness meant I was going to have to face the trio up front, first thing in the morning. Not only would they need to bring the patients back and get them settled, but I also hadn't been able to do a thorough read-through of the first patient's file.

As I made it to the mouth of the hall and passed by the break room, I steeled myself against the gossip I might find.

I didn't think anyone had seen Melody in her bloodied state yesterday, but neither of us was completely sure. I didn't think I'd be able to keep myself quiet or professional if they said anything about the incident while I was there.

"Melissa," I called. She was so focused on the computer screen in front of her, the sound of my voice made her jump.

Immediately suspicious, I moved from the side to directly behind her, but she hit buttons on the keyboard to make the screen minimize.

Visions of a horrible scenario bloomed in my mind. What if, somehow, someone had gotten a picture of Melody yesterday on their phone and emailed it around to the whole office?

What if all of these women are fucking laughing at her behind her back?

Rage built inside me immediately, and I could tell by the throb in my hands that my blood pressure was through the roof.

Goddammit, I have to know.

Stepping forward and lowering my voice to a controlled growl so the patients in the waiting room couldn't hear me, I dove headfirst into a grisly line of questioning.

"What were you looking at, Melissa?"

"Nothing, Dr. Cummings."

I lowered the volume of my voice even further. "Don't fucking lie to me."

Her eyes widened in fear. "Okay, I'm so, so sorry."

I prepared myself.

"Just show it to me."

God, how am I going to break this to Melody? How am I going to deal with this? Am I going to have to fire everyone and just start all over? Jesus, what a nightma— Wait... Is that a cat with sixteen kittens wearing lipstick?

"What the..."

Definitely not a compromising picture of Melody. Just a BuzzFeed article about kittens.

"I'm so sorry, Dr. Cummings. I know I'm supposed to be working. I swear this won't happen again."

I froze, widening my eyes as I tried to figure out how to play this off.

Fuck. Okay…um…

"Good," I muttered as calmly as possible. "See that it doesn't."

Backing away slowly, I didn't even bother telling her to bring a patient back. I'd just wait for Melody.

Safely back in my office, I sat down in my chair and thought about the implications of telling the office about Melody and my relationship. If I'd been that fired up to rain hellfire on Melissa without even having confirmation of her crimes, I could only imagine what I'd be like if someone actually did something to Melody in the future. No one would ever trust me to be impartial, and to tell the truth, I didn't even know what HR's take on our relationship would be. Would she be allowed to keep working with me directly?

Fuck. Relationship aside, she was a brilliant nurse, and I didn't want to lose her.

Maybe we shouldn't *say anything.*

Melody stepped through the door of my office just then, a brown paper Starbucks bag in hand. "Is it safe to come in? I come bearing muffin."

I rolled my eyes. "I guess they're talking about me up there?"

"Yep. Apparently, Dr. Cummings hulked out in a rage this morning over a picture of kittens."

I shook my head as I considered whether I should tell her the truth or not.

I couldn't see a way out of it, so I went with it. "Yeah…I kind of panicked, thinking she had a picture of you from yesterday. That's where the anger came from."

Her face softened into a smile.

"Someone's protective of me, huh?"

I shrugged. "More than I knew. Though, I'll note I was nowhere near the Hulk. If you'll notice, my clothes are still intact."

She laughed, easy and free, and three little words swelled up inside me until I couldn't contain them anymore. "I love you, Mel."

Her laughter cut off abruptly.

"I realize it was kind of ridiculous to tell you in a text message, but…" I shrugged. "It just popped out. I've been trying to tell you for weeks."

"Will…"

"And I've been thinking. I don't think we should tell people here."

Her face shifted from happy to confused, her eyebrows pulling together. "But I thought…"

"I don't want things to change. I don't want things to be more difficult for you in the office—and they will—and I don't want the shine of your ability to dull because of assumptions."

"Assumptions?"

"You slept your way to the top assumptions."

"Will—"

"I love you, Mel. But I'm also seriously impressed by you. You make my life easier when you're not twenty minutes late…"

She rolled her eyes.

"And I'd miss you if you weren't with me all the time."

"We're going to have to tell them one day."

"I know." I wanted to. I wanted to desperately. But for once, I was thinking about the consequences of my actions for someone other than me. "We will one day. I promise."

"Okay," she agreed with a nod.

I pulled her close and touched my lips to hers, wishing I could keep her there forever.

"But, Will?"

"Yeah, baby?"

"You should know I love you too."

Like a vise, my arms constricted around her.

Forever.

CHAPTER *twenty-six*

THE DAY HAD STARTED OUT AS A COMPLETELY NORMAL SATURDAY AFTERNOON IN New York.

I'd woken up to the fresh smell of coffee and Will's naked butt in the kitchen. I'd given him a kiss after he'd handed me my mug. And after we'd had sex on the kitchen counter, I'd gotten showered, dressed, and taken a nice stroll with Georgia and Cassie toward Mirabelle's auction house to bid on some items for the charity function I'd been planning for the practice.

I guess, in a sense, we'd be reauctioning the items I got today at the function, but since my auction was a silent one *and* for charity, I figured that couldn't be as bad as regifting. *Right?*

All in all, the day had been off to a fantastic start.

Will's sudden change of heart about telling the girls in the office about our relationship had taken me by surprise at first. It seemed like I'd done something or he'd developed some kind of doubts.

But when I'd left the haven of his office after exchanging I love yous, his reasoning made almost immediate sense.

Melissa had been doing the most work I'd ever seen her do in her life, but she'd also been ranting with an intensity I hadn't even known was possible. About how Dr. Cummings was biased, treating some people in the office one way and others another. Saying how she'd really gotten a rotten deal and how he probably needed to get laid.

All in all, it hadn't taken a whole lot of rational thinking to infer what she'd be like if she learned about our relationship that day. So, a delay had been warranted, and we hadn't discussed it again. It'd been a week and a half.

But I was happy. Happier than I'd ever been in my life.

At least, I *had been,* until we'd arrived at the auction house and things started to move toward violence.

"I'm going to kick that old lady's ass if she keeps bidding on all of the shit I want," Cassie whisper-yelled to me and Georgia. "That old goat is trying to start shit. I can sense it."

See what I mean?

Cassie has officially made enemies with an elderly woman.

Mind you, this woman couldn't be a day younger than eighty, and I'm pretty sure needs a walking cane to get around.

The bald-headed man sitting in front of us glanced over his shoulder, and a sharp "Shh" left his scowling lips. Immediately, a woman with a giant blue hat sitting across the aisle whispered her appreciation in his direction.

Good Lord, not only was Cassie in a bidding war with an eighty-year-old, she was now calling attention—*and not the good kind*—toward our threesome from other people. I looked around for the exit routes just in case the crowd went in together to bid on a lot of pitchforks and re-volted against us.

"Stop being so loud, Cass," Georgia chastised, but otherwise, seemed unconcerned as she popped another Skittle into her mouth. The bag of candy sat visibly on the top of her rounded stomach, and it was more than apparent her pregnant self gave zero fucks on what was deemed appropriate auction-house etiquette.

Note to self: Next time Cassie and Georgia want to go to an auction with you, strongly consider finding a way to avoid it.

"I don't think she's trying to start shit, Cass," I attempted to defuse the situation before it got out of hand. "I think she just has the same taste in art as you."

"Nope," Cassie refuted. "She's playing mind games with me."

She stared down her little, white-haired bidding opponent sitting in the aisle across from us. "Look at her," she whispered. "Why in the fuck does she want all of the pervy, naked pictures?"

"It's not pervy, Casshead," Georgia chimed in. "They're tasteful nude paintings. Most of which are by twentieth-century impressionist painters. They're worth a lot of money. She probably sees it as an investment. Not a ploy to give her husband nonstop erections."

Cassie scoffed. "Giving Thatch boners is way more important than a goddamn art investment."

Yeah, you heard that right, folks.

Cassie is bidding on anything and everything that has boobs with the motive of giving her husband, and this is a direct quote, "more boners than Viagra."

Georgia snorted. "You guys have the weirdest relationship."

"I know, right?" Cassie said with a satisfied smile. "We're the best. I love that giant idiot so much."

I was almost afraid to hear any more details about their relationship. It had only taken one five-minute conversation with Cassie to realize she and her husband let their freak flags fly like a goddamn eagle, but knowing and *knowing the details* were two different things.

Hell, during the walk to the auction house, she'd spent most of it sending him dirty texts and repeating them out loud to us. If the auction house would have been a block farther, she might've had time to pull her boobs out and send him a selfie.

"When's the charity function, Mel?" Georgia asked, and I gladly welcomed the distraction of small talk.

"It's a week away." Just saying how quickly it was approaching out loud made me shiver. Countless hours of work and creative thinking had gone into the planning of each and every detail, and I was so excited to see how it all came together.

The function would be a full-day event that revolved around raising money for women who were in desperate need of financial assistance. Free prenatal care would be available on site, but we'd also have a few semiridiculous activities to draw in a crowd in an attempt to accumulate money. I was trying to keep my approach two-pronged—short-term assistance with a chance for a long-term impact. The women this function was meant to benefit needed help for more than a day.

But I wasn't above calculating some of the plans based on my own enjoyment. I'd even managed the necessary equipment for a simulated-labor, via electrodes, booth. Call me slightly evil, but I was pretty excited to see Will's face while he experienced what contractions *really* felt like.

"That's really soon," she noted with visible interest. "What will the money go to?"

"Mostly toward aiding patients within the practice in getting financial assistance and the medical care that they need but haven't been able to acquire on their own."

"That's amazing," she said with a soft smile. "There are so many underprivileged women out there who need that kind of assistance."

"I know. I wish St. Luke's would open a women's clinic so that even more of the underserved population in the city could be reached, but I'm happy to at least be helping a little."

She nodded in agreement. "They really need to figure out a way to do that. It would be a huge positive for the city."

If only I could find a way to make it happen...

I'd been spending so many hours of my days—*and nights*—making sure our lower-income patients had everything they needed. But the fact that there was so little support out there for most of them was breaking my heart.

I was only one person.

I could only make so many phone calls.

I could only personally follow so many patients.

And knowing I could only do so much—and that there were so many women out there who needed help—was becoming an emotional hardship for me. What had started out as something that felt important had quickly morphed into something that felt a lot like my purpose.

I honestly think I needed those patients as much they needed someone like me. And somehow, someway, I felt like my career would eventually need to revolve around focusing less on just typical nursing jobs and more on case-managing women like Carmen.

"You're one of the good ones, Melody," Georgia complimented with a tender smile. "Those patients are lucky to have you. Hell, my brother is lucky to have you. He better not fuck it up," she added with a playful wink, and I laughed softly. I was pretty sure I was the one lucky to have Will.

The squeal of the microphone reverberating through the speakers pulled our attention to the front of the room. "Sorry for the interruption, ladies and gentleman," the auctioneer announced. "We'll now resume bidding on the last half of the lots. The next item up for bid is lot number 175. It's an oil on canvas called *Mademoiselle X* by famous French Impressionist painter, Maurice Ehlinger. He was renowned for his stylized nudes on canvas, and…"

Georgia and I both glanced at each other with wide eyes.

Jesus…not another nude…

"Here we go," she muttered before our attention shifted toward Cassie.

"Hey, uh, Cass," I tried, but it was too late, she was already glaring at the old lady—before the auctioneer had even opened up the bidding.

He pointed to the painting and proudly announced to the crowd, "We'll start the bidding at two hundred."

"One thousand!" Cassie exclaimed, and the auctioneer's eyes went wide.

"Uh…Okay…" he stuttered into the microphone. "Do I have eleven hundred?"

The old lady gave a quick raise of her hand to indicate her bid.

"Fifty-five thousand!" Cassie shouted. Understandably, the old lady just shrugged into her seat when the auctioneer looked in her direction. *Holy fuckballs, she'd just upped the bid by nearly fifty-four thousand dollars!*

"Fifty-five thousand going once…going twice…sold to the…well…the very exuberant lady to the left."

"Hell motherfluffing yes," Cassie cheered loud enough for all of New York City to hear. And she sealed the envelope of crazy by pointedly staring at her bidding opponent while moving two of her fingers between her eyes and the old lady's. "I'm watching you," she mouthed, and the little woman quickly broke eye contact.

I didn't blame her. I wouldn't have wanted to be on the receiving end of Cassie's wrath. Her kind of crazy appeared to have no limit or boundaries.

"Uh…" Georgia looked toward Cass. "You do realize that painting is only worth like two thousand, right?"

"So?"

"You just paid fifty-five thousand for it," I reminded her, and she shrugged.

"Thatcher paid fifty-five thousand for it."

"And do you think he'll mind that you've spent one hundred thousand dollars on paintings today?" Georgia asked.

Yeah, I should probably mention here that Cassie and Thatch are loaded.

Like, they could probably buy three yachts tomorrow, and it wouldn't even put a dent in their savings. I don't know if I will ever get used to knowing people that rich.

"No way," Cassie disputed. "I haven't spent that much today."

"Actually, you have," I added, but it didn't matter. Cassie's sights were already set on the next lot up for bidding, and like a homing device, once the auctioneer announced the item, her focus darted directly to the old lady across the aisle.

Honestly, it was like watching a car crash. I didn't want to look, but I couldn't look away.

God, I hope that little old lady makes it out of this auction house alive today.

With the motive of distracting myself from the fact that Cassie was one nude painting away from going what Georgia described as *fight club*, I pulled out my cell phone and sent a quick text to Will.

Me: I'm not sure if it was such a good idea to bring Cassie to this auction.

My phone vibrated with his response a minute later.

Will: Lol. I can only imagine…

Me: I think she's about to fight this old lady for nude oil paintings. She's convinced it'll drive Thatch crazy and give him "constant bonertimes." Her words, not mine.

Will: Jesus. What kind of auction are you at? I thought you were getting items for the charity event…

Me: *Get your mind out of the gutter. It's not like porno nudes. It's classic, 20th-century art. Mostly boobs, no crotch shots.*

Will: *Well... Thatch is a boob man.*

Yeah, that was obvious. I was certain everyone in this auction house knew Thatch was a boob man.

Me: *Yeah, well, Cassie is about to throw down on account of his boob obsession.*

Will: *I'd like to say everything will be okay, but...*

Me: *Help me.*

Will: *LOL. What's Georgia doing?*

Me: *Eating Skittles.*

Will: *In the middle of an auction?*

Me: *Yeah, I'm basically with Thelma and Louise. Only instead of driving the car off the cliff, Cassie's going to set this place on fire just to piss off the old lady who keeps bidding on all of the nudes she wants.*

Will: *I think you should record this. For future viewing purposes.*

Me: *You're zero help!*

Will: *You have to admit the entire situation is hilarious.*

In that moment, it didn't fucking feel hilarious. My palms were sweaty, and the stress had spurred a constant, sharp ache in my chest. If I weren't under thirty and my family hadn't had any known history of heart disease, I would've been convinced it was a heart attack. Sure, it might have seemed a little dramatic to be stressed over Cassie trying to buy everything nude or boob-focused, but seriously, the looks we had been getting from everyone around us weren't exactly friendly or welcoming. I felt like a caged animal in the zoo. Only, the people staring at me weren't excited, they were two seconds away from calling the cops.

I was just glad she hadn't tried to bid against me on anything. There's no telling what emergent medical episode would have befallen us.

Me: Yeah, maybe when you're an outsider. It's not when you're actually in the middle of it.

Will: Were you able to bid on enough items for the charity function? Or is Cassie outbidding you, too?

Me: Luckily, yes. Thank God, I was focused on sculptures and boob-less paintings of landscapes and flowers. Otherwise, Cassie might have killed me by now.

Will: Lol.

Me: I'm glad this is so amusing for you.

Will: Does it help if I say I think you're amazing?

It helped a little… but that didn't mean I had to tell him that. I typed out a two-letter response and hit send.

Me: No.

Will: What about… I'm so proud of you for arranging this charity function?

He really was so sweet to me sometimes.

But still, that didn't mean I had to tell him he was…

Me: Nope.

Will: You're the most brilliant woman I know.

Me: Still not working.

Will: Stay the night at my place tonight, and I'll eat your pussy for a really long, long time…

My brows shot up with intrigue the instant I read the text.

Hmmm… Things have started to get interesting…

Me: How long?

Will: I won't stop until you're begging for my cock.

Yeah, okay, a girl could only hold out for so long. I gladly gave in and sent him my agreement in the form of four letters.

Me: Deal.

Will: Lovely doing business with you, Ms. Marco. ;) See you tonight.

I put my phone in my purse and focused my brainpower toward imagining tonight with Will.

Will's face between my thighs… Will's mouth on my pussy… Lots of orgasms…

And, suddenly, the sounds of Cassie shouting outrageous bids on every nude wasn't so stressful anymore.

CHAPTER *twenty-seven*

Will

Today was the day. I was finally going to know what it felt like to have a baby.

Of course, I wasn't a medical marvel, and Melody, my would-be baby daddy, had been good about remembering to use protection, but as Melody placed the first electrode on my stomach, I geared up to feel labor pain all the same. She'd rented a machine that allowed men to feel stomach contractions via electricity, and from the looks of the line waiting to try it out, it appeared to be the biggest hit of the day.

She'd been organizing this charity event for weeks now, and as I looked around at the crowd, games, and crazy-long line at the booth where donations were made, I grew to nearly bursting with pride. Not to mention all of the pregnant women who'd come to get prenatal care for free. It was obvious there was a demand out there that needed a supply.

"You did a great job on this event, Mel."

"I know," she agreed with a smile, and I laughed.

She smacked another electrode sticker down, right on top of some hairs, and I groaned. "Oh man. That one is going to hurt when you pull it off."

She froze, her eyebrows nearly climbing to her hairline. "You're kidding, right?"

"What? No? Why would I be kidding?"

"Oh, Will. You're in trouble. Labor is going to hurt a whole lot worse than a tiny little waxing."

I hadn't understood the appeal of this kind of attraction, asking women to bring their men down for an experience in torture. But there literally had been a line of people waiting to do it all day long. The women looked positively gleeful. In fact, even Thatch and Cassie were getting set up a couple of beds down.

"What do you think, William?" Melody teased as she pressed on the last sticker and connected the wires. "Are you ready to have this baby?"

I laughed. "Normally, I'm telling women they don't have a choice."

"Exactly. This baby has to come out one way or another."

For the first time since I'd agree to this, I started to get scared. "But… there's not an actual baby in there."

"What are you saying?" she shouted in mock-anger. "Are you saying this baby isn't mine?"

"Mel…"

"I went on *Maury*, I took a paternity test, and William, I *am* the father."

"Mel…"

She hit the switch to turn on the machine, and I jumped as it buzzed to life. Oh God.

"Ready for your first contraction?"

"I'm not sure… Should I—" I started to ask, but she didn't wait or answer. Instead, she turned the dial halfway to the max and hit the button to start.

"Oh, Jiminy Cricket!" I shouted. She laughed. "Wow. That…that doesn't feel good."

"You thought it would?"

"Well, no…but, good Christ."

As the squeezing, cramping pressure settled in my stomach, she rubbed at my wrist. "Want me to turn it up?"

"Not really," I answered honestly, and she laughed again.

"You're not even in active labor yet."

"*What?*" I shouted, and her laugh turned into a cackle. People lingered around us as my shouts turned pained when she racheted up the dial and started my next contraction.

"Oh my God, I think my balls are swelling. Oh Jesus Christ in a tourniquet. Ooh. Oh, fuuuuudgesticks."

"Almost done," Melody wheezed out through a chortle. "Just breathe."

"How do women do this? I mean, I've always known. But I've never known. You just can't know until you know."

"Oh dear. And you haven't even gotten to the bowling ball out of a tube part yet."

Panic overwhelmed me as I looked to the countdown screen on my right and strongly considered crying. Another contraction was going to start in twenty seconds, and I wasn't going to be ready. Hell, I wouldn't be ready in twenty years, but time wouldn't wait for me.

"Titties and whipped cream!" Thatch yelled from two beds down. "What the hell setting do you have that thing on, woman?"

"What?" Cassie asked as a bead of sweat rolled off of his forehead. "You're a big guy. You make *big* babies. Just making sure you get the real experience."

I closed my eyes tightly and let my head fall back on the bed. The sound of the two of them was the absolute last thing I'd want to listen to during labor.

Meanwhile, a crowd was starting to form around my bed, patients and employees alike, and I wasn't sure I liked the feel of that either. "Is this what it's really like?" I asked all of them. "Just a crowd of strangers watching intently as you go through some of the most horrendous pain of your life?"

Several of them nodded and laughed. "For about twelve hours," one of them shouted.

"Wow. What a horrifying miracle."

Melody's laugh was contagious as she found humor in my torture. Honestly, with this woman, it didn't really ever matter what she was laughing about, even if it was about me, as long as she was laughing.

"Think you can take more?" Melody asked. I wanted to say no, but a sudden vision of her a couple of years down the road, laboring with *our* kid, made me reconsider.

"Go ahead," I offered. "Turn it all the way up. No reason to half-ass it. Plus," I teased. "I want to hold my baby."

She did as instructed, turning the dial to the maximum and grabbing on to my hand for support. "Just don't break my hand, okay?" she requested with a laugh.

I wanted to agree, but as the pain started to roll through me, like an actual violent wave that pulled me under and held me there, I wasn't sure I could follow through.

"Ahh. Holy hell." I grabbed my stomach and writhed. "Christ almighty, how is this natural?"

I had to admit, I didn't think I'd ever done anything that would give me as much perspective as this would. When women demanded the drugs, I'd be a lot more sympathetic to the speed with which it occurred—even if I had to drag an anesthesiologist up to the fourth floor myself.

Feeling normal again, Melody and I took our place in the free care tent to help out with some of the patients who'd made their way down, desperate to see us. Our first one was sitting on the table with her arms crossed protectively over her chest.

"Hi, Mrs. Kincaid," Melody greeted, a caring hand to Esmeralda's shoulder and genuine concern in her eyes. "What brings you down today? Have you had any prenatal care at all?"

Esmeralda shook her head, just slightly, embarrassed, and I glanced down at her bountiful stomach. I'd have to take a measurement to be sure, but she couldn't have been less than six months along. That much time with no prenatal care was risky, to say the least.

"That's okay. Don't be ashamed, okay?" Melody comforted. "You care about your baby, we know that. That's what brought you here today, right?"

The patient nodded, a tear dripping from the corner of her eye before she could dash it away. Melody pulled her into a hug immediately, whispering in her ear, "Don't worry. We're here for you now. And you've come to the very best place you could have. Dr. Cummings is the best, and he's going to do absolutely everything he can to help you."

God, I love her.

Her passion and completely genuine concern for these women shone out of her like an actual light.

These women needed her, and she needed somewhere to help them. I didn't think I could make it happen on my own, but as I glanced up to the crowd and spotted not only my sister and Kline, but Thatch, Cassie, Wes, and Winnie, I knew I didn't need to be able to.

I had fantastic friends in high places.

CHAPTER *twenty-eight*

MY FINGERS TAPPED GENTLY YET DETERMINEDLY AGAINST THE KEYS AS I FINISHED typing up a few notes on my last patient follow-up call. The office had been empty for well over an hour, and I savored the peaceful silence while I checked off the final items of today's to-do list.

This weekend's event had been a huge success. It had imbued me with pride and purpose and filled the tiniest hole in me that still needed filling—Will had managed to fill the rest.

But as much as it filled my void, and as good as it felt, it only drove me harder. I needed to work harder, reach out more, help more women.

Once Syreeta Johnson's chart was updated with our earlier conversation, I saved the file and crossed her name off the Post-it note of patients I needed to call. Before I could move on to the next, my phone vibrated across the table with a message from my mom.

Jazzercise Janet: Are you staying at Will's tonight?

Me: I'm not sure, I'm still at work. Why?

Jazzercise Janet: Just wondering.

That was a little weird, but I'd learned from the age of thirteen not even to bother with questioning Janet on her reasons or motives. Most times, I didn't want to know. And unfortunately for me, she appeared persistent on keeping this conversation going.

Jazzercise Janet: When do you think you'll know?

Me: I don't know, Mom. I'm still trying to finish up some patient calls before I leave for the night.

Jazzercise Janet: So...should I assume it's a good possibility that you will be staying at Will's tonight?

Call me crazy, but it seemed a lot like Janet wanted me out of the apartment for the evening...

Me: Do you want me to stay at Will's tonight?

Jazzercise Janet: Would it make me a bad mother if I said yes?

Yep. She definitely wanted me gone for the night, and I sure as fuck did not want to know why. Traumatic past experiences taught me that it most likely involved my father without pants.

Me: Considering I'm twenty-nine years old, I don't think so.

Jazzercise Janet: Okay, good. Could you stay at Will's tonight, sweetie? I'd really like some alone time with your father.

Me: Sure, Mom. I'll stay at Will's.

Jazzercise Janet: Yay! Your father brought home this *very sexy* movie, and he's going to be so excited we can watch it.

Ew. Gross. Sometimes it was truly a hardship having a mom who was so open and willing to tell you *everything*.

Me: Jesus, Mom. Let's just end this conversation before it steers to places I don't want to know anything about.

Jazzercise Janet: Pornography is a very healthy, sexual expression and outlet, Melody. It isn't anything to be ashamed about.

Me: OMG. Goodbye, Mom.

Note to self: Move out of Bill and Janet's ASAP.

Even though I stayed at Will's *a lot*, I really needed to get my own place.

If anything, it was a backup plan. A safe house. A place far, far away from walking in on Bill and Janet enjoying *very sexy* movie time. That was for sure one sight I did not want to witness.

Note to self: Schedule apartment showings ASAP.

I glanced at the time on my phone and saw that it was already half past six. The office was a complete ghost town, and I still had one more patient call I wanted to make before I left for the night.

Shit. I had to get moving if I wanted to be out of here before seven.

I pulled up Bethany Hyland's contact information and tapped the call button.

"Melody," she greeted with a smile in her voice. "I had a feeling you'd be checking up on me today."

The happiness in her tone had me grinning ear to ear. "How did your appointment with the specialist go?"

"It went really, really well," she answered, and I immediately breathed out a sigh of relief.

Bethany was twenty-six weeks into her pregnancy, and at her last ultrasound, we'd found a concerning spot on her baby's heart. We had to refer her to a Maternal-Fetal Medicine Specialist for further testing, but unfortunately for Bethany, her insurance was barely covering the additional expenses an evaluation like that would cost. And in her case, it was either go to the specialist or use the money to put food on the table for her family. Times had been hard for her family after her husband lost his job.

But after numerous phone calls and a lot of persistence, I'd managed to convince Dr. Wilton, a physician Will worked closely with on difficult cases that required extensive monitoring of the baby throughout pregnancy, to take on her case pro bono.

"What did Dr. Wilton say?" I asked, too curious to wait for the final report to come in from their office.

"She said that she has no current concerns and she doesn't think we have anything to worry about, but she wanted to follow me for the rest of my pregnancy," she explained. "Dr. Wilton was so kind, Melody. I'm so thankful you were able to find her for us. Sometimes, I wonder if you're an actual angel. I'm not sure you'll ever know how grateful I am for what you've done for me and my baby."

My heart grew inside my chest, and tears pricked my eyes at her kind words.

"I do know, Bethany," I said through the emotion clogging my throat. "And I'm so very happy your appointment with Dr. Wilton went so well today."

"Me too."

"Well, I'm going to head out of the office for the night, but I'll see you next week at your appointment with Dr. Cummings."

"Thanks again, Melody," she said.

"You're very welcome. Have a good night, okay?"

"You too."

I ended the call and with a thankful, happy smile etched across my lips. I closed up shop for the night, shutting down my computer and heading out of the nurses' office. As I pulled my purse out of my locker in the break room, a white envelope sticking straight out of the middle pocket stared back at me.

Fingers crossed this is my bonus for enduring the Goddess Cup of hell... I thought to myself as I dragged it out of my purse and slid my index finger underneath the seal. A folded white piece of paper with a key taped to the front sat inside.

My mouth crested into a huge goofy smile once I'd scanned the note scribbled inside. Immediately, I pulled my phone out of my pocket and sent Will a quick text.

Me: *The weirdest thing happened to me today.*

He responded a minute a later.

Will: What?

Me: While I was at work, some stranger put a note in my purse with a key to his apartment.

Will: No shit. What did the note say?

Me: "Dearest Mel, Meet me in my bed, naked, at 9:00 p.m. tonight."

Will: He sounds brilliant.

Me: I wish I could figure out who it was. I mean, he signed it, but his handwriting is complete shit. It might as well be a doctor's sig on a patient prescription...

Will: Lol. My girl's got jokes. I love it.

His girl. *Will's* girl. I felt like a complete sap for loving that so much.

Me: So, is dinner involved tonight, or are we just doing the sex?

Will: I'll pick up some takeout on my way home. I've got a board meeting at 7:30, but it shouldn't run too late.

Me: I'll only agree if the takeout is pancakes. Ohh! Make it chocolate chip pancakes!

Will: Pancakes? For dinner?

Why was that even a question? Breakfast for dinner was the greatest invention ever.

Me: Umm...YES.

Will: That's kind of weird.

Me: Get with the program, Will. It's the best dinner ever.

Will: Fine. I'll bring the pancakes. You bring that perfect little cunt.

His words sent a shiver up my spine. God, I loved it when he talked dirty.

Me: Deal.

Will: And Mel?

Me: Yeah?

Will: She better be bared and spread out on my bed when I get home.

Me: Or what?

Will: Tongue-lashings.

Me: That's not a punishment.

Will: I never said they'd lead to orgasm...

Whoa. Whoa. Whoa. Hold the phone. I wanted orgasms. I wanted lots and lots of Will-induced orgasms.

Me: Naked on the bed. Got it.

Will: See you tonight.

Since I had no desire to risk seeing Bill and Janet having "very sexy movie time," I hadn't worried about grabbing a change of clothes from their apartment and headed straight to Will's place after leaving work. Which explained my current situation—stretched out on Will's leather sofa, clad in only his T-shirt and my panties, while watching television and simultaneously scrolling through Facebook.

I wasn't really one to post a lot of things on social media, but I'd be a liar if I said I didn't enjoy reading everyone else's shit.

As I swiped my finger across the screen of my phone, flying past boring statuses about people's dinner choices and wedding countdowns and blah, blah, blah, one post in particular had me pausing at light-ning-quick speed.

Patty Lister: OMG. Who's watching The Doctor Is In *right now??? Are you seeing this??? Is Dr. OBscene going to sleep with Emily???*

I hadn't watched an episode since that night at Kline and Georgia's house, but for some insane reason, before I could stop myself, I had the remote in my hand, and I was typing in the channel that Will's docu-series was on. Instantly, his handsome face was on the screen. He appeared quite fucking cozy with a petite, blond nurse in a small alcove off to the side of the hospital hallway. His arm rested against the wall while he smirked down at her.

Jesus Christ, this kind of shit is still almost too painful to watch.

But I couldn't stop. I couldn't turn off the television. I couldn't fucking look away.

She whispered something into his ear, and he stared down at her with a heated look in his eyes.

Oh God. Please don't let this get any worse. I wasn't sure if my heart could take any more.

But, unfortunately for me, it did get worse. The camera flashed to shots of Will taking the nurse by the hand and leading her toward the doc-tors' on-call room. He ushered her through the door with a flirtatious tap to her ass, and she giggled as it clicked shut behind them.

By the time a commercial with a dancing goat took over the screen, I wanted to throw up.

I need to stop watching this. Stop. Watching. Mel.

I probably should've listened to my brain's wise words of advice. Actually, I *really* should've listened. But I didn't.

I wasn't sure whether I was a moron or a masochist.

Mindlessly, I stayed glued to the couch, and my eyes stayed locked on the television. Four commercials later, I was face-to-screen with shots of the closed call room door while the microphone caught the whispers and giggles and fucking moans of the two people inside.

My stomach dropped to my feet like an elevator without cables. I was listening to Will and a nurse named Emily have sex.

I'm literally listening to my boyfriend having sex with someone else right now.

Oh. My. God.

Honestly, I barely knew Emily. I'd only spoken with her a time or two while I was assisting Will with deliveries on the floor. But I knew Will. Hell, I knew him so well that I would've known those moans were *his* moans even if I hadn't had the awful opportunity of watching him walk into the call room with his work fuck buddy.

This hurts like a motherfucker.

That was an understatement. This was worse than the Goddess Cup opening up before I got it settled. This wasn't physical pain, this was soul-deep, heart-crushing, emotional kind of pain.

How in the fuck had I found myself watching this?

Time and time again, he'd basically told me the show had made things out to be worse than they were. He'd admitted to flirting with a few of the nurses during filming, but he'd never expanded on the fact that it was possible they'd caught more than just flirting—aka *fucking*—on camera.

Even after I'd told him that the show and the parade of flirtatious patients had started to make me uncomfortable, he had never opened up and told me everything, or *at least* told me that it was probably for the best if I didn't watch any more episodes. He'd had more than enough opportunities to be open and honest with me about how things were during the filming of the show—how *he'd been* before we'd started dating.

I mean, I wasn't completely unrealistic. I understood that filming occurred prior to our relationship, but what I didn't understand was how he'd completely missed the part where he filled me in on his sexual relationship with our hospital coworker so I didn't look like a fucking fool.

Or maybe I was a fool for being so upset by it. I honestly couldn't tell.

But, justified or not, I couldn't ignore these feelings.

264 · max monroe

It felt like Eli all over again. Cavalier and brushing things off that should have been talked about and discussed.

Will should have given me a heads-up. He should have told me.

But he didn't.

I tried to take a deep breath and think for a minute. I didn't think he was out cheating on me.

But I was upset.

This felt exactly like the bullshit my ex used to put me through.

The second I'd made the decision to end things with Eli, I promised myself that I would avoid getting involved with men who were careless with my feelings.

God, what if this was why he didn't want to tell the people in the office? What if I really was just another work fling, one in a line of flings he'd been having for ages?

Maybe he'd actually done me a favor. I would have looked like a fucking fool in public. Now, I only had to feel like a fool on the inside.

Like a moth to a flame, my brain sprinted toward the irrational need of dissecting every single moment that had ever occurred between Will and me. *Have I missed something along the lines, here? Some kind of red flag?* Within seconds, my mind pulled a memory out of storage and pushed it before my eyes. It was Will and me, in the office, inside of an empty patient room and seconds away from having sex.

"What? There are perks to doing this here," he'd said through a laugh and with a condom held between his fingertips.

The way he'd joked about it, having sex while he was at work, had taken me by surprise and stunned me silent. Immediately, he'd noticed, though, and answered my unspoken question of *"Have you ever done this at work?"* with, "Never."

He had looked me directly in the eyes and said *Never.*

And yet here I sat, listening to Emily moan at the work of his above average penis.

Goddammit. He'd lied to me.

Instantly, my body revolted at the thought. My stomach clenched, my heart ached, and my eyes filled with tears.

Why couldn't he be honest with me?

It was truly amazing how an answer compiled of five letters could fill your head with doubts and instantly caused you to question your trust in someone.

Fucking hell, I hated the way it made me feel. I was wrong—this wasn't like my relationship with Eli. It was a million times worse.

Right then, in that moment, I didn't want to be anywhere near him. I didn't want to be in his apartment when he got home tonight, and I didn't want to have a long, exhausting conversation where he did his best to resolve the situation and I took the blame on myself in order to make it happen. I just…wanted to be anywhere else but with Will.

I hopped off the couch, tossed my scrub pants and shoes back on, grabbed my shit and headed out the door. And since I couldn't go home to Bill and Janet's, five minutes later, I was in a cab heading toward the Hyatt Regency.

Once I checked in to my room, I sent Will a quick text letting him know I wouldn't be there tonight, and I turned off my phone.

Me: Janet called. Needs my help. I won't be there tonight.

The lie tasted bitter on my tongue, but I didn't mind. I didn't have much of an appetite anyway. *Fuck Will and his fucking pancakes.*

CHAPTER *twenty-nine*

THE SUBWAY WAS A LITTLE MORE CROWDED THAN USUAL AS I RODE HOME FROM MY board meeting that night. I'd have said I was excited to see Melody, but I'd gotten a succinct text message from her during the meeting, and by the time I got out, she hadn't answered any of my calls.

And after I'd sent her a text that said, *If you don't at least send me a message and let me know everything is okay, you can't get pissed at me for showing up to Bill and Janet's unannounced...* ☺, she'd sent back a quick, *Everything is okay. See ya tomorrow at work.*

Her short response left me feeling unnerved, like something was going on, but I tried to not read into it. I knew Janet could be a little trying sometimes, especially if it had to do with some sort of Jazzercise emergency.

So, after approaching the board tonight with my idea for the clinic and having them turn me down due to lack of funding, I set my focus to moving on to Plan B.

Group messages with Kline, Thatch, and Wes weren't my normal MO, but if I was going to get them all in one place quickly, I figured this was my best chance. A phone call would open all of that air space up for too much bullshit and trash-talking.

Me: I need a meeting.

Thatch: Like, AA? Are you on the booze, William?

Christ. So much for cutting through the bullshit.

Me: No, Thatch. I'm not on the booze. And I'd appreciate if you didn't go spreading that around the medical community.

Thatch: I wouldn't worry too much about me ruining your rep, bro. I'm not into torpedoing already sinking ships.

Me: Fuck you.

Thatch: Aw, I love you too.

Kline: Maybe he means a psychologist. He did have all of that emotional trauma from watching his parents bang growing up.

Me: You too? Are there any adults in this message?

Wes: I haven't said anything.

Me: You're my new favorite, Wes.

Wes: I mean…I was thinking it. I just didn't say it.

Me: Screw you guys.

Kline: A meeting you say?

Me: Yes. With the three of you.

Thatch: I thought you hated us?

Me: I could be persuaded to change my mind…with a meeting.

Kline: I'm free tomorrow morning.

Wes: So am I. And I'm in the city tomorrow.

Me: Thatch?

…

Me: Thatch…

Kline: You know what he wants. Just do it.

Me: Sigh. I love you, mighty Thatch warrior. Your seed is the strongest in the land.

Wes: You must really want this meeting.

Thatch: My office, 8 a.m., fools. Cassie and I have a lunch bang that I don't want to be late for.

Ignoring his propensity for oversharing and refusing to engage, I left them with a simple agreement and backed out of the message.

Me: See you then.

Scrolling through my contacts to Melody's number, I hit send and listened as the call rolled to voice mail one more time.

Frustration creased the corners of my eyes, and I rested my head on the wall behind me. Her lack of response had the irrational side of my brain threatening to go haywire. Over the past few weeks, I'd found that even a single night without Melody lying beside me messed up my sleep pattern.

I wanted her here, with me, and quite frankly, I wanted it every night.

I have to convince her to move in with me. Another fight for another day, I mused.

But for now, after a long day, I wanted nothing more than to sink myself into Melody and fall fast asleep, but thanks to her disappearing act, the latter would have to do.

I'd had three late nights this week with work, and two more provided by the aforementioned naked-time with Melody, and as a result, I was fucking exhausted.

I could barely keep myself awake as the lull of the train rocked back and forth while it screamed through the darkened tunnels of the New York City tracks. Light flashing like a kaleidoscope made me open my eyes just as we pulled into my station.

Up and off, I moved with the crowd, weaving my way up the steps and down the quiet block to my apartment.

It felt different as I climbed the steps and walked into the noticeably empty space. So different that I paused and looked around for a moment, spinning in a circle. Nothing seemed out of place, but something still felt off.

She isn't here, my mind whispered.

I chuckled softly to myself and shook my head over the fact that Melody Marco had burrowed herself under my skin and into my heart so deep that coming home to a Melody-less apartment didn't feel right.

With the motivation of making the Melody-less night go faster and catch some much-needed sleep, I moved toward my bedroom, shucking out of my clothes as I walked, and eventually, fatigue took its toll and I fell face first into my bed, passing out straightaway.

"Good morning, my poppet," Thatch greeted as I strode through the door to his office and took a seat next to Wes and Kline in the chairs of the little mini conference table he had set up in one corner. I'd managed a shower, clean clothes, and one hopeful tongue depressor in my pocket before stepping out the door.

Your tonsils are almost as big as your heart.

I was hoping it conveyed what I wanted it to. But I had to get what I wanted out of this meeting first.

I gestured halfheartedly and sank into the leather like I was melting.

"You look tired," Kline remarked.

I waved him off, but I was. I was fucking exhausted and pissed that apparently my body wasn't built for sleeping on its own anymore. My brain was still having a hard time comprehending why I felt like my world had been turned upside down. "It was a weird night."

Kline nodded, considering me carefully in a way that only he could. He was the master of reading people, but if he could figure out what was going on with me—when I couldn't even really figure it out myself—he could have at it.

"So why did you want to meet with us?" Wes asked, getting down to business. I was grateful.

Straightening in my chair, I did my best to perk up and make my pitch sound at least slightly marketable.

"I want to talk to the three of you about an investment opportunity."

"Ooh," Thatch said. "Money. I like money. Especially since my wife just spent two hundred and fifty fucking grand at an auction buying titty pictures." He rolled his eyes. "I have the best set of live art titties in creation. Why the fuck she thought I'd need pictures of other ones boggles me."

Kline shook his head and smirked. "The two of you really are perfect for one another."

Thatch smiled, leaning forward to buzz the intercom out to his assistant. "Mad, can you bring in some coffee?"

"Sure thing," she answered immediately.

Yes. Coffee sounded good.

"So what are you wanting us to invest in?" Wes asked, the only one with any fucking focus these days. I figured it had more to do with his stepdaughter Lexi than anything. She was an on-task kind of kid. And I wasn't kidding. Lexi hadn't even reached adolescence, and she could solve advanced calculus problems. Her brilliant little brain never stopped.

"Property?" Thatch offered.

"A start-up business?" Kline chimed in.

"What is this, twenty fucking questions?" Wes griped. "Let the man tell us himself."

I winced, knowing my prospect wasn't nearly as financially rewarding as those things…at all. But at the thought of Melody with these patients, women who needed her, I pushed on anyway.

"Actually, it's a clinic."

They stared.

"A free clinic. With about zero chance of any financial gain." I shrugged and went for it. "Probably a financial loss, to be honest."

Thatch laughed outright. "Well, you've got balls."

Kline smirked and leaned his elbows on the table. "And what's the purpose of this free clinic? If we're guaranteed to lose money, what's the draw here?"

"You'd be helping women, especially pregnant women, who can't afford medical care, get it."

"Does this have anything to do with your girlfriend?" Thatch asked.

I tried to look innocent, but with the way he hooted into laughter, I knew I'd failed.

"I was wrong. She's got you by the balls."

Kline smacked him, but he didn't look like he disagreed. I jumped to explain.

"Yes, this kind of patient outreach is Melody's passion. You should fucking see her with these women. But regardless of that, the city could really use one. There's a whole population of women out there who are underserved. I approached the hospital board, but they shot it down pretty quickly."

"Of course they did," Wes said with a chuckle. "It's a money pit."

Kline nodded. "Yep. All they saw was a love-sick idiot."

"They don't know about my relationship with Melody," I corrected.

"Sorry, dude," Wes apologized. "It's written all over you."

Disheartened, I stood up from the table and reached out to shake all of their hands. I couldn't say I blamed them. They hadn't gotten the kind of money they had by going around blowing it on dead-end investments.

They smiled and said their goodbyes, but none of them jumped up and shouted they'd be happy to give me their money.

I'd have to figure out another way.

CHAPTER *thirty*

SPENDING THE NIGHT IN A HOTEL WAS FUN AND EVEN A NICE LITTLE REPRIEVE FROM the real world when you were on vacation. But enduring a night in a hotel room after you'd watched—*well, mostly heard*—your boyfriend bang a coworker on *his* television, inside *his* apartment, with God knows how many other viewers? Yeah, that experience was fucking awful.

I'd spent most of the night tossing and turning, and when I'd finally managed to fall asleep, my dreams consisted of weird mashups of what I'd witnessed on *The Doctor Is In*.

My mind had played some seriously evil tricks on me, and I'd found myself wide awake and ready to escape the nightmares that hotel bed had brought before my alarm went off.

Which explained why, for once in my always tardy life, I was on time to work.

Groggy-eyed and numb from experiencing too many emotions in a twelve-hour period, I shuffled into the office after I'd made a quick stop at my parents' apartment for fresh scrubs and a trip to Starbucks for a coffee with three shots of espresso.

Considering my dog-tired state, I'd contemplated four shots, but I honestly wasn't sure if my heart could manage any additional stress. It'd already taken quite the fucking beating last night.

Once I set my stuff in my locker, I did my best to focus my brainpower on getting the office ready for a full day's worth of appointments. But as I set up each exam room with fresh paper and medical supplies, I couldn't stop my racing thoughts. I couldn't stop thinking about that episode. I couldn't stop hearing the sounds Will had made behind the on-call room door. I couldn't stop remembering how easily he'd lied to me. "Never," he'd said, and God had those words flowed off his tongue without any hesitation.

By the time the clock struck 9 a.m., and the rest of the staff—besides Will—had filled the office, I wasn't sure how much longer I could keep my composure. I wasn't sure how much longer I could physically stay at work. Hell, I wasn't even sure if I could successfully do my job—a job that I technically didn't even really want to do anymore. For the past month or so, I'd been struggling over the fact that I knew my passion wasn't working in a medical office. Sure, I enjoyed it, I loved taking care of women during pregnancy, but deep down, I wanted to make it so that all of my time was focused on those women who *really* needed assistance and advice and someone to support them. Women like Carmen and Syreeta and Bethany and…yeah, it was truly an endless list, and that was only in New York. But I'd stayed for Will. I loved seeing him all day long, watching him in action and thriving underneath his steady assurance.

Well, that's well and truly fucked now, isn't it?

No, really. Isn't it? Someone help me out here.

I fucking hate feeling like this.

Unfortunately for me, I didn't have a chance to find a way out of my internal hell.

Will walked through the reception doors with his briefcase in his hand while I was working on a computer in the hall, and the instant his reserved blue eyes met mine, a rush of emotions hit me all at once. Anger. Sadness. *Heartbreak.* I felt like the floor had dropped out from beneath me.

God, just the mere sight of him hurts like a knife to my already mangled heart.

Quickly, I averted my eyes and tried to switch my focus back toward the computer screen in front of me, but he didn't give me a reprieve. Out of my periphery, I watched as his feet moved in my direction, until they stopped directly beside me.

"Mel?" he asked quietly, concern etching his voice.

"Yeah?" I responded, but I couldn't find the strength to meet his eyes.

"I missed you last night," he whispered.

"Sorry," I muttered and racked my brain for a quick excuse to end this conversation before I started to sob in the middle of the hallway. "I was busy…with…uh…with helping Janet…" I lied. "Yeah…I was busy with Janet until late last night."

"Shit. Is she okay?"

"Uh-huh. She's fine."

I knew it was my fault, that'd *I'd* been the one to avoid *him* last night, but I really didn't want to have this scene out at work.

"Mel," he said, and his voice dropped to anxious. "What's going on?"

"Nothing," I lied and started to type out the rest of my nursing note into a patient chart. "Just busy trying to finish up charting on a follow-up call."

He placed his hands on top of mine, stopping my typing progress. "Can you take a quick break from that and come to my office?"

I glanced up from the computer screen and met his gaze.

"Please?" he asked and with the way his blue eyes had turned pleading, I couldn't *not* give in to his request.

I nodded, and silently, I followed his lead down the hall and inside his office.

He shut the door with a quiet click and set his briefcase beside his desk. Wordlessly, he stared across the room, into my eyes, with worry creasing his brow.

"What's going on, Mel?" he asked, and I shrugged.

"Nothing."

Everything.

I can't get the sounds of hearing you sleep with Emily out of my head. I can't stop thinking about the fact that you carelessly left me in the dark about what happened during the filming of the show. I can't stop wondering if there is more to the story on why you didn't want to tell the office about our relationship. I can't stop replaying and thinking about your lie over and over and over again.

I fear that I gave my heart to someone who, despite his best efforts not to, will crush it.

And that was the real crux of the issue. Despite all of his trespasses, I really did believe that Will thought I was the best thing for him. I just didn't know if he was the best thing for me.

"Talk to me," he urged, and his brow furrowed deeper when I gave him no response. "Melody," he said, and his long strides quickly closed the space between us. He pulled me into his arms and hugged me tight to his chest. "Please, tell me what's wrong."

I didn't react. I couldn't react. I just stood inside his embrace with my back stiff and my arms hanging limply at my sides.

"Just give me something…anything…" he whispered. "You're scaring me."

You're going to break my fucking heart!

"I can't do this," I blurted out, and Will stared down at me with wide eyes.

"What?"

I shrugged out of his arms and put some much-needed distance between us. "I can't do this," I repeated and gestured between the two of us with an impatient hand. "I can't do us."

"You don't want to be with me?"

"It's not like that." *I want to be with you too much. It makes me want to give up everything else I've ever wanted.*

"Then what is it like, exactly?"

"I don't think you're ready for a long-term relationship, Will," I explained, and his eyes squinted in confusion. "I made a promise to myself that I wouldn't fall into the same trap I did with Eli."

That was bullshit even to my own ears, but I went with it—to protect myself from him and to protect him from the mess inside my head.

His jaw dropped wide open, and a hint of anger tinged his already tired voice. "I'm not Eli."

"I know you're not, but—"

"But what?" he questioned in irritation. "You know I'm not him, but you're using your ex-boyfriend's fuck-ups against me anyway?"

Everything I'd been working so hard to contain bubbled up and boiled over.

"No," I said in a hostile tone. "I'm using *your* fuck-ups against you."

Outrage covered his face. "When did I fuck up?"

"I saw the episode, Will," I enlightened, and his back stiffened. "You know, the one where you and Emily stepped into the call room for a little afternoon delight."

"No, actually," he smarted. "I don't know. You know I've never had any fucking clue what they're going to air on the show or when they're going to air it."

"That's not why it upset me, Will!" I shouted back. "You had more than enough opportunity to be open and honest with me about what happened during filming," I said through gritted teeth. "But even after I'd told you that it was making me really uncomfortable to have to watch you flirt with nurses on the show and witness the parade of flirtatious patients stroll in the office, you never told me you slept with one." I paused, a horrifying thought occurring to me. "Or *more*."

"Jesus," he muttered. "I don't give a fuck about anyone but you. Can't you see that? Can't you see that I'm in love with you?" he asked and ran a frustrated hand through his hair. "I don't want anyone else but you, Melody. You're all I care about."

"Your actions speak louder than your words, Will."

"What in the hell do you mean by that?"

"If you cared about me so much, you would've acknowledged my feelings, and you would've made damn sure that I knew what happened during filming. You wouldn't have left me in the dark and let me get railroaded by it. I had to watch you…" Tears clogged my throat as I remembered it. "…on your fucking television, have sex with someone else. I had to hear it. Your moans. Her moans. All of it."

"God," he whispered, clearly tortured by the sound of my voice. "I'm so sorry, Mel. That's…" He paused, seemingly at a loss for words, and I answered for him.

"Fucking awful," I answered for him.

"But, Mel, I didn't know they filmed it. Of course I would have told you—"

"And you know what's even worse?" I asked, cutting off words I knew were an outright lie. "What's worse is when watching someone like that is how you find out that the one person you love can lie so fucking easily."

"What? When did I lie? What are you talking about?"

"Patient exam room six, Will," I explained, but he still didn't understand. "You know, that day you'd pulled me inside that empty room to have sex. The day you'd told me that you'd never done something like that at work. Do you remember that day, Will? I know I can't get it out of my fucking head." I mocked his words by lowering my voice into a poor example of his own. *"Never."*

He stared back at me with a plethora of emotions in his eyes. Sadness. Apology. Fear.

But I couldn't find an ounce of sympathy for him in that moment.

"A relationship needs honesty," I said, and he started to interject. But I held my hand in the air and continued. "I'm sorry, Will. I just can't do it. I can't be in a relationship with you."

In that moment, I wasn't sure what hurt more, Will breaking my heart or my having to end things with a man I'd honestly thought I would spend the rest of my life with.

"So…that's it?" he questioned and stared at me with an ocean full of hurt in his eyes. "You're just walking away without giving me a chance to explain? You're just giving up?"

I'm not giving up. I'm saving myself.

I had been able to leave my relationship with Eli unscathed. But I felt like if I stayed with Will, I was playing Russian roulette with my heart. And I knew he had the power to hurt me past the point of no return.

"I'm sorry, Will," I repeated, and before I could talk myself out of my next decision, I added, "Today will be my last day at work. Consider this my official resignation."

A shocked gasp left his lips, and I couldn't find the strength to meet his eyes.

Instead, without another word, I kept my head angled toward the ground and left his office.

And fifteen minutes later, I was sitting on the subway, heading home to my parents' apartment, jobless, Will-less, and feeling more lost than I'd ever felt in my entire life.

CHAPTER *thirty-one*

O
NE WEEK.

It'd been *one week* since Melody had left my office after quitting her job and ending our relationship in one painful as fuck swoop.

She'd seen an episode where I'd hooked up with a hospital nurse named Emily, and like a goddamn tic burrowing under a human's skin, the show from hell had succeeded in planting a seed of doubt into Mel's head.

She thought I was dishonest with her. No, that made it sound too nice. Like an honest mistake—which it was.

But what she thought was that I'd *lied* to her. Willfully and with intent.

Knowing she could think that of me burned deep inside, singeing my organs enough that I was in constant pain with absolutely no chance of respite from actual death.

But the worst accusation of all was that I'd been careless with her feelings. Again, willfully and with intent, as though I was the kind of person who couldn't see beyond himself.

And that fucking hurt.

If there was one thing I never wanted to do, would never on my life do intentionally, it was hurt her. In my world, the sun rose and set over Melody's smiles and laughs and anything else that made up the woman

I'd honestly thought was *the* woman for me. The one I'd settled down with. The one I'd marry. The one I'd spend the rest of my life with.

God, how in the hell did things go so wrong?

I'd spent the early part of this week trying to call her, trying to talk to her, trying to somehow get her to give me time to explain. But it was all to no avail. She either didn't answer or the calls went straight to voice mail.

Once, I'd even tried to ambush her at Janet and Bill's, but her mom had said she wasn't home. She'd had sad eyes as she said it, but I was still the enemy. No one fucks with a mama's little girl.

Basically, Melody was avoiding me, and I didn't know how in the fuck to fix this situation.

I wanted to—days without Mel were absolute hell. I just couldn't figure out *how*.

Fucking Dr. Obscene. I was really starting to hate that guy.

Too bad that guy is you…

"Congratulations!" Marlene cheered as I entered the office. "The show is finally over, and all of our new patient positions are filled. Thank God."

I attempted a half of a smile, but it didn't feel like the result was anything resembling happiness at all. Yes, the show was finally over. Yes, the focus would be shifting to Scott Shepard next week as episodes of the Dr. ER version of *The Doctor Is In* would start to air.

But I'd had a taste of everything I wanted—everything I really hadn't been sure I'd find out of life—and now I'd never have it again. Melody officially wasn't my nurse anymore, and even more officially, she wasn't my girlfriend either.

Fuck everyone and everything.

"Thanks. I…yeah. Thanks."

I shook my head and moved down the hall, but Betty didn't talk quietly enough to keep me from hearing the moment the gossip started up.

"God, he looks miserable."

"I knew that Load-y chick was bad news," Melissa chirped happily, like she'd won a prize or something. Goddamn rotten bitch.

"The whole reason I hired her on the spot was because she hadn't heard of the show. She wasn't lusting after him like all the other little tarts I met with. Clearly, that backfired."

"She probably wanted him from the beginning. Lied about not knowing about the show," Melissa proposed just because, without Melody here to defend herself, she could.

Going crazy from the comments but having literally zero energy to deal with them, I ducked inside the break room instead of going all the way to my office, tossed my briefcase down on a chair and sank my face into my hands.

Fucking shit, I don't want to live like this anymore.

Up and down, I scrubbed at the skin as if it could erase every miserable thing that had happened in the last week.

The show. The goddamn breakup. Life here, without her.

I hated all of it. And this one fucking week felt like it had lasted a year.

Frustrated that I couldn't get any relief from the terrible ache in my chest no matter how hard I scrubbed at my face, I snatched my brief-case from the chair and turned to leave the room when bright blue and pink icing caught my eye.

A cake, celebrating the end of the show.

Congratulations, Dr. Cummings, it read. *Dr. Obscene has cum to an end.*

Cute.

Obviously, I wasn't in much of a mood to gorge on sugar and celebrate the ending of a docuseries that had pretty much ruined my life.

All of the rage inside me built and broke at once, raising my arm with my briefcase up above my head involuntarily and bringing it down roughly…right on the cake.

Icing and perfectly moist crumbs shot out the sides and sprayed the fabric of my pants, the table, and everything else within a three-foot radius.

All of the women came running.

Marlene was actually the first to slide through the door—and start to cackle hysterically.

"Oh dear," Betty remarked.

Melissa and Beth just stood there, hands to their mouths.

Done with it all, I grabbed my icing-coated briefcase and headed back for the door.

"I'm taking the day off."

"Uh…" Melissa started as I shoved past her, forcing her to pull her body up and out of the way to avoid getting coated in icing. "But what about your patients?"

"I don't care. Give them to someone else."

And I didn't. I couldn't have cared fucking less in that moment if I'd tried.

Funny, I thought. *That damn show tried so hard to fuck up my career and failed. Until the last episode…where it broke two people's hearts.*

CHAPTER *thirty-two*

MY LIFE HAD BEEN REDUCED TO SIX CARDBOARD BOXES.
Sound familiar?

Well, it *was* familiar, only this time, I was moving *out* of my parents' apartment.

It'd been two weeks since I'd last seen Will. Two weeks since I'd quit my job at his practice and ended our relationship. Time had nearly stood still for the first few days. They'd gone about as awful as anyone could imagine they'd go for a twenty-nine-year-old woman, fresh off of another failed relationship, jobless, and still living with her parents. But, eventually, after I'd had time to isolate myself from the world and lick my wounds to a tolerable level of pain, I'd found a way to pick myself up off of the floor and put myself back on shaky, unstable feet.

It'd taken baby steps, but slowly and with determination, I found things to focus on, things to fill my days so that my mind didn't have much time to think about Will. And it had worked for the most part, besides when I'd lie in bed at night, without the warmth and comfort of his arms. It was those quiet, lonely moments when I'd realize just how much I missed him. Just how much I still loved him. But before I could do something rash like show up to his apartment and beg for him to take me back, I'd remember just how much he'd hurt me.

How much I'm willing to give up for one of his stupid smiles.

And that was still a very present reminder of why I needed to look forward, to *move on.*

My frugal money habits had turned out to be a positive force. Before quitting my job, I'd managed to save enough funds so I could put down a deposit on an apartment in SoHo. Of course, I was renting for cheap from a friend of the family and had only enough reserves to pay bills for six months until I figured out what my next career step would be, but it was something.

I wouldn't say life was good, but I was doing everything I could to make it better.

"Melody," my mother said as she peeked inside her work-out room, where I was putting the last of my clothes inside an empty box. "Do you want me to box up the microwave for you?"

I smiled and shook my head. "Thanks, Mom, but I don't need your microwave."

She'd been at this line of questioning for the past two hours. Like clockwork, every fifteen minutes, Janet would peek past the door and try to give me something from their apartment. First, it was the coffee table. Then it was the sofa. Although, Bill quickly interjected his opposition to that. My father lived for that leather sofa, and the worn-in print of his ass on the seat beside the window proved he'd spent more time on that piece of furniture than anywhere else in the apartment.

Basically, she'd been trying to give me everything but the kitchen sink. Though, I wouldn't have been surprised if she eventually offered to pack that up in a box, too.

Janet sighed and leaned her head against the doorframe. "I just want to help you somehow."

"Mom, you've already helped me enough," I said with a thankful smile. "Don't worry, I'm a big girl. I'll be just fine on my own."

"I guess I should just be happy that you're only moving a twenty-minute subway ride away instead of all the way across the country."

I grinned. "Exactly."

She slid open the door and walked toward me with a small white envelope in her hands. "Here," she said as she held it out toward me, and I tilted my head to the side in confusion.

"What is this?"

"Just a little something your father and I wanted to give you."

"Mom, seriously, you guys don't—"

She cut me off with a raise of her hand. "We do, actually. We want to give this to you."

I stared at the envelope. "I know it's money, Mom."

"Yeah, so?" She shrugged. "We're proud of you, Melody. And we just wanted to give you a little extra funds so that you have the time to find a job that you really love."

"Wow... I don't know what to say..."

"You don't need to say anything right now," she said with a soft smile. "Because there's actually someone here to see you."

Will?

My heart jumped into my throat at the mere thought of his name, but then it quickly plummeted to my feet when the person who replaced my mother in the doorway wasn't him.

"Need any help packing?" Georgia asked with a friendly grin and a motherly hand resting on top of her belly.

"What are you doing here?" I asked and hated that my voice held a hint of disappointment.

She shrugged. "Just wanted to make sure you're okay."

"Did Will send you here?" The words flew from my lips before I could stop them.

Jesus. Why couldn't my heart realize Will and I were done?

"No." She shook her head, but I didn't miss the faint spark that brightened her eyes and had her lips cresting into a soft smile. "Actually, Will didn't send me. I'm here because, even though you and my brother are no longer together, you're my friend and I want to be here."

Even though, Will and I had broken up, I'd kept in contact with Georgia *and* Cassie, mostly through text messages and phone calls, but also because those two were persistent as hell. So, it wasn't a surprise that she knew I was getting ready to move, but it was a bit of a surprise that she'd shown up, offering to *help* me move. Packing up boxes and moving shit didn't seem like the kind of strenuous activity someone who was four weeks away from her due date would want to engage in…

I searched her expression for an answer, and the nervous rap of her fingers against her belly had me wondering if she was here for more than just support.

"That's…uh…really sweet of you," I answered, but I really wanted to ask if this was some kind of ploy to get Will and me back together.

She flashed a knowing look. "You don't believe me."

"I guess I sort of believe you?" Honestly, I wasn't one hundred percent certain, but considering Georgia had schemed a few times just during the short time Will and I had been together, I wouldn't put anything past her.

"Trust me, I don't do favors for my brother." She giggled nervously, and my eyebrows quirked up. *Bingo.* She was definitely here to be Dr. Relationship and try to fix what had already been broken.

I grinned. "You really are a terrible liar."

"Ugh," she groaned. "And I thought I was getting better at it."

I laughed at that, and she offered an apologetic smile.

"Look," she explained and sat down in my favorite cozy reading chair that had been pushed haphazardly aside to the front of the room. "I'm here for both you and Will."

I flashed a skeptical look, and she held both hands in the air.

"I'm being completely honest."

"So you're here to convince me to get back together with your brother?"

She grinned. "Well, sort of, but mostly I'm just here because I wanted to make sure you were okay."

"Promise?"

She nodded, and this time, as her eyes softened and creased at the corners, I believed her.

"So, where did you end up renting an apartment?"

"I got real fucking lucky," I answered. "A friend of the family has offered to let me rent out one of their many investment properties in SoHo for an insanely low rent."

"That's amazing."

"I know, right?" I agreed as I used packing tape to close the filled box. "I'm excited to have my own place again."

"I couldn't imagine having to move back in with Dick and Savannah after being on my own."

"Trust me, it's fucking terrible," I said with exasperation in my eyes. "Honestly, I think Bill and Janet could give Dick and Savannah a run for their money in the inappropriate department."

Georgia laughed. "That's almost hard to believe. My mother is literally the most inappropriate person I know."

I grinned. "Believe me, it's no wonder they're friends."

I couldn't deny it made me feel sad to think of how well our families got along. Deep down, before Will and I had broken up, my heart had already been convinced that we were a forever kind of relationship.

"He misses you, you know," Georgia said into the quiet room, and I glanced up to meet her eyes. "He's been a complete mess since you ended things."

"I wish things were different."

"I know from personal experience that sometimes things aren't always what you think they are."

I tilted my head to the side, and she smiled softly.

"Kline and I," she explained. "Before we got engaged, I'd ended things with him out of assumptions. They were very, very wrong assumptions. And luckily for me, he didn't give up on us."

"He fought for you guys to get back together?"

She smiled like a woman who was madly in love with her husband. "Like you wouldn't believe."

The sad thing was, despite my happiness that Kline and Georgia had managed to find their way back to one another, all I could think was that if Will had been trying to fight for me, for us, I hadn't even given him the opportunity to do so. Since the moment I'd left his office, I hadn't answered a single one of his phone calls, texts, and one night, when he'd stopped by my parents' place, I'd made Janet tell him I wasn't home.

And the worst part of it all, I hated how miserable it made me feel.

I hated that there was a tiny little voice inside my head that whispered, *Did I make a mistake?*

CHAPTER *thirty-three*

Will

HEAD DOWN, WRITING OUT A PRESCRIPTION FOR THE PATIENT I'D JUST FINISHED WITH, I'd successfully talked myself out of tanking my entire fucking life for a woman.

Granted, she wasn't just *a* woman, she was the perfect fucking woman, but I wasn't going to think about that right now because when I thought about Melody, I got *pissed*.

And after seven days had passed without a returned call or text or fucking email from her, I realized that I had to go back to the drawing board and think of something else that would convince her to let me explain.

An "I can't live without you" gesture of some sort, but fuck if I knew what that entailed. Mel deserved more than just me standing in front of her door with something cliché like flowers that she couldn't even enjoy unless she wanted to break out in hives.

Melody deserved the world, and that's exactly what I wanted to give to her.

But after spending the last two hours of my day trying to rack my brain for the perfect gesture without any luck and riding the subway home with a cake-covered briefcase a week ago, I'd gone straight to my liquor cabinet, taken out a bottle of whiskey, and gotten the British version of pissed. So fucking sloshed, I couldn't lift my hand to pick up my cell phone, a cell phone I would undoubtedly have used to make a fool of myself if she happened to answer my call.

So sloshed that all this goddamn pain hurt less, if only just a little.

A week later, and the only step I'd managed in progress toward getting her back was step one of twelve where I put down the fucking bottle.

I was just ripping the paper off of the pad and pushing myself to stand when Thatch, a shit-eating grin on his face, stepped through the door.

"What are you doing here? How the hell did you get back here?"

Kline stepped through the door after him, followed by Wes, and my eyebrows pulled together even closer.

Wes rolled his eyes at my question. "Are you kidding? All that stupid giant has to do is wink, and women let him do anything."

Kline nodded. "Even after several case studies, I still don't understand it."

Thatch flashed a grin and smiled. "Come on. This face could sell fake titties to a nun, son."

Kline shook his head and stepped forward, dropping a thick stack of papers on my desk with a dramatic plop.

I looked down and took the weight of them into my hands as I asked, "What's this?"

"It's the paperwork for the clinic," he said simply, but the wave of shock nearly knocked me on my ass.

Huh? I squinted my eyes together in confusion. "The paperwork for the…?" *Did he just say clinic? As in, Melody's dream clinic?*

"*Clinic,*" Wes confirmed. "The one you talked to us about."

"But you guys said…" I paused and glanced around the room at each of them in surprise. "You laughed about this. Called me a love-sick idiot."

"We remember," Thatch spoke for the group.

"He doesn't realize love-sick idiots are our favorite," Wes stage-whispered.

"Oh," Thatch said with a laugh. "Well, they are. And we love the idea of the clinic. So long as my name is on it."

"Thatch, we talked about this," Kline said with a laugh.

"We did. We talked about putting my name up in big neon letters."

"Shut up, T," Wes muttered with a slight smirk on his face.

"No way. You can't shut me up. No one can shut me up! I am El Duce, and you are nothing but my minions."

"Jesus," Kline said through a sigh.

I shook my head, my mind spinning at how fucking amazing this was. How it would change countless women's lives—and dramatically improve the health of their babies. And then I thought about how the one person who wanted it most wasn't even here anymore, and my elation quickly faded. "It doesn't even matter."

"Of course, it matters," Kline replied confidently. But he didn't understand.

"No," I disagreed. "She's gone. From here. Probably from New York. She doesn't want anything to do with me."

"They always say that," Wes remarked.

"Mel isn't a part of a *they*. She's not like anyone else. When she said she was leaving, she meant it," I said, and fuck, the words tasted bitter on my tongue. "Believe me, I've spent the last two weeks of my life trying to get her to talk to me."

"They always fucking mean it," Thatch boomed, holding out his hand toward me and looking to the others in a gesture of *Do you believe this guy?* "But they very rarely want it. They just want you to stop fucking up."

Somehow, for some insane reason, I found myself looking to Thatch, of all people, for advice. "And how do I do that?" My voice sounded desperate even to my own ears.

"You don't. You're a dude. But you can work out a system where your fuck-ups line up with her tolerance, and everything comes together in a neat little package."

"Start by opening the clinic," Wes advised.

"We did already do all the paperwork," Kline mused.

"And ponied up the money," Thatch added.

Was it all that simple? Could a new medical facility and an honest effort on my part make it all better? Was it the *big* gesture? The kind of gesture that I'd been trying to figure out, but couldn't find...

"Uh-uh," Thatch clucked. "I can tell by your face you need to stop thinking right now. This isn't going to solve any of your problems. Not at all. In fact," he emphasized, "it's probably going to make it worse."

Kline nodded. "But only until you make it better."

Huh?

"I don't know what the fuck you guys are talking about. Is the clinic good or is it bad?"

They all looked to one another and smiled. *I'd love to know what's so fucking funny.*

"It's good," Kline promised. "But there's a chance she's gonna be pissed about it, but that only lasts until you can convince her it's a symbol of what you're willing to do for her."

"You see, William," Thatch cooed. "Women are very complicated creatures."

I flipped him off. Kline looked to the others and nodded to the door. "We'll get out of your hair. Just look through the paperwork and think about it, okay?"

"Me, think about it?" I asked. "You guys are the ones who are going to lose money."

Thatch turned back as he was moving through the door, his hands going to the top of the frame so he could lean back in. He filled the entire space. "Some things, young William, are worth the money," he said and followed it up with a wink and a smirk. "Plus, we could all use the tax deduction in the form of good charity and the ultimate gesture."

As they all filed out, giving waves and jerks of their chins, I looked down at the stack of papers on my desk and read the first few lines.

"Those do-gooding bastards," I muttered, the absurd amount of money they'd each pledged to the formation and operation of the clinic blinding me with the reality.

Frustrated by my own discord, by how conversely happy and twisted inside-out miserable I was, I banged around on my desk like it held important things and yanked open the middle drawer to toss some knick-knacks inside.

I didn't have a purpose, just a fuse to burn out, but as soon as the old drawer squeaked to a stop, so did I.

Right there, on top of everything else, was that very first tongue depressor.

Open wide! Everything you're looking for is inside yourself.

It was Mel. It was me. It was everything that was us, *together.*

And it was the only reminder I needed to make a plan.

It was time to get my shit together.

CHAPTER *thirty-four*

THIS SHOULD HAVE BEEN AN AWESOME DAY. I SHOULD HAVE FELT LIBERATED AND FREE and excited as I unpacked my belongings from their cardboard boxes and filled my new apartment with everything that was me, but I had never felt more alone.

It was a soul-crushing kind of loneliness, and it made it damn near impossible to set up my apartment without doing something ridiculous like painting everything black or impulsively running to the nearest shelter and bringing home a cat.

I didn't even like cats. I was more of a dog person, but I had a feeling me and a sassy feline would have more in common in this miserable moment than a happy, tail-wagging puppy.

I looked around my apartment, and it just didn't feel like home.

I honestly didn't know what was home anymore.

Will.

Ugh. One day, my heart would catch up with my brain and get the memo that it was time to move the fuck on from Will Cummings... *Right?*

It had been so fucking easy to move on from Eli.

Why in the hell was it so hard to move past Will?

Because you're in love with him, and love never makes sense. And deep down, you think you might have made a mistake...

Sigh. Thanks for the update, Subconscious.

Love was a real motherfucker if you asked me. It was single-handedly the best and worst thing that could ever happen to a person. It was bliss when things were good, but if shit hit the fan and you weren't with the one you loved, it left you pathetic, emotionally maimed, and wishing you could go back to a time in your life before that person stepped inside your world and made you realize how shitty everything was.

Once someone left their mark on your heart, it was permanent. It wasn't something that would disappear. And only time would allow for the discomfort to lessen until it became tolerable.

There is no amount of time that will make not being with Will tolerable…

Ugh. Jesus. I couldn't sit here and fixate on the past. I had to get out of this funk. I couldn't walk around my new apartment all day moping and doing nothing productive.

Music. I need music. Loud, obnoxious, mind-numbing music.

Jumping to my feet, I fired up my laptop and opened up my iTunes. Once Drake started to serenade me with "Hotline Bling," I worked toward finding my mojo and set my sights on unpacking my dishes and putting them in the kitchen cabinets.

Three Drake songs in and I was on a booty-shaking roll. Dishes were being stored, and the number of unpacked boxes was increasing at a slow but constant pace.

You've totally got this, Mel.

As I folded up a now empty cardboard box and set it near my garbage pile by the door, the sound of my phone ringing loudly reverberated off the empty walls and caught my attention. I snagged it off the counter and saw the name *Georgia* on my screen.

"Hey, Georgia," I started to greet, but I was immediately cut off by her heavy breathing and panicked voice.

"Mel! Oh my God… I think I need your help."

My eyes grew wide with concern. She didn't sound like her usual perky self at all. "What's wrong? Are you okay?"

"I think I'm in labor," she said through panting breaths. "Jesus, these contractions won't stop coming…"

Considering Georgia was still four weeks away from her due date, worry fell into my stomach like a bowling bowl.

"Holy hell… Where are you?"

"I'm actually downstairs," she breathed.

"Downstairs?"

"At your apartment," she explained in a tight voice. "I wanted to stop by and bring you a little housewarming gift, but holy hell, I think the extra blocks I walked to get your flowers pushed me into labor."

"Shit," I muttered. "Stay put. I'll be right down."

With lightning-quick speed, I tossed on shoes, grabbed my purse, and sped out of my apartment door, running down the two flights of stairs that led toward the main entrance. The second I stepped outside, I found Georgia sitting on the stoop with her hands clutching her stomach and her giant purse and a potted plant of daisies near her hip.

"How far apart are your contractions?"

"Like, four minutes, I think," she said and then groaned. "Jesus Christ, these hurt worse than last time…"

"Okay. Just take some deep breaths," I reassured and rubbed a soft hand down her stiff back. "I'll grab a cab, and we'll go straight to St. Luke's."

"Okay…Oh! Ow! *Motherfuckingshit!*"

Oh boy. Maybe Cassie was some kind of witch. It looked like Georgia was about to have her bundle of joy four weeks early.

CHAPTER *thirty-five*

MEL HAD OFFICIALLY MOVED IN TO HER APARTMENT AND OUT OF BILL AND JANET'S place.

Obviously, since she'd been pretty goddamn consistent about not answering my calls, I didn't find that information out from the source herself.

Rather, Georgia had been the one to fill me in, and even then, she'd done it reluctantly—the little traitor. Still, I didn't blame her. I liked Melody better than I liked me too.

I looked around the too quiet space that was my living room, and sadness clenched my gut. Everything sucked without Mel. My apartment. Work. My goddamn life. *Every-fucking-thing.*

I stared at the two lonely tongue depressors in my hand. I had no idea why I'd brought them home from work with me, but here they were, in my hands, and a constant reminder of what I'd lost when Melody walked out of my life.

I wanted her back in my space, back in my life, back *with me.*

I needed a plan.

Since the clinic, *her life's passion project,* had become reality, I needed to find the right way to present it to her. I needed her to understand that I would literally do anything for her, that I loved her, that I wanted to spend the rest of my life with her, and that no matter what happened between us, even if she still didn't want to be with me, I wanted her to be happy.

I'd been hoping Georgia would throw a surprise birthday party for Kline so that I could talk her into inviting Mel, but Kline didn't want to focus on anything but his wife and kid—soon to be *kids*—this year. I was disappointed, but reason told me Melody probably wouldn't have come—thanks to me—anyway.

Twirling my two lonely tongue depressors in my hand, I looked down at the screen of my phone again, but it gave me nothing.

No phone call. No text. No Facebook message to tell me how she was.

I just wanted to hear from her, even if it was only ten seconds to hear her voice. Every cell inside of my body felt starved for her—her presence, her smile, her laugh, basically anything that made up the woman I couldn't picture a future without.

Just then, a buzz made my skin hum as my phone danced across my leg. I looked at the screen for at least ten seconds before believing the name I read on the screen.

Melody.

Hope blossomed, filling me up like a balloon and lifting me off of my couch.

"Mel?" I answered, swiping to pick up as quickly as I could and shoving the tongue depressors in my back pocket so I didn't have to busy myself with holding them anymore.

"Will, it's—"

"I'm so glad you called," I interrupted because, fuck it, I'd always regret not putting my heart on the line. I already regretted having not done it sooner. I fucking *missed* her.

Her voice softened just slightly, but her overall tone was ominous. I braced myself. "Will, I'm calling for your sister."

Panic seized control of my veins and made them constrict.

"*Gigi?* What's wrong? Are you guys okay?"

"She's in labor."

Now? It was a good month early. *Shit*.

"Tell her to go to the hospital right now."

"Will, I know," she said, and a horn honking in the background filled the receiver.

Right, right. She's a nurse, for fuck's sake.

"Right. I'm sorry."

"No, it's fine. It's just…she's in the city. She was with me, actually. I'm taking her to St. Luke's. We're headed there now in a cab."

Launching myself over the back of the couch, I jammed my feet into my shoes sans socks, scooped my wallet and keys from the table by the door, and pulled it closed behind me before breaking into a jog toward the stairs.

"I'm on my way."

"We'll see you there," she said in a rush and ended the call.

I'd be calm once I got there and they did too, but this was my sister and my soon-to-be niece or nephew I was talking about. The more moving I did until then to keep me occupied, the better.

Down the stairs and through the lobby, I didn't even pause until the heavy glass door to the outside made me.

Forcing it open as quickly as I could, I maneuvered my way through the small crowd in front of my building and broke into a jog. The hospital was ten blocks away, but completely unwilling to wait for a cab or the subway, I ran every single one.

❦

"Gigi!" I yelled as soon as I spotted her in the waiting room at St. Luke's. They'd gotten her into a chair and Melody was with her, but I didn't understand why the fuck she wasn't back in a room yet.

"Oh, Will!" my sister sighed. "Thank God."

"What's going on? Are you okay?" I asked rapid fire, brushing her little blond ponytail off of her shoulder. "Is Kline on his way?"

Melody did her best to comfort me and take some of the pressure off of Georgia simultaneously. "She's okay. I tried to call Kline on the way, but it went to voice mail, so I left a message," she explained and glanced down at my sister. "But she wouldn't let them take her back to a room until you got here."

That was weird. Why the hell not? "Georgia?"

"I just panicked, Will." She shrugged but kept her hands tightly clutched to her belly. "I guess I just wanted you here first."

"Of course," I told her with a reassuring squeeze of her shoulder.

I met the eyes of the nurse on call, Gina, and signaled that I was going to take her back to a room. She nodded and picked up her phone as it rang.

Moving around Georgia's wheelchair, I took the handles at the back and started pushing her down the hall.

Gina covered the mouthpiece on her phone as we passed. "Room sixteen is open," she advised.

"Thanks."

Down the hall and into room sixteen in no time at all, I wheeled Georgia to a stop, locked the wheels, and then lifted her up and out of the chair and onto the bed.

"Will!" she yelled. "You don't have to carry me."

"Too late," I told her as she settled.

I moved to the corner to grab the fetal monitor, but Melody was already there, bringing it over. I smiled my sad smile of thanks, and her answering expression looked just as unhappy.

"Pull up your shirt, Gigi," I instructed. She paused, glancing to Melody behind me and then back again before complying.

"It's okay," I comforted. "I'm going to take care of you. Both of you."

She smiled a sweet but weird smile and finally lifted her shirt up to uncover her swollen belly.

I started hooking up the monitor, and Melody didn't hesitate to jump in and assist. I didn't even have to direct her, such was the flow of us working together.

Have I mentioned that I fucking miss her?

"Will," Georgia called, and I had to physically force my eyes away from Melody to look at her.

"Yeah?"

"You know I love you, right?"

I smiled. "Of course. I love you too, Gigi. You and Julia and this little angel are my world."

Her smile turned watery. "I know. And you're a huge part of ours too. And that's why I hope you'll forgive me for doing this."

"For doing what?" I asked, and Melody stood up straight like a rod. I could see her body out of the corner of my eye.

Georgia reached out and stilled my hands at her stomach, gentling her voice cautiously. "I'm not in labor."

My eyebrows shot together. "What do you mean, you're not in labor?"

"I mean...I faked it."

"You *what*?" Melody said at a near shout.

Georgia's face pinched, the absolute picture of anxious as she fast-talked to explain.

"I'm sorry. I know it was a really terrible thing to do to both of you, but I just want you together so bad, and you weren't talking at all… and… and I'm about to have this baby, and I can't deal with all of this discord…and now that Melody is my friend, I can't be objective…and the two of you have been stupid, and you need to talk." She gasped for air, and my eyes widened.

"Good God, that's a lot of information," I remarked as I got my bearings.

Melody stood beside her, breathing heavy and looking directly at me, and the pressure of it all came crushing down.

I turned my back to both of them, covering my eyes and trying not to lose my mind. My body didn't know how to cope with the mix of emotions. Frantic that Georgia had faked labor, relieved like all hell that she and the baby were okay, and crazily enough, even hopeful that I might actually have a chance to sort things out with Melody. All of it banged and swirled as my adrenaline crashed, and the sudden change in my chemical makeup made me feel like I might pass out.

Understandably, with all of that going on inside me, I didn't notice when Melody reached forward and pulled the tongue depressors out of my pocket. Only half of the stick fit inside, so the other half was sticking out, and my little mental breakdown had given her enough time to notice them.

"What are these?" she asked from behind me. The tremor in her voice made my heart jump as I turned around.

"Mel…"

"What are these?" she repeated, angry tears now moistening the whites of her eyes.

Now or never, Will.

Georgia, the little schemer, nodded encouragingly behind Mel's back. I didn't have to speak out loud for her to know what I was thinking.

"Will," Melody called, demanding my attention by shaking the tongue depressors almost violently. "I asked…*what are these?*"

Finally, I sighed, shrugging out a hand at the stupid things. "What do they look like?"

Georgia pursed her lips and shook her head rapidly behind her.

Not a good start, you idiot.

"Sorry. I've just…been holding on to both of them for a while, I mean," I corrected, softening my voice to something much more appealing.

"Why?" Melody questioned. "What were they for?"

"Well…" I paused. "That one" —I gestured to the one in her left hand that read *Open wide! Everything you're looking for is already inside of you*— "is the first one I ever wrote for you. Before the bouquet, before the first date…right after you turned me down, actually. I found it in my desk the other day." I laughed with a little self-deprecation. "I wrote it for you, but I never realized I might need it for me."

"For you," she stuttered. "Why'd you need it?"

"I thought it was obvious," I muttered. She shook her head.

I stepped forward and grabbed her hands as I said my next words. "Mel, I love you. Don't you know I've been lost without you?"

CHAPTER *thirty-six*

I'VE BEEN LOST WITHOUT YOU.

God, I knew the feeling.

The pressure inside of my chest made it feel like my heart was either attempting gymnastics or planning an emergency escape route from my body.

My heart wants Will.

Nothing had been the same since I'd broken up with him. I missed his laugh and his smile and the way his sense of humor always turned my day on its axis and pointed it directly at the sun. I just *missed* him, and my gut instinct told me that no amount of time would ever make that feeling go away.

But he'd hurt me. He'd hurt me really fucking bad.

"You hurt me so badly, Will," I whispered, and a pained expression formed his lips into a tight line.

"I know," he acknowledged with apology in his voice and remorse in his eyes. "I'm sorry I hurt you, Mel. God, you have no idea. The idea that I made you feel like I was hiding things from you or I was being careless with your feelings hasn't stopped tearing me up inside. I don't want to hide anything from you. I want to share everything with you. My life. I want my life to be *our* life."

"I just don't understand," I said. "When we talked that day in the exam room…" I glanced to Will's sister, slightly uncomfortable that she was listening to all of this, but she did her best to shrink into herself. "…You told me 'never.' You'd never *done that* at work."

He sighed. "I used to be different. Young, stupid…easy," he explained, and a self-deprecating smile crested his lips. "I know that doesn't exactly make me sound like the world's greatest catch, but I'm being honest. The sex with Emily in the on-call room wasn't even a memory. Truth is, it wasn't the first time I'd hooked up in the hospital, but it was the last. When I answered your question, I wasn't even thinking about that shit. I'd kept my dick out of the practice, and since the moment I laid eyes on you, I kept it out of everywhere else. I'd never done with anyone what we did that day. I've never done with anyone what we always do… You and I, we make love, Mel, even when we're fucking."

It wasn't the flowery apology I would have dreamed of with Scott Eastwood, but it rang a whole lot more true. Still, uncertainty clung to me like the bloodsucking leech it was.

"My past is my past, Mel," he said in a quiet voice. "I can't take it back. Before you, my dating status was a big jumbled mess of pointless flirting and occasional, meaningless hookups, and that's pretty much it. I wasn't even interested in a long-term relationship or marriage until you."

Marriage? He wanted to marry me?

He reached out his hand and linked it with mine and gazed deep into my eyes. "I'm sorry you had to feel like I lied to you. I'm sorry you had to watch that awful episode of the show without any type of warning. I know it's not the same, but I know what the rock in my stomach felt like every time they surprised me with something else, so I can only imagine what watching that must have been like for you. But mostly, I'm sorry I made you feel like I was cavalier and thoughtless with you, no better than the viewers' version of Dr. Obscene." His thumb rubbed at the skin on the back of my hand with steady strokes. "I'm so sorry I hurt you, Mel."

Just one simple touch and my body felt like it had finally come home. I looked down at our interlocked fingers and knew in an instant. *We belonged together.* The urge to sob became nearly relentless.

God, I felt like I'd been starved for his touch for one hundred years.

He gently gripped my fingers. "I know I fucked up, and I know you might never forgive me, but I promise, when it comes to you, I only want the best for you, Mel. I miss you, but if you think you're better off without me, that's what I want. Anything to keep you from hurting again."

"Will," Georgia whispered, and surprised, we both looked in her direction. She pulled a stack of papers out of her purse and held them out for him. "I think you need to show her these."

Once he'd taken the papers and his eyes scanned the first page, a sharp, humorless laugh left his lips. "Gigi, you're fucking insane. I honestly have no idea how you managed to get your hands on these. They were just signed yesterday morning."

She giggled and rolled her eyes. "Just show them to her, Will."

"Well," he started, but he paused when his gaze locked with mine. A million different emotions crossed his face. Uncertainty. Hope. Determination. But the one that stood out the most was *love.* "These are for you, Mel." He held the papers out toward me, and my heart skipped three beats in anticipation.

"What is this?" I asked as I glanced down at the crisp, white sheets.

"It's your dream."

I searched his gaze for a brief, poignant moment, but nothing had changed. His blue eyes contained an ocean's worth of love. I moved my gaze to the top page and scanned the document for an answer.

Oh my God.

A gasp left my lips at the heading alone.

Official Investors' Contract for The Melody Marco Women's Clinic

My dream.

Immediately, my eyes filled with more tears, and this time, they found their way out in a tiny stream. I'd been so focused on staying away from Will so that I didn't give up all the other things I really wanted, and the clever bastard had found a way to bundle those things together and pull them out of his pocket.

Baffled, I looked at Will. And then I looked at the contract again. I even skimmed over the entire document and found that Kline, Thatch, and Wes had been the ones who'd helped make this come to fruition. "You got the funding for the clinic?" I asked like a moron, my voice just above a whisper.

"I want you to be happy, Mel. Even if that doesn't mean I get to be with you, I still want the best for you." He tapped the second tongue depressor, still trapped inside the tight clutch of my hand. I shifted the papers and forced my hand to open so I could read it.

Your tonsils are almost as big as your heart.

"It's a lie, you know," he said, and I startled, my eyebrows pulling together.

"Your heart is way bigger."

I had to pull my lips in on each other to fight the sting of tears buzzing in my nose. "You did all of this for me?"

His response was immediate and without hesitation. "I'd do anything for you."

"God, Will," I whispered through the emotion clogging my throat. "This is… It's just…"

"You deserve this," he said and slid his fingers underneath my chin until my eyes locked with his. "This is your purpose, Mel. This is what you're supposed to do. And that's why this is now *your* clinic."

Somehow, Will had not only found a way to find investors for the one thing I'd become most passionate about, but he'd also named the clinic after me. It was almost too much information to process at one time.

"W-what do you mean, *my* clinic?"

He grinned. "I think it's safe to assume that The Melody Marco Women's Clinic has to be run by Melody Marco herself."

"God, Will." My lungs stuttered with each inhale and exhale. "I don't even know what to say…"

"Melody Marco, I'm in love with you," he said and, like a drum, my heart made itself known inside my chest. "I don't want anyone else. Just you. Beautiful, brilliant, perfect you. I know, without a doubt, that I'll never love anyone the way that I love you."

Each one of his words touched my heart, and like a thread, they slowly sewed the wounded pieces back together.

"You're everything to me," he continued. "You're the one and only person I want to wake up to every morning and the one I want to hold while we fall asleep at night. When I see you, I see forever, and I don't want a life without you in it."

I didn't want a life without Will either.

I wanted him. I wanted us. And I wanted forever, too.

"I love you," I whispered through my tears. "So, so much."

"Yay!" Georgia squealed, but Will didn't seem to notice.

He closed the space between us and enfolded his arms around my body until he lifted me off of my feet and wrapped my legs around his waist. "I love you, Melody. I love you so fucking much."

I burrowed my face into his neck and inhaled his scent—clean laundry, his soft cologne, *Will*. God, I'd missed him, missed this, missed *us*. The mere thought of thinking I could have lived a life without him made my breath come in short pants.

I'm finally home.

I leaned back, and when my teary gaze met his, he asked, "So, are you going to accept the position to run the clinic?"

I giggled through my tears. "I guess it'd be a little weird if Melody Marco were working somewhere else, huh?"

A soft smile slid across his lips. "Those patients need you, Mel."

"And I need those patients," I stated and wrapped my arms tight around his neck. "But there's something else I think I need even more."

"What?" I almost laughed at the fact that he looked genuinely confused, until I remembered that that doubt was doubt I'd planted there.

I leaned close and put everything I felt into one word. *"You."*

He brushed his nose softly against mine, excitement making his limbs flex into me. "You love me?"

I nodded. "I love you."

"Thank God," he muttered and melded his lips to mine. The kiss started out slow and tender, until we both felt the electricity of our special bond spark to life. Will's lips became more persistent, and mine followed suit as I kissed him hard and deep and without concern for where we were or who might have been watching.

"Aww!" Georgia cheered and clapped her hands excitedly.

Her voice brought us both back to the present, and I giggled against Will's mouth.

He pulled his lips away from mine and met my gaze. "I think it's time we got the fuck out of here."

"Uh…yes, please," I agreed on a laugh, and he smiled.

Just then, Kline came sliding in the door at a run, his long fingers reaching out and grabbing the doorjamb to help slow himself down. "Georgie?" he asked, concern stark in his features.

Will and I bugged our eyes out at each other at the same time. *Completely in sync.*

Georgia just smiled. "Hey, honey. Guess what? I finally got good at lying!"

Kline was a smart guy, so it never took him long to catch up. Plus, he couldn't have missed how unconcerned with Georgia Will and I were.

"I take it you're not really in labor?"

As Georgia shrugged, I turned my attention back to Will and got lost in his smile.

Georgia and Kline could work out their own problems from here. I wanted a reunion. "Take me *home*, Will," I whispered into his ear, but it didn't spur the instant, on-the-move action I'd hoped for. Instead, he paused, and his blue eyes locked with mine.

"You are my home, Melody."

Swoon. Yeah, those words were way better than anything else I could've imagined in my head. Even, the dirty, naked types of scenarios I'd started to picture…

God, I love him.

I pressed a gentle kiss to his lips and whispered against his mouth, "Ditto, Doc."

epilogue

Will

"No."

"Come on, Mel. You have to realize how cool this would be for me," I explained, and my wife snorted in laughter as if it was the most ridiculous thing she'd ever heard.

Yes, folks, you heard that right, we are officially married.

Mr. and Mrs. Will Cummings, or if you ask Mel,

Mr. and Mrs. Melody Marco.

It only took me one year after she took me back to get her to walk down the aisle.

And it'd only taken another six months after that

before she got pregnant.

Believe me, I already know.

I'm the luckiest bastard in the free world.

My beautiful wife and I had been having the same conversation for the past two weeks.

I wanted to deliver our baby and she thought I was out of my mind and needed to deal with the fact that I would only be there as "*support at the head of the bed, not face first with her vagina and guiding our baby into the world."* Her words, not mine.

"I do," she responded with an exasperated smirk. "What I'm not realizing is what gave you the impression you're at all important in this scenario."

It sounded bad, but in reality, I was surprised she wasn't saying worse. After all, she was thirty-eight weeks pregnant, and I'd been persistent in telling her that I planned to deliver the baby myself and have someone stand in for me as coach.

"I'd say I played an important role in the making of the baby."

She sighed and rolled her eyes. "In implanting the baby with a chromosome. *I* made this baby. Fed it and housed it for nine fucking months. My feet are swollen, my bladder is destroyed, and I'll never sneeze without peeing again."

"Mel…" I said, smiling so big I thought my face might split in two. She was very nearly miserable, but she was still as lovable—and beautiful—as ever. And she was all mine.

She huffed, melting just a little in the sweet heat of my smile. "If you deliver the baby, who's going to be my coach? And don't you dare say Marlene."

I laughed. "It's going to be kind of hard for Marlene to be your coach when she's busy being your nurse."

In a surprising turn of events, once Melody had taken over the position of running the Women's Clinic, she'd hired Marlene to keep the younger nurses on staff in order.

I'd had my doubts when she'd told me of her plans to hire the world's grumpiest nurse in America, but somehow, the two of them were just the right amount of sweet and gruff to keep the clinic running like a well-oiled machine.

Their outreach and charitable successes had far exceeded anyone's expectations, and to Thatch's delight, had made the men behind the big investment look like the saints of New York City.

"William Morris Cummings!" she exclaimed with an accusing index finger pointed in my direction. "I will *murder* you. Not to mention, she just put her resignation in the other day. One more month and Marlene will be retired. *Finally.*"

I chuckled. "Yeah, that's what you said six months ago, and she never actually went through with it. The day that woman retires will be the day they're putting her in the ground."

"Oh my God," she gasped. "That's an awful thing to say."

"Oh, don't act all high and mighty over Marlene. You know she will literally be a nurse until the day she dies. There's no way she could give up a job that allows her to complain about anything and everything."

I watched as she bit back her smile and shook her head.

"Anyway, Marlene's fake retirement aside, I was thinking more along the lines of Georgia to be your labor coach."

She groaned. "Eh, I don't know. Sometimes your sister stresses me out."

"I'll give her a pep talk beforehand, I promise. Nothing but positivity and light and unicorns and rainbows and shit."

"Oh my God." She sank her head into her hands. "It's gonna be like being coached by someone on LSD."

"At least she's been through it before, right?"

"I guess," Melody grumbled. "And she's probably the best person on our family roster...except for Kline. Maybe he would want to be my coach," she said with a calculated raise of her eyebrow.

She wasn't fooling me, though. There was absolutely no way my Mel would be comfortable having her brother-in-law coach her through labor. She didn't need to know I knew all of that, though. She just needed to think I was willing to do whatever she needed. "Maybe he would. I'd be happy to ask him."

Her eyes narrowed as she turned away and whined, "I really hate you."

I chuckled. "Why? Because I'm accommodating of your every wish?"

"Because you make me feel like a bitch! Why do you have to be so helpful? Why can't you be an asshole?"

"You want me to be an asshole?" I asked even though I knew my wife was full of baloney. She secretly loved the fact that I treated her like a goddamn queen. The joke was on her, though. She deserved to be nothing less than the center of my universe.

"Ugh. No," she finally admitted as she moved, well, more like waddled toward the hallway. But she only made it four steps before she stopped, clutched her back, and grimaced.

The way she was rubbing at her lower back made me take notice and get serious. "You okay, baby?"

"Yeah." She nodded. "Just…" Her eyes pinched in pain. "Ow."

I stood up straight in one smooth motion and was at her side between one breath and the next. "Are you in labor?"

"Stop," she sighed and waved me away with the hand *not* constantly rubbing at her back. "Don't be ridiculous. It's probably just something I ate."

Not even listening, I moved down the hall to my home office, opened the bottom right door of my desk, and pulled out the portable cardiotocography machine, otherwise known as an electronic fetal monitor.

A quick trip back down the hall, and I was pulling up Melody's shirt to strap the band onto her stomach.

"Oh my God. You're ridiculous. You don't think I'd know if I were in labor?"

I paused my work at her stomach to meet her annoyed gaze and raise just one eyebrow. She rolled her eyes. "Okay, so maybe I haven't done it before, but I have two more weeks to go."

"And babies sometimes come early. Another thing you already know," I teased.

She flipped me off as I finished getting her set up and hooked to the monitor. Fifteen seconds later, a contraction read out on the screen.

"Well, well, well, what do we have here?" I goaded as I palpated her abdomen with both hands. "And an extremely strong contraction, at that. I mean…I'm not a labor expert…or maybe I am?" I questioned, and she huffed out her irritation in one long exhale.

"Fine!" she finally admitted and threw both hands into the air. "So, I'm in labor, but we both know that there's still plenty of time before we need to go to the hospital."

I shook my head, unsatisfied with the wait-and-see approach when I'd spent so many years in school to know better. "Come on," I said as I picked her up and carried her down the hall. "We're going to check your cervix."

"No! Will!"

"Sorry, Mel. Just lie back and pretend we're playing out your favorite doctor fantasy."

"I don't have a doctor fantasy!"

"You should," I advised. "I hear they're really dreamy."

She growled at me as I set her down on the bed and pulled her shorts and panties down her legs. "Relax, baby. Just let me check, okay?" I soothed as I ran my hand up the soft skin of her thigh. "I love both of you. Just let me make sure you're both going to be okay."

Properly mollified, she relented. "Okay. Fine."

I helped her scoot up and onto the bed as she clutched her stomach and grimaced with another contraction. Once she was positioned comfortably, I sat beside her hip and she pulled up her legs.

I rubbed her clit in the hopes of making a little natural lubrication, and she moaned, startled.

I smiled. "Maybe there are some benefits to letting me be your doctor?"

She flipped me off again and lay back, but that didn't mean she wasn't noticeably wet.

Using the moisture to ease my entrance, I pushed my fingers inside and moved straight to the cervix. As the three fingers I'd inserted slid easily inside, my eyes got a little glassy with anticipation.

"You're already dilated close to four centimeters, Mel."

"What?" she all but yelled.

"Time to go to the hospital, baby," I directed, pulling my hand free and wiping her clean with a washcloth.

"Ah, fuck. Fuck, fuck, fuck," she chanted.

But I'd never felt calmer in my life. Everything that mattered to me in this world was going to be in my arms within the day.

And they'd be getting there safely—I'd make sure of that.

Melody

"More ice chips, Mel?" Georgia asked, and I shook my head.

I didn't need ice chips. I needed my epidural to actually start working.

Jesus, Mary, and the Beatles, this pressure is fucking terrible.

Okay, maybe it was working, but holy hell, it wasn't taking this insane pressure away. I might not have been feeling the contractions in my stomach and lower back, but I sure as hell was feeling them in my vagina. It was like a bowling ball was trying to slowly roll its way out of my body.

Four hours after we'd arrived at the hospital and I'd gotten an epidural and dilated to ten centimeters at a pretty quick pace. But the baby was still a little high up, and since everything looked good on the fetal monitor, I'd chosen to try to let the baby descend farther before I started pushing. The fact that my husband was intent on delivering our baby himself might have also influenced my decision to wait a while before pushing.

Normally, I was madly in love with Will. But today, I was kind of in the middle of having his baby, and he seemed intent on driving me crazy with his resolve to deliver our baby himself.

I mean, he's crazy, right?

I understand that my husband is an OB/GYN.

> *But what I don't understand is why he'd think he should be the one whose face is all up in my crotch while I push out a baby from my lady parts.*

Intimacy is one thing, but this is a whole other kettle of insanity.

At that very moment, Will made his entrance back into the room. He'd changed out of his jeans and T-shirt and into a fresh pair of navy scrubs.

Oh, for fuck's sake.

"How are you feeling, baby?"

"No," I retorted and pointed a finger in his direction. "If you're here for delivery purposes, you need to turn back around and move your ridiculous ass back out that door."

He completely ignored my demands, and I was too numb to get out of the bed to enforce them.

The bastard. Using this goddamn epidural against me.

Will chuckled and sat on the bed near my hip. "Has the pressure gotten more intense?"

"No," I said through gritted teeth, another contraction wreaking havoc on my body. If the pressure I was feeling was any indication of where the baby was, I'd say my little bundle of joy was about one minute away from peeking out and saying hello.

He quirked a questioning brow. "Are you sure about that?"

"Yes," I lied. I knew the baby was probably crowning at this point. What I didn't know was how long I could hold out until Will just gave up on the whole "I'm going to deliver our baby" thing...

Will ignored my response and grabbed a sterile glove from the supply cabinet by the monitors. Two seconds later, he was gloved up and trying to pull the sheet down with this free hand.

"No." I gripped the sheets and held them close to my chest.

"Melody," he chastised and flashed me a determined look.

"No, Will."

"We need to check you," he said in a tender voice. "You and I both know it's probably about time that you started pushing."

I ignored him. I was on the "No push until Will puts his street clothes back on" plan. It wasn't a traditional birth plan, but it was mine all the same.

"We *can* check me," I responded. "We, being any other physician on this floor that is not you."

"You really want Dr. Elders to come in here and check your cervix?"

Ugh. No.

I didn't respond, and he took that as a green light, pulling the sheets down and instructing me to relax my legs.

His eyes lit up before he'd even touched me. "It's time, Mel," he said and hopped off the bed to push the nurse call button.

"What?" I questioned with wide eyes. "What are you doing?"

He ignored me and pulled the sterile delivery table toward the bed.

"Will, you're not delivering our baby."

He came over to me and sat at the edge of the bed. "Melody, I need to be the one to deliver my beautiful daughter or son. I want to make sure that everything goes smoothly and that our baby enters this world healthy and happy."

The earnest look in his eyes had me folding like a house of cards. "Okay." I found myself agreeing before I could even think twice about it.

Even though my husband was exasperating and a bit of a weirdo for being so hands-on during my pregnancy, I didn't want anyone else to guide our baby into the world. Sometimes, deliveries didn't go smoothly. Sometimes, emergent situations happened when you least expected them. And I knew, without a doubt, that Will would make sure our baby was okay.

A nurse came into the room to assist, putting my legs in stirrups while Will got his instruments ready at the foot of the bed.

But I didn't have time to watch what was happening around me. Another contraction hit me harder than a Mack truck. "Oh, holy hell and tomato sauce," I groaned as the pressure had reached the point where the urge to push was unavoidable. "I gotta push, Will," I exclaimed. "I gotta push right now." Even though I was most likely already pushing. The body has a way of forcing that shit.

He looked up at me and nodded encouragingly. "Good job, Melody. If you keep pushing like that, our baby will be here any minute."

"Just breathe," the nurse reassured. "Take a few deep breaths, give your baby all of that good oxygen, and get rest until the next contraction."

"Oh God. The next one is already here," I moaned and started to push through the pressure.

"Good job, Melody," the nurse encouraged.

"You totally got this," Georgia whispered into my ear and brushed a lock of sweaty hair out of my eyes.

"Keep going, baby," Will instructed. "There's the head," he said as he guided our baby out of the birth canal. "One more big push like that, and our baby will be here."

I pushed and I pushed and I pushed.

And I pushed some more. Seriously, they call the miracle of birth "labor" for a reason.

Until the most beautiful cry I'd ever heard rang loud and clear in my ears.

"It's a girl!" Will said with awe in his voice.

"Aww!" Georgia cheered, keeping her voice low and soothing in such a way that I knew Will had given her instructions.

Tears ran down my cheeks as I watched my husband hold our baby girl in his arms, his eyes wet with emotion. "You did it, Melody." He placed our squirming baby girl on my chest. "You just made my life. *Again.*"

"I love you," I said, staring deep into his eyes.

"I love you, too," he whispered.

And when I looked down at the dark hair and pink cheeks and big eyes of our beautiful—perfect—baby girl, I whispered against her forehead. "And I love you, sweet girl. Happy birthday, Emma."

THE*end*

Love Will, Melody, and the St. Luke's crew?
Grab the next in the series, Dr. ER, and meet sexy-as-hell player
Dr. Scott Shepard.
P.S. If you scroll a little further, you'll be graced with Dr. Shepard
himself in the form of an exclusive excerpt from Dr. ER,
for your eyes only. :)

BEEN THERE, DONE THAT TO ALL OF THE ABOVE?
Never fear, we have a list of nearly FORTY other titles to keep you
busy for as long as your little reading heart desires! **Check them out
at our website: *www.authormaxmonroe.com***

**COMPLETELY NEW TO MAX MONROE AND DON'T KNOW
WHERE TO START?**
Check out our Suggested Reading Order on our website!
www.authormaxmonroe.com/max-monroe-suggested-reading-order

WHAT'S NEXT FROM MAX MONROE?
Stay up-to-date with our characters and our upcoming releases by
signing up for our newsletter:
www.authormaxmonroe.com/newsletter!

You may live to regret much, but we promise it won't be subscribing
to our newsletter.
Seriously, we make it fun! Character conversations about royal babies,
parenting woes, embarrassing moments, and shitty horoscopes are
just the beginning! If you're already signed up, consider sending us a
message to tell us how much you love us. We really like that. ;)

Follow us online:

Facebook: www.facebook.com/authormaxmonroe

Reader Group: www.facebook.com/groups/1561640154166388

Twitter: www.twitter.com/authormaxmonroe

Instagram: www.instagram.com/authormaxmonroe

TikTok: https://vm.tiktok.com/ZMe1jv5kQ

Dr. ER Excerpt

Scott

"Yo! Scott!" Justin, one of the day nurses, greeted me and I slapped him a high five.

It was the changing of the guards, the switch of the shift, and things in New York City were about to get motherfucking interesting.

Trust me, as a doctor of ten years, and the head of the Emergency Department at St. Luke's Hospital for the last three and a half, I'd seen just about any injury you could conjure in your depraved mind—and then some.

From stabbings, shootings, and muggings to broken kneecaps from a trip on the crowded sidewalks to sex toys trapped deep within the female genitalia—medicine in an emergent capacity knew no boundaries.

Fortunately for my patients, I didn't know many either. While *work* was the most important part of work—always—I didn't think that meant I couldn't have fun at the same time.

Most attending physicians would use their station as head of the department to get *out* of night shifts, but not me. The nights were when you met the most interesting characters, experienced the weirdest of cases, and I'd always been a night owl anyway. I did this shift as often as I could.

"Another day, another dollar," I shouted back as Justin pushed open the door to the locker room.

He paused with a smirk. "Do they shove them in your G-string, *Dr. Erotic?*"

I laughed. Not only was I comfortable with the nickname my ever-growing reality show fame had brought me, I lived for it. Nine weeks of being on the air, and I felt like I was on top of the world. Some might call me outgoing—others might call me an attention whore. Either way, I didn't mind living in the limelight.

"I guess it depends on how good of a job I do," I teased before signing off with a wave and picking up my pace. I wasn't necessarily late, but I had shit to do before my shift started.

Around the corner and into the thick of it, I dodged a bed in motion and high-fived the patient, an often-drunk man named Barney who showed up here when he got into more trouble than the actual big purple dinosaur. Believe me, this Barney didn't spend his days sitting around a campfire singing nursery rhymes. The man made a career out of drunken shenanigans that resulted in injuries I had to fix.

"Suck dick, Dr. Shepard," he called over his shoulder.

"Only if you pay me, Barn," I struck back.

We really liked each other.

No, really, we do. He just has a unique way of showing it. As for me… Is your job this entertaining? I didn't think so.

As soon as I rounded the corner, I made a beeline straight for the desk, teasingly shoving Sherry, a cute little nurse from Tennessee, out of the way on the computer, and logged in to my sign-in. As of now, 10:58 p.m., I was officially on the clock.

Now that the formalities of the facility were out of the way, it was time for *my* formalities. My routine, my comfort zone, my way to get ready for all of the gruesome things these overnight hours could throw at me.

The warm-up. With questionable vocals and dance moves better than most toddlers, I took to the open airwaves, using my diaphragm to project fully into the space.

"Oh, baby, when you talk like that," I sang, calling the attention of several nurses around me. I turned up the volume on the computer behind the nurse's station, and a slow Latin beat thumped an instantly familiar rhythm.

"My hips don't lie," I crooned along with Shakira after missing a few lines while I was busy climbing atop the desk chair.

Most of my coworkers smiled. They were used to my routine—I'd been doing it for years, changing out the song every week or so—a musical warm-up for the things to come on the night shift in St. Luke's Emergency Department. Though, I had to admit, Shakira found her way into the rotation the most. There was something about her that kept me mildly obsessed. *Probably all of the tongue control that comes with rolling Rs.*

There weren't many patients in here yet, the real mayhem of a weekend overnight in New York City was just starting up. But the ones who looked on with mild distrust and disbelief at my antics until the rest of the staff fell victim to participating one by one, the beat of Shakira too powerful to resist. I watched as some of their faces melted to amusement, while others skipped surface-level delight and jumped straight to recognition.

Yep, I'm that guy. Dr. Erotic, here in the flesh. There was a GIF of me out there hip rolling as I did one of these very warm-ups, something they'd featured heavily on the show, if I wasn't mistaken.

A few cell phones appeared, but I was used to that, me popping up on YouTube and Facebook and Insta-fuck and whatever else there was to post elaborately staged pictures of fake reality these days.

I'm not anti-social media like it might sound. I'm just a liver, a doer, a partier of sorts. I'd much rather be out and about than posting pictures of myself with my dinner plate. If Shakira appeared in front of me right now, I wouldn't waste my time taking her picture, if you catch my drift.

Although, when one of the episodes aired featuring her song, "Whenever, Wherever," she tweeted me, and I'd be lying if I didn't admit it thrilled me. I just wish "tweeted" meant something more physical—dirtier. Seriously, I'm down with whatever freaky shit she's into.

"Dr. Shepard!" Debbie, the head nurse in charge of admission yelled, completely interrupting the climax of my performance. In her midforties with a generic blond bob, serious hazel eyes, and little to no makeup, Deb was the walking, talking dictionary definition of "business." She meant it, she enforced it, and she got shit done.

In real terms, she was a pain in my ass.

"Geez, Deb," I grumbled as I climbed down from my perch halfway on top of the desk. "Why do you always have to undermine my performances?"

She smirked and shook her head. "Because they're terrible. And you're needed on stage B, aka Bay Two, for an actual patient, that has to do with your actual job."

"I'm offended, Deb. You should know better than anyone that the warm-up is a crucial part of my process. Working conditions are integral to success. Would you consider patient care without your gloves?"

"Scott—"

"I think not!" I cried, fake outrage making my voice carry. Several sets of eyes followed us closely.

"Stop making a scene," Debbie chastised. "Aren't you tired of making a fool of yourself?"

"I'll never tire of it, Deb," I vowed solemnly. She sighed. "Not ever."

"Fine. Then make a scene in Bay Two. But do it while you're sewing up a head lac, would you?"

"I live to serve you, my sweet emergency goddess."

"Jesus Christ," she grumbled, shoving the patient chart into my chest. "They don't pay me enough for this shit."

Fortunately, Sherry found me far more amusing than Deb did, if the glowing smile on her face as she looked on was any indication. I winked at her as a reward.

"Scott!" Deb yelled from across the room.

Whoops. Patient in Bay Two. Apparently, I wasn't moving fast enough.

"I sure hope you're close to bleeding out," I told the faceless patient behind the curtain as I approached Bay Two. "You've interrupted my performance, gotten me scolded by Deb—"

The chink of the curtain hooks rang out into the space as I yanked it back, and I immediately stopped speaking.

Well, I'll be damned. She's cute. Shoulder-length, half-curl-rumpled hair, sexy smoky eyes with glowing green irises, and a body that could kill. She also had a fucking mess on her forehead, a blood-soaked rag and both of her hands pushing into it, but that was just a surface detail.

"You know what?" I asked her rhetorically. "Strike all of that. Don't you even worry about interrupting me."

She rolled her eyes and sank back onto the bed. "I wasn't worried about you at all. The gushing, bleeding wound in my forehead? That concerns me."

I smiled at her candor and sarcasm and then nudged at her hands with my forearm. "I'm concerned too. Truly. So move your hands."

She narrowed her eyes, and I laughed. "I'm concerned. I promise." I made an X over my heart with one hand and grabbed some gloves from the tray beside the bed with the other. "This is my job."

"According to your argument with Deb, performing is your job—"

"No, no," I interrupted as I popped the second glove into place. "You can't actually use my argument with Deb as evidence. That's just routine. It's mundane, actually."

"Listen, Doctor…?"

"Shepard. Scott Shepard. You can call me Scott."

"Listen, Dr. Shepard…"

I laughed at her obvious disinterest.

"Can you just treat my injury?"

"Of course. If you just move your hands."

"It's fucking bleeding! I'm holding pressure. Everyone says to hold pressure."

"That's true. Until you get to the hospital. Where the doctor—" I pointed to myself "—that's me—needs to actually look at the cut to assess and treat it."

"But what if what it needs is pressure?"

"I'll apply some."

"Promise?" she asked, big, mischievous eyes turning doey right before my own. *Wow. That's talent.* Usually, my conversational opponents didn't have as much expression control as I did. I was impressed.

"Promise."

"Ow," she muttered as she pulled her hand with the blood-soaked cloth away. "Fucking ball sac."

I shook my head, amusement making my cheeks feel heavy. "And here I thought I was looking at a forehead."

"Shut up," she mumbled. Again, I found myself smiling at her.

Grabbing some cleaning solution and a swab, I cleaned up the area until the actual laceration was visible. Four, maybe five, stitches, tops.

"Oh, this isn't bad at all."

"Says the person not bleeding." She held up the rag in her hand as evidence, the corner of her mouth curling up in protest. "Look at this."

I shrugged. "Head wounds bleed a lot."

"Because they're a big deal," she hedged. Thanks to the head injury, she was careful with any expressive use of her eyebrows, but I could tell the restraint took effort. I'd never seen it done, but uninhibited, I was convinced her eyebrows would be able to contort themselves into an illustration of the middle finger.

"Only sometimes," I argued easily.

The patient's medical file that Deb had so gently shoved into my chest felt like it would slow the conversation down, so I did the Cliff Notes version of surveying any important, life threatening information and tossed it to the side and grabbed a syringe and suture kit. With a quick and gloved hand, I pricked the area with a fast-acting dose of numbing agent and gave it a few seconds to take effect.

"I'm really starting to dislike you."

"Only starting?" I asked with a mocking smirk. "I haven't liked you yet."

"I was being polite."

I laughed, poking at the area a couple of times to test her level of feeling. She didn't even flinch, so I grabbed my needle and thread and got to work. "Really? This is you polite?"

"Is this you professional?"

I shook my head with a frown. "Professional is such a dirty word. Stuffy and boring. Who the hell wants to be professional?"

"Most physicians."

I pretended to yawn. "Bor-ing."

Her eyes lit suddenly, the way they always did when people realized who I was. For the first time, maybe ever, something panged in my chest that wasn't excitement.

"Ohh. You're—"

"Scott Shepard," I finished for her, looping through the skin once, and then again.

Her eyes narrowed, but she smirked at the same time. The skin I was working on shifted slightly, but she showed no signs of discomfort. "Right. Dr. Scott Shepard."

"That's me," I agreed with a smile. "And you are?"

She rolled her eyes. "The lady with the head wound."

"You know it says your name in your chart, right? All I have to do is look at it." I'd given it a glance to assure myself that she had no allergies or serious medical history just before giving her the dose of numbing agent, but now, a more thorough perusal seemed pertinent.

"Yeah, but what fun is that, Dr. Shepard?"

"Fine," I agreed. "What should I call you, then?"

"How about *Bleeding Woman Thanks to Horrible Sex with a Guy with a Fancy Name*?"

I laughed a little before clearing my throat and wincing. "Well, it's a little long. But I guess I can work with it. I would love to know how someone gets a head lac from horrible sex. It sounds like a really nice story."

"Sorry. It's an awful story that I'll never relive. Not even for your amusement."

"Geez. Fine. It's like you want me to sew this up and leave you alone or something."

She smiled, and it consumed her entire face. So much so, I thought the corners of her mouth might loop all the way around to form a circle. "That would be nice."

I laughed again, completely smitten.

Jesus. I hadn't had this much fun talking to a woman in a long time. Hell, I hadn't even spoken this much to a woman in a long time. Usually, we exchanged several heys and then went straight to making out. Not entirely flawed when your goals were what mine were—a night of fun and fucking—but not exactly mentally stimulating either.

"Well, you're in luck," I told her as I tied the last stitch and clipped off the excess. "You're all set."

I, however, wasn't feeling that lucky at all. I didn't want to be done working on her yet. Too bad I hadn't thought to stretch it out a little bit. Her conversation was too engaging to leave brainpower for scheming.

"Great!" she chirped, sitting up in a hurry and swinging her legs around and off the side of the bed.

"Whoa, whoa, whoa," I urged with a hand to her shoulder. "Take it easy, Sex Victim. I've got to sign off on your chart, and you have to get discharged."

"But if you sign off on my chart, you'll see my name," she said. It could have sounded weird, but with the way she said it, it just sounded flirtatious. Enchanted by her cool, witty demeanor and the sweet swell of her breasts, I was more than willing to go with it.

"I won't look at your name," I promised easily.

Because I wouldn't.

At least, not until she was already gone. And, depending on how off my moral compass was at the time, I might even look at her phone number too.

Chances are good I'll be dialing those digits in the near future.

Truth was, that fucker very rarely, if ever, pointed true north.

Get the rest of Dr. ER in your hands and finish getting to know sexy Dr. Scott Shepard!

Acknowledgments

First of all, THANK YOU for reading. That goes for anyone who's bought a copy, read an ARC, helped us beta, edited, or found time in their busy schedule just to make sure we didn't completely drop the ball by being late. Yeah, that's us—sliding in fifteen minutes behind schedule. Thank you for supporting us, for talking about our books, and for just being so unbelievably loving and supportive of our characters. You've made this our MOST favorite adventure thus far.

THANK YOU to each other. Monroe is thanking Max. Max is thanking Monroe. This shouldn't surprise you since we've done this in every book we've published together so far. Or maybe it does surprise you because you don't ever read those acknowledgments. If that's the case, joke's on you. We happen to be hilarious, even in our acknowledgments. But you'll still have a chance to find out next time because we'll probably do this forever.

THANK YOU, Lisa, for being your amazing, hilarious, graciously accommodating, and eagle-eyed self. We'll try not to send the next book to you in twenty-five separate sections, and we'll try to actually complete the transaction on time. Good thing you're so awesome and flexible. ;)

THANK YOU, Peter, for creating the latest covers for St. Luke's Doctors! You crushed the deadline. The very tight deadline. LOL.

THANK YOU to every blogger who has read, reviewed, posted, shared, and supported us. Your enthusiasm, support, and hard work do not go unnoticed. We'd offer to get you an appointment with Will as thanks, but we've tried that a couple of times and Melody isn't fucking having it.

THANK YOU, to the people who love us. They support us, motivate us, and most importantly, tolerate us. Sometimes we're not the easiest people to live with, especially when there is a deadline looming. We honestly don't know what we'd do without you guys.

P.S. You don't know what you'd do without us either, so suck it.

THANK YOU, to our Camp members! You guys make us smile every day! Especially when we pop into camp when we're supposed to be doing something else and we're really easy to please. It's like being really hungry—everything tastes good. HAHA! J/k. J/k. You'd taste good even if we were overfull.

As always, all our love.

XOXO,

Max Monroe

Made in the USA
Monee, IL
24 January 2024